The Lost Souls of Angelkov

НОКТЮРН
("Разлука")

NOCTURNE
("Separation")

Транскрипция А. ВЛАСОВА
Transcription by A.VLASOV

М. ГЛИНКА
M. GLINKA
(1804 - 1857)

Commodo

LINDA HOLEMAN

The Lost Souls of Angelkov

RANDOM HOUSE CANADA

PUBLISHED BY RANDOM HOUSE CANADA

COPYRIGHT © 2012 Linda Holeman

www.randomhouse.ca

Random House Canada and colophon are registered trademarks.

This book is a work of fiction. Names, characters, places and incidents either are the
product of the author's imagination or are used fictitiously. Any resemblance to actual
persons, living or dead, events or locales is entirely coincidental.

LIBRARY AND ARCHIVES CANADA CATALOGUING IN PUBLICATION

Holeman, Linda
The lost souls of Angelkov / Linda Holeman.

Also issued in electronic format.

ISBN 978-0-307-36159-2

I. Title.

PS8565.O6225L68 2012   C813'.54   C2011-908179-2

Cover and text design by Terri Nimmo
Cover image: © Mark Owen / Trevillion Images
Printed and bound in the United States of America

10 9 8 7 6 5 4 3 2

In memory of my grandparents,
Theodor and Lyuba, who left me a rich Russian legacy

"Sans illusions, adieu à la vie!"
Motto from Reminiscences of a Mazurka
MIKHAIL GLINKA, 1847

"The hundred-year rise and fall of serf orchestras
had produced precious few serious musicians and only one
great composer who had been exposed to them—Glinka."
RICHARD STITES
Serfdom, Society, and the Arts in Imperial Russia

ANGELKOV ESTATE, PROVINCE OF PSKOV

Three days' ride from St. Petersburg

APRIL 1861

The day his son was stolen, Konstantin had noticed the difference in the air. It was a subtle smell, the first hint that spring might finally end the long winter. It is this he's thinking about—the smell of the air—when the men appear in front of him.

They arrive from the quiet forest—his forest—slipping and weaving between the slender, leafless birch and green spruce. How did he not hear the hooves pounding in the hard snow, the heavy breathing of the horses as they charged in his direction? He remembers that Mikhail had called out to him, *Papa, someone's coming*, yet he ignored the boy. Why? Would it have made a difference? Should he have stopped his horse and listened?

The men wear their tall fur hats pulled low, covering their eyebrows. Their wool jackets bear the distinctive Cossack insignia. Their noses and mouths are hidden with scarves. On their swift horses they appear huge, monstrous. They charge at him with their sabres drawn, the sabres Cossacks favour.

Konstantin drops the reins he holds loosely in one hand, grabbing at his own sword. He pulls it awkwardly from the scabbard as he shouts over his shoulder, *Ride, Mikhail, ride away!* But Mikhail can't control his horse.

Papa, Papa, I can't turn him. Mikhail is ten years old. He's not on his own small and gentle mare; he rides a frisky dappled gelding. Grisha, Konstantin's steward, had suggested the challenge would be good for the boy. *Damn Grisha.* Would it have changed things if Mikhail had his usual horse, the one instantly responsive to his commands?

There are three Cossacks, maybe four; it's happening so quickly, and his eyesight . . . it's no longer what it used to be. He's too old to see with the clarity he once possessed, to hear what he should hear. Suddenly his son is beside him; he catches a glimpse of Mikhail's thick blond hair, creamy skin. So like his mother.

Antonina, he thinks next, oh God, no, Antonina. She told him not to take the boy today, told him it was too cold, the child had been ill. *Don't take him out, Konstantin,* she'd begged, *please, Kostya, he shouldn't be out in the cold.*

He knows instinctively that whatever happens in these woods will destroy her. Her face rises before him, stricken, agonized, an expression he has never before seen. But it's too late. He knows it's too late.

Konstantin grabs the reins of Mikhail's horse, pulling up on them sharply so that the horse and Mikhail are close beside him. The gelding still prances nervously. The Cossacks circle Konstantin and his son.

This was all because he was stubborn—*you stubborn old man*, Antonina had said when he'd insisted on taking Mikhail with him. She'd called after him again, when he'd refused to have any of the servants accompany them on their ride, and then Konstantin saw her speaking to Grisha, pulling on the steward's sleeve. She was already unsteady, although it was only early afternoon. And then, after Grisha walked away, Antonina stood on the wide steps of the house, holding a pillar for support. She'd shouted at him one last time, her usually melodic voice hard and flat in the still, cold air, something about a hat for Mikhail. He looked away. A servant chased after them with Mikhail's *ushanka*, waving the ear-flapped fur hat.

He'd galloped towards the forest. Mikhail was a length ahead of him, and he admired the way his son's thick hair blew in the cool breeze.

And now... The leader of the Cossacks, taller and broader than the other men, brings his chestnut horse up beside Konstantin's silvery grey Arabian, shivering on its slender legs. The Cossack's horse worries its bit, nodding its head as if in agreement with whatever its rider will direct it to do. Konstantin's Arabian is taller than the Cossack's horse and yet it shies, throwing back its head as though it feels the violence in the air.

Konstantin lifts the sword he holds—how has it grown so heavy?—but before he's aware of movement from the Cossack, there's a sly whistle, and a thin, deadly blade slices into the back of his ungloved hand. His sword is gone.

He doesn't feel pain immediately, and manages to hold on to the reins of his son's horse with his left hand. He hears Mikhail's cry of distress, hears him shouting, *Papa, Papa*.

"It's all right, Mikhail," Konstantin says to his son.

Mikhail's face is ashen, his mouth trembling.

"It's all right, Misha," he repeats. "Be quiet." He feels that silence will help prevent the disaster about to take place. He also thinks he should have taken the hat: Mikhail's head is too exposed, too vulnerable. Somehow the hat might have helped the child.

"Count Mitlovsky," the Cossack in front of him states, his voice muffled by the scarf.

The Cossacks know him. Everyone knows him; he's the landowner. He owns the grand estate of Angelkov and the hundreds and hundreds of surrounding versts. He was also, until recently, the owner of thousands of souls, all his former serfs. So yes, it's a plan. How many hours have the Cossacks waited for him in the trees, in this damp, late winter cold, their toes numb within their high leather boots, their hair slick with sweat under their hats? How many days have they come to this place, waiting for just this moment: when Count Konstantin Nikolevich Mitlovsky travels, unaccompanied, through his own thick forest of pine and spruce and birch? When he rides, unsuspecting, along the isolated trail he had his serfs cut through the woods so that he might come out at the road close to the nearest village, saving a distance of five versts?

But in almost the same instant he realizes he *has* done this very thing every day over the last week. The weather has been so fine. Yes, alone, he rode this path yesterday, and the day before that and before that. The only difference today is that his son is with him.

His only child.

Konstantin tries to focus more clearly on the dark eyes of the man in front of him. He's now aware of a shocking, great throb in his right hand. It hangs loosely at his side, and blood drips from the ends of his fingers onto his grey woollen pant leg, onto the lustrous polished leather of his high riding boot, onto the packed snow beneath his horse. He's glad Mikhail is on his other side, and won't see the blood.

The Cossack peers around Konstantin, studying the boy. Something in the Cossack's eyes makes Konstantin close his own, sending a silent prayer towards the saints. "I have a number of rubles with me," he says, opening his eyes and again looking into the Cossack's face. His voice is raspy, as if just awakening from a long sleep. "Here." He makes a motion with his head, a nod at the side of his greatcoat, where a leather bag is attached to his belt. "Take it. And there's more. You know there can be any amount. Name it. Name it, and it will be yours."

Konstantin must continue to hope that what is happening is only simple robbery. That these men are taking what they feel is rightly theirs, another result of the unrest sweeping the country. The Tsar emancipated the serfs in February, and with their freedom has come a cost to those who once owned them. These men may not be true Cossacks, not soldiers of the Tsar, but newly free men angry with those who once dictated their futures.

The Cossack uses the tip of his sabre to slash through the leather tabs holding the purse onto Konstantin's belt. In one more deft movement of his sword he flips the purse into the air, grabbing it with his left hand and cramming it into the pocket of his coat.

But Konstantin isn't relieved. The men circle closer. He knows what will come next. A desperate, tipping weight makes him feel, suddenly, that he might fall from his horse in a way he hasn't since he was three years old and on his first small pony.

The Cossack puts the tip of his sword to Konstantin's neck. "Hand over the boy's reins."

Konstantin doesn't move, aware of that deadly point. "Please. Spare the child, I beg of you. What good is he—a boy, and not even a good horseman yet? He'll only slow you down. On God's name, I will give you what—" He stops, the tip of the sabre pressing so deeply into his neck that there's a tiny pop, a sound that echoes in his ears as if a bottle of chilled champagne has been opened in an adjoining room. His flesh burns as though a flame is held to it.

"Give me the reins," the Cossack says again. He lowers his sabre and reaches forward with his other hand, huge and corded, to rip the leather reins from Konstantin; the older man's strength is no match for the Cossack's.

As the boy's gelding passes in front of his Arabian, Mikhail stares at him. "Papa?" he says. He is not a particularly obedient boy, and yet at this moment he is waiting for his father to instruct him.

Konstantin sees the boy's name, *Mikhail*, embroidered in blue wool along the bottom of the back of his *talmochka*. He remembers watching Antonina as she worked with her needle and thread, her head bent over her son's quilted coat.

"Please," Konstantin begs, and even to his own ears his voice is feeble, an old man's voice. Helpless. He has no weapon now, no defence. He's one old man against three—there are only three, he sees—strong young Cossacks. Still, he leans sideways in his saddle, tugging at the Cossack's sleeve with his good hand. Cut off my hand, he thinks, cut it off, cut off both of my hands, so all will know I tried to save my son.

But the Cossack simply slides his sabre into its sheath, struggling to yank his arm from Konstantin's grip. Konstantin won't let go. The Cossack digs his heels into his horse, kicking its flanks, and it rises on its hind legs. Konstantin is thrown to the ground, and his horse bolts and gallops through the trees, ears back. The Cossack turns his own gleaming chestnut in the opposite direction. Guiding Mikhail's horse, he rides away, the others following.

Mikhail twists in his saddle to look at his father. Konstantin is already on his feet, and calls out to his son, "It's all right, Mikhail. Be a good boy. Do what they tell you. I will come for you later. I will come for you. Don't be afraid." He thinks his voice sounds certain and will reassure Mikhail. Does it? Mikhail's expression is panicked, his eyes wide, grey-green in the thin winter air, but he doesn't make a sound.

A brave boy, Konstantin thinks in an oddly suspended moment. "The ransom," he shouts, as the men ride farther into the trees. Mikhail is still slightly turned, looking over his shoulder at him. "The ransom! Any amount. Send word. I will pay immediately. Any amount, I tell you. I'll give you anything. Anything! Tell me!" He's watching the direction the Cossacks are heading as he looks in the thick trees for his own horse. He has to follow them.

At his father's shouting, Mikhail turns away, his small shoulders stiff and high, his hair a golden glow in the light streaming through the tall, swaying trees.

It's too cold for him to be without a hat, Konstantin thinks. *The child's mother was right, as always. I should have listened to her.*

The sound of hooves echoes behind him. He spins. It's Grisha, holding the reins of the grey Arabian.

"Grisha," he says. "Thank God. They've got Mikhail. They've got my son. Go after them, Grisha."

Grisha drops the Arabian's lead in front of Konstantin. Konstantin attempts to pull himself onto his horse with his good hand. He falls onto the bloodstained snow, tries to rise, falls again. His left hand trembles as he points west, into the thick forest.

Grisha gallops in the direction of the kidnappers, disappearing into the trees.

2

*A*ntonina is alerted by the screaming of a servant in the yard.

She holds up her wide skirt with both hands and runs towards the front door. She arrives in time to see Grisha helping Konstantin off his Arabian. He would have fallen had it not been for Grisha's firm grip.

She takes in the scene in an instant: her husband and Grisha. Something is wrong with her husband. Where is her son?

"Misha," she says. "Misha." Grisha, aided by Lyosha from the stables, half drags, half carries Konstantin towards the house.

"Let's go now, Grisha," Lyosha shouts, struggling under the count's weight. "I'll get the others. We can't give them any more time."

Antonina's mouth goes dry, dread gripping her with

such strength that she can't speak. Can't even say her son's name again.

Grisha hisses at Lyosha to shut up. "We've got to get him inside. Then we'll go back."

Antonina grips the door frame, staring at her husband's open coat, his bloodied shirt and hand wrapped in a scarf she recognizes as Grisha's. They push past her, and she smells the rancid odour of fear, the metallic tang of blood in the waft of air that follows the men. She is beside them as they lay Konstantin on the emerald silk settee in the drawing room.

Grisha straightens and looks at her, and suddenly it's as if the air in the room has stilled around Antonina.

Servants crowd in the doorway, pushing against each other silently, crossing themselves. Antonina sees her maid, Lilya, clutching her younger brother Lyosha's shoulder as if protecting him, even though he is taller than she, and she has to reach up.

If she moves or speaks at this moment, Antonina fears she will come undone and do something mad—whirl her arms like a windmill, or crash to the floor, kicking her legs so that her underskirts are revealed to all the servants. She'll wail—oh, she knows with certainty she'll wail like an old babushka, following a coffin to the cemetery.

No. She won't allow herself to do any of these things. Finally she says, "My son. Where is my son, Konstantin?"

When Konstantin closes his eyes and turns his face towards the back of the settee, Grisha says, "He was taken, madam. I was following the count and your son, as you instructed, but I stayed back. I knew if the count saw me . . . so by the time I arrived in the clearing and found him"—he indicates Konstantin with his chin—"the men had a good start. I followed the direction the count pointed out, but after only a short time it became impossible. There were too many trails, countess. I knew I had to get back to the count and bring him home. His hand . . ."

Lyosha steps forward from the crowd of servants in the doorway. "Let's go after them, Grisha."

Grisha stares at him until Lyosha takes a step back. Lilya puts her hand on her brother's arm. Grisha is the head man on the estate. He reports to the count. It is Grisha the others obey.

With no warning, a rush of acidy fluid is in Antonina's throat. She swallows, bringing her fist to her mouth. She won't disgrace herself in front of the servants. Her throat burns as she lowers her hand. "Taken?" she repeats, and clears her throat. "Taken by whom?"

"I don't know, madam. I didn't see them. There were three, the count says. He needs a doctor, madam."

Konstantin finally speaks, loudly. "No, there is no time for a doctor. Bring clean linen." He sits up and slowly unwraps the scarf, wincing.

Antonina looks at her husband's hand. The back of it is slashed through, tendons and veins a pulpy mess of congealing and fresh blood.

"But Count Mitlovsky," Grisha says, "it's bleeding too—"

"I said no doctor. There's no time," Konstantin says, grimacing. "*Chyort,*" he curses.

"Madam," Grisha says to Antonina. "His hand—please, madam. We await your orders."

"I give the orders," Konstantin tells Grisha. "Keep your mouth shut."

Antonina focuses on Konstantin's linen shirt: on its snowy surface is a spread of crimson. From Konstantin's hand, she thinks. Not from Mikhail. The blood is from Konstantin's hand. "Get something to stop the bleeding," she says into the room, her voice steady. She hasn't come undone. She sees a scrap of fabric protruding from Konstantin's uninjured hand.

"What is that?" She points. "What are you holding, Konstantin?" She goes to him and tries to open his fingers, but his is like the grip of a man already dead. "Konstantin," she says, low and fierce. He uncurls his fingers. A strip of wool with a small insignia sewn onto it in tight stitches lies on his palm.

"Cossacks," she says. Now her voice is a stranger's, hoarse and rough, as if she's been screaming for a long time. Cossacks, cavalry in the tsarist army with their lances, carbines, pistols and sabres, are fierce and predatory in time of war. But there is no war. The Cossacks should be fishing and breeding cattle, as they do during peace.

"Why would Cossacks take Misha?" she asks Konstantin. She thinks about the stories she's heard, of Cossacks recruiting their numbers by kidnapping peasant boys in time of war. "They don't need more boys now. And especially not a . . . Mikhail is of the nobility. Why, Konstantin?"

Konstantin pulls away his hand, his lips pursed, the skin around them white. The insignia falls to the floor.

Behind Antonina is the swish of skirts, the rasp and slap of heavy boots against the floor. The clock on the mantle ticks. There are murmurs. Then the old housekeeper Olga is wrapping a length of cotton around Konstantin's hand. But the bleeding continues, soaking the layers of cloth.

Antonina again clears her throat and swallows, tasting

the sourness of her own saliva. "It's for money? Is that it, Konstantin, a ransom demand?" Now her voice is hard. "All this unrest—they think they can just steal children and demand a ransom?" She looks at the crowd in the doorway, as if they, her own house servants, are somehow responsible. All of them except Lilya look at the floor; she comes forward, to her mistress.

"They will demand ransom," Antonina states, looking back at Konstantin. Her voice is loud in the eerie silence of the room. And suddenly she's full of terrible energy; there have already been too many wasted precious moments. "Ransom! Ransom—we'll pay the ransom. Of course." Her hands reach out, trembling.

Lilya stands beside her. "Madam," she says quietly, and at her voice Antonina drops her hands.

"Yes," Konstantin says. "Yes. They will want money, and we will pay them. That's enough," he says to Olga, who is fussing over the bandages and a sling she is attempting to tie. "But we can't wait to hear from them. We'll go after them now. Grisha, round up as many men as we have horses. We'll find them, Antonina. And we'll take back Mikhail."

"Kostya." She glances at his hand again. It is thickly bandaged and the cotton sling holds it against his chest, the index and middle fingers exposed, pointing towards his neck. "Is Misha—did they harm him? Tell me what happened to him. Tell me exactly what they said."

"They didn't hurt him," he says.

She wants to believe him. "Hurry, then, Kostya," she says, even louder, looking over her shoulder at Grisha. "Go, Grisha. I'm coming as well. Lilya, get my riding boots. Saddle my horse, Lyosha."

But Konstantin is staring at Grisha. "You," he roars, abruptly standing and pushing Antonina aside, as if he's taken energy from her. She loses her balance, but Lilya is there to catch her. Konstantin sways. "You gave him that damn horse. He couldn't handle it. It was too wild for him. Why did you give the boy such a difficult horse? You idiot." He raises his left hand as if to strike Grisha, but in the next instant he groans and falls back, sprawling heavily onto the settee, his legs wide.

Grisha hasn't moved. His face, as usual, shows nothing, apart from a slight flush. He doesn't apologize, doesn't drop his gaze.

"For God's sake, Konstantin, never mind the horse. Go on, Grisha," Antonina says. "Immediately. We can't wait. Every moment that passes . . . Mikhail, he's a child. He had a fever, only yesterday. He shouldn't have been out in this cold." She knows she's speaking too quickly but can't stop. "He needs to be kept warm, doesn't he, Lilya?" She looks at her maid, and the woman nods. "Soon it will be dark. We can't wait," she repeats.

Lilya picks up the countess's hand and chafes it between her own.

Konstantin stands again, his face chalky. "Hurry, you bloody fool," he yells at Grisha. "Gather the men and get moving."

Grisha stares directly into Konstantin's face as if he wants to speak. His face is even more flushed, his jaw tight.

"Which direction will we—"Antonina starts, pulling her hand from Lilya, but Konstantin grabs her wrist.

"You're not coming. Stay here and wait."

"I'm a better rider than most of the men. I'm going with you."

Konstantin grips her wrist tighter and leans into her face. His voice is low but carries through the room. "You're drunk. You can't ride the way you are. Stay here and sober up. Do you hear?"

Antonina draws her head back, blinking. There isn't a sound from the servants, not a cough, not the shuffle of a boot. Antonina lifts her chin. "Don't speak so, Konstantin. What is important right now is the safety of our son. I want to come."

"No. You will not." Konstantin strides past her, and the huddled group of servants in the doorway parts.

Lilya puts her arm around Antonina's shoulders. "Come. Come, madam. We will bring you tea."

Antonina looks at her as though she's speaking a foreign language. Tea? Why would Lilya think tea would be of any use? Lilya lowers her eyes—although not before Antonina sees something in them. Some great sorrow. Sorrow, and something else Antonina doesn't recognize. Nothing makes sense.

Antonina can't think of tea. Instead, she goes out to the wide front veranda. Grisha is there, his back to her. She sees a fresh slash, beaded with blood, across the back of his neck. He turns at her footsteps and, as she comes closer, puts his hand on her forearm in an unfamiliar gesture. "Madam," he says. "About the horse . . ."

"It was foolish of you, as my husband said," she says, her voice rising. "You know he's not yet a strong rider." Blood from the back of Grisha's neck stains the collar of his white tunic, and she knows Konstantin has done this.

What good would it do to punish him further? She needs him to help find her son.

ꓘ Grisha is still looking into her face. When she says nothing more, he nods. "We're waiting for everyone to be saddled. We'll spread through the trees in many directions, and we'll find the Cossacks, countess. We'll return with your son, unharmed."

At his words, spoken with such confidence, a tremble goes through Antonina. She looks down at his hand on her sleeve. For the first time since the servant's hysterical screaming in the yard, she feels she's not alone. "Thank you, Grisha," she whispers. "Thank you." To hear him say these words of comfort—and to believe him, as she stares into his face—is what she needs. Grisha is much younger than Konstantin, and strong; he would not be cowardly and weak, as Konstantin must have been.

It has been no more than two hours since Mikhail was taken. As Grisha has said, they will find the Cossacks, of course they will. Misha will be returned to her, cold and frightened, hungry, but unharmed.

I will have the Cossacks sent to the far reaches of Siberia. Antonina straightens at the thought. She always felt a certain pity for the prisoners sent east, across the country to the great stretches of barren land. She had, at times, studied their faces as she passed a wagon loaded with chained, bruised and wretched-looking creatures on the road, and wondered what crimes they had committed to be sentenced to such an exile. She will no longer feel pity.

Grisha takes his hand from her arm and hurries down the steps to the horse Lyosha has led from the stables.

Antonina watches the men leave, Konstantin in the lead.

She isn't wearing a coat but doesn't feel the cold. Only a few hours earlier she had stood in the same spot and watched her son ride away with his father.

Olga is gently pulling at her arm and Antonina allows the old woman to lead her into the house, and then to the drawing room, where Lilya is setting a tray with a glass of tea and a crystal bowl of jam on the table. Antonina stares at the tray as if it contains unknown objects, then sits on the burgundy velvet sofa, across from the bloodstained settee. Olga drapes a wool shawl over her shoulders. Tinka, Antonina's tiny Maltese lapdog, jumps up and lies quietly beside her, licking her front paws.

"Lilya," Antonina says. "Please. Bring me a glass of wine." But isn't this the reason Konstantin took Misha away from her that afternoon? Isn't it her fault that Konstantin took her son out riding? If she hadn't been drinking, she and Konstantin wouldn't have fought. *You disgust me*, Konstantin had said. *I don't like the boy seeing you like this.*

She had been in the music salon listening to Mikhail play, her eyes closed as she sat in a small armchair near the piano. She'd sipped her wine, letting the music wash over her.

The music came from him effortlessly; even though she too had the gift, her son was more advanced than she had been at his age. What pleasure he brought her, not only when he played but in their daily lives together. He was the first thing she thought about when she awoke each morning and was in her final prayers as she fell asleep. As she listened this day, she remembered the first duet they had played together, when Mikhail was four—Schumann's Kinderball duet— and how he had looked up at her when the final notes were played. He still looked at her like this when he completed a complicated piece and was pleased with himself and wanted to share the pleasure with her.

Today he was playing Glinka's Separation in F Minor when Konstantin's voice, loud and near, made her jump, spilling a few drops of the rich red wine onto her skirt.

"I'm taking the boy for a ride," he said.

She stood, clutching her glass. Mikhail continued playing. "Let him finish the piece," she said. "He hasn't been at the piano for a few days because of his fever."

Konstantin met her gaze. "So early, Antonina?" he said.

She lifted her chin. "I've been very worried about him. You know that." She lifted the glass to her lips and slowly drank, her eyes not leaving his.

She saw his lips tighten and then he raised his hand and knocked the glass from hers. It shattered against the stone fireplace, and sheets of music fluttered to the floor, some falling into the wine and broken glass. Mikhail stopped abruptly, jumping up and putting his hands over his ears. "Look what you do to him," Antonina cried. "Why must you upset him?"

"It's not me who upsets him," Konstantin said, his voice raised. "I'm ashamed for even the servants to see you in such a state."

Mikhail ran to Antonina, putting his arms around her waist. "Father, don't. Please don't make Mama sad."

"It's all right, darling," Antonina said, smoothing his hair. "I'm fine, really. Go back and finish the nocturne. It's lovely. You haven't forgotten a note. Go on, dear, go and finish it."

But Konstantin shook his head. "You're coming for a ride, Mikhail. You spend too much time indoors. You need exercise after you've been ill. Grisha has the horses readied. Come along."

As he strode away, Mikhail pulled away from her and looked up at her, then at the piano, distress on his face.

Antonina wanted him to finish the nocturne. A piece of music unfinished was like a sentence left hanging, half spoken, in the air. She hadn't always felt like this, so anxious, so easily undone. The trembling began just under the surface of her skin. And yet she couldn't bear the terrible look of confusion on her son's face.

"Go then, my darling. Do as your father says."

He nodded, but still looked troubled. She fought not to pull him back to her and hold him tightly. She wanted to feel the graceful bones of his shoulders, put her face into his thick blond hair and breathe in his scent.

She will always remember this: she sent him with his father. What if she *had* called him back, had said, *No, no, Misha. I won't allow it. You will stay here, safe, with me.* What if she had said this? Could she have stopped Konstantin from taking him?

Mikhail had grabbed his little leather music composition booklet from the piano and ran after his father. As Antonina took a step, glass crunched under her foot. She looked down at the sheet of music.

To Antonina Leonidovna on her name day. With great admiration and respect, Valentin Vladimirovitch. Dated March 14, 1849.

The page was spattered with brilliant crimson from the broken glass of wine. Seeing how Konstantin had ruined even this—her lovely Glinka score, a gift so special to her—made Antonina go to the sideboard and pour herself another glass from the decanter. She swallowed it in one draft, then set the glass down, wiping her lips with the back of her hand.

"Lilya," she called. "Lilya! Fetch Misha's jacket and hat. He's going riding."

But of course Mikhail didn't wear his hat.

And this is the last image Antonina has of that moment: her son riding away from her, her hand raised as she called out to Konstantin, *Wait, please wait. Mikhail needs his hat.* She saw how his hair blew back from his ears and she knew they would be cold.

Now Lilya, kneeling between the table and the sofa, puts a spoonful of jam to Antonina's mouth. "No wine just yet, madam," she says, and Antonina nods.

"You're right. No more wine today." She swallows the jam and takes a sip from the steaming glass in the engraved silver holder Lilya puts to her mouth. The glass is thin and as silky as satin on her lips. She is aware of the sweetness of the jam, the heat of the tea, but tastes nothing.

"When do you suppose they will find him?" she asks. "It will be before dark, certainly before dark. Don't you think so, Lilya?"

Lilya sets down the glass. "I'm sure of it, madam. There are a number of hours until dark." Her face is tight, expressionless. She looks unfamiliar to Antonina. She is closer to her than any of the servants, and yet she looks strange and distant.

"Don't distress yourself further, madam," Olga says now. "It might be best to sleep. If you rest—"

"Oh, no. I must go and watch for them," Antonina says, leaping to her feet, the shawl falling from her shoulders and Tinka jumping to the floor. Lilya, still on her knees, leans away so that Antonina's full skirt doesn't swing into her face. Olga treads on the dog's paw. Tinka lets out a surprised squeal and scurries under the sofa.

Antonina heads for the hallway, the door. Lilya scrambles to her feet and runs after her.

"Madam," she says, her hand touching Antonina's. "Perhaps Olga is right. You should go to your bed, and take one of your sleeping tablets."

Antonina shakes her head, crossing her arms over her chest. "No. I must be here for Mikhail's return. I want to be waiting when he's brought to me."

"All right. Then come back and have more tea. You've eaten nothing since breakfast. If you drink another glass of tea, and eat something, you will be . . . yourself, more quickly. Then you can properly attend to your son when he needs you. Come," Lilya says, and her voice lowers so that Olga can't hear her. "Come, Tosya. Please."

Antonina licks her lips. She sees the woman's crucifix and thinks of the icon of Saint Nicholas on a thin gold chain around Mikhail's neck, beside his own crucifix. Did she once really believe that Saint Nicholas could protect her son? The shock is taking over, and she shivers. "Yes, all right."

She goes back to the velvet sofa, wrapping the shawl around herself again. Lilya murmurs instructions to Olga as she pours another glass of tea. Tinka creeps out from under the sofa and Lilya picks her up and puts her on Antonina's lap.

While she drinks her tea, Antonina absently strokes the dog's back.

Olga reappears with a tray. Antonina looks at the cold mutton and the beet salad, the soft roll spread with creamy butter. She swallows. She can't imagine eating.

"Slowly, madam," Lilya says. "Just take a little to start." She breaks off a piece of the roll and hands it to Antonina.

Antonina takes it and puts it in her mouth. Then she cuts the mutton and eats, chewing and swallowing very carefully, as though she has something blocking her throat, until the plate is half empty. She gives a sliver of meat to Tinka.

Then she pats her mouth on the damask napkin. "Thank you, Olga," she says. "I'll keep watch at the front windows." The old woman takes the tray and leaves. Still holding Tinka, Antonina goes to the tall windows that look onto the front yard and stands unblinking, her back straight. Lilya kneels beside her and clasps her hands in prayer. "He will return soon, Tosya," she says. "And it will be as always. You, me and our Misha." She closes her eyes and bows her head over her hands.

Antonina puts her lips against the little dog's head and whispers her own prayers.

The men and horses thunder through the forest with Konstantin and Grisha in the lead. The back of Grisha's neck still stings from Konstantin's whip.

Should the count turn on his horse now, he would be surprised at the hatred etched on the face of the man he relies on to help him run Angelkov. Grisha is not a serf but a free man who is paid a salary for his work. Konstantin considers his treatment of Grisha to be generous and fair. Konstantin also believes he had always been generous and fair to all his serfs—all the souls he once owned.

But now everything is changing. The Russian world is tilting on its axis. The Emancipation Manifesto, handed down by Tsar Alexander II two months earlier, in February 1861, has changed life for both serfs and landowners. The serfs now owe the landowners nothing, neither *obrok*, the yearly tax they used to pay to the landowner for using some of the harvest to fill their own bellies, nor payment in goods.

Some of Konstantin's serfs have already left the estate, wanting to start their own lives in the villages. But he can't believe that Grisha would ever go. What would he have to call his own without Angelkov? Wasn't he luckier than most, to have the highest position on the estate? Doesn't Konstantin provide him with a cottage—a warm wooden cottage with blue shutters—that allows him to live on his own, away from the shared servants' quarters or, worse, the wretched village *izbas*, little more than hovels? Doesn't Konstantin himself sometimes seek out Grisha in the blue-shuttered house, bringing Imperial vodka and discussing politics with him, treating him almost as though he were of the same class?

As they ride, Grisha isn't thinking of the missing child. He's thinking of New Year's Eve, over three months earlier, and how Count Mitlovsky and he had discussed the promise— or threat, depending on the view—of the Tsar possibly issuing an edict to free the serfs.

"It's serfdom that holds Russia back," he had said to his master as they drank a glass of vodka. "Were we not humiliated in the Crimea? We pride ourselves on our military strength, and yet we were no match for the armies of France, or Britain or Turkey. With respect, Count Mitlovsky, feudalism was abandoned in most of Europe centuries ago."

The count, straightening his collar, pulling down his waistcoat and smoothing his beard, poured another round of vodka. He lifted his small glass and drank it in one shot. "Holy Russia is a God-inspired nation. Looking at the corrupt nations to the west can teach us nothing."

Grisha's left eye throbbed with the effort of keeping his temper as he was forced, yet again, to have the count use his home for an assignation. He can hear Tania, the laundress at Angelkov, moving about in the bedroom. *His* bedroom. And while she dresses, he must listen to Mitlovsky's posturing. He held his glass tightly but didn't drink. "I beg to differ, *Barin*. My lord. We can learn much from countries who have allowed their people to determine their own destinies. When men are slaves, there's no incentive to improve."

Konstantin laughed. "Slaves? The peasants are not slaves. I own my land, and the peasants work the land. Only in this way are they bound to me."

Grisha had to rise, bowing to the count, and then went to the window. It was black beyond the panes, and he saw his own reflection, his hair a wavy dark mass brushed back from his forehead, his eyes no more than slashes in the paler oval of his face. "Again, with all respect, Count Mitlovsky," he said to his own image. "You control the lives of the thousands of souls you own. You have the power to deny the peasants the chance to leave your land, and you can, at will, move or sell any soul to another estate, even if that means splitting families." He turned then, and saw that Konstantin's eyelids were heavy, his cheeks flushed. He kept his voice low, the tone even. "You may have them beaten, or without cause sent to work in the mines or to end their lives in Siberia. You dictate whom they may marry. Is this not slavery, *Barin*?"

Konstantin waved his hand in the air as though Grisha's words were unimportant, as if he'd heard them too many times to take them seriously. "Don't talk politics any further. You bore me. The Tsar is appointed by God. He will see sense. He will not carry out his ridiculous threat. Come now, it's the New Year. We will drink to our health, and to the health of those we love."

Grisha joined him, and the first boom of the estate's fireworks sounded as he drank with his master.

"Good night, my dear," Konstantin called through the bedroom door as he stood and set down his empty glass. Grisha heard Tania's murmured reply.

The count put a small pile of rubles on Grisha's mantle, then left to watch the display with his wife and son. Grisha stared into the fire. The vodka burned in his belly. Count Mitlovsky was wrong; Grisha was certain that the Tsar would hand down the Emancipation Manifesto within months. And when it happened, Grisha knew exactly how he would live his life when not under the thumb of Mitlovsky.

Tania came from the bedroom with an armload of linens. Her auburn hair was tidy, her long face emotionless as she picked up the rubles from the mantle and tucked them away.

Grisha poured another glass of vodka and held it out. "Toast the New Year with me, Tania."

"Thank you, Grigori Sergeyevich," she said, setting down the used bed linens and taking the glass. The lines between her eyebrows and around her mouth were deep.

He touched his glass with hers and raised it. "To freedom," he said, and tipped back his head and swallowed.

3

A few hours have passed. Antonina sits on a straight-backed chair in front of the window, leaning forward to stare into the dusk. She hasn't taken her eyes from the yard.

She jumps up as horses approach, handing Tinka to Lilya and rushing to the front door. She flings it open, but on the top step of the veranda stops so suddenly that Lilya bumps into her.

It is only Konstantin and Grisha.

She runs down the steps to them. "Why are you back? Mikhail—Misha . . ." She looks at Konstantin, slumped forward on his saddle, his mouth hanging slightly open, then to Grisha. "You didn't find him?" She knows this, but has to ask.

Grisha shakes his head. "Not yet, madam, but Lyosha and the others are still searching. They had a good lead while it was still light, as the tracks . . ." He stops, glancing at

Konstantin. "The count was weak from loss of blood. He can hardly remain on his horse. I had to bring him home. But the others . . . they'll find him, madam."

Antonina clutches the shawl at her chest with one hand as if a sudden cold breeze has swept through the yard. "But it's been too long. It's too long, Grisha. And now it's almost dark."

"No, not so long," he says, dismounting and coming to stand beside her. "Lilya! Call Pavel to help with the count." He touches Antonina's hand briefly. "Not long at all. And if he isn't found tonight, we'll begin again as soon as it's light, with fresh horses."

Again, his confidence and touch calm her. Konstantin's manservant, Pavel, arrives, and he and Grisha get Konstantin off his horse. They help him to his bedchamber. Antonina follows, and when her husband is lying on his bed, his good hand over his eyes, she moves to stand beside him.

"Husband," she says with authority, looking down at him. Konstantin takes his hand away from his eyes. "Speak to me, Konstantin Nikolevich. Tell me how you last saw Mikhail." She sees a fresh scab on the sagging skin under his earlobe. "Kostya," she says, louder this time.

He looks at her, but his mouth remains closed.

"Why will you not speak to me?" She grabs his shoulders and shakes him. As if in a dream, she sees herself from above, as wild as a *vedma*, perhaps Baba Yaga herself.

Konstantin stares up at her. His helpless expression fills her with rage. Grisha steps behind her and puts his hand on her shoulder, and she stops shaking her husband, ashamed.

Konstantin's mouth opens, a black square beneath his thick white moustache, and he whispers, "My son. Tosya, our boy." His eyes glisten with tears. "He was so brave."

Antonina puts her hand to her mouth, and Grisha lets go of Antonina's shoulder and steps back. She hears the door quietly closing. Pavel remains in place, ready to do her bidding. She hovers near the bed. But instead of Konstantin's tears invoking sympathy, they arouse even more fury in her. Her own tears come from this anger, and from the terrible fear.

"Tell me," she says, quietly this time.

"They . . . they just led his horse away. They didn't hurt him—they didn't touch him at all. He didn't make a sound. I told him to be quiet, and he did. He did, Tosya. He's a good boy. He was always a good boy, wasn't he?"

Antonina can't speak.

"He is a child of breeding, and of high intelligence. He will act in a noble way, as we have taught him. The Cossacks will see this. They'll respect him for it."

Antonina closes her eyes. Konstantin is a fool. *They've taken our child, and he talks about respect.*

"He sat so well on the horse, Tosya. I saw, as he rode away, that he had more control of it than I had imagined. He has the makings of a good horseman. All he needs is more riding—less time at the piano and more in the saddle."

Does he think I don't know my own son? I want to know what will happen next. I want to know when I will have him in my arms again.

"His head was held high, Tosya. He will not bow it to them. I have taught him well." At this Konstantin's voice quavers, and he begins to cry in earnest, sobbing like a boy. Antonina has never seen him like this. She wishes for arms around her, wishes for some kind of comfort, but doesn't move any nearer to her husband.

And because there's nothing more for her to do, she kneels and prays, looking at Konstantin. His eyes are closed and tears run down the sides of his cheeks, towards his ears, but he makes no sound.

Antonina requests that Pavel fetch the vodka from Konstantin's rosewood table near the fireplace. Unlike Lilya, Pavel obeys without hesitation. Grabbing the bottle from him, she pours herself a glass and nods at him. He bows and steps outside, although Antonina knows he will remain in the hall near the door.

She moves to the wide leather chair. Eventually she hears the clock on the landing strike the midnight hour. She pours from the bottle. She drinks through the first night of her son's disappearance.

At daybreak, Konstantin calls for Pavel and sends him to fetch Grisha. Antonina hasn't slept. She paces. She knows there is no news; had there been, Grisha would have come immediately.

When Grisha tells them that the search party returned near midnight, empty-handed, Konstantin orders them all to be beaten. He doesn't know how else to deal with his fear and guilt. Grisha nods, but has no intention of carrying out the order.

"Surely there will be a ransom letter today," Antonina says to Konstantin as she continues pacing in front of his bed. She wipes her lips with the back of her hand. "It will arrive today, and we'll know what to do to have Misha returned."

Konstantin's skin is grey. The bandage is crusted with dried blood and blossoming with fresh blotches of scarlet.

"You should have your hand seen to," Antonina says. "I'll send for the doctor."

"There's no time. We'll go out again," Konstantin tells her. "Pavel, help me dress."

"I'm going as well," Antonina says, and Konstantin doesn't argue with her.

By eight o'clock, they all set out in the overcast, damp April day.

They return to the clearing where Mikhail was taken. Antonina sees the churned mud and skiffs of hard snow, some of it spattered with Konstantin's blood. They move out in a spoke-like fashion. Antonina rides with Grisha. They ride slowly, their horses finding paths through the trees. Eventually they come out into a field, and cross it to the village of Tushinsk, owned by Konstantin.

There they dismount and tie their horses, walking through the few streets. "It's best if you stay with me, madam," Grisha says.

Grisha questions the villagers. They are wary of him, silent, shaking their heads. They bow from the waist to Antonina. She asks them questions as well, but the faces of the men and women, when she orders them to lift their heads, show nothing.

They ride on; they don't stop to eat or drink. With each passing hour Antonina feels more desperation. When they question a villager with a handcart on the road and he simply stares up at them, not responding to Grisha's questions, Antonina raises her voice at the man in frustration. Grisha leans close and lays a hand on her reins.

"It's growing late, madam. We should return to the estate. You're cold, surely." He looks at her wool cloak, blowing open in the cooling wind.

"I'm not cold," she says, pulling it around her. "Let's keep going."

Then a light drizzle begins, and Grisha insists they turn around and ride back to Angelkov.

"Not yet, Grisha. Let's keep going. Just another hour," Antonina says.

Grisha shakes his head, looking at her horse. The roan Antonina has named Dunia is weary, her head down as she plods on her delicate hooves. "Perhaps the count, or the others . . . perhaps Mikhail Konstantinovich is home by now," he says.

"I pray this is so, Grisha," Antonina says, and turns Dunia to ride with Grisha back to Angelkov.

They arrive home before the others to find there has been no word from Mikhail's captors.

Antonina goes to her bedchamber and changes out of her mud-spattered clothing. Lilya brings her one then a second glass of vodka, and afterwards Antonina stands on the veranda, shivering, arms wrapped around herself as she looks down the long treed drive, the linden branches still naked in the spring air.

Eventually she goes back inside, but within half an hour hears the sounds of men and horses, and races out in her slippers and thin woollen dress, running through the patches of dimpled, melting snow and frozen mud to the stable yard. She is willing her son to be sitting in front of his father. But he is not there.

She stares at her husband, her arms limp at her sides.

"Did a ransom note come?" Konstantin asks.

Antonina shakes her head.

Konstantin looks much older than he did yesterday. When he removes his hat, the shape of his skull, under his sweat-drenched hair, is too apparent in the dying light. He's sixty-one to her twenty-nine. He dismounts with difficulty, relying on his one good hand. Lyosha leads his horse away.

"Konstantin? Now what?" Antonina asks, but he doesn't answer immediately.

Finally he looks at her. "Tomorrow we begin again. That's all we can do—search, while we wait for word about our son."

She follows him into the house, where the servants have lit the lamps. There is the smell of beef, and the long, polished table in the grand dining room is set for two. Antonina walks past the dining room and up the curving staircase to her bedroom. Konstantin sits at the table and waits to be served, staring at the setting for Antonina, then at the spot where their son would have sat.

⸺

She doesn't sleep, once again keeping vigil with a bottle of vodka, and she is shaky when, the next morning, Lilya comes to help her get dressed. Antonina's thick, pale hair falls to her waist, but even her husband has never seen it completely undone. Normally it takes Lilya at least half an hour to brush through it and secure it into its fashionable style with the delicate combs Antonina favours. It's beautiful hair, Lilya always thinks, the weight of it in her hands a marvel. She loves to wash it as her mistress lies back in the large porcelain bath. Sometimes, alone in Antonina's room, Lilya tries to create the same style with her own dark hair.

But hers is too fine and the combs slide about, unable to find a hold. It doesn't matter. She could never appear with her hair in anything other than the usual, her braids wound round her head.

"Do it up quickly, Lilya," Antonina tells the woman. "I'm going out with them again. I don't want to waste any time." She sighs heavily as the brush slides from her scalp to the end of her hair with long, even strokes.

Lilya meets Antonina's eye in the mirror. "All the servants are praying for Mikhail's safe return," she says. "Even my husband says the Cossacks wouldn't hurt a child, especially not a child like our Mikhail."

There is a moment of silence before Antonina says, "And what does your Soso know of Cossacks and their ways, Lilya? What does he know of my child, of children at all?"

The brush stops, and Lilya takes a breath as if she is about to defend her husband, but says, "Let us believe, then, that God will care for His lamb." She lifts the brush again, but Antonina reaches up and grabs it.

"I will believe in men like Grisha and your brother Lyosha. If anyone can find Mikhail, they will. They will find him and return him, unharmed, to me. This is who I will believe in, Lilya. Not your crude husband. Not my weak husband. Not God."

Lilya's lips tighten. "Still, you should see to the count. Pavel says he's not well at all."

Antonina stares at the mother-of-pearl tray holding her combs.

"Tosya? Did you hear what I said?"

Antonina looks at Lilya in the oval mirror again. They're the same age, although Lilya looks much older. She has streaks of grey in her dark hair, and the small lines radiating from the corners of her eyes are visible even when she isn't smiling.

"Finish then, please, Lilya."

When Lilya is done, Antonina goes down the long, wide hall to her husband's bedroom. When she enters, she finds Pavel standing over Konstantin, a damp cloth in his hand. Another wet cloth is draped on Konstantin's forehead.

"Kostya?" she says. He's holding the bandaged hand against his chest with his left hand. As well as the old and new blood, there's ugly yellow matter on the bandage. She leans over him but immediately draws back at the smell of his breath. His dark eyes are flat and yet have a strange glitter. "Let me unwrap your hand and take a look at it."

Konstantin shakes his head.

"Then let me send for the doctor."

Konstantin sits up. "I must go out again. Help me, Pavel."

"Eat before you go," Antonina says. "You're no good to anyone if you let yourself grow ill."

Konstantin ignores her and, with Pavel supporting him, slowly stands.

Antonina leaves his room and goes downstairs to the drawing room and sends for Grisha. When he arrives, he bows.

"I want you to try and talk Konstantin into having his hand looked after. The wound should have been properly cleaned, and stitched. I'm sending to Pskov for the doctor, but you know how stubborn the count is. Will you speak to him, Grisha? Tell him he's too ill to ride. He must get better . . . he must be well to help bring our son back. He listens to you."

"Yes, madam," Grisha says. "Shall I go to him now?"

"Please. He's in his room. Without him . . ." She stops. "When the kidnappers make their demands, they will be to the count." She stands in front of Grisha, looking up at him. He's taller than her husband. "Why hasn't there been a ransom note, Grisha?"

Grisha looks away from her, towards the crackling fireplace. "I'm certain it will come today, madam."

Antonina clutches his sleeve. "You truly believe this?"

"These men . . . they're simply making you suffer. In this way they can be assured of your desperation." He looks at her hand and she takes it back. "They're biding their time so that there will be no hesitation in you following their orders."

Antonina lets out a long breath. "It makes sense. They wouldn't hurt Misha, would they." It's not a question.

"Why would they hurt the child when they will return him, madam?" Grisha asks, his voice softening. "Your son will not be hurt."

She nods, and she is grateful to Grisha for his confidence that Mikhail is safe, and that the ransom note will come. Still, she can't help but cry; it is as if the steward's calmness and strength allow her to weep. She turns her head away, ashamed of her tears in front of him.

"I think you should stay home today," he tells her, his voice still soothing. "In case a note comes."

"But I want to help find him." She turns to face him. "I want . . ." She stops as Grisha shakes his head.

"I do believe, madam, you would be more useful here. In case your son is returned, or a ransom note comes. Whichever it is, you should be here."

"Perhaps you're right," she says, and takes a handkerchief from her sleeve to dry her cheeks. As she takes a deep breath, Grisha is filled with respect for her. She is handling each day

with dignity and stoicism. He knows the depth of her dedi-
cation to her son. He can guess at her despair.

⁓

As Grisha predicted, the ransom note arrives mid-afternoon.
Pavel has to waken her—she fell into a light sleep on the sofa
in the music salon.

The head stableman, Fyodor, is at the back servants' entrance, waiting right where Pavel had said he would be. She
smells Fyodor's manure-covered boots as well as the grease
and sweat wafting from his heavy jacket and the hat he holds in
one hand. She notices the man's missing left ear as he bows
from the waist, his face parallel to the floor, holding out a paper.
What happened to the ear? she wonders. She knew, once.

She snatches the paper from him and unfolds it, her own
hands trembling. It's poorly written, but the details are clear.
She reads it once, twice, and then presses it against her chest.
Fyodor is still bent in front of her.

She is so thankful for the note that she forgets to ask him
who gave it to him. "You may leave, Fyodor," she says.
"Thank you."

The man straightens, although he keeps his eyes on the
floor. He backs away until he is out the door. He still acts as
a serf; it will take a long time for the habits of a lifetime to
disappear.

Antonina stays where she is. The note demands a huge
sum, to be delivered by the estate steward the next morning
at a specific time and place in the forest. The note adds that
no one can accompany the steward; if others come, the kidnappers will not hand over the boy. But if the demands are
carried out as asked, the child will be returned.

Antonina drops to her knees and crosses herself, whispering a prayer of gratitude.

※

The search party comes back to Angelkov earlier this day than the previous days. When she hears the horses, Antonina rushes outside to give Konstantin the note. He reads it and passes it to Grisha; a steward must be able to read to do the accounting for the estate.

"We'll have him back tomorrow, Konstantin," she says. "Tomorrow."

"Who brought this?" he asks, and only then does Antonina realize she hadn't asked. She tells him Fyodor delivered the note, and he and Grisha go towards the stables.

Antonina eats a few mouthfuls of dinner that night in her room. She asks Lilya to prepare a bath for her, and allows the woman to wash her hair, sighing as she sinks back in the tub of hot water. She wants to look as she always does for her son when he comes home.

Once Lilya has left her for the night, she takes a bottle of vodka from the usual place in the back of her wardrobe. She looks at it, then puts it back without opening it. She knows she will sleep without it. Mikhail Konstantinovich is coming home.

※

She is up well before dawn. She can't bear waiting for Konstantin to rise, and goes to his room before seven. When she opens the door and steps into the darkened room, the putrid odour is even stronger.

Pavel rises from a pallet at the end of Konstantin's bed.

"Konstantin Nikolevich," she says quietly. "Please. Do you have the money ready for Grisha?"

It appears difficult for Konstantin to open his eyes, and when he does, he looks at her with vagueness, as if unsure whether he's awake or dreaming. There's sweat on his forehead, and the front of his nightshirt is damp.

"The doctor will come today," she tells him.

Konstantin nods.

"Is all in readiness for Grisha?" she asks again.

"I'm going with him," Konstantin says, and pushes back the bedclothes, swinging his legs to the floor and then rocking slightly to gain enough momentum to stand.

Antonina stops him, her hand on his chest. "No. The note is very clear, Konstantin. You can't. Nor can I. If either of us go, we'll ruin everything."

"I won't let them see me." Konstantin sways as he stands, grabbing her shoulder for support.

Pavel steps up behind her.

"Look at you. You can hardly stay on your feet. You can't ride. You're ill, Konstantin. Let Grisha do as the Cossacks have asked. You mustn't go, Kostya," she says, louder. "I won't let you."

"I saw my son being taken, and I will see him returned," he says, pushing her aside with his good arm. "Stay out of my way. Pavel, get my clothes."

Antonina shakes her head. "Don't you understand that by going you'll—"

"Get out," Konstantin growls.

Antonina opens her mouth to speak further, but there is nothing more to say.

She slams the door as she leaves.

She waits on the veranda. Three hours later, Grisha and Konstantin return. Both men are on Konstantin's tall Arabian, Grisha seated behind Konstantin, one arm around the older man's waist. Konstantin's head hangs forward, his chin on his chest as though he's asleep. When Grisha stops the horse and removes his arm, Konstantin falls, slowly and ungracefully, onto the dirty snow of the yard. Grisha dismounts awkwardly. He's hurt, one cheek already swollen and his left eye puffy and blackening. His lip is cut, and drying blood cakes his chin. His coat is gone, his tunic torn.

They do not have Mikhail.

Antonina goes down on one knee beside Konstantin. "Where is he? Where's my son? What happened?"

But Konstantin is unconscious. At her voice, so high and thin and filled with panic, servants run from the house, from the stables and barn and greenhouse and storehouses, from the chicken coops and blacksmith shed. Men lift the count and carry him inside the house.

Antonina looks at Grisha. "Tell me what happened."

Grisha sits in the kitchen, his glass full and a bottle of vodka in front of him. Antonina stands on the other side of the table, clasping her hands to quell the shaking. It's hard to breathe; she feels light-headed and pours herself a glass of the strong, clear liquid. She holds it tightly with both hands while she waits for Grisha to speak.

"I asked—begged—the count not to come with me," Grisha finally says, taking very small sips from the glass, wincing as the alcohol touches his cut lip. "Once I had persuaded him to give me the packet of rubles—the ransom money—I rode away from him at full speed, hoping to get to the appointed spot well before him, to give over the money and retrieve the young master. I didn't think the count would be able to keep up with me—as you know, he could barely ride."

Antonina keeps nodding, her head moving up and down as if she has no control.

"I did get to the place the Cossacks had instructed me to come to, and—"

"Mikhail. Did you see Mikhail?" Antonina interrupts.

Grisha shakes his head. "No. I'm sorry, madam. Your son was not in sight. But three Cossacks were there. Their faces were hidden from me. As I approached, I called to them, *Where is the child?*

Do you have the money? one shouted back. *Have you come alone?*

"Yes, yes, I told him, but without the boy there is no payment. *Show me Mikhail Konstantinovich Mitlovsky and I will show you the money.* One of the men turned his horse and started towards a thicket. I heard the snicker of another horse from there, madam. I think—"

"Yes? What do you think, Grisha?"

"I think Mikhail was there, hidden."

Antonina sucks in her breath. "But you didn't see him?"

Grisha has already answered the question. "At that moment, the count rode into the clearing. He was hardly able to stay in the saddle. He was confused, madam, shouting things that made no sense."

Now Antonina's voice is barely a whisper. "And?"

"When they saw him, they set upon me. They pulled me from my horse, the three of them, and beat me. I fought back, but they ripped off my coat and took the money from it." He isn't looking at Antonina but studying his hand, gripping the glass. Antonina sees the torn skin on his knuckles, the bruising already beginning.

"I fought them, madam," he repeats. "I said, they had the money, why did it matter if the count had arrived? They were disguised—he couldn't recognize them. Give me the boy, I told them, and it's done. You wanted the money, and you have it. Now give me the boy." Finally he looks into Antonina's face. "They took my horse. I ran after them, but I was no match on foot. So I ran back to the count and pulled him from his horse and rode after them. But they had already disappeared. I rode in circles for some time, madam, and then went back to where the count lay and . . . and we came home."

The kitchen is quiet except for steady thumping as Raisa, the cook, punches down dough. Something is bubbling on the stove; it rattles the lid of the big pot.

"So if Konstantin hadn't arrived, Mikhail would be home with me now," Antonina says slowly. She lifts her glass and drinks, never taking her gaze from Grisha.

Grisha gulps his vodka. He touches his torn lip with the tip of his tongue. "I believe so, madam. This I believe." He can't look at the countess any longer. The anguish on her face reminds him so much of another woman.

What has happened in these last few days is bringing back the old memories.

He pours more vodka. He drinks to numb the pain from his injuries, and to wash away his mother's image.

4

*I*n 1827, Grisha had been born Timofey Aleksandrovitch Kasakov in Chita, a village in the eastern province of Irkutsk in Siberia. The town closest to the west was the Buryat enclave of Upper Vdinsk.

When Grisha, or Timofey—Tima—as he was then called, left Chita for the small city of Irkutsk, the five-hundred-mile journey taught him something about his own resilience. He was fifteen years old, and he left home on his horse, Felya, carrying a small number of rubles, saddlebags of food, two heavy yak-hair blankets, the few pieces of clothing he owned, a small collection of books, his father's crucifix and his mother's Tibetan prayer wheel, and a wooden flute his brother, Kolya, had given him. He also carried the far heavier burden of guilt.

It was June, and along the rough, muddy trail to Irkutsk, Tima encountered thunderstorms that rolled across the steppes with terrifying power, and midges that drove him nearly mad as he slept under the stars, rolled in his blankets. Walking, stumbling, fighting to keep his footing, he led Felya through quagmires and rushing streams. When he ran out of food, he bought what he needed from the hamlets he rode through.

One afternoon, two ragged men accosted him as he stopped to let Felya drink at a narrow river, grabbing at his saddlebags. He escaped them easily, but felt threatened for the first time in his life. At the next village he bought a long-handled knife. Every day he was thankful for his Don horse. Felya was agile, with the immense endurance of the Russian horses bred for harsh climates and conditions.

When he finally arrived at Irkutsk, two weeks after leaving Chita, he stood on one of its main streets and looked around him in wonder.

He planned to spend only one night there, buying more food and then riding on. He had to take advantage of the weather. He wasn't sure how far he would get before Siberia's early autumn descended, but once it did, he would have to stop and find work. He could easily die travelling in the winter months through the isolated steppes and wooded taiga of Siberia as he attempted to cross the low Urals leading to European Russia.

Irkutsk tempted Tima with sights and sounds he had never dreamed of in tiny Chita, but he knew he couldn't stay. He needed to get as far west as he could, as quickly as possible. Nikolai—Kolya—was somewhere in Irkutsk. He couldn't take a chance on his brother seeing him.

He pushed away thoughts of Kolya for this one night in the exciting city. He spent some of his carefully hoarded kopecks to board Felya. He bought cabbage soup and a dish of marrow and peas and drank four bottles of cheap, sour beer. He was walking, slightly unsteadily, back to the stable, thinking he'd spend the night in the straw with Felya if no one threw him out, wondering if Felya had been given the oats he'd paid for or if he'd been cheated and the horse was munching low-grade hay.

A young woman in a doorway beckoned to him.

Heady from the beer, flushed with the exhilaration of the wooden streets with their oil lamps and bright storefronts, Timofey went to her. He allowed her to take his hand and lead him through the doorway and into a room partitioned with hanging blankets. Timofey tried to ignore the moans and whispers in the hot, stinking room.

"What's your name then, *moy sladki*? Eh, sweetheart?"

"Grigori," he said after a moment. "Grigori Sergeyevich Naryshkin." He combined the names of three of his father's old friends. He did not want to be Timofey Aleksandrovitch Kasakov anymore. Although he knew there was almost no chance of anyone recognizing his father's name, he wanted a new start. He no longer wanted to be thought of—even by himself—as the son of a revolutionist and the brother of the sweet, trusting boy he'd betrayed.

"Ah, Grishenka, my beauty," the girl said. "Haven't you got some eyes, eh? All the girls must love those eyes."

"How much?" he asked, trying to keep his breathing even. He was a virgin but didn't want this girl to know.

She named a price and he nodded, handing her the money. She tucked his kopecks under the thin mattress, giving a little laugh before shrugging out of her frock and pulling Timofey on top of her as she lay in her patched chemise.

Her hair was an odd red colour and Timofey liked the sound of her laugh. He could see her nipples, small and as pink as her cheeks, through her chemise. Such was his inexperience and excitement that he climaxed almost as soon as he'd released himself from his trousers and pressed against her. She cried out in annoyance, pushing him aside and fussing at him for soiling her chemise. Then she sat up and gave a brittle laugh.

"First time?" she said, and Timofey drew back at the stink of raw onion on her breath, noticing the silvery streaks stretched down the slight sag of her belly.

He stood awkwardly beside the bed, humiliated and angry, hating her laugh.

She rubbed at her chemise with a foul-smelling rag, and then tossed it to him. "Here, clean yourself up. You paid for an hour. I'm tired. I'll sleep for the rest of it." With that, she settled onto her side facing him. Within moments she was emitting small puffing sounds from half-open lips.

Timofey watched her sleep. He wanted to smack her for laughing at him. Instead, he listened to the stifled, rhythmic groans behind the blanket separating them from the next pallet, hearing the damp slap of flesh on flesh. After a few minutes of listening, he ran his rough fingers over the woman's thinly covered nipple, and then climbed on top of her, pushing up her chemise again. She made an irritated sound as she squinted at him in the dim light.

He shoved himself into her, not stopping as she said, *Wait . . . let me just . . . my hair is caught . . .*

"I'm sorry," Timofey murmured as he forced himself not to focus on the warm, welcoming softness of her.

He did not let himself think of the road back to Chita, or the one that lay ahead. He did not let himself think of his brother Kolya.

He especially tried not to think of the woman under him. This time he moved in an unhurried fashion, determined not to embarrass himself again.

"Well, you figured it out that time," she said when he'd finished and was sitting on the edge of the bed. "Just keep at it, and smile that pretty smile of yours. Will you come back to visit me, *moy sladki*?" She reached up to draw her index finger down his cheek, but Timofey recoiled from her touch. He stood, pulling up his trousers and stepping into his boots.

He discovered there were women to be had for next to nothing in every little village and hamlet along the way. Some of them sensed something—they weren't sure if it was suppressed violence or simply indifference—and were wary. Some of them were attracted to his guarded silence and dark looks. On his lonely journey, he wanted the comfort of a woman in the dark. But never did he allow himself to be moved by any of them.

⇁☞

He decided to stop in Krasnoyarsk, northwest of Irkutsk, for the winter. He got a job unloading timber. It felt good to use his muscles again after so much time astride Felya.

From Krasnoyarsk, he wrote two letters and sent them both to his dead father's friend. The man was a Decembrist who had been with his father in the uprising in St. Petersburg in 1825. One of them was for Timofey's mother, who couldn't read. In it he told his mother that he had not been able to find Kolya in Irkustsk, and that he was not coming home to Chita. He told her that the friend would explain about the money from the sale of the cooperage, the family business where Timofey had worked alongside his father until his death.

It had been a thriving concern, making barrels for Chita and the environs. The money would be enough to last her as long as she lived. *I embrace you and bless you. Tima*, he ended it.

The second letter asked the friend to sell the cooperage and give the money to his mother. He also asked him to look out for his mother should she need help. *I will not be returning to Chita. My life is elsewhere*, he wrote, signing it *Timofey Aleksandrovitch Kasakov*, knowing it would be the last time he used this name.

He left on the day the last crusty mounds of snow were

Over that winter, sharing a drafty hut with ten snoring, coughing, flatulent men, he heard stories about their lives as prisoners in distant *katorgas*, working to cut timber or, like his father, in the mines. From those who were released or those who had escaped, he understood, for the first time, that Siberia was its own prison, and grew anxious for the spring.

He left on the day the last crusty mounds of snow were melting in the shadows beneath the spruce trees, setting off for the next major town, Novosibirsk.

As he travelled the slick, muddy spring roads, Timofey— Grisha now—fought not to think of Kolya. Most days he didn't, but occasionally he'd see a thin, fair-haired boy and his heart would give one painful thump. Once he passed a man trudging down a narrow road, merrily playing a tune on a rough wooden *svirel*—a peasant flute—and this also caused a dark pain.

If he spent the night in a village hovel and could not avoid thinking about his little brother and how he'd betrayed him, he would take out the little flute with *Tima*—his own former name—carved clumsily onto its side. Kolya had made it for him as a gift. He couldn't play it, but his brother could. Then he would drink a bottle of cheap vodka so he could sleep without the familiar nightmare. If he was on the road when he thought too much of Kolya, he'd whip Felya to a gallop, fleeing from his thoughts.

He was a week east of Novosibirsk when he was surrounded on the road by a crew of rough-looking men in grey tunics. They questioned him and asked for papers.

Papers? What papers?

Papers that showed he owned the horse, they told him. You don't look like the kind of young man who could afford such a horse as the well-fed Don. You've stolen it, they told him, and pulled him off. He fought them, but all it earned him was two broken fingers and a ringing in one ear that lasted ten days. They threw him into the back of a cart with three other men. The men in the cart said nothing as he was chained in beside them. But as they jolted and bumped through the night and most of the next day, the man beside him told how a nearby work camp had suffered a loss of men from dysentery. The low government officials who had broken his fingers and temporarily partially deafened him were arresting any able-bodied men they could find on the road that day in order to meet the required quota of cut timber.

Grisha cursed his bad luck. At first he was most angry over the loss of Felya, hoping whoever owned him next wouldn't mistreat him. He didn't imagine the false arrest would come to anything more than a week or two of hard work, and then he would be on his way again, although this time on foot. He was used to hard work. But when he arrived at the camp deep in the forest of conifers, and saw the haunted expressions on the sallow, lined faces of the other men, and the chains securing them to their wheelbarrows and saws, he felt a deep thump of dread.

As the first weeks passed, all he could think of was his father. His father, at the time not as young and strong as Grisha, had survived in worse conditions for over a year, farther north, in the mines. At least Grisha was outside, breathing clean air. In the thick taiga of summer the men found berries and occasionally wild mushrooms to supplement the meagre rations they were given after twelve hours of cutting trees. He was allowed to keep what he brought with him, apart from his knife. In his sack Grisha still had a few of his books, the crucifix and the prayer wheel, and the *svirel* from Kolya.

During the following winter, Grisha watched men all around him die from overwork, cold, malnutrition and illness. All night, every night, men coughed and moaned and prayed, but Grisha refused to pray. When his partner on the crosscut saw, his fingers numb from the cold, lost his grip for only a moment, the sharp, angled teeth bit deeply into his thigh. Grisha watched, helpless, as the man bled to death in the snow, and knew he no longer believed.

Prayers wouldn't bring bread, or another blanket or warm boots or safety from the teeth of the saw. He believed that the others were wasting their time praying for comfort. As he learned to survive in the camp, he knew he was also learning to survive outside of it. He would work for or steal what he needed, depending only on himself.

As spring approached, he made a plan with two other men, both a few years older than him. He'd been in the camp nine months, and knew if he didn't make his escape soon he'd be too weak. The three men waited for the perfect conditions: a moonless, balmy night, the guards outside their hut drunk and arguing. They killed first one guard and then the second and ran through the darkness into the thick forest. Which of them drew the knife, made from a broken saw blade, across the men's stubbled throats remained their secret: they were all guilty. They separated once they were three days from the camp, not wanting to be reminded by each other of what they had become.

Grisha made his way west, his small sack strapped on his back. He crossed the rest of Siberia by walking and begging rides in carts. Through that spring and summer he stole what he could from gardens, living for days on the first tiny spring onions and bulbs of garlic. He stole from the backs of rough carts delivering grains and from horses' feed bags. He stole clothing hung to dry; he once stole boots from the feet of a sleeping drunk. Some of what he stole he sold for a few kopecks in the next village. He fought senseless arguments with his fists after too much vodka.

The one thing he would never allow himself to do, the one thing that he knew would be the last step to truly make him the animal he felt he was becoming, was to take a woman against her will. When he wanted a woman but didn't have enough to pay for her, he shrugged and walked away.

As the cold weather once again descended, he passed the marker that stood on the border between Siberia and western Russia. He thought of his father as he stared at the rough cylindrical stone symbol, taller than him by a head. Although Aleksandr Kasakov had never spoken to his son of his brutal time in the mines, he did say that when he and the cartload of chained prisoners passed that marker, on the way into Siberia and away from everyone and everything they knew and loved, many of the men—strong and dignified—put their faces into their hands and wept.

Unlike his father and those wretched men, Grisha was travelling west, not east. As he looked over his shoulder, he allowed himself one final goodbye to his mother and his lost brother. He swore that he would not live with guilt, guilt for what he had done to them, and to the prison guards, and to all the people he had wronged in order to survive. It was the only way he could live his new life.

He put his hand on the cold stone marker, resisting the old urge to cross himself, and then stepped into European Russia.

5

*D*r. Molov arrives at Angelkov a few hours after Antonina left Grisha in the kitchen. She is in Konstantin's room when he is shown in, and stands beside him as he listens to Konstantin's heart and then slowly moves a candle back and forth in front of his eyes. Konstantin allows the doctor to do as he wishes.

"Countess Mitlovskiya," the doctor says, setting down the candle and facing her. "I'm very sorry for the tragedy that has come upon your home. It's spoken of throughout the villages and on the neighbouring estates."

Antonina nods.

"The fever," Dr. Molov says, "when did it begin?"

"I don't know. Maybe yesterday," Antonina says, swallowing at the strong smell of garlic on the man's breath. "His good hand and his feet have been bathed in cool water and vinegar, but it isn't bringing down the heat."

The doctor again bends over Konstantin and begins to unwrap the dressing. When the last round of linen is pulled away and the smell is fully released into the room, even he reacts with a small intake of breath. Antonina presses her handkerchief to her nose and mouth.

"This should have immediately been well cleaned and stitched," Dr. Molov says. "How many days since he was hurt?"

"Four." It's been four days since she's held her son, she thinks.

The doctor shakes his head, opening his bag and pulling out a small leather case. After he's worked over Konstantin with warm water and disinfectant, needle and thread, he and Antonina go into the hall. He tells her he will check on the count's progress in the morning; there is nothing more to be done this evening. He has ridden to the estate from the city of Pskov, and will stay overnight at Angelkov.

Antonina nods. "Thank you, Dr. Molov," she says, and goes down the long hall to her bedroom.

Tania has waited until the doctor and the countess have left Konstantin's bedroom. She enters with stacks of towels and bed linens. "Will he recover?" she asks Pavel.

"The doctor has done what he can," Pavel says as the woman sets down the clean laundry. Pavel knows about her relationship with Konstantin. Everyone on the estate knows, including the countess. Pavel watches her. She is very like Konstantin's first wife, dark-complexioned and raw-boned, the same age as the first Countess Mitlovskiya. The count started to make his demands on Tania six months after his wife succumbed to a lifelong stomach ailment.

Tania leans over the count and strokes his cheek. "Kostya," she whispers. She hopes he recovers. After thirteen years, she is used to the small pleasures the extra weekly rubles from her master bring.

He doesn't stir, and Tania, without looking at Pavel, goes downstairs and back to her room in the two-storey stone building behind the manor that houses the servants of Angelkov.

In her bedroom, Antonina thinks about how she could have had her son back by now. She could have, if not for Konstantin. Her anger at him is too intense to let her sleep.

The next morning, Antonina pulls herself out of bed, her head dull and her eyes gritty. The horror of it all, the sleepless nights and too much vodka are taking their toll. She knows she has to see to her husband, but even the thought of walking down the hall is daunting. She holds Tinka against her, pressing her face into the little dog's warm fur. When Lilya comes in, she gently guides Antonina into the chair in front of the dressing table and pins her hair haphazardly for the time being. She speaks to Antonina as she wipes her face with a warm, damp cloth, but Antonina can't quite make sense of what she's saying. It's as if she is underwater.

As Antonina moves slowly to her door to go to Konstantin's room, Lilya stops her, putting a robe over her nightdress and then a shawl over her shoulders, clasping it with a sapphire brooch. She stoops and picks up Tinka, who tries to follow Antonina.

Grisha is standing outside the count's room. He bows to

Antonina and opens the door for her. Antonina enters. Her husband is as motionless as he was the evening before, although now his eyes are closed. There is dried matter on his lips. Dr. Molov is sitting on a chair beside the bed, holding Konstantin's injured hand. The edges of the wound, under the new stitches, are swollen and reddish-purple, pushing against the thread. Through the stitches seeps a fluid, bloody and yet not entirely blood.

"It's worse?" Antonina asks. The words are measured. She has no saliva, and her lips are slightly numb.

"Yes," the doctor says, glancing up at her and frowning. "He's in a state of unconsciousness."

"What's happened? Why is he like this?"

"We can't say just yet." The doctor wraps fresh gauze around Konstantin's darkening hand.

"We?" Antonina repeats. "What do you mean? What can't we say?" Does it take a very long time for these short phrases to come out, or is it just her drowsiness that makes her voice sound so dull and slow?

The doctor again looks up at her. "Countess Mitlovskiya, it's too soon to predict. But should the fever continue . . ." He stops, tying the strip of gauze. "Has he been taking liquids? Has he been passing his water?"

Antonina sees that Konstantin has two spots of hectic colour on his unshaven cheeks. "I don't know."

"Neither," Pavel says from the foot of the bed.

"Why not? Why have you not been giving him fluids?" the doctor asks the servant.

"I have tried, sir, many times. But he won't drink."

"Won't? Come now," the doctor says sharply. "Are you so incapable of a simple task?"

At the annoyed tone of his voice, Antonina's head clears a little. She knows how devoted Pavel is to Konstantin; he's been his manservant for over twenty years, long before she came to Angelkov. He has not left Konstantin's side the last few nights. And now this doctor is speaking to the elderly man as though he were a child, rebuking him for his lack of duty.

She would like a cup of hot sweet tea. "You attempt, then, Dr. Molov," she says. "You try to force open his lips and make him swallow."

The doctor frowns at her. "Countess, I only stress how important it is, in the case of blood poisoning, to—"

"Blood poisoning?" Antonina rubs her forehead. "You didn't say this."

"I've done what I can for now." He stands. "I have commitments today, but will return tomorrow. It's most important that Count Mitlovsky have fluids. This will flush out the poison, countess."

Antonina nods.

The doctor closes his bag and then says, in a kinder voice, "Surely your son will be returned. It's a time of great instabililily: the Emancipation Manifesto has thrown the country into chaos. Nobody understands what it will mean. The serfs . . . the newly freed people, haven't yet been told how they'll be affected, or how to deal with their freedom. There's fear, confusion and too many rumours. There have even been some minor uprisings on other estates. The thugs who kidnapped your son will soon realize . . ." He stops.

Antonina waits. Although more focused now, she still feels as though she's stepping out of a strange twilight. "Will realize what?" she finally asks.

The doctor opens his bag again, taking out a small square

bottle. "Laudanum, countess. It will help you cope for the moment. It's better than—I believe it will help you." He turns to Pavel. "Force fluids into him as best you can, and keep bathing him in cool water to bring down the fever." He picks up his bag, nods to Antonina and is gone.

Antonina lowers herself into the wide leather chair. She closes her eyes and puts her head back, exhausted, although she has done nothing more than walk down the hall and listen to the doctor.

As the doctor closes the bedroom door behind him, Grisha steps forward. "Will he recover?" When the doctor doesn't immediately answer, Grisha says, "I am the steward, Dr. Molov. I must know what to expect, for the sake of the estate."

The doctor nods, then reaches for Grisha's arm to guide him away from the door. "I'll speak the truth with you— I can see that she's of little use."

"What do you mean?" Grisha asks, looking down at the short, huffing man.

"The countess. Is it a muted form of hysteria? Last night, and now this morning . . . she doesn't appear fully in charge of her senses." He nods at Grisha. "I'm glad there's someone in charge here."

"Countess Mitlovskiya has had a great deal of distress," Grisha says. "But what of the count?"

"It's not good at all. Because the wound wasn't cared for properly, it's become infected. There is poisoning of the blood, and it's working its way up his arm. We don't want it to go into the rest of the body."

"Will he live?"

The doctor shrugs. "It's in the hands of God now. All we can do is wait." He turns and starts down the staircase.

Grisha watches him go.

⤳

That night, Antonina dismisses Pavel to allow him a proper rest. She sits by Konstantin's bed with Tinka in her lap; she knows that, for her, there's no point in attempting to sleep. She had taken a number of spoonfuls of the laudanum throughout the day. The blended potion of opium and alcohol allowed her to drift, and she hadn't wanted to emerge from the dull, dreamlike sensation the murky liquid gave her.

Now she sits in the dark, her cheek resting on her palm, elbow propped on the wide arm of the chair. The other hand rests on Tinka's head. At some point she thinks she hears Konstantin murmur something.

She pulls herself up, holding Tinka against her with one hand, then kneels beside the bed. "Speak, husband," she whispers. "If you can, for God's sake speak."

In the darkness, she can't tell whether Konstantin's eyes are open or not, but she definitely hears him whispering something. "What is it? What are you trying to say?" She puts her hand on his shoulder. It feels bony, as if the flesh is falling away.

And then she hears him say a name.

"Grisha? But he's not here—it's the middle of the night. Why do you want Grisha?"

"Grisha knows," Konstantin says. The second word is a long-drawn-out sigh.

"Knows what? What does he know? I've spoken to Grisha. He's told me everything that's happened."

"Knows," Konstantin repeats, so quietly that Antonina has to put her ear to his mouth.

"Knows what?" Antonina asks again, but Konstantin is silent. She firms her grip on his shoulder to try to wake him, but it's no use; he has fallen back into a state of deep sleep, or unconsciousness.

Antonina knows that the poison from the wound is making him this ill, that it might have been prevented had he allowed his hand to be looked after properly right away. Or if he would take in fluids. In effect, he's killing himself. And in the manner Konstantin has always lived his life— with narrow-minded, dogged perseverance—she knows that in this, he also wants to complete what he has begun. He wants to die.

"I see what you're doing," she whispers to him. "You can't live with your guilt, and so are choosing the coward's way out. You lost our son because you wouldn't listen to me, and now you choose to leave me to deal with the aftermath. To leave me alone to hope, to watch at the window for Misha, to pray until my knees bleed. And as you force me to carry this unbearable weight, you also wish to put on me the burden of widowhood."

Of course, he doesn't respond, and there is nothing for Antonina to do but rise and return to her chair.

The next morning, Antonina doesn't allow herself any more of the laudanum—she needs to be alert—although later in the morning she quickly drinks one glass of wine. She has sent for Grisha, and the wine is just to steady her hands while she waits for him in Konstantin's study.

"What now, Grisha?" she asks when he arrives, noticing the dark blotches of colour on his bruised face. She's sitting on a chair in front of the fire, and Grisha stands near the fireplace. "What do we do now?"

Grisha concentrates on kicking some ashes back towards the grate. "We will continue to search for Mikhail Konstantinovich, of course, madam. We were out all of yesterday, and Lyosha and the others are out again today. There were many issues for me to deal with here, but I gave instructions for the men to spread out in wider and wider circles among the hamlets and villages. And we have reported the kidnapping to the authorities in Pskov."

"Is there any news at all, Grisha?" Antonina speaks quietly. She has no energy to raise her voice.

He doesn't answer immediately. "No one has actually come forward and said they have seen the young master," he says at last. "But the villagers are frightened. Of course, they may have been threatened and are afraid to speak up. And so we will continue to look. We won't give up, madam. And you know your son is strong, and clever. You must comfort yourself with that thought, madam: that he is all right. He is all right," he repeats, more loudly.

Antonina nods, but doesn't look convinced. "Perhaps they took him to the city—to Pskov. Or even all the way to St. Petersburg."

Grisha shakes his head. "I feel strongly that he's nearby, but well hidden. We will search the whole province, madam."

"Will they send another note? Will they ask for more money?" This is the question Antonina has been wondering about since yesterday. She hoped Grisha would mention it first, in his usual firm way. "Because Konstantin foiled the first attempt, will there be another chance?"

Does his expression change, ever so subtly, now? Antonina remembers how Konstantin had murmured Grisha's name in the night. *Grisha knows.*

"It is certainly a possibility, madam. Men like these . . . they're corrupt and greedy."

His answer doesn't bring as much relief as she'd hoped. "So we just wait?"

"And continue to search, madam."

There is silence, except for the snapping of the fire. Grisha stares at the flames.

"Last night, Grisha, Konstantin spoke to me," Antonina says.

Grisha doesn't react for a moment, then turns from the fire to face her. "He regained consciousness?"

"For a moment."

Grisha is very still.

"He said your name. It sounded like he said, *Grisha knows.* What did he mean, Grisha?"

Grisha doesn't answer immediately. "I thought I recognized one of them. The Cossacks. As they came for me, I called out a name."

Antonina rises from her chair. "You know him?"

But Grisha shakes his head. "As I said, madam, I thought so for a moment. I could only see his eyes, and as they beat me, his scarf came away, and it was not the man I thought. But Konstantin . . . he heard me call a name. This is what he must have spoken of."

Antonina, standing in front of her chair, studies Grisha's dark eyes. "Thank you," she finally says, when a log drops heavily. "You may leave, Grisha."

Grisha bows and turns. Once out of the study, he leans against the closed door. As negative as his feelings are for Konstantin Nikolevich, he doesn't want him to die.

The kidnapping had not gone as he expected.

And death was not part of the plan.

6

*H*ad Grisha suspected how terribly wrong it would all go, how Soso would deceive him, he would never have agreed to it.

He now knows—although he had never seen it in all the time he'd known Soso, Lilya's husband—that in the same way he hates Konstantin, Soso hates him. Konstantin had no clue of the deep, dark anger Grisha felt towards him for his superior air and expectations, the casual demands. And now Grisha is having done to him exactly what he wanted done to Konstantin. Soso is punishing Grisha, as Grisha sought to punish Konstantin—by blackmailing him, extorting money.

When Soso invited Grisha to a game of cards in the servants' quarter one night early in January, Grisha should have been wary. Because of his lofty position at Angelkov, the other men treated him with cautious deference. It was he, after all, who supervised all the serfs on the estate, who reported their infractions or disobedience to the count, and who meted out their punishments. Grisha knew he made the serfs uneasy; when he was around, they had to be on their guard. He wasn't a man who needed the company of either men or women, and he had never particularly liked Soso, but the winter had been harder than usual, each evening long, dark and frigid. The idea of a night of cards and vodka unexpectedly appealed to him, and so he let down his guard. He said yes.

By the time they started the second bottle, Soso was talking about his burning resentment towards the count, citing recent incidents that still angered him: selling two of the storeroom workers to another estate, which put an extra workload on Soso, and berating and humiliating him about a spilled bag of oats—even cutting his wages over it.

"He acts as though we're of less importance than his bloody horses," he ranted.

And Grisha agreed. Count Mitlovsky was pig-headed and cruel. Some landowners treated their serfs with kindness and patience. Mitlovsky did not: to him, they were, as Soso said, little more than animals. "He thinks," Soso said, throwing down his cards, "that tossing us a handful of extra rubles at Christmas and a few bottles of vodka a year—the man has his own distillery, for God's sake—makes him a saint." He spat on the floor.

Grisha drained his glass, feeling his own anger growing. "I'm the one who runs Angelkov, who makes sure he understands the accounting. He asks my opinions on matters dealing with his finances. Was the estate this successful under the last steward? No. He has much to be thankful to me for, and yet he acts as though I'm the one who should be thankful." He didn't mention that the count used his home—and

Grisha's own bed—for his trysts with Tania. Yes, the blue-shuttered house belonged to the count, but that he would take this liberty was, to Grisha, the most despicable affront.

He reached for the bottle and filled their glasses, then raised his. "To honesty," he said. Aware that it was inspired by the vodka, he nevertheless felt camaraderie with Soso as they sat in the chilled dimness of his room in the servants' quarters. Soso was one of Angelkov's hardest-working serfs. He looked after the storehouses, ensuring they were properly stocked with food to supply the huge estate. Grisha had known him since he'd come to work on the estate with Lilya and her little brother a decade earlier, just before the count's son was born.

Grisha had always had a grudging admiration for the man. Soso was a few years older than him, strong and tire-less. He worked without complaining—usually—and so to hear him talk so freely about the count made Grisha feel that Soso also trusted him enough to confide in him.

"Freedom is coming, and I'm not going to walk away from a lifetime of work with nothing," Soso said, his glass raised towards Grisha's. "If Mitlovsky thinks he can get the same amount of work out of us once we're free men, he's wrong." He drank. "I'm working on a plan, something that will give us—you and me—what we deserve. Something to help start a new life." He stared at Grisha, frowning, his eyes almost disappearing under his heavy, short-lashed eyelids. He dug his little finger into his ear and rotated it. "We'll get money from him, a lot of money. You don't plan to stay and work for the old bastard, do you?"

Grisha shrugged. "I'm not a serf. It's different for me."

"He treats you like one. I've seen it. You want to keep taking it? Eh? Are you in?"

Grisha didn't respond for a moment, thinking of Tania emerging from his bedroom with the dirtied linen. "It depends," he finally said. He knew he was drunk, and wiped his mouth with his sleeve. "What are you thinking of?"

"I haven't worked it out yet," Soso said. "But if I know you're with me, it will make it easier. And I have some friends . . . they'd help us."

Grisha shrugged and rose, leaving the servants' quarters and walking unsteadily back to his own house down the road.

The next day, his head sore, Grisha remembered the conversation as simply the drunken solidarity of men puffing themselves up with random thoughts of revenge.

But when Soso came to him after emancipation had been declared, and asked if he had been serious about extorting money from the count, Grisha told the man he would have to think about it.

"I told you, I have friends. I can vouch for them—they're decorated former Cossacks," Soso said.

Grisha didn't even know if he could trust Soso, and didn't know anything about the man's friends, Edik and Lev. But it appeared Soso already had a plan in place: they would kidnap the count's son. Kidnap him, demand ransom, get the money, give the boy back. Simple.

Grisha didn't like it. He told Soso to come up with another plan. Not kidnapping. He didn't want to think of Mikhail Konstantinovich put into a dangerous situation. He had watched the boy grow up. Misha took after his mother in both appearance and character, and he was a winsome child. Grisha liked him.

He wouldn't be a part of it if it involved Misha.

Soso assured him that the boy wouldn't be mistreated, and would be fed and kept warm for the one or two nights he was held. That was all—a few nights, and then, when Grisha brought the money demanded by the ransom note, it would be divided four ways. They would each have more than enough to buy themselves what they needed to start their new lives: a plot of land or a small business. They would never again answer to a master.

Soso said he, Edik and Lev were ready to go forward. Still Grisha refused. But only Grisha could make sure the kidnapping went smoothly, Soso argued. Only he had inside information as to the count's movements. If Grisha wouldn't go along with them, they would still carry out the plan, but might have to resort to violence to take the child. There might be bloodshed. Who knew what might happen to the boy? "Lev and Edik won't wait forever," Soso added. It was on Grisha's head now—did he want this guilt?

Guilt. Without knowing it, Soso had chosen the right tactic. And so Grisha agreed that he would alert Soso when the circumstances were right—when there was an opportunity to take the boy. "But," he told him, "I'm going to make sure you don't harm Mikhail Konstantinovich."

He also stressed that while the boy was still a few months from turning eleven years old, he was very clever. And while he wouldn't recognize the Cossacks, he knew Soso; he was Lilya's husband. There could not be even the slightest indication that Soso—or of course he—was involved.

Soso told Grisha he understood, and would comply.

"And what of Lilya?" Grisha added. "Will you share this with your wife?" Grisha knew how dedicated the woman was to her mistress, and to the child. He so often saw the three of them—Antonina, Lilya and Misha—together.

Soso slowly shook his head. "Lilya? I couldn't trust her with this. She will know nothing." He wiped his nose with his fingers. "Nothing," he repeated. "Only the four of us are in on it."

The actual kidnapping—Grisha had been sitting back, watching through the trees—had not gone as smoothly as Soso had promised. Grisha was angry over the count's injury. He had been promised, hadn't he, that no one would be hurt.

After that, it had all grown far worse. When he took the ransom money to Soso and the others a few days later, Mikhail had been there.

It haunted him how the child's face had lit up when he appeared in the clearing; the old memories from Chita flooded back. "Grisha!" Mikhail had cried out. "Grisha! Take me home!"

Grisha had nodded. "Yes, yes, Mikhail, you will come back to Angelkov with me now." He had ridden towards Soso, who, like Edik and Lev, had his face hidden.

But when Grisha held out the packet of money, the men surrounded him, dragging him off his horse and beating him. It happened so unexpectedly that he wasn't prepared. He fought back, hearing Misha calling his name, then crying *Papa*, and then there was nothing more. As he regained consciousness, he found his horse gone and the count on the ground near him, his Arabian nosing about in the half-frozen undergrowth.

He was furious with Soso, and confronted him later that day. Soso, lifting heavy bags of grain in the storehouse, simply shrugged when Grisha demanded to know where Mikhail had been taken.

"You have your money," Grisha said. "I don't care if you won't give me my share—just give me the boy."

With his take, he'd planned to add a last piece of good land to the versts he had already bought. He had come to understand, many years ago, that he needed to possess something of his own. And now he did. He would build a house and hire some of the former estate serfs to work for him. He'd been training Lyosha to be *his* steward. He planned to leave Angelkov as soon as the wretched business with the kidnapping was over. It wasn't about the money for him; it was only about his anger towards Konstantin. Now he wondered why he had been so vindictive.

"Give back the boy," he said, making a fist, although he involuntarily winced. Two of his ribs were broken, and in spite of his bluff, he knew he wouldn't be able to stand up to Soso.

"The others want more money."

"More? They got what was agreed upon."

Soso dropped the bag with a grunt. "It's not enough."

"Then send another note and ask for more ransom. But don't think I'll deliver it without getting the child back first this time."

Soso leaned against a stack of filled sacks and lit his pipe. "A bit more money is all they want."

"And where is Misha?" Grisha asked him again.

"Safe. Get me money, and I'll get you the boy."

"Do you think I'll get you more money if the child is already dead? Am I that much of a fool? Unless I have proof he's alive, there will be no more money. Get me some proof."

"I'll talk to the others," Soso said, and sucked on his pipe. He crossed his arms over his chest and stared at Grisha. "When I'm ready."

Grisha knew then that Soso had him in exactly the position he wanted. He saw that it wasn't only about the money for Soso, just as it hadn't been for him. It would bring Soso pleasure to make him wait.

A week after the kidnapping, Antonina sits beside Konstantin's bed.

He is in a deep sleep, his lips cracked and peeling, his cheeks sunken. Antonina wonders what he is capable of thinking, of understanding, in this fevered state. Is he suffering over his son? Of course, he loved his child, even though he was not the son he had dreamed of.

His first marriage had been long and childless. He had wanted the son Antonina gave him to be more robust. He urged the boy to take chances, to ride difficult horses through the meadows and to practise dives, over and over, in the lake on the estate. Konstantin forced Mikhail to skate on that same lake, frozen in winter, until the child's face was ghostly with exhaustion. He had been proud of the boy for his outstanding musical ability, yes, proud that by the age of five Mikhail could compose melodies. But it wasn't enough for Konstantin.

"Is that all he's interested in?" he asked Antonina when Mikhail was seven. "It's abnormal for a boy to care more for music than the thrill of the hunt, the horses and dogs, rifles and hunting bows. Look at Lilya's brother from the stables. Lyosha. He's still a boy, and yet already so accomplished. Grisha told me that only last week he got three grouse and a fox within an hour."

"Lyosha is much older than Mikhail. Don't compare him to our son."

A few years earlier, Konstantin had seen Lyosha kicked by one of the horses. Luckily, it was a small filly, and it was just the edge of her hoof that caught the boy or he might have been seriously injured, even killed. Lyosha was knocked unconscious for a few moments. As he came to, with two of the older stablemen kneeling over him, he grimaced but insisted on getting to his feet. Konstantin later learned that the child's collarbone and arm had been broken, but he hadn't made a sound. He had been impressed by the boy's strength and stoicism.

"Mikhail should spend more time outside, instead of all the hours at his lessons or at the piano," he said.

"Misha is extremely musically gifted," Antonina had argued. "You're aware of that."

Konstantin grunted. "I'm not suggesting the boy give up his musical studies. But I want a son who can ride and hunt with me, not just compose piano trifles. I want him to have a career in the army."

"The army?" Antonina was dumbstruck.

"The training will be good for him. He can join one of the noble cadet schools in St. Petersburg when he's thirteen. It will guarantee him entrance into an elite branch of the Russian military service. By the time he's twenty, he could be a lieutenant, and move steadily forward. I have always dreamed of a son who becomes a general."

Antonina knew that nothing would be gained by arguing with Konstantin. Mikhail was only seven; she had a number of years to change her husband's mind. She would not let him give up his musical career for a rifle, no matter what Konstantin said.

I despise him, Antonina thinks, looking at her husband. For all his self-indulgent life Konstantin has done whatever he wanted to do, regardless of the cost to others. Even worse than taking Mikhail out against her wishes the day he was kidnapped, he did not obey the Cossacks' demands, and as a result destroyed the chance of her child's safe return.

She dismisses Pavel and takes a pair of nail scissors from the dressing table. She stands over Konstantin, wanting to press the small, sharp blades into his lips, pry them open so that the answers she needs to hear will spill out. *How hard did you fight if only your hand is injured? Would you not fight to the death for your son?*

She will not imagine Mikhail dead. He is not dead. She would know if he was dead. He is her son.

"Je t'aime, Maman," he always told her as she tucked him into his bed. Antonina had encouraged him to speak the second language of Russian nobility since he was a toddler. *"Je veux beaucoup de baisers,"* he would add, and she would answer, "How many? How many kisses do you wish?"

Sometimes it was five, sometimes ten, sometimes twenty. It was their bedtime ritual. She smothered his cheeks and hands with kisses, and he laughed and told her that her lips tickled.

She realizes now that it's not her husband's lips she wishes to cut open. She wants to puncture his neck, push the blades into the scab already there, into the slowly beating and vital artery. She wants to see a satisfying spurt of thick blood leap into the air, an arc of life that if left to pulse long enough will, eventually, lead to death. She wants to do this so badly her hands tremble.

But to what end? Yes, it would be vengeance, of course, an absurd and illogical retaliation for Konstantin's lack of respect, for his stupidity. But Antonina also knows there can be nothing gained from his death. Killing Konstantin would be a mortal sin, sealing her fate in the afterlife. Worse, it would do nothing to return her child.

Still, she allows herself to slowly press the blades to his neck. His eyes open, as if she has called his name, and he looks up at her. There's no surprise or fear in his eyes. What she sees is hope. *Do it*, his eyes say. *Kill me, Antonina Leonidovna. I beg of you.*

And when she understands that this is what he wants, she removes the scissors. Of course, she will not grant his wish. It simply gives her momentary relief to think of something besides Mikhail's sweet chin, his smooth high forehead, his clear grey-green eyes. Instead, she presses the blade into the skin on the inside of her forearm, just below the lacy edge of her sleeve. She pulls it in a slow, hard line, as though the blade is the nib of a pen and her skin the parchment. As she does this, she continues to watch Konstantin. He stares at her arm, and she looks down as the beads of blood rise up along the slice in her flesh.

She feels no pain, and yet the cut has brought some hard, dark relief she can't name. She throws the scissors to the floor and retreats to her chair.

The following day, people move about the bedroom as though it's a hive. Konstantin is no longer the dull drone Antonina often believed him to be, but a useless queen. As in a hive, it's as though all lives depend on that one life.

A second doctor joins Dr. Molov; Antonina doesn't know his name and doesn't care to learn it. The two of them bleed and cup the count. They force fluids into his body with a glass tube.

Father Cyril, the priest from the estate church, has become a permanent fixture, taking the chair in the opposite corner of the room from Antonina. And as well as Lilya, there are always too many servants. Antonina stays in her darkened corner in Konstantin's high-backed leather chair, watching the endless movements around his bed. Tinka is in her lap.

Lilya had looked at the cut on the inside of Antonina's arm, silently washing away the drying blood. She wrapped a strip of linen around it, brought her soup and tea with jam. She regularly bathes Antonina's face and hands with a warm damp cloth and keeps a shawl around her shoulders, a blanket over her legs. She gently lifts Tinka from Antonina and takes her outside a few times during the day; she gives the dog food and water and brings her back.

Lilya is her maid but also her companion, her friend and Mikhail's *nyanya*—his nanny. Since Antonina had come to Angelkov and found her again, Lilya has looked after her every desire, seeming to understand a need before it is spoken.

Antonina does not say anything now, except to ask every few hours, or perhaps every ten minutes: "Has there been another message from the Cossacks?"

Nobody answers her. After a while nobody looks in her direction when she asks her question, over and over.

7

*T*hat night in the bedroom, Lilya asks, "Shall I get your laudanum, Tosya?"

Antonina nods.

Lilya brings the bottle and a spoon, and Antonina opens her mouth and swallows, three times.

"Now a glass of wine," Antonina says.

"You don't need wine with the laudanum."

"I do," Antonina answers.

Lilya pours her a small glass. Antonina drinks it, sitting on the edge of the bed, and then hands the glass back to her maid.

Lilya helps Antonina out of her clothes and puts a nightgown over her head, doing up its many tiny buttons. She settles Antonina under the fresh sheets and turns down the lamps so there is only the faintest glow illuminating the shadows. She opens the tall windows just enough for a cool, fresh spring breeze to billow the curtains. Antonina feels the night air on her face.

Does Mikhail smell this same breeze? Is he in a clean bed?

She looks at the journal on her bedside table. She hadn't wanted to go to Mikhail's room, somehow thinking that if she left it exactly as it had been, it would help him come home. But this afternoon she could no longer sit in Konstantin's busy bedchamber with its whispers and unpleasant odours. She suddenly wanted—needed—to be close to Mikhail's belongings.

When she opened his door, something between a moan and a sigh escaped her lips. She looked at it all—his bed and wardrobe, his bookshelf and desk, the low footstool near the fireplace where he liked to sit, his boyish collections of rocks and jars of dead insects and the pictures he'd painted—and held on to the edge of the door frame. When she was no longer dizzy, she closed the door and went to his bed. She lay down on it, burying her face in her son's pillow. But the servants had changed the linens and all she could smell was laundry soap and starch. She got up and went to his wardrobe, pulling out tunics and jackets. She held each to her face, weeping. She carried one tunic—there was a splotch of ink on the cuff, so she knew it had somehow escaped laundering—back to the bed. She lay down again and held it against her face, breathing. Finally, in the unwashed tunic, she could smell her son.

After some time, she got up and sat in front of his desk. She ran her fingers over Mikhail's lessons books, stopping at a journal with a soft calfskin cover. It made her think of his small leather music composition booklet, which held some fugues and nocturnes of Glinka's she had transcribed into easier keys for him. Of course, now he could play the originals with ease, but he had kept the book, using it to write down his own melodies. He carried it with him always, along with a little sharpened stick of charcoal, because, he had told her, he never knew when he would hear something beautiful in his head. She thought, suddenly, of how he had grabbed the booklet from the piano as he ran from the music salon. Did he still have it?

She picked up the calfskin-bound journal, running her hand over its soft cover. It was a gift given to him at a neighbouring Christmas party that year. When he showed it to Antonina, she said he should write down his thoughts on its stiff, creamy pages. She told him she had always kept a journal, and that it is a lovely thing to write what one is thinking or wondering about.

A week later, Mikhail sat at the breakfast table across from her, writing in it while she read and drank her morning tea.

When Konstantin came in, he asked, "Are those lessons, Mikhail?"

"No. I'm writing my thoughts in my journal, Papa."

Konstantin slammed his hand on the table. Antonina's tea sloshed into the saucer. "Men do not waste time on such things, Mikhail. This is a woman's pastime. Put it away."

Mikhail very slowly set his pen on the table.

"Close that book, I said."

"I'm waiting for the ink to dry."

"Don't let me see you with it again," Konstantin threatened, then left without eating breakfast.

Once the front door slammed, Mikhail picked up his pen and dipped it into the ink.

Antonina drank her tea.

She opened the leather journal and drew in a deep breath.

His handwriting. His words. His thoughts. She closed the book and put her hand over her eyes. Eventually she rose, leaving the journal on the desk, and went to her room, separated from Mikhail's by a large linen storage closet. She took the vodka from her wardrobe and a glass from her washstand and carried them back to his room.

She filled the glass and took a drink, and then another, and finally read the first entry, dated January 8, 1861.

My friend Oxana Alexandrovna gave this book to me for Christmas. Mama has said that I should use it to write what I am thinking about.

Mama told me I must not be shy, and to write about the things that make me happy and things that I do not like. She said that it is private, and no one need ever read it.

Antonina stopped and took another drink. She touched the uneven lines and splashes of ink.

Mama told me it would be good practice for me to write in French, but I don't want to. I still make too many mistakes in my French. Monsieur Thibault tells me this every day.

I don't like writing out my lessons for him. I always get ink on my fingers and on the pages, and he shakes his head and looks sad. And then when it is time for Monsieur Lermontov to hear my practising, he makes loud, angry noises with his tongue, and says my hands on the keys do not look like those of a careful boy.

Starting today I will try to be more careful.

Antonina finished her vodka and poured another glass. She has not seen the tutors since the day Mikhail was taken. Are they still in their rooms in the servants' quarters, waiting for Mikhail to return, waiting to be summoned to resume their work with him?

There are pages torn from the journal. The next entry was three weeks later.

> *I have been practising, but I am not any neater. Monsieur Lermontov will be very cross when he arrives later today. When he is like this I have a bad feeling in my stomach, like when I eat too many of Raisa's poppy seed rolls, and then I do not play as well. He sometimes tells Papa when my practising doesn't go well, and knowing Papa is displeased makes my stomach feel worse.*
>
> *But if Papa isn't home and he tells Mama, she nods at him but then makes funny faces at me when he's not looking. Mama never gets angry with me.*

Antonina pulled her handkerchief from her sleeve and held it to her eyes for a long moment. Then she took another drink and continued reading. The next entry was at the end of February.

> *I like my room, but it is very big and sometimes noises come from the fireplace. Last year I told Lilya I was too old for her to sleep on her cot at the foot of my bed anymore, but some nights I wish she was still here like before. When I was very small and had bad dreams she would carry me to Mama's bed and I would stay the night with her. But if Papa came in from his room in the morning and saw me*

*there he would grow cross with Mama and tell her I was
not a baby and that I must sleep in my own bed. Papa calls
me a little soldier and says soldiers do not sleep with their
mothers, and they do not cry.*

*I try not to cry because I know it makes Papa cross.
But I don't want to be a soldier. Mama told me her brother
Viktor Leonidovich was a soldier and he died. I don't want
to die like Uncle Viktor.*

*When I was a very little boy and Papa went to the city,
I always slept with Mama and Tinka. Sometimes Lilya
would stay with us too, sleeping on Mama's settee, and in
the morning when I woke up and saw Mama and Lilya
talking and laughing I always felt happy. Mama doesn't
call me a soldier. She calls me her petite souris.*

March 14
*I have five friends: Andrei Yakovavich and Stepan
Yakovavich (they are brothers) and Oxana Alexandrovna
and Yuliana Philipova. There is also Ivan Abramovich.
I don't like him as much because he is mean sometimes but
he is blind in one eye and Mama says maybe that makes
him sad and maybe that's why he is mean so I must be kind
to him anyway. All my friends live on other estates and we
only get to play together sometimes.*

*At home I like playing with Lyosha. He is much older
than me but he is nice. He is Lilya's brother. He shows me
how to tie special knots in ropes, and he tells me stories
about the horses. He works in the stables with Fyodor, and
sometimes, after I have done my practising and finished my
lessons, Mama allows him to take me to the stables. Lyosha
shows me how to hold my hand flat with a carrot on it and*

let Dunia eat the carrot. Dunia's lips are soft and whiskery and tickle my hand.

I try to remember not to speak French with Lyosha. Mama told me it was not polite, because the servants don't speak French and if we do that in front of them it might make them feel left out. It is all right if we're alone, Mama says. But Papa speaks French when the servants are with us.

Once, when Mama and Papa took me with them to visit Prince Usolotsev, his boys ran away from me and hid and didn't play with me. Mama found me and hugged me and said she was sorry I was left out. She said she knew how sad that felt, because sometimes she feels left out too. I don't know who makes her feel left out. I won't ever speak French to Lyosha because I don't want him to feel sad like I did. Or like Mama.

March 22

My two favourite things to do:

1. Anything with Lyosha.

2. Playing the piano, but not with Monsieur Lermontov. When I play alone, or with Mama, I feel very quiet inside. Even if the music tells me it needs to be fortissimo and my fingers are very hard on the keys, I still feel quiet. I feel the way I do when Mama hugs me tightly, or the way I used to feel when I was so little and Lilya sang to me in bed at night.

I have always played the piano. Mama says that when I was only a baby she held me on her lap while she played. She says that I must have heard the music she played even before I was born, when I was still an angel, and that's why I can play the way I do. I don't remember being an angel, but I do remember being very little and sitting on Mama's lap in front of the pianoforte and Mama putting my fingers on the keys. I also remember when we played our first duet together. Mama cried, but she said it was not because she was sad. She said sometimes people cry when they are very, very happy. But I think that maybe only girls do that. I have never wanted to cry when I am happy.

I always hear music in my head, and I can make that music with my fingers. It is very easy, and it pleases Mama so much. It is my best time, after my dinner in the nursery with Lilya, when I come downstairs to the music salon and play for Mama and Papa. It is the only time I see them both smile at the same time.

Papa smiles when he stands on the veranda and looks at the fields, or when he puts me on the tallest horse and I hold the reins very tightly and pretend I'm not afraid. He also sometimes smiles when Grisha talks to him about the papers they look at together at Papa's big desk in his study.

Mama smiles more than Papa. She smiles at everything I say or do, and she smiles when she talks with Lilya and with all the servants.

Sometimes, especially when it rains all day, and I come to Mama to kiss and hug her good night and tell her je t'aime she smiles, but her eyes are wet. Once when I asked her why her eyes were wet she told me that she had looked at the rain too long. I believed her when I wasn't as old as I am now. Now I know that can't happen. It probably was because she was very, very happy.

March 23
I hope that I get a dog for my birthday or for my name day. I had a lap dog, a Bolonka like Tinka, but he got sick and

*then he died. That was just before Christmas. I was very
sad, and Mama said that as soon as it is spring and the
weather is warm I will get another one. I want to get a bigger
dog this time. It will be a boy dog, and I will call him Dani.*

April 6
What I am most afraid of:
   Being a soldier.
   The noise the wind makes in my fireplace sometimes.
   Papa when his mouth is straight.
   When the dogs in the yard bark too long at night.
   Something bad will happen to Mama if I am not with her.

That was the last entry.

When Antonina couldn't cry anymore, she took the book
and went back to her bedroom. Now, in the near darkness,
she caresses its cover with her hand and thinks about her son
and a dog named Dani.

"Tinka?" she calls. She hears the dog's short claws scraping at the edge of the bedcover. At almost twelve years old,
Tinka is no longer able to jump up onto the bed. Lilya picks
up the little cream- and caramel-coloured Maltese and sets
her beside Antonina. The dog licks the back of Antonina's
hand and then walks to the end of the bed and turns in a
circle four times before lying down.

Antonina remains still as Lilya moves about the dim
room, putting away clothing and straightening bottles on
the dressing table. There is nowhere for her to be, nothing
for her to do. She is just waiting. Waiting takes a huge
amount of energy; she is so tired all the time. She knows
the men search the same trails, ride through the same

villages. She doesn't ask to go with them now; she doesn't have the strength.

Outside her door, there are hushed voices and many footsteps. Very quietly a man says, *Countess Mitlovskiya?* It might be one of the doctors, or the priest.

Lilya goes to the door, opens it and speaks, then closes it and comes back to the bed. "Nothing important," she says, looking down at Antonina. "You must try to find peace, sweet Tosya." She brushes Antonina's hair from her forehead, and then leans over, kissing the smooth, warm brow. Her lips stay an extra few seconds on Antonina's skin, and at that Antonina draws in a quavering breath.

"But how can I find peace, Lilya? How can I ever feel peaceful again?" she whispers. "I'm so frightened."

At this, Lilya lies beside Antonina, putting her arms around her. Antonina buries her face against Lilya's shoulder.

"I'll help you," Lilya tells her. "I will always be here with you." Her voice, although barely above a murmur, is confident.

After a few moments, Antonina's breathing grows soft and even. The laudanum, aided by the wine and the vodka she drank in Misha's room, is working. Lilya moves her head back so that she can see the other woman's face. She touches Antonina's cheek, and then leans towards her and softly, softly, so as not to wake Antonina, kisses her mouth, tasting the laudanum on her lips.

8

*T*he first time Lilya kissed Antonina was when they were thirteen years old, and she a village serf on Antonina's father's estate.

Antonina was the daughter of Prince Leonid Stepanovich Olonov and Princess Galina Maximova Olonova. Although it was difficult to remember the very distant royal lines so many of the aristocrats laid claim to, Russian nobility was divided into ranks, Grand Duke being the most senior title, reserved for members of the imperial family, followed by thousands of princes, counts and barons.

Prince Olonov had an opulent home in St. Petersburg but preferred to spend his time on his sprawling, luxurious country estate built in imitation of an English manor. The Palladian mansion in the province of Pskov had an imposing facade and separate wings, attached to the house by corridors. Outside were verdant parterres and *allées*. Spreading for hundreds of versts in all directions were dark forests of birch and pine, and rolling meadows, ponds and rivers, as well as rich fields that, every year, with the labour of his serfs, turned from black to green or golden and yielded all manner of crops: wheat, corn, sunflowers and sugar beets. Prince Olonov owned thousands of souls, the male and female serfs living on the estate or in the many small villages that dotted the countryside.

Antonina was the last of four children. There were three boys before her, the youngest brother already eight years old when she was born.

Lilya was the daughter of a blacksmith and a fieldworker. Lyosha, ten years younger, was her only living sibling; six children had died between Lilya and Lyosha. They lived in one of eighty-nine single-roomed izbas in Kazhra, the village closest to the manor house.

⁂

One afternoon in early May, Antonina rode through her father's forest, accompanied by Kesha and Semyon. They had been her guards for the last three years, ever since she had begged her father to let her ride away from the fenced fields near the house. Antonina stopped so her pony could nose at some soft underbrush; the new grass was just appearing after the long winter. Kesha and Semyon stayed well behind her, as Antonina demanded. She resented their constant presence, and longed to be alone, truly alone, although she knew it could never be allowed.

Antonina sat on her supple leather saddle as her pony munched the fragrant grass in the quiet afternoon air. After a moment she frowned, pulling up the pony's reins to stop his chewing, and turned her head. Signalling the two men to stay where they were, she rode slowly in the direction of what sounded like weeping.

In a clearing, a girl knelt, hugging a small cloth-wrapped bundle against her chest. As Antonina watched, the girl laid the bundle, very gently, in a shallow depression hollowed from the soggy, dead leaf–strewn ground, and started to brush the damp soil over the cloth. Lost in her grief, she didn't hear Antonina until she had dismounted and walked a few steps towards her. As a dry branch cracked under Antonina's foot, the girl's head jerked up.

"What is that?" Antonina asked, stopping between the slim, naked birches. "What are you burying?"

The other girl jumped to her feet, brushing her hands down her apron. Antonina saw how red her hands were, the nails broken and rimmed with dirt. The girl immediately bent from the waist, her face parallel with the ground.

"Rise," Antonina said, and the girl straightened.

Although she was afraid to look into the princess's face, the girl studied the strange clothing she wore. The Princess Olonova, daughter of the man who owned her and her brother and mother and father, their hut and village and the land they worked, was dressed as a boy: trousers and a belted tunic and boots and a short jacket. Yes, the trousers were of luxurious brown velvet, and the white linen tunic fine, with stitching of the most delicate design down the front; the belt and boots were of soft, pliant leather, the jacket a rich dark green wool. But still, this was not the clothing of a princess. Her blond braids were coming out of their bindings, and the loose hair—she wore no hat at all—was stuck to her forehead with perspiration. Her eyes were wide and grey-green, her mouth also wide, her nose perhaps a little too long. She looked slightly annoyed. For one instant the village girl in her ankle-length skirt and embroidered blouse and apron and kerchief thought that she herself looked cleaner and tidier than the princess. She silently asked for forgiveness, knowing she would confess her sin of pride that evening at church.

"I asked you what you are burying."

Finally she glanced into the princess's face, but only for a second. "It's Romka. He was my puppy."

Antonina went to the edge of the little grave. "What happened to him?"

"He ate poison put out for the rats in my father's shop," the girl said. She raised her head, although her eyes were lowered. "I didn't know my father had set out the poison." She drew in a ragged breath. "Poor Romka. He cried so loudly at the end." She wiped the tears from her cheeks with the ends of her braids.

Antonina crouched, patting the earth over the slight mound. "Shall we say a prayer?" she asked, looking up at the girl, who stood motionless. "Shall we?"

The girl gave a small nod, blinking.

"What's your name?" Antonina asked.

"Nevskaya, Lilya Petrova," she answered.

"You know who I am," Antonina stated, standing again.

The girl bowed low, her hands clasped in front of her. "Of course I know who you are, Princess Olonova," she said, and then, with a slight hesitation, she looked up again. She was a little shorter than Antonina. She had dark auburn hair and eyes that were golden brown. Her skin was darkened from the spring sun and wind.

Antonina liked the colour of the girl's eyes.

"I've seen you when you ride through Kazhra," the girl added, as if the princess was waiting for an explanation. "Where I live."

"Oh," Antonina said, studying her. "How old are you?"

"Thirteen. Exactly three months older than you. To the day."

"How do you know my birthday?"

Lilya's mouth moved in a very small, uncertain smile. Her eyes were still damp. "Everyone knows the birthdays of the prince and princess and their children," she said. "Each family in the village is given a celebratory bottle of vodka on the birthdays and the name days."

"I didn't know that." Antonina studied Lilya. "So we are the same age. Do you have many friends in the village?"

"Oh yes, princess."

"What do you do with them?"

"Do?" Lilya asked, growing more and more uncomfortable. She had never before been in the private presence of her landowner or any members of his family, but knew the importance of subservience to them.

"Yes. Do you play games with them?" Antonina thought of the yard boys on the estate and the confusing games they played with pigs' knuckles and rocks and sticks. But she wasn't to speak to any of them, unless it was to give an order.

Lilya frowned. "We work together in the fields, princess." She was afraid this wasn't the right answer, and tried to think of what might please the girl. "But when we stop for a drink of water or to eat, we talk. Sometimes when we walk home, if we aren't too tired, we sing hymns. I like that, the singing."

Antonina nodded.

She doesn't appear too displeased, Lilya thought, and looked at the grave again. She wanted the princess to mount her horse and ride away. She made her anxious with all her questions.

"Did you love your puppy very much?"

"But of course, princess."

There was silence.

"I suppose you have many dogs," Lilya finally said, when it appeared she was expected to speak.

"My father and brothers have dogs for hunting." Antonina thought of the three elegant, aloof borzois, lounging on the red velvet sofa or on the thick wool rug in front of the fire. She was not allowed to touch the dogs, although her father daily brushed them. In the spring he used a strong boar brush, urging out the soft undercoat that thickened in the colder months. When she had been very small, she remembered leaning against her father, watching him as he crooned and sang to his dogs while he worked over them.

Lilya licked her lips. Was it her turn to speak? "But you don't have your own dog?" she asked.

Antonina shook her head.

"That's too bad," Lilya said. "I will get another puppy soon. My father promised." She again looked at the grave; she didn't know where else to look.

"Let's say the prayer for Romka, then," Antonina said, standing beside her now, and Lilya felt a surge of relief. This was as it should be—the princess deciding what was to be done.

Together they bowed their heads and clasped their hands. "Which one?" Antonina asked, and Lilya hesitantly began: *"Into Thy hands, oh Lord, I commend the soul of Thy servant*

Romka," and Antonina joined her in the Prayer for the Dead, *"and beseech Thee to grant him rest in the place of Thy rest, where all Thy blessed Saints repose, and where the light of Thy countenance shineth forever."*

Then Lilya added, "And I beseech You, oh Master, be merciful to Romka."

"Amen," they both said, crossing themselves.

Lilya gathered some tiny wild spring hyacinth and knelt, laying the little purple blossoms on the earth. Her kerchief had slipped to her shoulders, and Antonina looked at the whiteness of Lilya's scalp through her dark hair as she bent over Romka's grave.

"The next time I come by the village, will you show me your new dog?" Antonina asked.

Lilya quickly got to her feet, her head bowed. "Yes, if it is your wish, princess." Cautiously, she looked up. "But . . . why?"

Antonina shrugged. "I don't know," she said, and it was true. She didn't know what made her want to keep talking to Lilya, what made her feel that she didn't want to leave.

At a horse's snort, they turned to see Kesha and Semyon. Though Antonina had ordered them to stay behind, they had come nearer, pulling Antonina's pony with them. They were close enough to hear the conversation.

Antonina shook her head, annoyed. But she understood that this was their duty. Should anything befall her, Kesha and Semyon would pay with their lives.

Lilya lowered her head again, even more uncomfortable. The two burly men might think she was at fault for talking to the daughter of the landowner. "Have I permission to leave?"

"Yes."

"Goodbye then, Princess Olonova," Lilya said, bowing from the waist before she turned away. When she had taken ten steps through the grove, Antonina called out to her.

"When do you get your new puppy?"

Lilya had to turn around and bow again. "Next week. Today my father showed me a litter, almost weaned. He said I can pick one."

Antonina thought of her own father. Would he do this for her? She didn't know. "Then I will come to Kazhra next week, to see it."

Lilya performed another small bow. "As you wish, princess."

But Antonina wanted something more. "Lilya Petrova," she said, and Lilya cocked her head. "Do you *want* me to come?" Antonina asked.

Lilya pulled her kerchief up, tying it firmly under her chin. She looked over Antonina's head at the softly swaying branches with their small, furled buds. Her eyes skittered past Kesha and Semyon. When she finally looked at Antonina, her face was tight, suspicious.

"I don't understand, princess," she said.

Antonina raised her shoulders. "What don't you understand? I asked if you want me to come to Kazhra and see your puppy."

"But . . . but . . . if you wish to come, you will come. It is not my choice."

It wasn't the answer Antonina wanted.

Lilya saw that she had annoyed Princess Olonova. "If this is what you wish, princess," she said quickly, aware of the clenching in her stomach, "then, of course, it is my wish too." She held her breath.

Antonina smiled.

Yes, her nose was a bit long, Lilya thought, her eyebrows so much darker than her hair, but when she smiled, the stern expression disappeared. She was pretty, really.

"All right," Antonina said. "I'll come to the village. Look for me."

Lilya let out her breath. She had chosen the right words, then. "Perhaps . . . perhaps it would be better if I bring the puppy here, to the clearing. And princess? It must be on this day, at this time."

"Sunday afternoon?"

"Yes. It's the only day I'm not at work, and allowed my own time—Sunday, after church." Lilya couldn't imagine what her father would think should the daughter of Prince Olonov come to their izba; surely it would cause trouble. He wouldn't understand.

Lilya didn't understand herself. But it was the princess's order. She smiled back at Antonina, a small, forced smile.

Her front teeth were short, the eye teeth longer and pointed, and Antonina saw the tiniest bit of her pink upper gums. With her slightly slanted golden eyes and sharp incisors, Lilya Petrova had the look of a small and wary yet intelligent animal.

A fox. Yes, a fox.

9

*A*ntonina lived in the huge and glorious country manor with her father and brothers. Her father hired nurses and governesses to watch over her, and tutors who taught her to read and write based on religious and Biblical texts: the Psalter and the books of hourly prayers and the Gospels. She was a quick learner but difficult to keep on task, working carelessly, easily distracted and often gazing longingly towards the windows during her lessons.

Her favourite time was at the piano. She had taken her first lessons on the small spinet in the corner of the music salon but quickly advanced to the beautiful rosewood Érard square piano, imported from Paris, in the centre of the room. Her teacher, the elderly Monsieur Fadeev, told the prince that his daughter showed great eagerness for a four-year-old, and had a definite gift. He had Prince Olonov come into the music salon, where Antonina sat on a high tufted cushion placed on the piano bench. The old man played a simplified Mozart sonata and Antonina played the tune back easily, her small fingers stretching surprisingly to reach the keys.

Prince Olonov smiled proudly at his daughter, fondly, perhaps, but the fact that she was talented musically was of minor importance. Playing the piano was one of the requirements of young ladies of the nobility. By the time they were ready to be courted, they were expected to have a repertoire pleasing to the ear. They would play at small soirees and gatherings for the pleasure of family and friends and, hopefully, a future fiancé. However great a musical talent a Russian noblewoman might possess, it was simply a form of entertainment within the confines of the home. Professional performing was relegated to the serf troupes trained specifically for this purpose.

For women of Antonina's class, singing, the reciting of poetry, skill with the needle, lovely penmanship, cleverness at cards, or playing the piano with a deft touch were all part of a package, one designed to attract the proper suitor. In Antonina's case, her dowry was so large that it wouldn't have mattered if she'd possessed the face of a horse and played the piano as though her fingers were wooden pins—there would be a line of men eager to wed her for her riches, and Antonina's father imagined that he would marry her into further money.

Whatever her father's thoughts about Antonina's abilities, she progressed quickly in her insular music career, and derived great daily pleasure from her hours at the piano. She happily learned the thundering chords of Bach, which reminded her of the darkly scented world she knew from church. She loved the complicated trilling of Beethoven and the lighter crescendos and diminuendos of Schubert, which made her think of the sounds of the forest. But her favourite composer was Mikhail Glinka, his music redolent with delicate nuance for her.

A Russian aristocrat who studied in Milan and Berlin, the young Glinka had produced the first Russian operas in the years following Antonina's birth. She loved the village sounds of his music, especially those with the falling fourths that Glinka referred to as the soul of Russian music. By the time she was twelve, Antonina had memorized a number of his mazurkas and polonaises as well as the longer, more haunting fugues and nocturnes that became, to her, tiny epiphanies of private emotion.

Although her father occasionally sat, smiling, and listened to her play, her mother never entered the music salon unless she was hostessing one of her own soirees.

Antonina's mother preferred city life. She occasionally stayed with her husband and children at the country estate during the pleasant summer months, but she chose not to leave her St. Petersburg social circle when winter covered the countryside in snow.

Princess Olonova had given her husband children because it was her duty, nothing more, and she had left their care and rearing to wet nurses and nannies. She found the three boys rowdy and annoying, and often smelling unpleasantly of the fields and stables. She would occasionally hold Antonina and stroke her hair as though she were a doll or a charming pet when she was a baby, but as the girl grew older, she lost interest in her as well.

Galina Olonova was known for her beauty. She was also flighty and fickle. She cared only about the latest gossip, what she wore and the next fete. All of the princess's concentration was directed towards herself and her own pursuits: shopping, having a new wardrobe designed and sewn for each season, the planning of elaborate, week-long parties and the various forms of entertainment these celebrations demanded, and the endless stream of company that arrived and sometimes stayed for months at a time in the grand St. Petersburg house with its views of the Neva River. She also spent considerable time on her romantic dalliances. She took lovers. Her husband knew but turned a blind eye, for he had his own affairs.

They lived their lives as if not married to each other, or, more specifically, as if unmarried and free.

When Antonina's mother came to the country estate for a few summer weeks now and then, the huge house came alive with company. Princess Olonova arranged dances and musical evenings and dinners for thirty or forty friends. She even carelessly entertained her various lovers at the estate. She had had the walls and doors of her bedchamber covered in layers of felt under the wallpaper, so that any illicit sounds would not be heard by the house serfs. She never worried about her husband coming to her room; that hadn't occurred since she first learned she was carrying the baby who was to be Antonina.

Her husband was more discreet, and enjoyed a different kind of game. Unlike his wife, who usually picked men of her own class for her trysts—although she wasn't averse to a quick rendezvous with anyone young and good-looking, no matter his station—the prince definitely preferred women of the lower class. But he was above using his own house serfs for his pleasure. As a young man in his father's home, he had seen it too many times. His father had used and discarded his female house serfs at will. As little more than a boy, the prince observed that it was a game for the old man: when a fresh-faced girl working in the fields caught his eye on one of his rounds to see the progression of the spring planting or the autumn reaping, she would be summoned, given a household uniform and thrust into life in the estate house. Within weeks, she fully understood the rules of the manor—and her role there.

The young prince had seen that these girls never stayed long. Some were sent back to the village because they simply couldn't adapt to moving from life in a hovel and field to the routines of a household serf, trying to learn to serve dishes with never-before-seen foods or launder and iron expensive silks and linens or dust precious porcelain and polish heavy family silver. Some were let go simply because they proved too difficult to deal with, weeping for their mothers and disappointing the old prince in his heavy-handed attempts at seduction.

If one did respond as he wished, and settled into the life of the manor, she was dismissed, too, as soon as she showed the earliest signs of pregnancy. She would be sent back to her village to live in shame, spoiled and unmarriageable, with an eventual illegitimate offspring.

The younger Prince Olonov simply didn't want to deal with such messy and time-consuming pursuits. No—for him, the serf actresses were the perfect solution.

Like many landowners of large, wealthy estates, Prince Olonov had his own serf orchestra and serf acting troupe, which he used for his own entertainment and also hired out to other landowners who didn't have the means to possess their own orchestras. He had a theatre for performances on the property. While serf orchestras were only male, the acting troupes were both male and female. The men and women who rehearsed their music or lines for the stage lived in quarters on the estate, and relationships between them were forbidden. They were not allowed a family life.

While the serf actors and actresses—mostly selected on the basis of their pleasing appearance—were usually trained when they were young adults, the serf musicians were picked at a much younger age. Sometimes a landowner would recruit his own serfs, or send maestros to scour the countryside for boys gifted with musical abilities. Those chosen were bought and taken from their families and given formal musical instruction. All those in the serf theatres and orchestras knew that if they embarrassed their owners by forgetting their lines or performing off-key in front of a crowd of guests, there could be disaster. Depending on the personality, mood and whim of his master, a serf would either be harshly punished with severe lashings or, even worse, be demoted to a low job on the estate or sent to a miserable village izba and work in the fields. It was a terrible fate for a trained musician to have his instrument torn from him, knowing he would never again make the music that had been his life. Within a day, the hands that had controlled a cello or violin to such a delicate crescendo that women wept would know only the handle of a shovel or axe or plough or scythe.

The actress who failed to meet expectations would forfeit fine costumes and life on the stage before an appreciative audience. If dismissed, she might spend the rest of her days chopping beets and potatoes in a humid kitchen, or, like her male counterpart, be relegated to punishing physical work in the fields.

Many of the actresses were worldly, having lived in Moscow or St. Petersburg for their dramatic and vocal training, where they experienced a less supervised and slightly bohemian existence. They knew how to entertain a man, and were knowledgeable not only about the lure of sex but also about how to keep themselves from the family way. Should one of them whisper to Prince Olonov of an accident— entirely her fault, of course, she would add—all he had to do was hand her a wad of rubles and she would deal with the nuisance herself.

The prince carried on his dalliances at his summer dacha a few versts from the manor, which he kept heated through the winter. It was charming and beautifully decorated, although it lacked the grandness and elegance of the manor home. He treated his women with a certain respect, buying them pretty clothing and baubles and arranging elaborate private meals with the most costly of wines. He romanced them, flattered their beauty, their talent. He felt a surge of pride as he watched his woman of the moment perform on the stage in his theatre at the end of the larch *allée*, glancing at the audience to enjoy their reactions. Some of his mistresses he kept for over a year, developing genuine feelings for them.

But eventually he would grow bored, his eye turning to another, more recently purchased member of the troupe. He would gently but firmly inform his current lover that her time with him was over. In most cases the woman agreed, knowing there was no point in protesting. The occasional one who refused to cooperate—to rid herself of a child or leave behind the lovely pleasures of the dacha—disappeared quickly. She would be spoken of only in whispers, as if the mere mention of the rebellious woman's name might bring on a similar fate.

~

While Antonina grew up in the care of those hired to look after her physical needs and those hired to train her mind, she was intrigued by her older brothers, Viktor, Marik and Dimitri. She did what she could to keep up with them. While young, she was often as unkempt as they were, her boots muddied and her hair loosened from its ribbons and hanging down her back in an impossible tangle. The nannies despaired, and at their master's request tried to tame her. They buttoned her into fancy dresses and laced her feet into soft silk or satin slippers. They brushed and curled her hair, trying, as the prince ordered, to impart some femininity to his only daughter.

But Antonina didn't make it easy for the women attempting to teach her the role of daughter of a prince. She attended daily prayers at the church on the estate, and spent three hours every Sunday listening to the intonations of Father Vasiliy. But none of this helped. She showed no signs of the good and gentle spirit expected of a well-born young lady. She liked spending time in the kitchen with the old cook, or following the head housekeeper, with her ring of keys, up and down the many stairs. From them she learned peasant songs.

Antonina's brothers treated her as though she were a puppy, playing with her when they found her engaging, pushing her away as she grew older and more demanding and perhaps less winsome. They cheered her on when she demonstrated stoicism in the face of both pain and distress, praising her for not crying when she fell from the tree they had encouraged her to climb. When they swam in the icy lake at the edge of the estate, they instructed Antonina to take a deep breath and then held her under the water until she saw bright bursts of colour. She quickly learned that they would only let her rise, choking and gasping, when she stopped struggling and went limp. They nodded approvingly when the rifle they taught her to shoot left painful dark bruises on her shoulder.

When she was twelve, they encouraged her to drink vodka with them, laughing uproariously at her first signs of inebriation. But she would not be laughed at, and practised drinking the strong, clear alcohol on her own. There were so many varieties, from caraway seed and dill to cherry and sage and pear. There were bottles of it in her father's study, in the dining room, the library, the sitting room—everywhere throughout the manor. It was easy to help herself to a glassful—or two or three—on afternoons or evenings when she was bored or restless. She learned not to taste it as she let it run down her throat, and by age fourteen she was able to control her behaviour while matching her brothers shot for shot. They showed first surprise and then respect for their sister.

Although her parents paid her little heed, caught up in their own affairs and desires, she took this as a normal state. She had her brothers, and until she met Lilya she hadn't felt any particular need for a friend her own age. The serfs working the land thought her slightly mad, dressed as a boy, galloping at full speed down dusty roads in summer with her guards behind her, or picking her way through the deep, muddy ruts caused by soft spring rain or hard, driving autumn torrents.

Although she was fond of many of the house serfs, the peasants outside the estate were part of the landscape to Antonina. Bent over in the fields or under bundles on the roads, they were mostly nameless and faceless.

Meeting Lilya changed that.

That second Sunday, Lilya did bring the new puppy, a little spotted male with a small white star at the base of his spine. Lilya had named him Sezja.

At first, Lilya was stiff and uncomfortable, but she thawed slightly as Antonina laughed delightedly at Sezja's antics.

When Lilya told Antonina she must return home, Antonina told her to come back the next Sunday. Lilya had to obey the princess. The third visit went more comfortably for Lilya, and by the fourth Sunday, Lilya looked forward to her weekly escape from the tedium of her village Sundays.

After that, she was often waiting when Antonina arrived.

Through the long, warm spring and hot summer of 1845, Antonina learned about the true lives of the serfs through her clandestine friendship with Lilya. At first, when she asked Lilya what she did in the fields and how she spent her winters when there was no outside work, Lilya answered slowly and carefully, afraid of saying the wrong thing. She wondered if the princess was trying to trick her, to find out if she and her family were not working hard enough. But as she grew to realize that Antonina was genuinely interested, she lost her suspicion. More than that, she started to enjoy Antonina's reactions to her stories. Eventually Lilya grew to savour telling the princess about her life, feeling a small burst of pleasure each time she saw the princess's mouth open in disbelief.

"Well," Lilya said, settling more comfortably on the fallen log they usually sat on, "this story is about my mother having a baby in the field."

"The little brother—Lyosha—you talk about?"

"No, no. This was only last fall, during harvest. It was a girl. But she died."

Antonina studied her, but Lilya's expression hadn't changed. Whether she was telling how she and her mother had to take turns tying Lyosha on their backs as they worked—the days he was too sick to walk beside them and they couldn't leave him lying in one spot in case he was cut by a swinging scythe—or how many poisoned rats she'd picked up and thrown out of her father's blacksmith shop the night before, her face always looked the same. Now she'd just told Antonina about a dead baby sister, and she didn't look sad at all.

"But . . . why did your mother have her in the field?"

"When she told my father her pains had started, he said she couldn't stay home. We had the *obrok* coming—pay to your father—and if she didn't work, we would be further behind."

Antonina swallowed. She wanted to ask Lilya what *obrok* was. Why did Lilya's parents have to pay her father? It didn't make sense—they worked for him.

"So when she couldn't stop the baby from coming and there was no time to get one of the other women, she had to hold on to my shoulders and push it out. It fell onto the ground. But it was already dead—it was blue. I used the edge of my scythe to cut it free from my mother."

Antonina hadn't blinked.

"And after that, the blood wouldn't stop coming, and my mother couldn't walk, so I had to run and get my father to bring a cart to take her home. He was very angry. He missed hours of work, and she couldn't work for another two days. Then she worked slowly for a week. He beat her, but it didn't make her work any faster."

"He beat her?" Antonina echoed. "Because she had a baby and couldn't work?"

Lilya shrugged, picking up Sezja and rubbing his head with her knuckles. "He always beats her. And me. Not Lyosha yet. Lyosha he just slaps a little."

They sat in silence, Lilya enjoying the shock on Antonina's face.

Antonina was imagining a tiny blue baby lying dead on the ground between rows of waving blue flax with the blue sky overhead. Everything was blue. It was a horribly sad picture, and yet somehow, in Antonina's mind, the blueness rendered it unreal. She felt as she did when she read a beautiful passage in a novel. She took Sezja from Lilya and buried her face in his side, not wanting Lilya to keep looking at her.

Each Sunday, after hearing Lilya's stories, Antonina prayed her thanks to the Holy Mother for all the gifts bestowed upon her. She knelt in the corner of her bedroom filled with candles and her collection of icons blessed by Father Vasiliy, and was thankful.

On a sultry, overcast July day a few months after she met Lilya, Antonina made her first kill. It was a red deer, deep in the Olonov birch forest, and Antonina's shot had been clean, hitting the doe in the chest. The animal dropped to her knees gracefully, her head still lifted in surprise, but by the time Antonina rode close and dismounted, the doe lay on her side.

Antonina knelt beside her as she drew her last breaths, took off her gloves and stroked the soft head, seeing the deer's eyes film, her tongue, slightly protruding, stiffen.

"A marvellous killing, little sister," Viktor said, and she looked up at him, proud. "Strange," he then said, and Antonina frowned.

"What's strange, Vitya?"

He was studying the doe's swollen belly. "It's far too late for that—most of the young were born long ago."

Antonina put her hand on the rise of it, and in that instant felt the smallest of movements. Her mouth opened as she looked up at her brother.

He lifted one shoulder in a casual shrug. "It doesn't matter. They'll both be dead in another moment. Come now, we will let the others dress it and bring it home. Tonight at dinner we will raise our glasses in a toast to you, our Artemis, our little hunter." He smiled fondly.

But something had happened to Antonina in the moment she felt the dying thing in its mother's womb. She thought so little about her own mother, apart from occasionally studying her as she stood in a receiving line in the grand entry, and wondering if she really looked as Princess Olonova had looked when much younger—as her father had once told her. Feeling that small, feeble movement within the doe, Antonina thought of Lilya, cradling dead Romka. She thought of the blue baby dropping onto the flax field. She thought of her own mother putting her hand on her distended belly, with her moving inside. And Antonina was filled with sadness unlike any she'd ever known. She had killed a mother deer and her baby, and for the first time she missed her own mother, who was in her bedroom in

St. Petersburg, spooning a generous dollop of the finest caviar into the mouth of a handsome young lieutenant.

That evening at dinner, Antonina stared down at the succulent loin of pork on her plate. What of the tiny fawn? Did it hang on a hook beside its gutted mother? Would it be prepared for a future meal? A wave of nausea swept through her. Without picking up her knife and fork, she asked to be excused from the table, saying she was unable to eat. But her father scolded her, telling her she must stay until he and her brothers and their guests were done. At the far end of the table sat an elderly baron and baroness who were visiting for the week. They were both hard of hearing and napped much of the day, showing up for meals and eating with surprising gusto.

Usually Antonina obeyed her father. But this time she said in a loud voice, "I'm not feeling well. It's my woman's time, Papa."

It was shocking to speak so before not only her father and brothers but also the baron and baroness. And it was a lie. Her time had not come; it would not for another few months. Antonina tensed, waiting for her father to reprimand her for acting in such an indelicate manner.

But her father didn't berate her. Instead, he looked uncomfortable, glancing at her brothers as if for explanation. But they all lowered their heads, cutting and chewing with great energy, as if they had never before eaten pork loin. As if they had never considered that their little sister was a female.

The baron and baroness didn't appear to have heard the small drama playing out at the other end of the table. Both continued their meal, smiling in a vague manner.

"Papochka?" Antonina said. "May I go to my room?" She stood and put her hand to one side of her abdomen for further effect, mimicking the younger house serfs when they begged the housekeeper to lighten their workloads on particular days of the month.

Her father glanced at her, scrubbing his moustache with his napkin. "Yes, yes, of course," he said, his eyes darting about the table as if looking for the salt cellar or the butter dish.

Antonina lay on her bed in the darkening bedroom, thinking about the doe, and about her mother.

After that, Antonina no longer joined her brothers on their hunts. Her taste for killing had ended with the one incident, and she would not be cajoled or shamed into joining them. Instead, she grew silent, watching the overdressed and highly scented women her brothers sometimes invited over for a social evening.

Antonina—the little sister of these tall, good-looking young men—would no longer be drawn into gossipy conversation, or play the piano as bidden, or recite poetry or act out a scene from a play in the drawing room. She shook her head, her chin raised. She would not perform like the trained bears in their chains, padding behind the wagons of the Germans on the roads.

Where once her brothers had flattered her, complimenting her on her stoicism and bravery, on her riding abilities and her capacity for vodka, at the ends of these evenings they told her she had shamed them.

"You have such a miserable expression," Vitya told her. "Why don't you smile more often?"

"I'll smile when there's something worth smiling about," she retorted.

After a time, Antonina found it was easier to stay in her room when her brothers entertained. She fit nowhere; she was neither as hard and aloof as a man nor as soft and flowery as her brothers' female friends.

On one of their Sundays together, Lilya confided in Antonina that if she could do anything she wanted, she would go into a convent to be a Sister of Righteous Elizaveeta. The village priest had once spoken of these women of virtue in a sermon, describing the lives they had devoted to God. "Imagine living every day in a clean, beautiful place, with candles and icons, the smell of incense. My own cot in a cell, my days filled with praying and serving God," she said.

Antonina had quickly discovered how intelligent Lilya was; had she not been, Antonina wouldn't have been interested in her. She thought of Lilya's ability to learn Bible verses from simply listening to the village priest read them— more verses, Antonina suspected, than she knew.

"But my father says it's not for peasant girls, only the nobility. And he told me even if I could be a sister, he wouldn't allow it. He says women should leave the Church to men, and do God's work in bearing children and working for the good of the family." She shrugged. "What do you dream of doing?"

Antonina blinked. "I . . . perhaps . . . playing the piano."

Lilya had never seen a piano. The only music she heard was the discordant sound of the village church bells. "Will your father not allow you, either?"

"Oh, I *do* play the piano, every day. But I would like to play in front of many people, at a concert. My parents have taken me to concerts in Moscow and St. Petersburg."

Lilya didn't know what a concert was. She had never been to a city, and thought she probably never would. But for a princess, anything was possible.

"Surely you will."

"No. Only men are allowed."

This Lilya could understand.

⁓

Of course, Antonina couldn't tell her father that she was spending a few hours every Sunday afternoon with the daughter of Kazhra's blacksmith. She couldn't tell her brothers that she and Lilya took the puppy into a fallow field at the edge of the forest and taught him to fetch a stick and offer one paw for tiny bits of black bread. He barked when he ran after the sticks, barked when he chased his own tail, and barked when he put his small front paws on Lilya's boots, begging to be picked up.

Naturally, Kesha and Semyon were always there, and after a time their presence no longer disturbed Lilya. The two serfs never spoke to Antonina's father; their role was to keep his daughter from harm. They saw no harm in their young mistress playing games in the forest clearing or a stubbled field with a kerchiefed village girl and a clumsy, noisy *laika* pup, a dog named after its most common pastime—barking. They found it highly peculiar and definitely in poor taste. But they found many things about the prince and his family peculiar. They had one job to do—guarding the young mademoiselle—and they did it.

Antonina's friendship with Lilya continued through the summer and into the autumn. The trouble began after they had known each other for six months.

10

*T*he mid-October Sunday was overcast and gloomy, the air chilled. Within ten minutes of Antonina and Lilya meeting, the rain started. Lilya cringed with each boom of thunder and jagged flash of lightning.

"I must go," she said, picking up Sezja and holding him against her. The dog trembled, whining, and Lilya glanced nervously at the sky.

"Come," Antonina said, holding out her hand. "Come with me. I'll take you back to the village." They ran, hand in hand, to her horse. Semyon pulled a heavy cape from his saddlebag and dismounted, settling it around Antonina's shoulders. She helped Lilya up, and climbed in front of her. There wasn't really enough space for two girls in the saddle, but they were both slight, and Lilya was pressed against Antonina's back.

"Hold tightly," Antonina said, and Lilya wrapped her arms around Antonina's waist, the puppy between them.

Antonina urged the horse into a quick trot. They were at the edge of the village within ten minutes.

"Please, Antonina Leonidovna, let me down here," Lilya shouted above the downpour. She had stopped calling Antonina "princess" long ago, and sometimes even called her Tosya.

"No, no, I will take you directly to your house," Antonina said. "Which one is it?"

"Please. Here is best," Lilya said, but Antonina wouldn't listen. Finally Lilya pointed down the muddy, deserted road. It was dark and wet and miserable. All the wooden doors were closed and the windows shuttered against the storm. When they stopped in front of a small hovel, Kesha and Semyon behind them, the door opened. A man and a woman looked out while rain poured onto them off the slanted roof. A little boy, his scrawny legs dirty and bare beneath a short, tattered tunic, hid behind his mother, clutching her skirt. He coughed in a phlegmy way, his mouth open. He was perhaps two or three—Antonina couldn't tell, he was so thin. The mother pushed him farther behind her and the child was hidden from view, the choking wet cough the only indication he was still there.

The man and woman stared with consternation, their mouths open. Then they bowed from the waist, rain bouncing off their backs. The child coughed, over and over.

"Kesha," Antonina called. "Come and help her down."

As the man dismounted and held his arms up to Lilya to help her off the horse, Antonina saw the woman in the doorway, still bent, cross herself and then kiss her fingers.

"Are these your parents?" Antonina asked, although she knew that the man dressed in the leather tunic of a blacksmith, his great arms and thick hands stained black, was surely Lilya's father.

"Yes, princess," Lilya said, reverting to the old title as she stood beside the horse. She then bowed as she hadn't in a long time. "My father Petya—Pyotr Ivanovich—and my mother, Leepa Stanislavova."

Lilya's father spoke to his boots. "My deepest apologies, Princess Olonova. Whatever my daughter has done, she will never again repeat. She will be beaten for her misbehaviour."

The rain was lessening now. Antonina frowned. "Look at me, Petya," Antonina said. The man straightened. His mouth was still slightly open, and Antonina saw from the way his lower lip caved in that he had no bottom teeth. "She has done nothing wrong." She glanced at Lilya.

The girl's eyes were unnaturally wide, her expression somehow pleading, as if she wished Antonina to understand something. Her hand around Sezja's muzzle so he couldn't bark, she stood beside her father. But now he narrowed his eyes, looking at his wife, who was still bent over, and then at Lilya. He spoke so low that Antonina couldn't hear what he said. Lilya shook her head, also speaking rapidly in the same indiscernible murmur. The father responded with a slight rise in tone, as though arguing. Lilya finally looked up at Antonina.

"My father says that you must take Sezja."

Her father hissed something and Lilya dropped her gaze to the mud again.

"What? Why would I take him?"

"I told him that Sezja was almost swept away in the stream." Looking down, Lilya was speaking louder and more slowly than usual. "That you had your men grab him and save him. That you worried about Sezja—that's why you brought us home." Although Antonina couldn't see Lilya's face, she knew from the odd, stiff voice that Lilya was begging Antonina not to correct her.

Antonina didn't understand why Lilya had fabricated this lie and yet knew it was somehow important that she go along with it. "Oh. Oh, yes. It was simply a fortunate situation, us coming by just as little Sezja slipped on the muddy bank. I'm only happy my men saved him from certain death."

Pyotr Ivanovich brusquely grabbed the puppy from Lilya. It yelped. He held it by its throat, swinging it up to Antonina, his head still down, although Lilya now looked up. Antonina saw the back of his thick neck, the line of grime just under the collar of his tunic. "You must take it, princess. Our daughter says you like the dog, so you must have it."

Antonina opened her mouth in protest, but at the sight of Lilya's face, so pale and troubled, she nodded, taking Sezja. "Thank you," she said, then stopped. She had been about to say "Lilya Petrova" but now realized it would not go well for Lilya should her father realize she knew anything more about her.

Without another word, she turned her horse and left the village, Sezja held tight against her. On the ride home she thought of Lilya's face, so ashen, and the little boy's bony legs, the knees too large.

***

That night, Antonina slept with Sezja in her bed. She had brought him up to her room under her cape, and fed him a big plate of rich beef covered in gravy, taken from the kitchen after dinner. Twice in the evening she set the puppy outside on her balcony and watched him run in circles, sniffing busily before squatting to relieve himself near one of the posts. The second time, he looked through the balcony railings, stiffening, then let out a long series of sharp little barks. "Shh, shh, Sezja," Antonina said, grabbing him up and holding his muzzle as Lilya had done. She crouched down with him, seeing Borya, the head stable serf, leading a horse across the yard. "You will have to learn not to bark at everyone here. You will have to learn to be a good and quiet little dog," she whispered against his warm ear.

Antonina fell asleep with the puppy in her arms, but at some point she became aware of him moving restlessly and whimpering. She sleepily stroked him and murmured to him, falling asleep again. In the morning she saw that during the night the little thing had been sick, leaving a slimy mess of barely chewed beef at the foot of her silk bedcover.

The puppy cried louder now, circling the edge of the high bed, unable or afraid to jump down, and Antonina picked him up and hurried him out to the balcony again. As the puppy quivered, obviously in pain, crouching in a piteous way as he tried to rid himself of the rich food, Antonina realized she had made him ill with the abundance of beef and gravy.

"My poor Sezja," she murmured, stroking the dog's head and back when he had finally finished and lay, head on his paws, staring in what Antonina thought was a mournful way through the balcony railings.

The dog looked up at her, and she felt a jolt of remorse. Did he miss Lilya, and his meals of dry bread crusts, perhaps his nest of straw near the stove?

"Are you sad, little boy?" she asked, picking him up and holding him against her. He struggled to free himself, and she set him down. He went back to look between the railings, and this made Antonina feel worse. She knew she had been unkind to take him from Lilya, and from his home, but what choice did she have? Lilya had made it clear.

After the maid had helped her dress and had done her hair and taken the ruined bedcover away as Antonina instructed, she took Sezja down to the drawing room, where her father sat reading in front of the fire.

"Look, Papa," she said, cradling Sezja, holding his muzzle.

Without lifting his eyes from his book, the prince said, in a distracted manner, "What is it, Tosya?"

"I have a puppy. Look," she said, pressing her lips onto the dog's head. He squirmed.

Her father looked up, removing his eyeglass. "What? What is this? Where has it come from?"

"I . . . I found him in the woods. He was all alone, Papochka, and hungry. I brought him home. I want to keep him."

Her father rose, coming closer and looking at the dog. "No," he said.

"Papa. Why not? I'll look after him. I'll feed him, and make sure he doesn't cause any trouble. We already have dogs. What's one more?" She looked at the three borzois. They were quiet yet alert at the scent of the puppy, their long noses lifted from their equally long and delicate front paws. Three pairs of eyes were fixed on what Antonina held.

"My wolfhounds are trained hunting dogs. They have a purpose. They're treated well because they earn it. We have the guard dogs in the yard. They too know their place, and what they're expected to do. But that dog has no purpose."

Antonina looked at the borzois again. There were always three of them; if one fell ill or was killed in a hunting expedition, her father would have it replaced as soon as possible. The dogs were carefully bred, with a powerful instinct to chase a moving object. Although they hunted any small game, they were particularly adept at running down a wolf. The three of them, Antonina knew, could catch a wolf and hold it by its neck until her father or brothers or any of their guests arrived to kill it for themselves.

Antonina had always been warned that the borzois didn't understand simple amusements such as fetching thrown objects or rough play. They were aloof and gracious, silent, and also sensitive, nervous around too much activity. They didn't understand children, with their unexpected movements and noise, her father had explained. Should she approach them suddenly, they might snap at her. Now, even though she was no longer a spontaneous child who might invoke anxiety in the dogs, she had nothing to do with them. They were her father's dogs. She knew their names, and that was all.

"Your village cur is an ill-bred *laika*. All he'll ever know is how to bark and how to pull a load. He has no pedigree. Do you know that these dogs—my dogs—cannot be purchased?"

Sezja pulled his muzzle free and gave a short yap. All three borzois instantly rose, glancing at their master for permission. Sezja barked again, struggling, and Antonina set him down. The borzois tensed, looking from their master back to the *laika*.

"Down," he said, and they dropped to the ground as one, but remained poised as they watched the puppy.

"They're bred by the Tsar," her father went on, as Sezja sniffed around his boots. "His dogs are given as gifts to those landowners who have shown themselves worthy, with great tracts of land and an abundance of souls and all taxes paid on time. *Aiii!*" he suddenly shouted, kicking the puppy away. Sezja had grabbed the toe of his leather riding boot between his tiny, sharp teeth. "Look—already he's showing predictable behaviour." He pointed the boot with its row of tiny teeth marks towards Antonina as she knelt, holding Sezja. "None of my dogs have ever been guilty of such behaviour."

"I never ask anything of you, Papa," Antonina said. "Please?" She let go of Sezja again and stood, looking at her father with her chin down and her eyes tilted up at him. She had used this tactic before, although not since she was much younger.

Her father gazed at her wearily, then nodded. "Fine. But you must keep him in the stables."

Antonina frowned. "He's still a baby. He's too young, Papa. He'll be lonely all by himself. And he might be stepped on by a horse. Please, Papochka. Please, let me keep him with me until he's older," Antonina begged.

Sezja scampered towards the larger of the male wolfhounds, yapping. The older dog growled a warning, and at the low rumble Sezja threw himself onto his back, whimpering.

"Do you see?" the prince asked Antonina. "He's a grovelling serf dog, this little *laika*. He has no fight, no spirit. He's not meant to be an estate dog."

Antonina hurried to pick him up, and Sezja let out a series of yips, as if complaining to her. "I'll keep him away from your dogs, truly, Papa."

But the prince wouldn't relent. "No. The barking will annoy everyone. He's an outside animal. Take him to Borya at the stables. You can visit him when you like. That's the end of the matter, Antonina."

He sat down again, picking up his book, his wolfhounds unmoving but ever watchful. From outside came the sound of the wind in the trees nearest the house.

Antonina knew her father would not change his mind. She took Sezja to Borya, who looked disgruntled when Antonina told him he must look out for the puppy.

"Please clean out the empty stall in the corner, and put in fresh straw for him to sleep in," she told him. "Also one of the horse blankets. I'll come to feed him and play with him every day, Borya. All I ask is that you make sure you keep the stall door closed so he can't get out and under the feet of the horses, or into the yard. And keep him away from the guard dogs."

Borya nodded, and Antonina waited while he forked out the soiled straw and threw in a fresh, fragrant bale. Then she spent time fashioning a little bed for the puppy in a warm, dry corner of the stall in the high-ceilinged stable.

Four days later, Antonina ran to the stable to play with Sezja as she had done for the last three days. The stall gate was open.

"Where is he, Borya?" she asked, seeing the serf currying one of the horses at the far end of the stable. "Where's Sezja?"

Borya didn't look at her or stop the rhythmic brushing of the horse's bulging side. "I'm sorry, princess," he said, frowning as he brushed harder. "I tried to watch him. But he's a puppy. He wouldn't stop barking and whining. It was too much. I let him out—only for a few minutes—thinking he would quiet down if he was near me. But somehow he got into the yard and . . ." He stopped talking to change brushes, and began to work on the horse's mane.

Antonina stood very still. "And what, Borya?"

Finally he looked at her. "It was one of the guard dogs, princess. The puppy made a nuisance of himself. The older dog had no patience, and . . ." He turned away again. "He snapped the neck. It was over in an instant—the little one had no time to suffer."

Antonina put out her hand to steady herself, feeling for the edge of the stall. "He's dead, Borya? Sezja is dead?" Her voice was barely a whisper.

Borya nodded. "I'm sorry, princess. I did what I could, but it isn't my job to be nursemaid to a *laika* pup."

Antonina was weeping now. "Where is he? The body— where did you bury him?"

At this, Borya shook his head. "Bury? He was a dog, princess, not a child."

"But then . . . where . . . what did you do with him?"

Borya didn't answer for a moment. "Princess Olonova. We burn the bodies of dead animals. You know that."

Antonina pressed her hands over her mouth. She turned from Borya and ran back to the house. Her father was on the front veranda, buttoning his topcoat. The barouche with their family crest waited for him, the driver on the high front seat.

"He's dead, Papa," Antonina cried, rushing at him. "You see? You see?" she repeated. "You made me put him in the stable, and now he's dead." She beat against his chest with her fists. "I told you. I told you he was too little."

Her father grabbed her hands. "Stop it!" he shouted. "Stop it this instant. What kind of behaviour is this?" He leaned close to her, his voice low but harsh. "All the servants can see you. Have you no shame?" His hands were iron shackles around her wrists. "Since you cannot behave in a manner fitting your station, go to your room."

Antonina wept, looking at him.

"Go to your room," her father repeated, his voice very low. "Stay there until I return. You are forbidden to leave your room while I am away for the day. Do you understand me? Do you?"

Antonina nodded, unable to see for the tears. "I understand," she gulped. "But you don't. You don't understand what you've done."

"I understand one thing," the prince said. "That I have a wilful and discourteous daughter who shows no sign of becoming a proper young woman. You disappoint me in so many ways, Antonina. Now go inside. I'll deal with you when I return." He let go of her wrists and turned away from her. The footman held open the door of the barouche, his face showing nothing.

Without looking back, Prince Olonov stepped into the carriage and the footman shut the door. As the barouche left the yard, a freezing rain started, turning to sleet within a few moments. Antonina stood there watching, weeping still.

﹋

Antonina didn't know how she would tell Lilya. That Sunday after church, she didn't go to their usual meeting spot in the forest.

But she knew she couldn't stay away forever. It wasn't

fair to Lilya that she simply disappear. The following Sunday, the first day of November, skiffs of the early first snow melted in unexpected warmth. Antonina slowly rode into the forest, trailed, as always, by Semyon and Kesha.

Lilya was there. Antonina dismounted and walked to her.

The girl smiled, coming towards her. She had a long scabbed cut on her jaw, and a yellowing bruise on her neck. One eyelid was a faded violet.

"Lilya," Antonina said. "What happened?"

Lilya gave a lopsided smile. "I'm so clumsy. I was helping my mother load the last of the wood and I fell off the cart."

Antonina studied the girl's injuries. "Does your face hurt?"

"No. Everything is healing."

Antonina reached into her saddlebag and pulled out a cloth bag. "I brought you a jar of strawberry jam."

Lilya took the jam and opened it. She dipped in two fingers and licked them. "Umm. It's so good. I'll share it with Lyosha later. Thank you, Tosya."

All Antonina could think about was Sezja. Lilya hadn't asked about him yet. "His cough? It's started again?"

Lilya nodded her head. "It disappeared over the summer, but as soon as the cold weather begins, so does Lyosha's cough. My mother puts poultices on him daily, but still he coughs all night. I missed you last week. I waited."

"I'm sorry I couldn't come." Antonina walked to the fallen tree. "Let's sit down—I have a lot to talk about. About Sezja," she added, trying to smile. Her face ached as if her own jaw were bruised.

Lilya said nothing, studying Antonina in a cautious way.

"Well. I must tell you that he has outdone himself in his ability to learn tricks," Antonina said. "Just yesterday he finally mastered turning in circles on his hind legs. He holds up his front paws in such a dainty fashion, and pirouettes quite prettily. Even my maid claps her hands in delight."

"But Antonina," Lilya said. "Antonina, I—"

Antonina ignored her. "Did I tell you that he sleeps on a velvet pillow at the foot of my bed? Oh Lilya, you should see him. He is like a small prince, so handsome and proud."

Lilya hadn't taken her eyes from Antonina's face, and now something in her expression made Antonina uncomfortable. "What is it, Lilya?"

"Antonina Leonidovna," Lilya said, looking at her hands in her lap, still clutching the bag with its jar of jam, as if embarrassed. "Over a week ago, Sezja came back to the village."

A cry escaped Antonina's lips. "He's alive?" she whispered. "Sezja is alive? Is he well? Oh Lilya, is he all right?"

"He must have been in the forest for some days before he found his way home. He was so thin and dirty, his little paws covered in cuts. I heard him crying outside our house as I lay in bed. I brought him in, and fed and cleaned him. He's well again, Antonina. My father punished me. He thought the dog had displeased you and so you turned it out. I couldn't believe that you didn't want Sejza. I thought he must have run away."

"Your father—he punished you because Sezja came back?" Antonina asked, staring at Lilya's neck and jaw, her eye. "You didn't fall from the cart."

Lilya still hadn't looked up.

Antonina stared at Lilya's bent head, and then put her face into her hands. She was hot with both shame and sorrow.

"Antonina Leonidovna," Lilya said. "Please. Don't be upset with me."

Antonina lifted her head. "Upset with you? No. I'm sorry I lied to you about Sezja. I'm so happy—relieved—that he's alive. I couldn't bear to tell you . . . I wasn't allowed to keep him with me in the house. My father insisted he live in the stables. But I visited him every day, Lilya. I brought him food and brushed him and played with him, every day, for most of that first week. And then one day the stable serf told me he'd been killed by one of the guard dogs. He said he'd been killed, Lilya. I was so sad. Not only for poor Sezja's suffering, but knowing that I would have to tell you. I couldn't, Lilya, and that's why I didn't come last week." She knew now that Borya hadn't wanted to tell her he didn't know what had happened to the pup; maybe he thought she'd stop bothering him about it if he told her it was dead. Or perhaps her father had told him to get rid of it. She would never know.

"But Lilya, more than anything, I hate that because of me you were beaten. I hate that little Sezja suffered because of me. You know I would never have turned him out. You know I loved him."

Lilya moved closer to her on the log, glancing behind her at Semyon and Kesha. They were talking, smoking their pipes and paying no attention to the two girls. Lilya put her arm around Antonina's shoulders. "Don't cry, Tosya. Don't. It's all right. I'm glad he's home with me. My father's beatings don't worry me. I'm used to them."

But Antonina's tears kept coming. "And today, when I knew I must see you, I was a coward. I didn't know how to tell you."

Lilya still had her arm around Antonina's shoulder. "Sezja has brought us both sorrow."

Antonina nodded. "But it's all right now. You have your dog back. He was never mine. I'm glad he's with you, as he should be. And you must tell your father that you saw me. Tell him the truth—that the dog simply ran off."

Lilya shook her head. "I cannot tell my father that I have seen you. Or that I speak to you."

"But if you tell him what happened, he won't be angry with you anymore."

Lilya took her arm from Antonina's shoulder. She stood and looked down at her. "Antonina Leonidovna," she said, and something about the way she said the name filled Antonina with dread. She also stood, facing Lilya.

"My father is already over his anger," Lilya said. "And . . . I have liked our times together so much. Sometimes I think that it must be a dream. How could it be possible that you wanted . . ." She stopped.

Antonina waited. She understood what Lilya was trying to say, but had nothing to reply.

"You saw my father," Lilya finally said. "He could never understand that you chose me as a friend. Even I can't understand it, Tosya. It's not the natural order of life as God has decreed it, that you and I would be friends. If I tried to explain, it would only confuse my father, and make him angrier. I can no longer see you," Lilya continued. "This is the last time. It's colder now. We can't meet outside in the winter. And I can't take the chance . . ." She reached into the pocket of her apron and held out a little amulet. "Please. I want you to have this, to remember me by."

Antonina took it. It was a small, poorly rendered metal icon of Saint Nikolai Chudotvoret—Nicholas the Wonderworker, most merciful of saints. Antonina didn't know how Lilya had come to own it, but knew it must be her only piece of jewellery and how difficult it would be for her to part with it. Tears came to her eyes. "Thank you, Lilya Petrova," she said. "I will always keep it." She pulled a small ring, a simple gold band with a tiny garnet in the centre, from her finger. "And you must have this in return, as a keepsake."

Lilya looked at it, sucking in her breath and then shaking her head. "I can't, Antonina. If my father ever discovered it . . . Thank you, but I cannot."

Antonina understood. She put the ring back on her finger. "Will you kiss Sezja for me?" When Lilya nodded, she said, "I'm so sorry for what has happened to you. I'm sorry that we cannot be friends any longer. But perhaps one day, when some time has passed, we . . ."

But Lilya shook her head. She stepped close to Antonina and flung her arms around her neck. She hugged her with a quick, hard press of her chest against Antonina's, her cheek against hers. "Goodbye, Antonina Leonidovna," she whispered.

Antonina hugged her back. They stood that way for a long moment, and then Lilya moved her head and gently kissed Antonina on each cheek. Antonina pulled back to stare into Lilya's eyes, and the girl slowly kissed her on the mouth. Lilya's lips stayed against Antonina's, warm and soft, for a long moment. And then she turned and ran, her kerchief a bright splash of colour among the leafless birches.

Antonina felt strange—weak, somehow—after Lilya's unexpected kiss. She stood for a long time, thinking. Eventually she looked down at the icon in her hand. She turned it over. It had a tiny number engraved on the back: 962. She carefully wrapped it in her handkerchief and tucked it into her waistband and rode home.

She went directly to the blacksmith's hut on the estate and had him make a tiny hole in the icon, and added it to the chain around her neck.

Antonina kissed it, as well as her crucifix, before she went to sleep that night. She thought about the sensation of Lilya's lips on hers. She couldn't believe she would never see her again.

$\mathscr{A}$ntonina missed Lilya. Lilya had become a part of her life, and she longed to see her every Sunday.

She became restless, filled with a heaviness that made her uninterested in her usual winter pastimes. She didn't feel like skating or going to the yearly winter fetes at other estates, and none of her books interested her. She found comfort, as always, in the piano, but all the songs she played made her think of Lilya. And of her kiss.

Seven weeks after she had last seen Lilya—at Christmastime—Prince Olonov frowned at Antonina as she sat across from him at the breakfast table. He carefully set his fork and knife on his plate.

"Come here, daughter," he said, and Antonina rose and went to stand in front of him. His bristly grey moustache was stained in two yellow-orange lines from his nostrils, evidence of the endless cigar smoke he exhaled.

"What's this you're wearing?" he asked, his fingers brushing the raised figure on the metal oval beside her crucifix.

"It's Saint Nikolai, most merciful of saints."

Her father shook his head. "I know who it is. But where did you get it?"

Something in his voice made Antonina wary. She never imagined her father would notice—or care—what she wore around her neck.

"I asked you a question, Antonina. Where did you get this icon?"

"Someone gave it to me," she said, thinking that would satisfy him.

His face darkened. "Who gave it to you? One of the house serfs?"

She couldn't think of an answer with her father staring at her in such a strange way. "I don't know."

"What do you mean, you don't know? Are you such a simpleton?" Antonina was shocked at the threatening tone. "Tell me, Antonina Leonidovna."

Antonina would not make any more trouble for Lilya.

Her father stood and took hold of her shoulders. "Which serf gave it to you?"

Antonina's mouth opened. She closed it. "Why do you think it was a serf?"

Her father's hands were hard on her shoulders as he stared at her intently. "This is what each of the new souls on my estate is given at birth. The steward informs me of the family, and the child's name is added to the record, with an individual number. If we purchase new serfs, they are also given an icon with their number recorded." He reached out and pulled on the amulet, forcing Antonina to stretch forward.

The chain bit into the skin on the back of her neck. He turned it over, squinting. "I need my eyeglass to see the number properly," he said, and Antonina's heart thudded. "What is it? Tell me the number, Antonina."

Antonina swallowed, putting her hand over her father's, pushing his fingers off the icon, pretending to study the tiny inscription of 962. "I found it, Papochka, in the fields, a long time ago, before the snow. I thought it was pretty, that's all. The number is five-one-one."

At this, her father stepped back, and his face relaxed. "You found it? But you said someone gave it to you."

Antonina licked her lips. "I . . . I just pretended someone gave it to me. That I had a friend, Papa." She tried to look downcast.

It worked. "Well. You should always speak the truth. You can see that you upset me. If you had been honest, there would have been no need for me to be angry with you."

"I know, Papochka," Antonina said, picking up her father's hand. "I'm sorry," she said, pressing it against her cheek.

"All right, daughter," he said, pulling his hand away. "You must give the icon to Kyrill and ask him to return it to the serf who lost it. Five-one-one, you said? Besides, it isn't pretty at all. You have your own jewels. That icon, a cheap bit of nothing owned by every soul on my estate, is unfit for the daughter of a prince."

"Yes, Papa," Antonina said. "I will give it to Kyrill right away, Papa."

She curtsied and left the room. But she did not go to seek out Kyrill, her father's steward. She went to her bedroom, removed the icon from her chain and buried it deeply under the velvet lining in the bottom of her jewellery box.

A few days later, her father summoned her to his study. He was staring out the window at the falling snow as he sat in his wide chair behind the mahogany desk.

"You gave the icon to Kyrill, as I asked?" he said as soon as she entered the room, and Antonina's heart thudded at his words. She looked at her father's profile—his long, straight nose, the slight bulge over his eyebrows.

When she remained silent, he swung around in his chair. She couldn't read anything on his face. He held out his palm. "Is this the icon you gave him?" he asked, and now Antonina swallowed. "Take it," he said to her.

She came to the desk, picking up the small metal oval from her father's hand.

"Turn it over and read the number to me," he said.

Antonina knew what the number would be. "Papa, I—"

"Read the number," he said again, his voice quiet and hard.

Antonina turned it over. "Five-one-one," she whispered, staring at the three figures. They swam as though her eyes were watering. She blinked to clear her vision.

"Am I to thank you for being honest, and turning the icon over to Kyrill as I requested?"

She couldn't look at her father.

"Of course not," he said. "Again you are lying, Antonina Leonidovna. Kyrill came to see me about another manner. He mentioned something about your horse, nothing of importance. I asked him when you'd last spoken to him. He said over a week ago. So I had him check his records. This icon you hold, five-one-one, is owned by a serf in a tiny hamlet near here. I had Kyrill go and see this serf. It's an old woman, near to death. He brought me her icon. The one you hold."

The icon felt like a shard of ice on Antonina's palm.

"Will you tell me the truth now?"

Antonina closed her hand around it.

"I want the icon you wore, Antonina. Go and fetch it, now."

"I threw it away." She spoke boldly to cover the slight tremble she was afraid her father would detect.

"How can I believe you? How will I ever believe anything you say?"

When Antonina had no answer, her father continued. "Do you understand why I'm dealing with this matter in such a way, Antonina?"

Antonina shook her head.

"Speak. Don't shake your head from side to side like a dumb animal."

"No, Papa. I don't understand why the icon matters so much. Or why you're so angry that I had it."

"Do you think I know nothing? I have uncovered your deception. First the dog, then the icon . . . You're involved with a serf, aren't you, Antonina?"

A second of silence—time for two quick heartbeats—passed in the still room. "No, Papa. I'm not involved with any of the serfs." This question was easier to answer. She and Lilya were no longer friends. She met her father's eye.

"How old are you, Antonina?" he asked.

"You know I'm fourteen."

At that, he stood so abruptly that his chair clattered backwards, and Antonina jumped, dropping the icon. She had never seen her father this angry—not with her. Not even when she'd struck him when she thought that Sejza was dead.

He came around the desk and took hold of her upper arms. "This cannot go on. I've let you run wildly, let you do as you wish for too long. You're no longer a child. I married your mother when she was not quite sixteen. You will not be ready for marriage in another few years, no thanks to her."

"I don't want to get married in a few years," Antonina said.

"That isn't the point. The point is that you don't know how to behave as a proper young woman. I don't want you influenced by any of the serfs." He hadn't let go of her.

"Why?"

"Why? Because they don't possess brains such as we do, Antonina. They can't feel things the way we do. It's impossible for them—they've been bred by the same families for centuries. They're uneducated and illiterate. Quite simply, they're born with a lesser intelligence and less capacity for emotion."

Antonina pulled back slightly. Her father's grip hurt her arms. "That's not true, Papa. Not true at all."

Her father stared at her. "And what makes you say this? You think serfs have the same abilities we do? The same abilities for mathematics and languages? That serfs could run an estate? Run a country?"

"I didn't say that."

"You're saying they're the same as the nobility? The same as blood descendants of tsars?"

"I . . . I'm just saying . . ."

There was baying from the dogs in the yard, then the sound of hooves on the hard-packed snow. Antonina glanced towards the window, hoping her father would leave her to see who had arrived.

But he ignored the noise from outside and gave her another

slight shake, so that she was forced to look at him again. "Well? What are you saying, daughter?"

Antonina thought of Lilya, with her clever face, her sudden smile. She remembered her words: *the natural order of life as God has decreed it.* She thought of the sadness in Lilya's golden-brown eyes as they said goodbye, the way her thin arms had clung to her.

"You know life as the daughter of great nobility, Antonina. You must know how to continue this life in your own home, with your husband and your children." His mouth tightened. "You will owe your allegiance to your husband. You will have to know how to deal with the servants. You cannot befriend them. And more importantly, you cannot squander your affections with low-class lovers, cuckolding your husband. Who is he, Antonina? Who is this man?"

"Man? Papa, what do you mean?"

"I'm not stupid." His voice had risen. "Do you think I don't know the ways of women, even my own daughter? All women are slaves to their romantic notions."

"Papa. No. I . . ." Antonina's face was hot. How could her father imagine this of her?

"Silence, Antonina Leonidovna. Silence," he shouted, then abruptly dropped his hands.

Her upper arms throbbed. The next day, each would be bruised with a band of dark purple.

Prince Olonov sat heavily behind his desk. As Antonina's face had flushed with embarrassment at her father's suggestion, his had become pale. He studied the book on the desk in front of him, running one finger up and down its cover.

"I am not Mama," Antonina said then, her voice barely above a whisper.

Her father's finger stopped moving.

"I am not like her, Papa," Antonina said, her voice stronger. "I would never behave as Mama does. Never."

Now Prince Olonov closed his eyes and put one hand over them. "I want to believe you, Antonina. But you have told too many lies, acted too impulsively. Although I've been negligent, there is still time for me to drive home to you the importance of proper behaviour. There must be some sort of punishment, or at least chastisement." He took his hand away from his eyes and looked at her. "It's impossible for me to allow you to carry on, keeping secrets, lying. You must conform. Your marriage and your future depend on it. You must go to your husband in a . . . a clean state, Antonina."

He turned to look out the window so he didn't have to face her. "It should be your mother's job to discuss these things with you." He cleared his throat. "Russia is changing. We must fight to keep it as it is, to make sure our culture remains intact. Some, especially those who have travelled abroad extensively, have begun suggesting political experiments. They have spoken of the issue of serfdom, and its evils. But serfdom isn't evil—it is necessary."

His voice had fallen on the last sentence. "Where would we be without the serfs, and them without us, Antonina? Where would we all be without this established order? Would the serfs be happier without our direction, without our support? No. They're like children, and we—the noble landowners— are their fathers. We treat them well when they follow the rules and punish them when they don't. They must understand the importance of the system, just as you must understand."

He looked back at her. "The serfs have no ability to run their own lives independently, let alone a country. It's us,

Antonina Leonidovna, men like me, and the future wives—you, daughter—who will keep the country pure. You defiling yourself with a serf can only lead to a downfall."

"Defiling? Papa . . ." She looked down. "I didn't . . . I haven't done anything wrong, Papa." Then the memory of Lilya's lips rushed back.

There was silence. Antonina didn't know which of them was more embarrassed. She studied the pattern of the deep red and purple rug. The dropped icon glittered beside her right foot.

Prince Olonov sighed, long and deep. "I want to believe you, Antonina. But you've lied to me too many times. You must speak the name of the serf you've been seeing."

Antonina looked up. "I have told you the truth, Papa. There is no man."

Her father stared at her for so long that Antonina had to concentrate to not look away.

Prince Olonov at last nodded. "You're stubborn. Perhaps you imagine you actually have some true feeling for him. You'll eventually tell me."

"How can I, when there is no such man?"

Her father tilted his head. "If you wish to play it like this, you leave me no alternative. We'll flush him out. You're living in your fairy stories. You imagine it's love, and you will be loyal to him. You'll see. A serf doesn't have the capacity for loyalty, or real love. A serf will speak in order to save his own skin. I've seen it too many times. With the touch of the knout on their backs, they all sing."

Antonina thought of Lilya's bruised jaw and neck. Something small and cold wormed through her intestines. "What do you mean?"

"You know what I'm saying, Antonina. We'll start here, on the estate. Next we'll move to Kazhra—it's the closest village. We'll question every soul, ask what people have seen. Someone always sees something. There are no real secrets. Someone can always be persuaded with either rubles or a threat. You may imagine it will be a difficult task to find this man, Antonina. Trust me—it won't."

Antonina swallowed. "You cannot, Papa. Please."

"You will speak his name. Otherwise, many of the serfs will suffer. Then we'll see if this young man is as wonderful as you imagine him to be. You'll be disappointed. This I can swear to you."

"You won't do this, Papa. I know you won't. You aren't a cruel man."

At this, Prince Olonov stared so long and hard at her that Antonina could no longer stand it. She put her face into her hands.

"You're right, Antonina," her father said after a moment. Even though his tone was different, his voice softer, something about this change made Antonina even more fearful.

She raised her face, clenching her hands in front of her now.

"I wanted to see if you could be honest and forthright with me. But you can't. It's so simple. All I have to do is ask Semyon and Kesha. They know that if they don't speak the truth about what they know—where they've gone with you, and whom you spend your time with—they'll not only have to fear losing their positions, they may lose their lives. They'll give me the answers I need."

Antonina was hot, too hot, and her father's face floated, a strange, pale rectangle apart from the darkness of his beard, threaded with white.

"You can't hide anything from me, Tosya," he said.

She felt for the chair behind her, and sat in it. "All right, Papa. All right—I will tell you everything. But it's not a man. It's a girl. Just a peasant girl, that's all. Surely you don't feel the same about me talking to a peasant girl. There was no harm in that. It's as I told you, there was never—has never been—a man."

"A girl?" her father repeated, and Antonina tried to smile.

"Yes. Just a girl. You were right—it was her puppy, and she gave me the icon. I haven't seen her for a long while."

"Who is this girl?"

Antonina shook her head. The movement hurt. "It doesn't matter. I told you, we haven't seen each other for some time. I just wanted . . ." She stopped. She knew she couldn't try to explain to her father how she and Lilya had become friends, or why.

"It matters."

"Why?"

Her father rose. "I've explained it all. And I'm tired of this nonsense. I'm going to summon Semyon and Kesha."

"All right, Papa," Antonina said, jumping up. The sudden movement gave her a jolting pain in her temple. "Her name is Lilya Petrova Nevskaya. She's the daughter of the blacksmith in Kazhra. Now that you know . . . that's all you want, isn't it? For me to tell you her name? To speak the truth?"

When the prince didn't answer, Antonina stepped closer to him. She looked up into his face. "You won't punish her, though, Papa. It's not her fault. It's mine. I told her she must meet with me, and talk to me. She didn't want to. She truly didn't want to. It's not her fault. You must not punish her," she repeated. "Promise me you won't punish her, or her family, for what I wanted. What I did."

She stared at her father, willing him to nod, to say, *Yes, yes, daughter, I understand now. I give you my pledge no harm will come to the girl or her family.*

"No," he said. "I'll promise no such thing."

＊

That night, her father's last words—*I'll promise no such thing*—repeated over and over in Antonina's head, increasing the ache that wouldn't go away. She couldn't sleep for worrying what might happen to Lilya. She lay in the dark, staring at the black square of the window.

When morning finally came, she went downstairs to the breakfast room. Her father was at the table, reading a newspaper and eating egg pie and cold roast beef.

Antonina sat across from him. "Good morning, Papochka," she said carefully.

He glanced at her. "Good morning." He picked up a small gold bell from beside his plate and rang it. Immediately the door opened and two uniformed servants in white gloves entered. One brought in a tray with a silver covered dish and set it in front of Antonina, removing the lid with a flourish. The other servant poured her a cup of tea from the samovar.

"Thank you," Antonina murmured, looking at the pie and meat. Her stomach churned.

"Eat, Tosya," her father urged her. "Eat while the pie is hot."

Antonina picked up her fork and put it into the egg-filled pastry, staring at it. Then she looked at her father. "Papa."

"Hmmm?" He was still reading.

"Papa," she said again, louder, and this time her father put down the newspaper and looked across the table at her, a small, easy smile on his face. "What of Lilya?"

"Lilya?" he said, as if he hadn't heard the name from her lips the afternoon before. "Oh, the daughter of the blacksmith. They've been dealt with."

"Dealt with?" Antonina echoed.

"Yes. The blacksmith I had whipped. To punish the wife, I sent the girl and the other one away."

Antonina swallowed. "Sent them away?" she whispered.

"Yes. The girl and the filthy child." He spoke casually. "I wouldn't have bothered with the boy, but at the last minute I felt sorry for the girl. Actually, I rather admired her. She accepted it well—did not make a fuss when she understood what was to happen to her. As a reward, I let her brother go with her." He looked at Antonina, his eyebrows raised. "I am not as hard-hearted as you might think me, daughter."

Antonina tried to speak, but her mouth was too dry. She lifted her teacup. Her hand shook, and scalding drops of tea fell on the back of her other hand. She needed two hands to set the cup back on the table. "Papa, Lyosha, the little boy . . . he's barely four years old. He's sickly. He needs his mother to care for him."

Her father concentrated on cutting his beef. "That's not my concern. The punishment fit the crime."

Crime, Antonina thought. "Where did you send them?"

"That's not information you need, Antonina. You have learned a lesson: your actions have consequences."

Antonina imagined the hovel in Kazhra, the mother screaming as Lyosha, coughing and wailing, was torn from her arms, the father perhaps unconscious from the lashing.

Sezja barking without cease. And Lilya? At this, Antonina covered her face with her hands. Lilya would know this happened to her family because of Antonina. That Antonina had revealed her name.

"So," Prince Olonov said, looking at her across the table, "we will speak no further of this unfortunate situation. Pass the pepper, please, Tosya."

When Antonina didn't move, he asked her for the pepper a second time. She stared across the table at him. "I know now what kind of man you are," she said. "You spoke, only yesterday, of acting as a father to the serfs, saying that they are like your children. Would you treat your own child so? Would you treat me in a way to bring such unhappiness into my life only to make a point? Why would you?"

Her father's face had grown darker, his lips thinner. Antonina knew she was driving him to fury, yet she couldn't stop herself. Her head pounded; she had to shout to hear herself over the heavy drumming.

"You only make their suffering worse. You are a tyrant."

Was she screaming? He rose and came around the table. Antonina stood. Her father stepped towards her, raising his open hand.

Antonina closed her mouth, willing herself not to shut her eyes or draw back. She wanted him to hit her; she wanted to understand what the servants understood. To know what Lilya had felt from her father. She counted the beats—the thud in her head matching the pulse of the blood in her veins—her father's face undergoing a series of expressions in that tiny and yet somehow unending period. After five beats, he made his hand into a fist and lowered it.

"What would you like to do, Antonina? Will you go and

live in a peasant hut? Yes? This would make you happy? Then go. Go and live with the serfs. See how long you last, sleeping with the pigs to stay warm, your head jumping with lice, your flesh crawling with fleas."

Antonina flinched, deflated. Of course, he was right. She had no power to change anything.

"You have no idea of anything, you foolish girl." He turned and walked away, his shoulders slumped, both hands hanging loosely at his sides in defeat. At the doorway, he said, "Go to your room. Stay there until tomorrow. You will not be brought your meals."

Antonina didn't respond.

"Do you understand the position you put me in, Tosya? I cannot allow your disrespect."

Antonina could not speak as she watched him go. She thought of Lilya, and dropped to her knees, praying that the girl could find a way in her heart to forgive Antonina for what she had done to her family and her life.

12

MARCH 1849

*A*ntonina's name day was March 14, not exactly winter and yet not spring in the Pskov region; each day the weather changed, unsure of its season. To celebrate Antonina's name day the year she would turn eighteen, her mother came to the country estate to put on a fete.

Arranging parties was Galina Maximova's forte. In the autumn she had orchestrated two *bals blancs* to introduce Antonina into St. Petersburg society. Antonina, dressed in white, had danced with a number of eligible men. The balls resulted in two marriage proposals, but neither suited her father because the men weren't influential or wealthy enough. And Antonina had been relieved. There *had* been one man, a slender, dark-haired young soldier from a good family whom Antonina found interesting and thought she might like to speak to further. She reported her interest to her mother, and the princess invited the soldier to a small tea. But the soldier sent a note of apology, saying he was previously engaged. He hadn't tried to set another date. Princess Olonova told her daughter this meant he wasn't interested in pursuing anything further with her. Antonina had been nothing more than slightly annoyed with the soldier for his insult.

She had last seen her mother in St. Petersburg two and a half months earlier, when she and her father had gone to the city for Christmas and New Year's, as Princess Galina Maximova hadn't wanted the cold isolation of the country estate during the holiday festivities.

Antonina's brothers had all left the manor. The oldest, Viktor, had joined the army, and Marik was married with a young child and lived on a smaller estate on a far corner of their father's land. The youngest, Dimitri, had moved to St. Petersburg to live with his mother. The princess complained that Dimi was only interested in gambling and frequenting the drinking establishments around the city. Antonina had seen, over the holidays in St. Petersburg, how Dimitri never rose until mid-afternoon, and was pale yet dark around the eyes, his face slightly puffy from the vodka and late hours.

At the time, her mother had kissed her and told her she would organize a big party for her only daughter in March. The princess was in a wonderful mood; Antonina noticed that she wore a large and new emerald ring.

The princess kept her promise, arriving a week ahead of the scheduled three-day party so she could finalize the events she had planned and make sure the manor was ready. Although Antonina had invited some young people her age from nearby estates, and Marik and his wife and Dimitri were in attendance—Viktor couldn't get leave—most of the more than one hundred guests were her mother's friends from St. Petersburg and Moscow. They would stay in the dozens of guest bedrooms of the estate.

The prince's theatre troupe would perform, and because he had sold his serf orchestra the year before—complaining it was enough to house and feed one troupe—the Yablonsky serf orchestra was hired. It took the sixteen men in the Yablonsky orchestra two days of travel to get to the Olonov estate. They were housed in the servants' quarters and allowed a full night's sleep after their journey. Then they came into the ballroom to rehearse the pieces Galina Maximova had selected. Antonina heard the first strains of their music and went to watch the rehearsal.

The men were dressed in the usual belted tunics and full trousers and felt boots worn by the peasantry. Antonina's gaze kept returning to a violinist, the youngest member of the troupe. He appeared to be about her age. He had a narrow, sensitive face and curling, dark blond hair. She couldn't see the colour of his eyes across the grand expanse of the room, but his eyebrows slanted downwards at the outside edges, giving him a slightly melancholy expression.

Antonina moved closer, keeping to the wall; the room was bustling with servants setting up chairs and arranging ribbons and candles and hothouse flowers. She leaned against one of the smooth round pillars that rose to the soaring ceiling. Now she could see that the violinist's eyes were dark blue. He had delicate hands with long, tapering fingers, and a wide mouth. As well, he had a puffy, burgundy bruise on his left cheekbone—new, still swollen.

He lowered his bow and turned a page of the score. Antonina looked away in case he glanced up and saw her staring at him. She studied the elaborate cornice above one of the windows. When she looked back, he was playing again. His eyes were closed, his face radiant, the shadows of his lashes on his cheeks. What was he thinking of?

The first night of the celebration, after dinner and before the orchestra played, Antonina looked out a tall window at the end of the drawing room. Although a crush of guests circulated around her, she stood alone. In the dark glass she could see her reflection and the wavering shapes of others against the candlelight that filled the room behind her. The air was stifling, the fireplaces at either end of the long hall roaring, and the odours of the guests' heavy perfumes and pomades, underlaid by perspiration, were thick. There were too many voices, too much laughter as the guests drank fine champagne while they waited to dance.

She had a headache just behind her eyes, brought on by the heat, the noise and tension, and the imported champagne. She had drunk a great deal of it, but found it overly sweet. She preferred the clean, smooth taste of vodka. She leaned her forehead against the cool pane, closing her eyes. Where was Lilya living now? In another dank, cold peasant hut, like the izba in Kazhra, or worse? She thought of the little boy, Lilya's brother, with his bare bottom and knobby knees and filthy feet, holding on to his mother's skirt. The wet depth of his cough. Was he still alive? Had Lilya managed to care for him as well as carry out whatever job she had been assigned?

She didn't want to think of that terrible time, over three years earlier. Instead, she focused on the orchestra; soon they would assemble and tune their instruments. She envisioned the young violinist with the bruised cheek.

She opened her eyes, startled, as a hand gripped her shoulder. In the glass she saw one of her mother's friends, Prince Khrutsky. Her mother had introduced Antonina to him earlier than evening.

"All alone, princess?" he asked, needlessly. "This isn't proper, the special girl alone on the first night of her own party. Do you wish to come into the ballroom and dance when the music begins? I can tell you're light on your feet." He smiled at her.

Without facing him, she returned his smile with a very small, polite movement of her lips. He came even closer and very subtly pressed his knee against the back of her thigh. She moved, just enough to turn and face him without having to touch his body. Prince Khrutsky looked even older than her father: hairs protruding from his nostrils and ears, spotted hands, his left eye aimed slightly to one side so she couldn't be sure if it was actually looking at her.

"Well? Will you save me a dance, mademoiselle?" he said. His breath was fishy and dark with the stink of caviar.

She shook her head. "No, thank you, Prince Khrutsky. I don't think I'll dance tonight. A bit of a headache. I'm off to my room soon."

"Abandoning your own fete? That's impossible. Come now, a glass of champagne will clear it away, my dear. Come, have a glass. You're all grown up now—time for champagne." He laughed as he spoke, and Antonina saw one fish egg, no bigger than a poppy seed, caught between his greying front tooth and eye tooth. Time for champagne, he had said, as though she were a child, unused to drinking. Did he not realize how repulsive he was to her? His hand, still on her shoulder, was hot and heavy. She moved again, dipping her knees and turning her shoulder just enough to extract herself from his grip.

He raised his hand to summon a servant with a tray of Baccarat champagne glasses.

"Thank you, prince, really, but I believe I'll go." As he reached to take two glasses from the tray, she slipped away and hurried across the room.

The prince followed. She heard him calling: *Princess Antonina Leonidovna. Mademoiselle, please. Don't run from me. I only wish to enjoy your company. We don't have to dance if it is not your desire. Mademoiselle!*

Glancing over her shoulder again, she saw Prince Khrutsky bearing down on her. She turned a corner and ran to her father's study. She slipped behind a painted screen of Oriental vines and flowers and pushed, firmly, on a panel in the wall. It opened soundlessly. She stepped in and swung it closed behind her. Immediately she was in darkness. She put her hand out and slightly up to the right, and yes, they were still there: the candle and flint. It had been a long time since she had used this passageway.

Her brother Dimitri had first shown her the hidden stairways in the huge manor when she was five or six, and Antonina had been delighted and curious to explore. The doors were nearly impossible to discern even when you knew where to look. She spent endless hours moving about these secret places as a child, popping out and frightening the servants. This one, in the study, led to her mother's bedroom. Although Antonina was told they'd been built for safety reasons, should there be some threat to the family, she couldn't imagine this ever happening. After all, the house was full of faithful servants and the whole estate guarded with more trusted serfs and fierce dogs.

She struck the flint and lit the candle. The space smelled stale, and was strung with cobwebs. Under her slippers, old scatterings of mouse droppings crunched with tiny popping sounds. She sat on the second step of the narrow, steep flight of wooden stairs, careless of her satin skirt. She put her arms on her knees and rested her forehead on them. The champagne had left a sour taste in her mouth. She waited, listening to the far-off, muted voices and laughter, thinking that in another few minutes she would blow out the candle and step back into her father's study. Prince Khrutsky would have found someone else to flirt with. She would slip out of the study and run up the graceful curve of the centre staircase to her bedroom without being seen.

She had survived the meal, and been toasted and congratulated and kissed by her family and her friends and her parents' friends. Once the dancing began, no one would notice her absence.

She heard her father's voice, slightly muffled, by the door. "Khrutsky," he said. "Not enjoying the champagne?"

"I was looking for your lovely daughter, Leonid Stepanovich. I thought I saw her scamper in here—I wanted to extend my good wishes to her on this special occasion. I've been studying your sword collection. Very impressive, old friend."

Antonina sat up to listen, their words clear through the thin panel.

"She's like a shadow, that girl," her father said, "always slipping about. Here—I recently had this Madeira shipped in. Join me, won't you?"

She heard the clink of glass against glass, and next smelled the rich odour of cigars. How annoying: she was truly trapped now. It would be impossible to emerge without embarrassing herself and angering her father.

The candle was only a stub; it would last another five minutes at most. Antonina didn't want to remain in the dusty, dark place. She thought about her bedroom, and the copy of Goncharov's *A Common Story* waiting for her. She had only the last few chapters to finish, and wanted so badly to take off her layers of clothing: the silk chemise covered by the tightly laced corset that pressed painfully against her ribs to mould her waist, the layers of petticoats and the heavy satin gown of deep green, which her mother insisted brought out the colour of her eyes. The thought of putting on her cotton nightdress and curling up under her heavy wool coverlet to finish the novel was unbearably tempting. She had another of these tedious social evenings to deal with tomorrow. Apart from the music, which she loved, it was simply too much rich food and drink, the same overly loud laughter, the same conversations.

Her father and Prince Khrutsky were now on to uninteresting talk of land and crop production. She wondered how long she would have to wait for them to finish their drinks and their cigars and leave.

Of course! Antonina rose and carefully started up the stairs that led to her mother's bedroom. From there, she could simply hurry through the maze of upstairs hallways to her own room. Instinctively stepping over the fourth step, which she remembered made a dry and alarming creak, Antonina climbed. When she was almost at the top, the candle sputtered, diminished but still alive.

In near darkness but for the smallest glimmer, Antonina put out her hand and her fingertips made contact with wood. She pushed gently on the door, disguised as a wallpapered panel in her mother's room, hoping one of the servants hadn't moved a dressing table or heavy chair in front of it since she last used it so long ago. But it swung open easily, silently.

Bending over so as not to hit her head on the lintel, Antonina stepped into the long room. As she straightened, she heard a sound.

She stopped, letting her eyes adjust to the dim light. There was a dull glow from the fireplace, where a hard log of oak softly crackled. She was across from the foot of the bed, and saw a tangle of bed linen. At first she could only make out a bare back, long and white. In the next instant she knew it was her mother by the red blossom in her thick, fair hair. It was still pinned up, although some of it fell from its combs to hang below her shoulder blades.

Holding her breath, Antonina straightened, her eyes never leaving her mother's back.

Galina Maximova Olonova moved in a slow, easy rhythm as if on her favourite horse, her spine undulating slightly with each forward and then backward motion. Antonina stood, transfixed not as much by the damp, pearly sheen of her mother's naked back, the dying fire throwing shadows onto it, as by the sight of the hands around her mother's waist. The fingers were long and smooth, the nails short and clean. They held her mother loosely—not in the grip of possession or passion, but with confidence.

Antonina stood frozen, still holding the candle.

She pressed her lips together and watched as her mother rode faster and faster, beginning now, with each movement, to emit a small cry. There was no sound from the owner of the hands, nor was there, from what Antonina could tell, any movement on his part. It was her mother who was the flame, bringing the heat and desire, her mother who at one point held on to the man's hands, wrapping her own around them fiercely, forcing them to hold her more tightly. In the next moment she let go of the hands and cupped her own breasts, throwing back her head so that the loose strands of hair cascaded to the middle of her back.

It appeared, to Antonina, that her mother might indeed have been alone, except for those disembodied hands.

Then her mother gave a long, trilling cry, and after a few seconds of stillness she folded forward. And it was then, over her mother's form, her hair a light mass on the man's chest, that Antonina was able to see his face. He was partially propped on a silk-covered pillow. She looked at him, and he looked back at her.

It was the violinist from the serf orchestra, the young one with the bruised cheekbone. He stared at her as her mother lay on him, making small, pleased sounds now.

She knew her face was illuminated by the tiny flame of the candle. She was aware of the sleek, silken warmth of wax dripping onto her hand. The candle burned itself out, a tiny stab of pain in the warm tallow melting into the web of skin between Antonina's thumb and index finger. She became aware of an odour: not just the familiar strong scent of her mother's eau de cologne, but also of sweat, and something musky. The smell of sex, Antonina instinctively knew.

The young man didn't make a sound, nor move. He didn't look away from Antonina's steady gaze. His face, so expressive as he played, held none of that joy and passion. Now it showed nothing—no pleasure, no shame.

"My pretty boy, I feel you—still firm and ready. You have boundless energy, it appears." The princess gave a low, throaty laugh. "Even after our stolen hour this afternoon, you're nevertheless more than capable. How delightful you are, as I sensed you would be." She stroked his shoulder. "Come, Valya, tell me how beautiful I am, and how you have never before had a princess as a lover. I have more to offer than the silly village girls who must throw themselves at you. Tell me how much more I am. Tell me, Valya."

The man hadn't taken his eyes from Antonina's, staring at her over her mother's shoulder. The princess reached out with one hand to cup his chin and turn his gaze to hers. She then fell to one side, pulling the violinist with her so that they were face to face. "Tell me what I want to hear before you have to go," she said, and Antonina saw one slack breast drop as her mother raised her arm to push away the hair stuck to her face. "How tiresome that you are needed downstairs."

Antonina backed, barely breathing, into the passageway, and just as soundlessly closed the door.

Her legs were weak. She sat in the dark on the top step. Her heart was a steady flutter, her face damp in spite of the chill of the passage. She realized that she herself was giving off an odour, something sweet and hot, as though that same smooth, warm wax that coated her hand now ran through her body. Although disgusted with her mother, Antonina was aroused at the sight of her with the man. But only because she suddenly realized she wanted that—to be doing just that—with the young serf violinist.

She crept back down the stairs. There were no voices in her father's study. She pushed open the panel and hurried through the empty room. The guests were now assembling in the ballroom, and she ran up the stairs without having to speak to anyone.

In her own room, she closed the door and leaned against it, breathing heavily—not only from the hurried pace, but from what she had just experienced.

⁂

Late the next afternoon, her father's acting troupe put on a play—a love triangle with a few rather predictable comedic overtones—but Antonina found it difficult to concentrate. The production was followed by hors d'oeuvres and some organized rounds of whist and *vint*. The one hundred and twelve guests were eventually treated to an elaborate dinner and more champagne, to be followed by another night of dancing.

Antonina had slipped away from the dinner as the orchestra's musicians were tuning their instruments, readying for their performance. As she had at the rehearsal a few days before, Antonina watched the orchestra, this time slightly hidden as she sat in a high-backed settee with curving sides. The room reverberated with the cacophony of keys, strings and woodwinds.

She openly studied the young violinist, sitting with his violin and bow, his music stand empty in front of him. The cellist spoke to him, and it was clear to Antonina that the violinist was lost in thought. The cellist had to touch him on the shoulder before he looked up at the older man. Antonina saw the fine curve of his lips as the violinist spoke, the way his hair gleamed in the light of the candelabra. She thought of his hands on her naked hips as they had been on her mother's.

⁂

Twice Antonina, on the arm of a friend's brother, threaded her way through weaving mazurkas with three other couples, and then danced a waltz with an unknown young man who held her lightly enough that she wasn't uncomfortable. She liked to dance, and even though she had no interest in her dance partners, she smiled unconsciously as she danced a polka and then a quadrille.

Every time she whirled past the orchestra, she caught the eye of the violinist. When she declined another polka with a lieutenant in too-tight trousers, claiming that she needed to rest her toes, she took her glass of champagne and stood in a cluster of unmarried young women from neighbouring estates. They fanned themselves and spoke in high, breathless tones, watching the dancers and discussing the charms of certain men. While Antonina smiled, nodding at their conversation, she tried to keep the violinist in her line of vision.

The orchestra rested their instruments to prepare for another number, and Antonina saw her mother flirting openly with the lieutenant in the tight trousers, touching the rim of his ear and laughing gaily, then whispering something against his cheek. The lieutenant laughed heartily, squeezing her waist. Antonina looked at the violinist. He was also watching her mother, his mouth tight as he busied himself with stroking his strings with a block of resin.

Antonina was ashamed for her mother, and angry at her for so pointedly demonstrating how very unimportant the violinist was to her.

"Mother," Antonina said, going to her, pulling on her hand so that Galina Maximova had to reluctantly leave the lieutenant. "I want the orchestra to play Glinka's Separation in F Minor. It's my favourite."

Her mother waved her hand in the orchestra's direction. "Give them the order, then."

They stood near the violinist. Antonina looked at him. "Excuse me," she said, stepping up to the low platform.

The violinist put down his resin and stood. He studied her, and then her mother, with a steady, cool gaze. "Mother," Antonina said, "I believe the two of you have met. Isn't this so?"

Neither her mother nor the violinist answered her, but the young man bowed to Antonina. "I am Valentin Vladimirovitch Kropotkin." He lifted his head and looked into her eyes. It was the same look he had given her over her mother's shoulder.

Antonina's breathing quickened despite her efforts to control it. "I told my mother that I wished the orchestra to play Glinka's Separation in F Minor. Would you play it for me?" Standing so close to the violinist was making her heart pound. Without waiting for him to answer, she looked back at her mother. "I'm sure, Mother, that you can persuade him to do anything you wish. Can't you?"

Galina Maximova frowned, glancing at the violinist and then back at Antonina. "What do you mean, Antonina?"

"You know what I mean, Mother. Haven't you already asked him to do your bidding?"

"Mademoiselle, it is of course up to you," the violinist said, ignoring Galina Maximova and speaking directly to Antonina. "It is your party, after all. I will talk to the maestro about the change."

Antonina's mother stopped a server, taking a glass of champagne from the tray.

"It would be a great pleasure to play something special for you at your name day celebration, Princess Olonova. We have all of Glinka's music. We shall play it as the finale, if that is to your liking."

Antonina liked the sound of his voice. She also liked that he was ignoring her mother. "Yes. Thank you," she said, unsmiling. "Valentin Vladimirovitch," she added, giving him the respect of calling him by his proper name.

As the orchestra finished their last waltz at three in the morning, the guests, damp with perspiration, moved to leave the ballroom. But the conductor loudly tapped his stand, calling out, "Ladies and gentlemen. If I may, we have one last piece. It is not a dance, but a special performance for the Princess Antonina Leonidovna, our gift to her in celebration of her name day."

He looked at her, and Antonina bowed her head in thanks. The rest of the guests stopped where they were, a few still talking, and watched the orchestra.

The conductor turned back to the men and lifted his baton. Antonina smiled openly at the violinist. He smiled back at her.

She pressed her fingertips to her lips as she watched his face, intense and expressive as he accompanied the pianist. She thought again how she had seen his hands so loosely set on her mother's slightly fleshy hips, and wanted to feel them on her own bare skin.

When the last note of the nocturne had faded, she, along with the others, clapped enthusiastically. The orchestra rose as one, bowing deeply. Still Antonina watched the violinist. As he straightened, he tossed his head to swing a lock of hair from his forehead and looked directly at her.

The guests left the ballroom, but still Antonina lingered as the orchestra began packing up their instruments. As she hoped, the violinist came to her, a sheaf of music in his hand.

"I have asked the pianist to allow me to present you a copy of a number of Glinka's pieces," he said. "Although they are well used, and you may already own some of them, perhaps, when you play—I assume you play?" he asked, and when Antonina nodded, he added, "—you will remember your name day."

I will remember you, Antonina thought.

"May I inscribe them to you?" he asked, and she nodded again, flustered.

"There is pen and ink in the vestibule," she said, "near the guest book."

"If I may . . . ?" Valentin asked, and Antonina turned and went into the huge, echoing hallway, with the violinist following.

There he bent over the top page, writing. As they waited for the ink to dry, Antonina read what he had written: *To Antonina Leonidovna on her name day. With great admiration and respect, Valentin Vladimirovitch. Dated March 14, 1849.*

"I know this gift cannot in the smallest way match any of your others," Valentin said, gesturing at the table with its riches of celebratory presents Antonina had received from her guests.

She picked up the pages. "I believe this music is the most special," she said, shocked at her forwardness. "Every time I play it, I will remember who gave it to me." His handwriting was very fine.

"Perhaps, after we perform at the final luncheon tomorrow, you will do the honour of playing for me," Valentin said.

Antonina smiled at him.

She didn't see her mother studying her, her brow slightly furrowed.

The sheets of Glinka music sat on her dressing table. Antonina thought of the young violinist while she fell asleep. She slept deeply, and arose happy at the thought of seeing him again that day. She gave much thought to which piano composition she would play for him.

When she went downstairs, she avoided the guests enjoying breakfast in the huge dining room, slipping into the breakfast room for a quiet cup of tea. She was surprised to see her mother and father sitting together, talking quietly, in the sunlit room. They stopped when she came through the glass doors. Antonina wondered why they weren't with their house guests for breakfast.

It was odd to see them together, looking strangely pleased, Antonina thought. As if they had, for once, agreed upon something. While she ate a sweet roll and drank a cup of tea, her parents spoke briefly of the success of the evening before.

"What time is the luncheon and performance scheduled for today?" Antonina asked, hoping the question appeared nonchalant. She reached for another roll.

Her mother's eyelids lowered slightly. "Actually, I have dismissed the orchestra. They left an hour ago." Then she smiled at Antonina, an open, careless smile. "The luncheon will be at one o'clock."

Antonina pulled her hand back from the plate of sweet rolls and opened her mouth to protest. Staring at her mother, she closed it again. What could she protest? She hated her at that moment.

"I want you to come to my study," her father said then.

She rose, avoiding looking at her mother.

13

*A*ntonina fingered the smooth roundness of the globe on her father's desk as she had done since first coming to his private study as a child. He sat behind the desk in his creaking leather chair.

Being summoned to her father's study was never a good thing. As a little girl, she was chastised for being rude to her tutors or hiding from her nanny. When she was older, she had been scolded for riding her brother's favourite horse without permission and for sneaking off to swim in the lake without a chaperone and for giving away one of her mother's simple day gowns to a young house serf to be married in.

The last time had been the event with the icon.

Although no longer a child, she once again felt like one, standing in front of her father's wide mahogany desk, imported from London. Was she to be reprimanded for refusing to dance with the annoying Prince Khrutsky two nights before, or for attempting to humiliate her mother in front of the violinist?

"Sit down, please, Tosya," Prince Olonov said.

"Thank you, Father," she said, and lowered herself into the brocade chair. The seat sagged slightly: it needed restuffing. She realized there had been no new furniture or decor changes at the estate for some time, and the study had grown slightly shabby. The navy silk curtains were discoloured, the sun having created strips of lighter blue in the folds. One of the swags had loose threads hanging from it.

"You're quite grown up now," her father said. His forehead shone damply, and again she thought of that time, over three years ago, when he had exiled Lilya and Lyosha. The room was cool, a fresh March breeze blowing through the slightly open window behind the prince's desk, lifting the faded draperies.

Then he stood; Antonina also rose respectfully. His behaviour was confusing. Antonina could almost believe, in a strange twist, that she was making him uncomfortable.

"And so I have arranged a marriage for you," he said.

"What?" When her father didn't immediately answer, still standing behind his desk, she licked her lips and spoke again. "But . . . who? And why? Why now?"

"It's time," he said.

Antonina walked around his desk and stood in front of him.

"You will be married to Count Mitlovsky."

For a moment, Antonina thought she must have misunderstood him. "Count Mitlovsky?" He had been at her name day celebration; Antonina had seen him a few times over the last two days, but she hadn't done more than accept his gift and curtsey to him. "No . . . no, Father." Her voice grew louder. "He's an old man!"

The prince's lips pursed. "He's not yet fifty—six years younger than I am. And he's an honest man. I've done business with him before."

"Business? That's what this is, then?"

Her father stared at her. "Antonina, you're old enough to understand that these things—the merging of families—is for the betterment of all concerned."

"How is it for my betterment?"

The prince shook his head in an impatient manner. "Konstantin Nikolevich is an influential man. He has a large estate close to the city of Pskov. He owns many versts and many souls. Most women would be thrilled to be married to him—there have been any number of interested widows. He's willing . . ." He stopped. When he spoke again, it was as if he was weighing his words. "He has been a widower for the last few years, Antonina. He's looking for another woman to share his life—and his wealth. His first marriage, although long and, according to him, happy, produced no children. His wife wasn't a well woman for much of her life. And he would like children. The widows who have made their desires apparent aren't young enough to ensure this."

"He wants me to give him a brood of children?"

"Stop your foolishness. He finds you attractive and interesting, or he wouldn't have made the offer."

"*He* made the first offer? Not you?"

At this, the prince looked at her for a long moment, and then looked down at his desk.

Antonina noticed the bald spot on the top of his head. Was Count Mitlovsky bald as well? No. He still had thick, wavy hair, although it was grey.

She tried to summon memories of the count, who'd simply been one of her father's guests who sometimes came for a weekend or a week-long visit. She vaguely recalled his auburn-haired wife, a rigid and rather disdainful woman with a bony frame. She had the faint scars of smallpox on her cheeks, which she tried to cover with a thick layer of powder. At some point Count Mitlovsky had come on his own, wearing a black armband, so Antonina had known his wife had died. Standing in front of her father now, she remembered the count arriving on a blustery January afternoon, just after their most recent New Year celebrations in St. Petersburg, and spending some hours with the prince in his study before Antonina was summoned to dinner. It had been only the three of them at the long, gleaming table.

The scene came back to her now in all its details. As she had entered the dining room to join her father and Count Mitlovsky for dinner, the prince had said, "And we are agreed upon souls—the full hundred?"

Count Mitlovsky stood, bowing over Antonina's hand and then kissing it lightly. As he pulled out her chair for her, he said to the prince, "The time for discussing business is ended, now that your lovely daughter has joined us. Do you not agree?"

"Certainly," Prince Olonov answered.

"Are you selling serfs, Father?" Antonina asked, and when her father didn't answer, she turned to Count Mitlovsky. "I hope not. He feels he has the right to separate families, which causes great heartache."

Count Mitlovsky opened his mouth to reply, but Antonina's father spoke to her first. "Please, Antonina Leonidovna. Don't show such disrespect in front of our guest. These are matters for those of us who have full understanding of the situation."

But Antonina wouldn't be silenced. "I hope you don't agree with this barbaric practice, Count Mitlovsky." She settled herself in her chair.

The count took his seat as well, and the door swung open. Servants entered carrying silver trays with bowls of soup and plates of thinly sliced onion and salted, pickled cucumber, and began to serve.

"Do you, Count Mitlovsky?" Antonina persisted. "Because when I ride through the villages, and notice how—"

Her father interrupted her, his voice smooth. "The count is our guest, dear daughter, and he has requested that we not speak of business during dinner. You will of course respect his wishes."

Antonina sat back as the servant lifted the silver cover from the steaming soup in front of her. "Yes, Father," she said.

They had finished the dessert, a tart of preserved berries with thick whipped cream, and the samovar had been brought in when Prince Olonov asked Antonina to recite part of Pushkin's *Yevgeny Onegin* for Count Mitlovsky. "Just the opening of Book One, Antonina," he urged.

"Please, Father," she said, not wanting to stay at the table any longer. "I'm sure Count Mitlovsky has heard many, many stanzas of *Yevgeny Onegin* far too many times. It would be tiresome for him."

"Oh, I can assure you, Antonina Leonidovna," Count Mitlovsky said, "that I would indeed care to hear it. It's been many years since a young woman recited poetry for my benefit." He smiled. Although slightly stained from tea and tobacco, his teeth were straight, and his smile was almost charming. "I am sure you have a highly compelling voice."

"Yes, come, Tosya," Prince Olonov said, fixing his eyes on her.

She put down her napkin and stood, clearing her throat.

"Your hair, Antonina Leonidovna," her father said.

She reached up, feeling long strands against her cheeks. She tried to push the stray locks into their pins.

To his guest, her father said, "You may be assured, Konstantin Nikolevich, that although my daughter lacks certain feminine understandings, she is very compliant."

Antonina looked sharply at her father, both angry and shamed. Although her father was correct about her lack of interest in her hair and the latest fashions, the second part of the statement was an outright lie. He knew how stubborn she was.

"You have brought enchanting colour to Antonina Leonidovna's face, my old friend," Count Mitlovsky said then, and she clenched her hands and hid them in the folds of her skirt.

The ormolu clock ticked loudly, and there was the rasp of the swinging door and the tiniest tinkle of porcelain as a servant entered with a tray of cups and saucers and a pot of sugar chunks. Antonina stood in the almost silent room, waiting while the man put out the cups and saucers and sugar then bowed and left.

"Perhaps you will first pour the tea, daughter," her father said. "We will enjoy it while you entertain us."

As she'd set the cup and saucer on the heavy damask tablecloth in front of Count Mitlovsky, he'd unexpectedly taken her hand. "Do you not wear gloves when you ride, Antonina Leonidovna?" he asked, and she looked at him, then at her father, then back to Count Mitlovsky. What a peculiar and rather personal question. How inappropriate that he touch her.

"If I choose not to," she said.

"Your skin is roughened by the cold." He turned her hand over, looking at the palm. "My dear, such calluses from the reins. You should take better care of these young hands."

Something about the way he held her hand, so lightly and yet possessively, unsettled her. She extracted her fingers from his and again looked at her father, wanting . . . something, some form of support—even an expression that told her she wasn't wrong in being uncomfortable with the unwanted attention from this man. But her father wore a small smile.

"I'm terribly sorry, Count Mitlovsky," Antonina said, "I cannot stay to recite for you. There is something I must do."

She ran from the dining room and up to her room.

Later that evening, after the count had retired, her father came to her and reprimanded her for her rudeness. He went on, yet again, about appropriate behaviour. He also told her that it was particularly important that she display excellent manners while in Count Mitlovsky's presence.

"Why do you care so much about him?" she had asked, but her father had simply shaken his head, frowning, and left her room.

Since then, she had pushed from her mind the disturbing thoughts of Count Mitlovsky's hand on hers. She hadn't thought of him again or paid any attention to his presence among the guests over the last few days. And now her father was telling her she would marry him.

Her father's chair creaked as he sat down again, resting his hands on his desk. "The benefits of this marriage are great for you, Antonina. You will continue to live a charmed life, with the finest of possessions, opportunities for travel, and invitations to all the most influential events of each season. But it will be as a wife, not a daughter. Do you not see what a wonderful opportunity this is for you? Do you not see that your mother and I are thinking of your future?"

Antonina walked around to the other side of the desk again. "I'm not marrying him. You can't make me." Of course, this wasn't true. Prince Olonov dictated Antonina's life. He *could* make her.

Now he leaned back. "Have you a husband in mind, Antonina Leonidovna?" he asked. "I haven't seen any suitors arriving at our door. The *bals blancs* your mother arranged last fall came to nothing. I'm not aware of you expressing much interest in going to dances or musical evenings when invitations from other estates arrive. In fact, you have refused all such invitations of late. Am I to believe that you think you will just stay on here, spending your time in idle pursuits, until . . . until when, Tosya? Are you not a normal woman who desires her own home, a husband and children?"

Antonina remained motionless.

"Well. This is an interesting turn of events," her father said, reaching for a cigar. He clipped the end. "For once, my daughter has no opinion: Antonina Leonidovna Olonova, with nothing to say for herself." He lit the end of the cigar, puffing vigorously.

His daughter had no idea how desperate he was, how unmarriageable she might soon be.

For the last few years Prince Olonov had managed to hide the grave errors he had made with his finances. His expenses were astronomical. The cost of running the estate was huge in itself, and he also had the grand house in St. Petersburg to support, along with his wife's rampant spending. He supplemented the incomes of all his sons, and Dimitri had lost huge amounts of money in gambling that he'd had to clear. Taxes to the government were high, and he was far in arrears. He was deeply in debt.

He had taken note of Count Mitlovsky's interest in his daughter since the count's bereavement. He explained to his old friend that he would be happy to have Antonina Leonidovna become his wife, but that with the crushing expenses he was incurring he could no longer supply the significant dowry expected for such a marriage.

Konstantin Mitlovsky had nodded, telling the prince that due to their long-standing friendship, and because fortune had smiled on him for the last number of years, he had no need of a dowry. The gift of the prince's lively daughter was certainly enough to satisfy him. So eager was he to have a young and fertile wife that he had agreed to purchase a number of versts from an estate that adjoined the prince's property. He would make a gift of these, along with the one hundred or more serfs living there, to the prince. The waning Olonov fortunes would be increased.

When the prince brought this up with his wife, she agreed completely. Antonina's mother was more than anxious to have her daughter taken to another man's home.

She didn't care about Antonina's moods or wayward behaviour; she wasn't around to notice what her only daughter got up to. She was more concerned that the girl, although not conventionally beautiful, had a certain charm, and that comparisons would inevitably be drawn between a beauty past its prime and one coming into full flower. For the last two years she had not allowed her daughter to stand beside her in the receiving line when she welcomed guests to the house in St. Petersburg or at the country manor.

This unfortunate merging of Prince Olonov's financial losses and his wife's self-absorbed fears created Antonina's destiny.

14

*A*ntonina did not go quietly into the arranged marriage. She protested to her mother, beseeched her father, and threatened to run off. She was bluffing, and her parents knew it; where would Antonina go? Still, she used every verbal tactic she possessed to persuade them that she did not wish to be married to Count Mitlovsky. It did no good: both the prince and princess knew that this was their only opportunity to carry on in the manner to which they were accustomed.

Besides, they told each other, Antonina would become almost unmarriageable as she approached twenty. It would be cruel to condemn her to the life of a spinster, living with her parents or her brothers' families. This was a fate no woman wished. They were helping their daughter, as any concerned parents would, they said to each other in a rare show of harmony, shaking their heads at their daughter's ungrateful spirit.

The wedding was to take place in the city of Pskov. Count Mitlovsky's request was that the ceremony be held in the grand and picturesque Trinity Cathedral within the medieval walls of the citadel. Pskov was only a three-hour carriage ride from his estate of Polnokove, and he didn't wish to travel the nearly three hundred kilometres farther to St. Petersburg, as the princess had hoped. She'd wanted all of St. Petersburg society to see her daughter married to the wealthy Count Mitlovsky, but agreed with her husband that they must not argue over any of the count's suggestions. There wouldn't be another offer such as his for their unruly daughter.

Two days before the wedding, during the final fitting, Antonina spilled a glass of claret down the front of her wedding gown, a costly effort designed by her mother and stitched by the finest seamstresses Pskov had to offer. The ruby liquid irreparably stained the bodice and voluminous skirt all the way to the hem. Why she had held the claret during the fitting was odd to the seamstresses, and how she had been clumsy enough to tip the full glass on herself was a mystery.

Princess Olonova had screamed as the claret spilled, and had then slapped Antonina across the face. The many seamstresses stood with open looks of horror on their faces. Which were they more shocked at: the ruining of the gown they had worked on for over two months, sewing thousands of tiny seed pearls over the entire skirt and train, or the behaviour of the supposedly well-bred woman?

Antonina didn't react to the slap. She'd apologized to her mother and the seamstresses, saying that surely the wedding would have to be postponed, as there was no time to make another gown. In a harsh whisper that nevertheless carried to all the dressmakers, her mother said, "Don't think I am so stupid as to not recognize what you are doing." She then handsomely bribed the head dressmaker to give them another young woman's almost finished gown. It was a beautiful tulle, and while not as glorious as the original, it would do.

It did not fit Antonina, too tight in the bodice and too loose at the waist, but there wasn't time to fix it.

Count Konstantin Nikolevich Mitlovsky and Princess Antonina Leonidovna Olonova were married at the soaring cathedral in Pskov in September 1849. As the priest droned on and on about vows and commitments, Antonina was aware of a breathlessness, caused, she was sure, by the tightness of the bodice with its many satin-covered buttons. She thought about the young woman who had lost her wedding gown due to her own childish behaviour, and was ashamed of herself. She hadn't planned to ruin anyone else's wedding, just her own.

Later, she saw the hard, pleased look on her mother's face as she kissed her daughter after the ceremony and wished her a fruitful life on the far-off estate of Polnokove.

Antonina's father's expression was somehow uncertain, although covered by a jovial smile.

She didn't let herself think about the night ahead.

Count Mitlovsky and the new Countess Mitlovskiya spent their first night together in the sumptuous suite of an inn overlooking the lovely Velikaya River that ran through Pskov.

A maid had helped her out of her gown and into the ribboned, high-necked, long-sleeved ecru silk nightdress.

Exhausted by the stress of the day and her anxiety about what was to come, Antonina climbed into the wide bed and sat there, her hair still piled on her head and threaded with strings of tiny lustrous pearls in the elaborate arrangement that had held her veil.

She was certain she wouldn't fall asleep but did almost immediately, propped against the pile of lacy pillows. When there was a quiet knock on the door between the two adjoining bedrooms, Antonina was startled awake. "Yes," she said, blinking, and cleared her throat. "Yes," she repeated, a little louder. "Come in."

Konstantin entered and stood awkwardly beside the bed in his nightshirt and robe and slippers. "Are you comfortable, my dear?" he asked, wiping his lips and moustache with a handkerchief he pulled from the pocket of his robe.

"Yes, thank you," Antonina said.

"It was a fine wedding," he said then, putting the handkerchief back into his pocket. "Don't you think?"

"Yes, very fine."

"I thought that we would go to the Monastery of the Caves tomorrow, just outside the city, if it suits you. It's very interesting. Pilgrims come from all over Russia to see its wonders."

Antonina nodded, although what would suit her would have been to be back in her bedroom surrounded by her familiar things: her many books of history, fiction and poetry, her sketches of horses hung on the walls, her atlas and memoirs of adventurers' depictions of exotic, faraway places, and, most especially right now, the flask of vodka hidden behind the padded window-seat cushion. Although she had drunk two glasses of wine at the wedding dinner,

Konstantin had, she noticed, given a sign to the server that she not be given any more.

She was trembling ever so slightly, as though a cold breeze blew through the open window, chilling her. However, it was a beautiful, warm autumn evening, and there was no breeze.

"Immediately after breakfast, we'll go back to Trinity Cathedral. I always start the day with prayer, as I'm sure you do," he said. "You'll enjoy my Church of the Redeemer at Polnokove. I insist on daily morning Masses for the house serfs, and of course ourselves and visitors. It's quite a beautiful chapel. I had the stained glass imported from Italy."

Antonina didn't answer. She did go to Sunday Mass on her father's estate, and said her prayers at night to her icons, but that was all she'd ever done in the way of observance.

"And directly after we've enjoyed the Mass, we'll have the carriage take us to the Pskov Gardens before driving out of the city to the monastery. It's still early enough in the fall for the colours to be bright. The following day, you can visit a dressmaker. I'm sure you'd like that."

"But I don't need anything," Antonina said.

Konstantin smiled. "Need? But I know women, my dear. It's not a question of *need*. Surely you will want to have some new clothing made, and perhaps purchase some jewellery before we return to Polnokove."

Antonina nodded then, thinking it best to agree, at least for tonight, but she had no intention of spending any time in Pskov being fitted for more gowns. She had spent enough time in that pursuit over the last few months with her mother in St. Petersburg. Her father had scolded Galina Maximova, telling her that the count would have a new wardrobe fashioned for his wife and there was no reason to spend any

more. As usual, Princess Olonova ignored him, and glee-
fully filled box after box with new gowns and hats and slippers and gloves and cloaks for her daughter. It was the first
time, Antonina thought, that her mother appeared to be
enjoying time spent with her.

Antonina's new nightclothes alone filled a trunk.

"But there is something I'd like," she said to the count. "A
dog." After the unhappiness surrounding her short time with
Sezja, she had never again brought up having her own puppy.

"A dog? But of course. You shall have whatever dog you
wish."

"Thank you." She smiled at her husband.

He smiled back.

Now she waited. She could smell Konstantin's moustache
wax, and the slight, lingering odour of cigar smoke, which
reminded her of her father. She didn't want to think of anything but sleep. She wanted to be left alone.

"May I extinguish the lamps, my angel?" Konstantin asked.

"Yes," Antonina said, but the word came out flannelled,
as though a filmy web coated her larynx. Again she cleared
her throat. "Yes, of course," she said, more firmly.

As each of the lamps was turned further down, then off,
the room was left in darkness but for a faint line of light showing between the curtains over the wide windows. Antonina
closed her eyes, and opened them to see Konstantin's shape
climbing into her bed.

She moved to the far side, holding her breath when he
pulled back the bedclothes. When Konstantin lay down on
his back, Antonina did the same. Her neck was tense, and
her ankle itched. The white satin ribbons on her wedding
slippers had been tied too tightly. Where she had been chilled

only moments earlier, now she felt too warm, but she didn't want to move.

The silence stretched. She thought that maybe Konstantin had fallen asleep. She listened to his breathing, but didn't know what he would sound like if he was asleep. She eventually closed her own eyes, and felt her anxiety ebbing. Her itchy ankle annoyed her. Sleepily she reached down to scratch it, and at the same time there was a movement and rustle of the bedclothes. Konstantin found her face in the dark, and put his lips against hers.

His moustache tickled, and the fruity smell of the wax was strong. Konstantin moved his lips, opening them slightly. She kept hers firmly shut, and let him kiss her. More than anything, she was afraid the smell of the wax would make her sneeze.

Finally he stopped kissing her, moving his lips to somewhere between her cheek and her ear, and gently put his hand on her breast. She froze. He left it there for a long moment, squeezing it a bit as though testing for something, and then his fingers grew still.

"May I?" he said, and she didn't know what he was asking permission for.

When he waited, she said, "Yes."

He slowly moved to lie on top of her. "Is that all right, my dear?"

It wasn't all right. He was heavy, but again Antonina said, "Yes."

Konstantin did everything slowly, tentatively, as if Antonina was very fragile, or he was very uncertain.

He planted his lower body between her legs, forcing them apart, and fumbled to pull up her nightdress to just above her knees. She drew in her breath at the sensation of the hair on his legs, scratchy against hers. And then she stayed immobile, hardly breathing, as if by her held breath and stiff body she could preserve herself. His stomach pressed her further into the soft mattress as he rhythmically moved against her, and she also felt the warmth from his flesh between her thighs, even though the fabric of their nightclothes was between them. This rubbing through their nightclothes seemed to go on and on; she kept her eyes closed and took small gulps of air when she could no longer hold her breath.

But at one point, she opened her eyes. What she saw made her close them again immediately. Konstantin's face was so close that even though the room was dark, she could make out his features. His eyes were closed, and there was a look of concentration on his face, as if he were contemplating a deep philosophical question. For that moment, in the dark, strange room, she was suddenly frightened—not exactly of Konstantin, but more of a sensation of imprisonment, of this intimacy with a near stranger.

A distressed moan forced itself from between her clenched lips, and she struggled, pushing her hands against Konstantin's chest. His eyes flew open, and his expression changed, becoming familiar. He rolled off her with a sigh that was weighty.

"I'm sorry, Antonina Leonidovna," he said quietly. His apology confused her. "We are both tired. I'll let you sleep. Good night," he said, "my angel." It was the second time he had addressed her in this way. He rose and pulled down his nightshirt. Slipping on his heavy robe, he left the room.

Antonina was at first relieved that she hadn't been made a true wife; the thought of the act with Konstantin had worried her. But once he was gone, and she was alone and able to turn over and let sleep come to her, she felt a stab of sadness. She had wanted to feel something. She had dealt with her wedding night the way she had learned to deal with the physical pursuits her brothers had forced onto her as a child. Perhaps the closest she could come to describing her feelings for those long, unpleasant moments was being held under water, holding her breath and waiting to surface.

She thought of her mother, moving atop the violinist with such obvious satisfaction. She thought of Valentin Vladimirovitch's face as he had stared at her over her mother's shoulder.

She wondered whether Valentin ever thought of her.

Antonina found it awkward to greet Konstantin the next morning in the private dining room reserved for the newlyweds, but he acted as though all was normal. He questioned the server about the freshness of the thinly sliced veal, then smiled at her across the table. She forced herself to return his smile.

Later, after the morning Mass, as they were walking through the pretty *allée* of ornamental trees in the Pskov Gardens, Konstantin said, "As a gentleman, it's probably not best that I bring this up, but I'm sorry that last night was . . . as it was. Although I suppose the blame can be placed on the fact that you are young."

"It was my fault?" Antonina said, trying not to sound too indignant. The air smelled peppery from the many marigolds still in bloom.

"You're pleasant-looking enough, but too slight, too fair. I prefer a taller, stronger woman, like my late wife."

Antonina stopped, so surprised that she didn't have time to be hurt. She thought of his mannish, raw-boned wife.

Konstantin stopped as well, pulling a small knife from his pocket. He opened it and looked down at his fingernails. "You are not yet very interesting, Tosya." Antonina stiffened at the insult. "Although I know that you are highly accomplished at the piano"—he paused—"you are still inexperienced and empty." He pared the nails of his left hand, speaking as casually as if he had just announced that he didn't like horseradish. "One can only hope you'll become less ordinary as you mature."

Antonina stared at him, heat spreading through her, slowly at first, like fire under moss. But then it caught, flaring up with a kind of relief, and she moved from beside him to in front of him. "How can you say this to me?"

Konstantin gave her no more than an unconcerned glance, then held his hand in front of him, surveying his fingernails.

"You believe I'm empty? *Empty?*" The word hit a sharp staccato note. A couple strolling by looked at them, then hurried on. "Empty as in a fool, as in stupid, with no more brains than a sturgeon? If you thought that, then why did you reward my father so handsomely for me? Why, Konstantin Nikolevich?" When he didn't answer, she said, "I am sorry you feel that way, husband. That I am somehow to blame for what was clearly difficult for both of us in the bed."

He put away his knife. "That's enough, Antonina," he said in a low tone. "Decent people don't discuss such private details."

But Antonina wasn't finished. "You are the one who brought it up. I can no more change my physical self than that statue," she said, gesturing to a marble figure in the middle of a circle of begonias, "but you and I both know that you are very wrong about my intelligence. There's no need to be mean-spirited simply because you're disappointed." Softer than before, she carried on. "As for how I felt while you lay on me last night, you might consider—"

Konstantin's head shot up and he squeezed her forearm. "I have just requested that you don't speak like a common woman, and yet you refute me. You are Countess Mitlovskiya. You will learn to behave in a proper manner, and set aside your wilful and childish ways. You're no longer that child. You are a woman, my wife, and the new countess of my estate," he said, letting go of her arm.

Antonina fought the urge to rub the tender area.

Konstantin wiped his forehead with his gloved hand. "Antonina, I believe we are both weary from the last few days. Don't let us argue on our first day as man and wife. I only want us to be happy. Let us speak of more pleasant topics." He smiled at her. "I am renaming my estate in your honour."

His comments about her intelligence still stung, but she saw that he was trying to make amends, trying not to let his impatience with her spoil their day.

"Oh? To what?" She attempted to smile back at him.

"Angelkov. For my angel."

She smiled again, pressing his hand between hers, although the heaviness inside her hadn't lessened.

At Angelkov, it took Antonina over a week to learn her way about the house and gardens and surrounding out-buildings, and to memorize the names of all the house serfs.

Her husband had made much of his money from a private vodka distillery he had on his estate, complete with a cooperage to build the vats and barrels for the liquor, which he sold around the province and beyond.

She had chosen Tinka from a weaned litter before she and Konstantin left Pskov, and the little dog was a comfort to her in her new home.

Antonina didn't miss her father; things had changed since the incident with the icon. Her mother—well, there had never been any love between them. As for her brothers, they hadn't been part of her life for the last few years, apart from occasional visits. The only people Antonina did miss were a few of the servants from her home. When she left, she had kissed their cheeks, pressing rubles and religious icons into their hands as she said goodbye to them.

Other than the belongings from her bedroom, she had asked her father for one thing from home: the lovely rosewood Érard square piano she had played since she was four years old. He'd had it sent to Angelkov, and it was waiting for her when she arrived.

Konstantin gave her permission to see to the decor of her own bedchamber, a former guest room—not, he said pointedly, his late wife's. Antonina unpacked her belongings, putting her books on shelves, setting out her small glass and china collections, and requesting that new bedcovers and draperies be sewn in her favourite colours, green and ivory. She liked to sit on the broad, cushioned seat built under the wide window, looking up from her book at the gardens below, and farther, at the countryside spread out before her. In October, the trees lost their leaves almost overnight, and the air was frosty in the mornings. Raisa, the cook, who was married to the head stableman, Fyodor, was agreeable to her requests for meals, and Olga, the head housekeeper, was kind and patient as she tried to explain the ways of running a household.

The only servant Antonina had difficulty with was her personal maid, Varvara. The older woman was cold and pious, and Antonina always felt she was being criticized, even though the woman never openly said anything disapproving. Antonina knew she had been the first Countess Mitlovskiya's maid.

Antonina didn't see Konstantin during the day, although they ate dinner together most evenings. As well as the distillery, he was involved in a number of businesses that took him from Angelkov into the city of Pskov, and occasionally as far as St. Petersburg. And so she filled her days much as she had at her father's estate, reading, playing the piano for hours and riding. Some evenings they had company for dinner— Konstantin's friends—and Antonina took part in many lively conversations, and then played whist and *vint* with the guests after dinner. In most ways it was as though she were still living her former life, apart from the added responsibilities of running a household: assigning chores for cleaning and maintaining the manor, organizing menus, writing out invitation and calling cards, and arranging and coordinating small parties. But she was lonely in a way she hadn't been in her father's home, she realized, because she no longer had vague, undefined but somehow optimistic thoughts about a future.

This *was* her future. She was a married woman, with a husband who came to her from his own bedroom, down the long, wide hall, every few nights.

Antonina remained a virgin for a full three weeks, although not for her husband's lack of trying.

15

*L*ilya had never expected to see the princess again after she and Lyosha were sold by Prince Olonov to their new landowner, Count Konstantin Mitlovsky.

Lilya and Lyosha were taken away in the back of a *taliezhka*, a rough, open wooden cart, its wheels replaced by runners for the winter, and drawn by a long-coated horse with a ragged collar and rope harness. It was bitterly cold. The driver, a youngish man with half his face stained with a burgundy birthmark, threw Lilya and Lyosha some flea-infested wolf hides to keep off the cold. Lilya was grateful there were two goats tied in the back of the cart as well; although they stunk, Lilya and Lyosha pushed against them for the warmth they generated.

The driver wore a wolf coat and hat and hunched over the reins, his head down as he drove through the cold wind and occasional snow. He smoked a pipe or chewed sunflower seeds, spitting the shells into the wind. Sometimes they landed on Lilya and Lyosha in the straw behind him. Lyosha cried quietly for the first hour of their journey, then stopped. He fell asleep wrapped in Lilya's arms, and she prayed he would continue to sleep as long as possible. When it grew dark, the young man drove the horse and cart into a low-ceilinged stable heated by a stove in one corner. When he opened a sack and took out a slab of dark bread and handed it to Lilya, he stared at her intently. Then he took a piece of dried fish and two boiled potatoes from the same sack as the bread.

"You like some of this?" he asked, and Lilya nodded. "Maybe," he said, and then, in front of her and Lyosha, ate one of the potatoes. Lyosha coughed, over and over, as the man chewed. As he raised the second potato to his mouth, Lilya understood. She nodded, and he stopped.

"When he's asleep," she said. The driver disappeared. She gave Lyosha the bread and watched while he ate it. Then she held him, humming, until he fell asleep.

The driver returned, lighting his way with a lantern, carrying the sack.

She held out her hand. "The fish and potato first."

"I don't have to give it to you," the young man said.

"God is watching," she told him, crossing herself. "And you must bring us hot millet and tea in the morning."

He crossed himself as well, then handed her the sack. She put it beside Lyosha. When one of the goats began to nibble on the burlap, she moved it. She was shivering from the cold and from fear, but Lyosha needed more than a dry crust of bread to sustain him. "Will you bring it tomorrow? The millet and tea?" she asked, and the young man nodded. "Hurry up, then," she said, "and don't wake him."

She took off her outer shawl and gently put it over Lyosha so that his head was covered. She lay back in the straw, and when the driver took her, she bit the shoulder of his foul-smelling coat so she didn't cry out and wake her little brother. She was just fourteen, and Lyosha only four.

The journey took another two days. Once Lyosha had exhausted himself coughing and fell into a deep sleep each night, Lilya gave herself to the driver in order to have decent food and another blanket. The village the prince had sent them to was a straggling collection of thatched huts along a road. They were dropped off in front of an izba similar to the one they'd left behind, a one-room hovel made of logs caulked with jute soaked in tar. The man and woman who came to the door cursed their ill luck. They had lost their three children to a fever the year earlier, and while they mourned their deaths, they had also seen it as a blessing from the saints. At least they didn't have to watch their little ones suffer from lack of food and wretched conditions. The man and his wife could work longer hours and have more food. Their prayers since then had been that God wouldn't see fit to have the woman bear more children.

So when Lilya and Lyosha were set down outside their door, the small sack of their few extra clothes thrown beside them, the man and his wife shook their heads in irritation.

"We won't be responsible for the boy," the man said to Lilya.

Lilya nodded. "I'll look after him." She put her arm around Lyosha's shoulders and he clung to her, both arms around her skirt, shivering with fright in the frosty air, his lips mauve with cold. "I'll work to help bring in what we eat. All I ask is a roof from the snow and rain." Lyosha had stopped asking for his mother the second day in the rocking wagon. Lilya had told him they would never see her again, and that she would be his mother now. "I am Lilya, and this is Lyosha."

"We are Masha and Osip," the woman said, and turned, going back into the izba. Osip followed. Lilya, holding Lyosha's hand, picked up the sack. Without looking at the driver, she and her brother went into their new home and closed the door.

Did Lilya miss her parents? The blacksmith and his wife had never given her any affection; they were worn out from hard work and disappointment. She did, however, want to be back in her home, where she knew everyone and everything. On the journey from her old hovel to this new one, she'd told herself she would never care about a place again, since she could, in a moment, be sent somewhere else. The one thing she would never let happen was to be parted from Lyosha, the only family she had.

She thought, at times, that she would die for him.

Lilya was also sad at the thought that she'd never have another glimpse of Antonina Leonidovna. She had never known anyone who smelled sweet all the time. Sometimes, as they sat and talked, she took deep breaths, marvelling at Antonina's scent. During the time of their friendship, she scrubbed her face and hands and arms to the elbow and rebraided her hair every Sunday. Her parents thought she was cleaning up for church. She was glad she didn't have to explain why she changed out of her patched weekday skirt and blouse and put on her Sunday clothing, a newer, cleaner version of the same outfit.

At night, with her parents asleep on the long, wide stove, warm in winter and cool in summer, and she and Lyosha on ragged blankets on the floor, she thought only of Antonina.

When Antonina pushed up her sleeves in the heat of summer, Lilya stole glances at her arms. The hair on them was slight and pale, almost invisible, and Lilya was certain it would be silky to the touch.

She also thought of Antonina's lips, and the way they felt when she kissed them. Lilya had ended their friendship, and yet it hadn't protected her after all. She didn't know why Antonina had told her father about their friendship, but she knew it was because of it that she and Lyosha were sent away.

When Prince Olonov had burst through the door of their izba followed by his men, she jumped up from the bench. "Lilya Petrova?" he said, and she swallowed.

It was as though she had waited for this. She had committed a sin by loving the princess, and she knew that in some way God would punish her. Everything went very still as she watched what happened next. Even when her own father cried out as he was whipped, and her mother and Lyosha screamed in fear and confusion, she couldn't hear them.

In their new home in the village owned by Count Mitlovsky, Lilya cared for Lyosha in the same way she had in their izba in Kazhra. Every night she slept beside him, waking when she felt him stirring in his sleep and guiding him to the pail near the door, keeping him steady as he relieved himself. The one time she hadn't wakened in time, he'd wet the piles of rags they slept on. This had earned her a hard slap from Masha as the acrid odour filled the low-ceilinged hut.

In the mornings, she wiped his face and smoothed down his dark hair with her damp hands. She made warm plasters for him, patting them over his narrow chest each evening to lessen his cough. She darned his clothing, and found replacements when they grew too small or patched. Shivering, wrapped in all of her shawls, she'd be on the church steps in the middle of the night on the day the monthly charity baskets were scheduled to arrive. She was first to grab what she could of the winter items—boots and socks and coats sent to the villages by the landowner.

Lilya's life on the new estate was much as it had been in Kazhra. Osip and Masha were not cruel, but deadened. They were, as Lilya's parents had been, worn out from a lifetime of hard work with no reward but the hope of a better afterlife.

For those first frigid winter months, when there was only the white blankness of the fields, Osip carved wooden spoons, the sugary, musty odour of his cheap tobacco filling the izba. Masha tatted delicate lace with a shuttle. She taught Lilya how to do this, and Lilya quickly surpassed the woman in both speed and ability. Some of the finest pieces Lilya and the woman produced were given to the church for vestments; other, more substantial pieces were sold at the weekly market in the next larger village, along with Osip's spoons.

In the spring, they got up at daybreak and went to the fields, planting wheat and corn, sunflowers, sugar beets and flax. Like the other children too old to be carried but too young to work, Lyosha followed Lilya up and down the rows. They came home as it grew dark, prepared a simple meal and spoke little.

During their first summer, the villager Iosef Igorovitch, called Soso, put in a request to the landowner that he be allowed to marry Lilya Petrova. His first wife had been a sour, lazy thing, and had died after four years and as many miscarriages. Ten months had passed since she'd succumbed to typhus, and he wanted someone to cook his meals and warm his bed at night. There were no other single girls in the tiny hamlet, and so when Lilya arrived, he kept an eye on her, watching to make sure she was a hard worker. When he learned that the child always at her side was her brother, he didn't like the idea of another mouth to feed, but still, he couldn't be choosy.

When his appeal to marry the recently purchased serf was granted, he came to the door of the izba and told Osip that after harvest he would marry the girl living with them.

"You have to take the child as well," Osip said.

Soso looked into the dim hut. Lilya had stopped chopping carrots on the wooden table and was staring at him. The boy was on his knees under the table.

"All right," he said. Osip held out his hand, and Soso shook it.

Lilya studied Soso. He was tall and barrel-chested, his shaggy dark hair cut in an unflattering bowl shape under his peaked cap. But his clothing was cleaner than that of most of the villagers, and instead of the crude sandals made from the bark of lime trees, he wore leather boots. Lilya suspected he wore his Sunday clothes, and was glad he had bothered to dress in his best to be introduced to her as her future husband.

He smiled, and although he appeared confident, the slightly tremulous smile told Lilya that he was nervous. The clean clothing and smile were enough. She had to marry someone soon. She estimated he was ten years older than her, but at least he didn't have a litter of lice-ridden children she would have to take on. Without hesitation, she nodded her agreement.

After that, Soso came to the hut every few evenings. He didn't say much, and Lilya thought him dull. Sometimes he brought a wrapped fish or a pocketful of boiled eggs. But on one visit he squatted in front of Lyosha and reached into his pocket to pull out a small chunk of hard sugar. As he handed it to him, Lyosha gave Soso one of his rare smiles, and Lilya thought he might not be so bad.

Lilya and Soso were married a month after her fifteenth birthday; Soso was twenty-six. She and Lyosha moved into the single-roomed hut Soso had lived in with his first wife. It had the same oven made of clay on an earthen floor, the same rough table and benches against the walls as every izba. The only ornamentation was a small shelf for the tallow candles that were lit on holy days, and a stamped metal icon of the Holy Mother in its frame.

On their wedding night, Soso found out that his new wife wasn't pure. He stopped, looking down at her, and slapped her, hard, on both cheeks, then continued. It was never spoken of.

He treated Lyosha with indifference, neither kind nor cruel. He was sometimes annoyed by the attention Lilya gave to her little brother, but felt he was fortunate to have been given permission to marry such a pleasant-looking, hard-working woman. Like her brother, she didn't smile often, but when she did, he felt something like pride.

He imagined their lives would continue forever as they

were now. He and Lilya would work the fields, and Lyosha would soon be old enough to be of real help. They would have their own children, but not too many who lived, he hoped, because that would prevent Lily from working, and be more mouths to feed.

16

*A*ntonina had been the Countess Mitlovskiya for a month when she first saw Lilya. It was early October, and the day was uncharacteristically warm and humid.

Antonina, with a manservant behind her, was slowly riding down one of the roads that ran between the golden fields. The peasants were reaping wheat, and some had stopped for their midday meal of boiled potatoes and raw onions and slabs of dark bread.

Antonina noticed a young woman tilt back her head to drink, water running down her chin and onto her neck. The woman tapped a cork back into the flask with the heel of her hand, then shaded her eyes as she looked up at the figure on the horse. Nobody came down this muddy track between the fields, well off the main road, except the estate owner or his visitors.

"Lilya," Antonina said, and Lilya dropped the flask. It bounced on the ground and lay at her feet.

She looked directly into Antonina's face without smiling. Around her, other peasants were bowing, their skirts and tunics rustling.

"Leave us," Antonina said, and with the same rustling the peasants backed away until it was only Antonina and Lilya, the manservant and his horse a few paces away.

Finally, Antonina smiled at Lilya, although Lilya saw that her expression was slightly uncertain.

"Why are you here, Princess Olonova?" she asked, conscious of her sweat-soaked blouse, her tattered kerchief. She attempted a smile of her own. "Do you visit the count?"

It wasn't the smile Antonina remembered. It was awkward, as if Lilya had forgotten how to move her mouth. "No," she said. "I'm not visiting. You're working here?" she asked as she dismounted.

"Yes. I've lived on the estate for almost four years," Lilya said, and Antonina felt a thump of distress.

"This is where my father sent you?"

Lilya nodded.

There was a moment of silence as the women just looked at each other, each lost in her own thoughts. Finally Antonina asked, "Lyosha?" She was afraid the child had died.

Lilya was glad to have something else to speak of. "He's getting tall, and too skinny, but he's as healthy now as any of the other boys."

"Good. That's very good," Antonina said. The silence again. "How are you?" It was an inane question; she was acutely aware that Lilya didn't look well. "It's very warm today," she added.

Lilya wiped her forehead with the back of her arm. "Yes. A warm day for October, princess," she agreed with that same unnatural smile.

"Oh. Lilya, I'm no longer to be addressed as princess," Antonina said. "I . . . I am Countess Mitlovskiya."

At this, Lilya's eyes widened. "You married the land-owner?"

"Only last month," Antonina said. Lilya was so thin, her pallor almost grey. Under her eyes the skin was smudged a deep violet, as though she hadn't slept in a long time. Her face and the front of her blouse were soaked from her exertions.

When she first came, Lilya had seen the landowner occasionally, with his haughty wife at his side. She couldn't imagine Antonina married to such an old man. "We knew he remarried, of course. We heard it was a young woman from another estate in Pskov. The marriage . . . it was your wish?"

Lilya knew she was being bold, but until Antonina made it clear she shouldn't address her so informally, she would ask what she wanted to know.

"It was best for all involved," Antonina said, and at that she saw something in Lilya's face soften.

"Not a love match, then?"

It was as if the last four years fell away with Lilya's abrupt question, and Antonina was with her friend again. She shook her head.

"And are you . . ." Lilya stopped, and licked her lips. "Are you pleased with your husband?"

"It is very early to speak of such things, Lilya."

A slight line appeared between Lilya's dark eyebrows. "I am married as well."

"Your husband is kind to you?" Antonina asked, glancing away from her to the bent backs of her fellow labourers.

"Soso—Iosef Igorovitch—is strong and hard-working."

"Well, I hope he's also kind, Lilya Petrova. You deserve kindness."

Another silence fell between them, comfortable this time, and then Lilya asked, "Do you have your own dog yet?"

At this unexpected question, Antonina felt such relief that she laughed, and Lilya herself made a strangled sound that could pass for laughter.

"I do. Her name is Tinka, and she's still a puppy. She's a very sweet little thing. She follows me everywhere, and demands to be held whenever I sit."

"That's good," Lilya said.

Antonina looked at Lilya's painfully thin frame. "Do you have children?"

Lilya's face lost any animation. "No, countess. And I must return to my work—I'm slowing the others down."

"Of course."

Lilya picked up her scythe. It hurt Antonina, this deliberate display of wanting—needing—to return to work, when all Antonina wanted was for Lilya to talk to her.

"Goodbye, countess," Lilya said, and bent to her work.

Every time he came to Antonina's bedroom that first month of their marriage, Konstantin would lie beside her in the dark and kiss her hand. Then he would stroke her hair and face, and finally, after some sort of fussing with his nightshirt, he would ease himself on top of her. But it was always as it had been the first time in Pskov: he was unable to accomplish the task.

With each of her husband's attempts, Antonina squeezed her eyes shut and held her breath, until finally, one night, he said, "My dear angel, please. You must put on some show of tenderness."

His voice, for the first time, bore a trace of actual sadness. He had visited Tania the evening before—as he had each week since he had begun with her, six months after the death of his first wife. Never, before this second marriage, had he experienced the difficulty he did with Antonina. Tania reminded him of his wife in age and appearance, and that was enough. He had enjoyed the physical side of his marriage with the first countess, and he felt powerful and virile with her—Irina Denisovich—and then with Tania. But this girl . . . something about the way she behaved with him made him feel old and powerless.

Antonina knew she had a duty towards her husband. The marriage bed, from all she understood in her novels, was the place where the act of love occurred. But she felt no love for Konstantin, and in no way could she imagine the embarrassing joining of their bodies as pleasurable. She often thought of her mother and Valentin. What did her mother feel that made her act so freely? She clearly didn't love the young violinist, and yet that didn't prevent her from enjoying what they did.

Antonina knew what was expected, and that it would have to happen if they were to have children—the reason he married her.

"Do you not . . . is there nothing I can do, Antonina?" Konstantin said in a tone of exasperation, rolling off her. But instead of leaving, he arranged two pillows against the headboard and propped himself against them, crossing his arms over his chest.

Antonina sat up and did the same, her shoulder resting against his in the darkness.

"I know you're young, and high-spirited," he said finally. "I don't, for one moment, fool myself into believing you are pleased to be married to me. I'm certain you didn't expect to find yourself here. Like this."

He spoke the truth. There was nothing for Antonina to say.

"But Tosya," he said, once he realized she would not dispute his words, "I want to have a child—a son and heir. It was my life's greatest disappointment that my first wife did not bear any children. There is a chance now. Is there nothing about me you find appealing? Nothing?"

The added *nothing*, uttered with a hopeless air, stirred a sense of pity in her. She wasn't attracted to him in any way. She was bored with his outright determination, pushing against her all these nights to no avail. But something—perhaps the defeat in his voice—made her feel sorry for him.

"I enjoy when you speak to me of the estate at dinner, and when your face shows that you enjoy listening to me play the piano." She cleared her throat. "I know you didn't mean what you said, that first day after the wedding—about me being empty. You didn't really mean it, did you, Konstantin?" Somehow it was important, at this moment, that this man—her husband—find her intelligent.

He didn't answer, but looked at the bedside table. "What is this book?" he asked, picking it up.

"*Eugénie Grandet*, by Honoré de Balzac."

"Would you read to me? Just for a few moments," he said, handing her the volume and then lighting the lamp. The request pleased Antonina; while reading, she was somewhere else, and safe. She opened the book where she had left off, and read aloud in French.

After ten minutes, Konstantin kissed her cheek and rose. "I was never one for reading. Figures are my strength. Have a pleasant sleep."

"Thank you, my dear husband," Antonina added, knowing it would please Konstantin for her to address him like this.

After he had gone, she felt a small glimmer of something that was close to pleasure.

In the fourth week of their marriage, Konstantin came in as Antonina's maid was braiding her hair for the night. "Pin it up quickly, please," Antonina said quietly, and the maid did so, winding the thick braids around Antonina's head and securing them with hairpins.

Nobody but her maids had seen Antonina's hair loose since she had been fourteen years old and stopped wearing it tied back with ribbons. It now reached to her waist, and she worried that Konstantin would think that with it down she looked too young.

He was carrying a small red box tied with a white bow. She tried to hide her disappointment that he had come to her. She was weary. She'd ridden the whole afternoon, had had her bath, and now wanted nothing more than to turn out the lamp and let her tired muscles relax. She had no energy for the same fumbling with nightclothes, the same endless pushing against her without any success, and finally, his disappointment palpable, Konstantin's silent rising from the bed and quiet shutting of her bedroom door as he returned to his own.

He sat in a chair by the fireplace in his robe. When the maid had been dismissed, Antonina stood, and he did as well, holding out the box to her.

"What's this?"

"I saw it when I was in Pskov yesterday, and thought of you."

"Thank you," Antonina said, taking it from him and untying the bow. Inside was a music box of lovely polished cherry with an inlay of mother-of-pearl on the lid. She turned the tiny brass key and it played a little Mozart sonata. It reminded her of the serf orchestra; they had played the same sonata at her party over six months earlier. She thought of Valentin's hands around her mother's naked waist, and felt a soft warmth, low in her abdomen.

She set the music box, still tinkling, on a table. "How pretty. And how thoughtful, Konstantin."

He nodded, turning down the lamp on the dressing table. The only light came from the fire and a candle beside the bed.

Antonina looked at him quizzically.

"Let us dance," he said.

"Here, in my bedchamber?" Antonina smiled. "So late at night?"

He didn't answer but stood in position, his arms extended, and Antonina went into the circle of his embrace.

He led her about the room to the music, easily sidestepping the furniture. The fire cast wavering shadows on the walls. "I remember the first time I saw you dance," he said. "It was at a party at your parents' estate. You were probably thirteen or fourteen. You were a fetching child."

Antonina looked at him. He was only a few inches taller than she—not an imposing height, but he held himself proudly.

"I noticed you a number of times after that, as you grew older. How lightly you moved, and yet warily, as though you might at any moment dash away from your partner."

Antonina laughed at his description. "Depending on whom I was dancing with, indeed I may have been imagining myself a wild animal from the dark continent of Africa, trying to escape my captor." They took another turn about the room. "I have a book on Africa, Konstantin, with drawings of the most amazing animals and strange, dark-skinned people. I would like to venture there someday. Do you suppose we could ever go all the way to Africa?"

"Africa? You're a funny girl."

The smile left her mouth. "Please don't call me a girl. I'm your wife. A woman."

"You're right," he said, letting go of her so she could wind the music box again. "You are an accomplished and clever woman."

There. The apology Antonina had wanted for almost a full month. Again he took her in his arms. In the dim glow, the lines around his eyes and mouth were softened, and suddenly Antonina saw what he would have looked like as a young man. It pleased her, and she kissed his lips, a small, light kiss. "Thank you, Kostya," she said, and at the use of his diminutive he lowered his head and kissed her back with passion.

Antonina kept her eyes closed, pretending it was Valentin who held her, who was pressing his lips against hers. She saw the violinist's face as he stared over her mother's shoulder at her from the bed.

She imagined herself sitting atop him as she had seen her mother do, and kissed Konstantin back. Encouraged, he moved his lips to her cheek and then her neck, pressing against her. Still she didn't open her eyes, imagining Konstantin to be the young and handsome Valentin Vladimirovitch.

"You see, my angel?" he said, his lips against her neck. "It's not so difficult." Gently, he directed her to the bed. When the back of her thighs touched the mattress, Konstantin easily lifted her and laid her down.

"Yes, husband," she whispered back, keeping her eyes closed, hearing Konstantin wind the music box again. Yes, Valya, she thought.

With her eyes closed, she imagined it was Valentin who now touched her breasts through the thin nightdress, and her nipples rose. She imagined his delicate hands and strong yet slender body, and it was Valya who lifted her nightgown and positioned himself over her as she wrapped her arms around his back and held him closer.

And at last Konstantin was able to move into her, very slowly.

"I don't wish to hurt you," he whispered.

"It's all right," she said, willing him to remain silent.

There was a brief, searing pain; Antonina tightened her lips so as not to cry out. Soon the pain dulled to a discomfort, as endlessly Konstantin continued his rhythm, his breathing growing heavier and heavier. And then he began to move faster, his breath rasping in his throat. Finally he stilled, then shuddered, letting out a muffled groan. After this he lay so heavy on top of her that for one brief moment she wondered if he had died. But then he stirred and lifted himself off her, getting out of bed.

With a slight intake of breath, she cautiously pulled the bedcovers over her and drew up her knees. She was sore, and longed for a hot bath.

Konstantin still stood beside the bed. The candle had burned low, and she watched as he smoothed his nightshirt and patted his hair and beard. "Thank you, my dear," he said. "You are all right?"

"Yes, I am well," she answered, and at this he smiled.

"Good," he said. "Yes, it was a successful night."

She nodded. The silence became awkward.

"I shall retire to my room, then, shall I?" There was something—perhaps reluctance—in his voice. Did he think he would stay here with her? Sleep in her bed? She wouldn't be able to sleep with him beside her. She had never slept with anyone, and couldn't imagine it.

"Yes, of course," she said, "you must find comfort in your own bed, husband."

He immediately performed a small bow from the waist, as if he had just brought her back to her chair after a lively mazurka. *"À demain,"* he said, with the hint of a smile.

To please him, Antonina replied, *"Oui, mon cher. À demain."*

Once the door closed, she rose and stripped off her soiled gown and tossed it over the back of a chair. She poured water from her pitcher into the washbowl. Then she slowly and carefully washed herself with the cool water, thinking about what had just transpired. She put on a fresh gown and spread a towel from the washstand on the sheet, covering the disturbing, pinkish wetness left there. She hated to think of the maid seeing it and her stained nightgown the next morning.

Was this what was called love in the novels?

Surely it wouldn't be the same with her violinist.

As she climbed back into bed, the candle guttered with a slight hiss.

The next morning, Konstantin appeared very pleased with himself, laughing heartily at the smallest things and treating Antonina with casual affection. He came to her bedroom three more times in the next week, and each time he thanked her, telling her he was pleased at their success.

The fourth night, as he moved on top of her, Antonina pushed at him and he rolled to his side. "Have I hurt you, my dear?" he asked.

"No," she whispered, and pressing on his shoulder until he lay on his back, she put one leg over to straddle him.

Konstantin sat up so quickly that Antonina fell to the side. "What are you doing?" His voice was shocked.

"I thought it might be . . ." Antonina stopped, propping herself on an elbow to look at her husband. It might be what? Each time Konstantin had come to her, she had managed to open herself to him by imagining she was with Valentin. This night she had wanted to pretend it was Valentin in the position she had seen him in with her mother.

But Konstantin sat up, shaking his head, his forehead wrinkled and the lines around his mouth deep. "You disappoint me. No, it's more than that—you disgust me. What kind of respectful wife would act in such a common manner? Such behaviour is sordid."

Antonina reached up to make sure her hair hadn't loosened. "I didn't know it was wrong. I thought it might please you."

"And how, I ask you, would you even think of such a thing? In all my years with my first wife, Irina—a good and dignified woman—she took her wifely duties with quiet acceptance." He shook his head again, thinking of Tania, who, although common, still behaved with modesty. His voice rose. "Now I wonder at your innocence. Perhaps this is why your father was so anxious to have you married."

Heat surged up Antonina's chest, to her neck and into her face. "You know perfectly well I was pure when I married you, Konstantin Nikolevich. I cannot believe you could think such thoughts about me, when all I wanted was to give pleasure to you."

"And who instructed you on the ways to please a man? Could it have been your mother? Everyone knows of her reputation."

Antonina's mouth went dry. "Get out," she said, low and hard. How had Konstantin guessed the truth? "Leave me alone."

"It would be my pleasure," he said, and slammed the door as he left.

Konstantin ignored Antonina for days after that night. He used Grisha's house to bed Tania more than usual, infuriating Grisha while pleasing Tania with the extra rubles she earned.

But then Antonina realized she was pregnant with the child who would be Misha.

17

*A*ntonina didn't see Lilya again until she was in the early stages of her pregnancy. In December, the empty fields covered in snow, Antonina rode through one of the villages. She came towards a group of women walking down the main street, carrying woven baskets of kindling on their backs, and recognized Lilya.

Lilya looked up at her, the weak winter sun on her face. "Good day, countess," she said. The other women bowed.

Lilya didn't bow. She seemed to have gained a bit of weight, although it might have been the padded coat and thick shawl wrapped around her. But she no longer appeared as exhausted as the first time Antonina had seen her. Her eyes were clear and her cheeks quite pink in the December chill.

Antonina wanted to tell her about her pregnancy. She had shared it with Konstantin, and sent a letter to her father. Of course, the house serfs knew—there was no hiding anything from them. Varvara had witnessed her morning nausea and immediately recognized that the countess was with child.

Antonina had so many questions for Lilya about the last four years. More than anything, she wanted to beg forgiveness, to tell her what had happened in her father's study. But they were no longer girls, they were married women, and as once Antonina had been the daughter of the man who owned Lilya, now she was the wife of the man who owned her. She could not demand, a second time, that Lilya be her friend. And it was clear that Lilya no longer felt the same way about Antonina as she had then. How could she? Antonina had betrayed her, and had her and her brother torn from their home and parents.

She nodded to Lilya and the women and rode on.

A few months later, Konstantin told Antonina she should be thinking of a wet nurse and a nanny for the expected baby. He had given her a list of suitable women who had worked on neighbouring estates, and expected her to pick one of them.

But Antonina set off down the snowy roads in a troika, to the village where she'd last seen Lilya. She asked a peasant on the street where she could find Lilya Petrova, married to Soso. She was directed to a hut at the end of the village. When the coachman helped her step down from the troika, she told him to wait for her. "You'll enter the hut, countess?" he asked. "Alone?"

"Yes," she told him, and walked to the door and knocked. The coachman followed her anxiously. When the door was opened by a boy Antonina knew must be Lyosha, she smiled. "Is this the home of Lilya?" she asked, and Lilya's face appeared behind her brother's shoulder. She looked, in that instant, frightened.

"May I enter, Lilya?" Antonina asked, and when she nodded, Antonina turned to the coachman and again told him to wait in the troika. He did as he was told this time, but he didn't look pleased.

"This is Lyosha?" Antonina said as she stepped into the hut.

The boy bowed. "Yes, madam," he said. His voice was high and clear.

She glanced around the dark room, seeing a tunic, a skirt and two pairs of socks drying on a rope across the ceiling. There was a stove with a bubbling pot of what smelled like buckwheat porridge. Apart from a table holding lengths of fine white skeins and a wooden shuttle, there were two benches and an icon on the wall over the stove. Nothing more.

"I won't keep you from your work," Antonina said, looking back to the table.

"I make lace for the extra kopecks," Lilya explained, still with that anxious look.

Antonina went closer. "May I look at it? You may rise, Lyosha." The boy straightened and went to stand beside his sister.

Lilya held out the end of the small strip of lace.

"It's lovely," Antonina said. "So delicate. I could never master tatting." Now she was here, she wondered whether it was wise even to think of this, but she forged ahead. "I've come to ask a favour of you."

"A favour?"

"Yes. I carry a child, and will, in a few months, need a nanny." Before Lilya could say anything, she continued, "I know you haven't had children, and my husband won't approve of me hiring a woman with no experience, but I will—"

"I've had children," Lilya interrupted.

"But you said you didn't."

"They no longer live."

Antonina's throat grew tight, and she put her hands on her belly, suddenly light-headed. "I must sit down," she said, and Lilya came to her and put her arm around her and helped her to one of the benches.

Lilya was, for the first time, close enough to breathe in Antonina's scent. It was still attar of roses.

"What happened to your children?" Antonina asked once she was seated.

Lilya took a deep breath. "I had daughters. Twins. They died—one in her second month, the other three weeks later."

"I didn't know . . ."

"How could you know? The last one—her name was Klara, the other Lena—had died only a few weeks before we met, during the harvest."

"May God have mercy on their souls," Antonina murmured, crossing herself. "But you will have more children, surely."

Lilya's eyes were strangely flat. "I will be honoured to be a nanny to the child you carry. But there is one condition." Her voice faltered as she realized how she was speaking to the woman whose husband owned her.

Antonina didn't seem taken aback. "What is it?"

But Lilya was silent for a moment. Why was God rewarding her so richly? Did she deserve such blessings?

"Is it your husband?" Antonina asked. "But of course, I won't separate you. I'll have the steward find him a job with the livestock or in the storerooms. You'll be given a room in the married servants' quarters."

Lilya drew a deep breath. "Oh—Soso," she said, as if just remembering him. "Yes, he'll be glad of a better job. But it's Lyosha I worry about, countess." She looked at the boy beside her. "I won't leave him behind in the village. I'm the only mother he remembers now."

Ah. Here it is. Antonina felt a huge surge of guilt, and pain. "Of course, he must come as well. He's your family. Yes, bring him. He's how old?"

"Eight. He's very quick to learn, very even-tempered. A good boy." Lilya said this as proudly as if she were his mother.

"He works the fields?"

Lilya nodded. "But"—she took a breath—"he loves horses, countess."

Antonina looked at the boy. He stared back, saying nothing.

"Then I'll get him a job as a stableboy, cleaning out the stalls, oiling the saddles and so on. As he grows older, he'll advance if he's as clever and quick as you say."

"And he will live . . .?"

"With you and Soso. Lyosha?" she said, addressing the boy directly. "Would you like a job in the stables?"

The boy bowed again. "Yes, countess."

"Then it's done," Antonina said to Lilya. "He will come with you."

"You're certain this will be all right with the count?"

Antonina shrugged and gave a sudden, bright smile, and all at once she was the girl Lilya remembered from the forest. "I am the countess. In certain areas I can do as I wish." She would deal with Konstantin's questions as to why she had hired a village woman and insisted her family be given work on the estate.

Lilya wrapped her thin arms around herself, smiling back at Antonina. "It's a dream come true, Tosya. Truly. Lyosha, do you believe our good fortune?"

At the sound of her diminutive, which Lilya had used so naturally, Antonina felt a surge of joy. She had found her friend again, and had also found a small way to try to make up for what had been done to Lilya and her little brother.

Maybe someday she would be forgiven.

Within a month, Lilya and Soso and Lyosha were settled into the servants' quarters. Soso was given a job in the storehouses for the estate, and Lyosha, as promised, had become one of the youngest of the stableboys.

Even though the baby wasn't expected for another two months, Antonina had Lilya spend as much time as possible with her. Soon the two young women were talking and laughing as they had almost five years earlier.

Antonina enjoyed having Lilya with her so much that she moved Varvara into another job, and promoted Lilya to the role of her personal maid. She was relieved to no longer have Varvara hovering over her with a look of disapproval. Antonina knew that she would never fill the dead countess's shoes, not only for Varvara but for Konstantin too.

Lilya quickly learned about the layers of clothing Antonina wore, and how to help her into them one by one. Following Antonina's instructions, she was eventually able to sculpt her hair as Antonina preferred it. It was tricky for her, and sometimes both of them laughed at her earnest attempts, but a woman who could make fine lace could also learn about the intricacies in dressing a noblewoman's hair.

One evening, Lilya was helping Antonina bathe in front of the fire in her bedchamber and gently ran her hand over Antonina's extended belly. A small heel protruded beneath the tight skin. She let her hand rest there, smiling at Antonina, and this gave Antonina the courage to ask Lilya about the births of her daughters. Antonina was ashamed of her own ignorance about childbirth and had no one else to ask.

Lilya, her hand still on Antonina, didn't immediately respond.

"Lilya?"

Lilya looked into Antonina's eyes then back to her own hand, slowly caressing the other woman's skin. "Your skin is so fine," she said, barely above a whisper.

Antonina shrugged. "My body doesn't feel like my own anymore. But please, Lilya, would you stay with me throughout the confinement?"

Lilya pulled her hand away and picked up a warm, dry flannel. "Come, it's time for bed." As she helped Antonina stand, she said, "You will be strong, I know. If I could survive it, with only an old woman from the next izba to help me as I laboured on a blanket on top of the stove, surely it will be so much easier for you, Tosya. You will have the doctor and any number of women to help. And of course, you will have me as well. I will always be here for you. Always." She patted the flannel over Antonina's shoulder blades, then rubbed more firmly in the small of her back.

"Yes, that feels marvellous. Your touch is so comforting," Antonina murmured, and Lilya closed her eyes for a moment.

Later, when Antonina was in bed and Lilya was hanging

her loose day dress in the huge wardrobe, she stroked one of the many beautiful fitted gowns there. "I'm sure you'll be happy to be wearing these again soon."

Antonina nodded. "I suppose. I can't imagine how I ever will." She patted her belly, laughing.

Lilya, on the pretence of straightening the dresses, leaned into the huge wardrobe and pressed her face against the delicate silk and satin, smelling roses.

18

SPRING 1861

After Misha is kidnapped, Lilya sleeps on the window seat in the countess's bedroom, and every day tries to encourage Antonina to bathe. If Antonina agrees, Lilya slowly and carefully pats the warm, soapy cloth over Antonina's body. She knows that it hurts Antonina to be touched too strongly. A number of times a day she tempts her with dishes of her favourite foods and sweet tea. She brings the first spring snowdrops and hyacinths. Every evening she has Antonina sit in the comfortable chair by the fire while she changes the bed linens. Sometimes, after she settles Antonina into bed, she lies beside her, humming to her, stroking her back, her brow, her hair, until Antonina falls into what passes for sleep.

Lilya. What a good and loyal friend. At times it would appear that these are strangely happy days for Lilya, in spite of Misha's absence. The count lies in a dazed state in his room. She has Antonina all to herself.

In Konstantin's bedroom, Olga has set out dishes of chopped garlic to try to stop the fever. But Konstantin has grown worse, muttering and calling out in delirium as the wound on his hand putrifies.

Antonina watches him through several long nights as he convulses with chills and then lies still, panting as if he's run many versts. At times he moans. Pavel tends to him with gentleness, bathing him with cool cloths hour after hour.

Even though he lies so still as to appear almost lifeless, each time Pavel holds a spoon or cup to his mouth, Konstantin's lips seal themselves into a thin line. It's as if they're darned with the most gossamer of blue silk, as if his mouth has been sewn shut.

When the doctor removes the dressing from Konstantin's hand, he shakes his head. "I'm afraid it's critical, Countess Mitlovskiya. There is still no urine output?"

Antonina shakes her head.

"Soon his kidneys will fail. We must give him vodka, with milk, every few hours."

"But he refuses."

"Then I shall try. The vodka and milk, as well as quinine, and tincture of the chloride of iron," he says, turning from her fixed expression, looking through his bag, pulling out small bottles and vials.

"And if this doesn't work?"

Konstantin's hand, she sees, is even more swollen, the skin around the wound livid, with streaks of burgundy and plum radiating up into his wrist and forearm. She stares at it, unaware that the poison is making its way into her husband's body.

My son. Is he being fed? Is he warm? Does he call out for me?

The doctor follows her gaze. "There's no way to stop the infection except . . ." He pauses. "Not yet. For now, we will try forcing him to ingest the medicine." He glances at Olga, who has brought hot water. "Where is your priest?" he asks, and Olga gasps.

The old woman doesn't comprehend the doctor's medical talk, but she does understand what the presence of a priest means.

"It's all right, Olga," Antonina says. "Send for Father Cyril."

As she leaves, Olga mutters, "The Father's prayers will surely heal the master." Her eyes flicker to the doctor, holding a long, slender tube. "Prayers we can always rely on," she says, giving him a pointed look.

Antonina does not apologize for the servant.

The quinine and chloride prove no use. Dr. Molov next brings out a jar of fly maggots. "It sometimes helps," he tells Antonina. "I'll place them in the open wound. They will consume only the dead flesh, leaving the living tissue unaffected. Perhaps this can stop the spread. But I want you to be aware that it's the last attempt."

Antonina looks away from the squirming white larvae. "The last attempt before what? If the maggots don't work, what then?"

"Countess Mitlovskiya," Dr. Molov says, "it has become gangrenous. There would be but one option left to try and save the count's life."

"Yes?" Antonina says, although the doctor thinks she appears rather uninterested.

"Amputation, before the infection is carried even further into the body. It will be clear, in the next day, if the maggots are effective."

The amputation takes place two days later.

Konstantin is tossing restlessly, and the bedroom is even more foul-smelling. Dr. Molov has opened a wooden case with a number of tools: various pincers and knives, as well as a small saw with an ebony handle.

"I will put the count into a sleep with chloroform," Dr. Molov says. "Its vapour depresses the nervous system. But it's difficult to find the right balance. Not enough and there will be the pain. Too much can lead to . . . Well, as I say, it's a delicate balance. To be safe, I need two men to hold him down, should he start to feel the amputation."

He uncorks a tall, narrow glass bottle. Antonina is near enough to detect a slightly sweet odour. Suddenly she notices a bucket of sawdust on the floor beside the bed. Why sawdust? Is this for the amputated arm? It will be cut off just below the elbow, the doctor has told her. Antonina's mouth is dry; it's as if she has been eating the contents of the bucket.

The doctor says, "Pavel, stand on one side of him, and you on the other . . . Grisha, is it?"

Grisha is watching Antonina. "You shouldn't be here, countess."

"You needn't touch him yet," the doctor instructs the men, who have moved into position. "Just be prepared." He lifts Konstantin's head and passes the bottle under his nose. Konstantin turns his head away fitfully, but within a moment it seems as though the anaesthetic is exciting him. He looks about, his eyes wide now, muttering syllables that make no sense. But in the next instant he slumps in what appears to be an insensible state.

"All right," Dr. Molov says, rolling up his sleeves. He unwraps Konstantin's hand, and Antonina covers her mouth and nose against the smell of the blackened, rotten-looking hand, the fingers bloated, the nails ebony and embedded deeply in the puffy flesh.

"I believe it best you go, countess," Grisha says again, and she looks at him gratefully and leaves.

But even in her room, she hears Konstantin's shrieks. She covers her ears with her hands and paces. Finally, all is quiet. She stands, looking out the window. There is a knock on her door. When she opens it, Grisha tells her, "You may see him."

She goes to Konstantin's room. His eyes are closed, but he is turning his head from side to side, as if in the grip of a nightmare. The bedclothes are drawn to his neck. Pavel and the doctor sit on either side of the bed. There is no evidence of the trauma that took place hours earlier. The window is open and a cool, fresh breeze blows in.

She looks down at Konstantin's face, waxy and damp. She nods at the doctor, and returns to her room.

The day after the amputation, Dr. Molov tells Antonina that her husband has voluntarily taken some nourishment, and has spoken her name. He doesn't tell her that, while delirious, Count Mitlovsky more frequently cried out for someone named Tania. The second day after the amputation, he says, "The fever is gone and the stitched area looks as well as can be expected. There is nothing more for me to do apart from regular visits to check on the healing. The recuperation should go smoothly, but the labour will be for the count to learn to use his left hand."

Antonina finds it difficult to visit Konstantin. He closes his eyes or stares at the window when she comes to sit beside his bed, ignoring her when she asks if he has pain or needs her to do anything. Eventually she doesn't go to his room, but asks Pavel how the count is doing. His answer is always the same: *As well as can be expected, madam.* He tells her that the tincture of chloroform mixed with opiate the doctor left helps her husband deal with the pain.

A month after the kidnapping, Grisha comes to Antonina in the music salon, where she sits on the chair beside the piano, her hands limp in her lap. He tells her he feels that, with her permission, they might give up the daily searches. They have questioned the serfs in a radius of over two hundred versts, he tells her, but his face is a blur to Antonina, his voice coming as if from a long distance. The kidnapping has been reported to the authorities in the city of Pskov, and those authorities have also notified the correct office in St. Petersburg. Nobody has come forward to speak of the appearance of an unknown child, or to report seeing or hearing anything out of the ordinary.

"There appears little else we can do," Grisha concludes, and reaches out as if to touch her, but stops himself. The expression on her face is as if she has just received shattering news, a startled look of disbelief.

"There must be something more we can do. There *must* be, Grisha," she repeats. "We can't just stop looking for him. As if . . . as if he's . . ." She can't continue.

"I understand," he says gently. "But the estate must continue to be run. Do you wish me—on my own—to continue to look?"

"Yes. Let the others return to their duties, but please, you continue with the search." She turns and walks from the music salon, going to her bedroom, where she sits on the bed. Such darkness engulfs her that she thinks, for the first time, of ways to die. She can't bear to think that her son is suffering.

There is no comfort save one: there has been no body. She will not believe her son is dead until she sees his body.

The silence of the house strangles her. The servants walk as though their feet are encased in cotton wool, and their voices never rise above a whisper. The spring—it is now May—has been exceptionally rainy. The trees are breaking into glorious colour, and yet there is a sodden, saturated feeling underfoot, and in the air. Perhaps she is drowning. Yes, she feels as if she is drowning: she can't breathe. Antonina is glad the days are overcast; the light is of no use to her.

There are no words that make sense, no Bible passages that bring comfort. Lilya never stops praying, and tries to persuade Antonina to do the same.

"You must pray, Tosya. Come and kneel with me," she says every day. "God will help you understand why He has chosen this path for you. He will bring you comfort."

Antonina shakes her head. She *has* prayed. It does nothing to bring her relief, or to bring Mikhail home to her. When Father Cyril requests a visit, she refuses to see him.

⁓

Every morning, she sets out the wine-spattered Glinka music—the music from the violinist Valentin—in her ritualistic manner on the piano's music stand. She knows all the pieces by heart, and yet it comforts her to see the first page, with the inscription, as she plays.

When she has finished the repertoire, she walks through the house: the morning room, the dining room, the conservatory, the library, the study, the billiards room, the gun-room, the drawing room. She touches all the beautiful, meaningless things: the glass ornaments, the black silhouette portraits in frames, the spines of the books on the shelves, the petals of hothouse flowers, the marble and polished wood tabletops.

"There has been no body," she whispers dozens of times a day. She touches the browning frond of an ornamental palm and whispers, "No body," then the heavy glass corners of the inkwell and again the same whisper. The servants are uncomfortable around her; when she enters a room, they bow and back out.

But she has to keep repeating the two words. They are her comfort. Her son's body has not been discovered. Therefore, there is the chance he is alive. And for this reason she will keep hoping.

Mikhail may be alive. She will not abandon the search for him.

The only way she can get through the day is with wine or vodka, but even so, her head hurts, her body hurts. It is as though her nerve endings have moved to the surface of her skin. Taking laudanum and a crushed bromide tablet with her wine or vodka before Lilya tucks her in at night affords her a few hours of numbness.

Antonina warily follows Dr. Molov to Konstantin's bedroom.

"Although he is not yet himself, countess, this will be my last visit. He does not need my talents any longer, and he is on the mend, but he appears to be unaware of what has transpired these last weeks." The doctor's eyebrows rise slightly. "He has been speaking of the November Uprising of 1830 against the Poles. He believes he was injured while fighting. Was he ever in the Tsar's army, countess?"

"No."

"Well, his body has undergone a great trauma. I'm sure his clarity will return. For now, it's best not to upset him with any truths or distressing news."

Antonina is strangely afraid of entering Konstantin's room; she hasn't seen her husband for the last week. To her great surprise, when she finally goes in, he is sitting up, his hair combed, his face shaved. He is dreadfully thin, and has become an old, old man. Whatever is left of his right arm is bound.

"Ah, Antonina," Konstantin says.

She sits beside the bed. She can't bear to look at the bandaged stump.

"I trust you have kept well," her husband says, and she tries to smile at this normal statement. But then he says, "It's good to be home. Bring in my boy. I'd like him to see that his papa has come home from the front."

Antonina looks at Dr. Molov. Pavel is holding the doctor's coat, and the doctor has one arm into a sleeve.

"Kostya, our Misha . . ." Again she looks at the doctor, and he shakes his head. "He is busy with his studies. He will come to see you later."

"Fine," Konstantin says. "After dinner, then," he adds, and closes his eyes.

Antonina follows the doctor out of the room and down the stairs.

"And you, countess? Are you sleeping?"

"A bit."

"You must try to keep up your strength. Your husband will need you more than ever now."

Antonina feels he is lecturing her. "I would like more laudanum."

He hesitates, then takes a bottle from his bag. "Use it sparingly."

Even though the site of the amputation heals, Konstantin continues to feel pain and itching in his missing arm. He complains endlessly, petulantly, demanding that he be given his tincture of chloroform.

Pavel complies. When the count had finished the first bottle and Pavel told him there was no more, he grew so agitated, shouting and struggling, that it took Pavel over an hour to calm him. Konstantin ordered him to procure more of the solution, giving him rubles from the small safe in his bedroom and telling him the name of a man in Pskov who would provide whatever he wanted.

One afternoon, as Antonina sits beside his bed and she feels he is lucid enough at last, she speaks of Mikhail. "You remember, don't you, Kostya, what happened to our son? That he was kidnapped?" Her voice is low in the bedchamber Konstantin doesn't want to leave.

"I remember." He is lost, staring at the fire. "He is dead, our son."

"No! No, Kostya, he's not dead."

"He's dead. How long has it been since he was taken?"

Antonina swallows. "Six weeks."

Konstantin turns to her, his pupils dilated. "You believe he's still alive? The Cossacks got their money. They killed him and left Pskov. It's over. Everything is over. Pavel!" he shouts, and the man appears with the bottle.

"He's not dead, Konstantin," Antonina whispers.

"Have a headstone carved for him, and place it in the cemetery behind the Church of the Redeemer," Konstantin orders. "Place it next to that of my Irina."

"Stop talking like this! Stop it. I won't hear of it." Antonina runs out of his room. She slams her own bedroom door and locks it, as if it can keep Konstantin's words out.

She sits on the bed, looking at her bottle of laudanum on the dressing table. She needs it to sleep at night, but it sometimes gives her horrid, panicked dreams. Over and over Antonina is running through thickets, searching, sharp thorns cutting her skin. When she wakes in the morning, it's difficult to think clearly, her eyes gritty and head throbbing. Her throat is dry until at least noon.

She gets up and takes a number of spoonfuls of the laudanum. After a few moments it puts her into a dreamy and unfocused state, but it makes her thirsty. She drinks from the decanter of wine on her dressing table. It's thick and warm on her tongue. She drinks earlier and earlier in the day now, not because it makes her feel any better, but to stop her hands from shaking and to take away the nausea she often feels if it's been too long since her last drink. Lilya tells her the nausea is from not eating, but Antonina has trouble swallowing food.

She sits on her bed, the wine decanter in her hand in the middle of that dark afternoon, the May rain pelting against the windows. Neither the laudanum, the wine nor the rain can wash away Konstantin's words. All she wants is to not think. She crushes some of the horrid white tablets of bromide and swallows them with another full glass of wine, and also takes a few more spoonfuls of laudanum.

She lies on her back at the edge of the bed, desperate for peace. Then she feels it, warm wings sweeping over her. Such a soft, feathery release—and she is relieved. Finally it will come, the old, untroubled sleep. The sleep she knew when her son lay in his bed in his room so near to hers. She welcomes it, inviting the wings to take her away.

But in the next moment, she has an odd, troubling sensation, and it's difficult to breathe. A bird, huge and frightening, is sitting on her chest. She can't—won't—open her eyes, afraid she will see an actual sharp beak. She tells herself it's a dream, a nightmare, and tries to move, but can't. She hears short, quick panting, as though the bird is leaning closer to her face.

Or perhaps it's her own breathing.

She knows that thoughts of the bird and its beak are irrational. It's the pills, the laudanum, the wine. A slow, bubbling sensation, perhaps a dulled panic, rises as she tries to think about how many pills she crushed, how much laudanum she swallowed. What if she dies?

She tries to open her heavy eyelids, no longer afraid of a phantom bird but of death. What if she dies, and tomorrow, or the next day, or the next week, Misha is returned to Angelkov? Would he be told that his mother was so weak she took her own life? She can't bear to imagine him thinking this of her: to be motherless because of her pathetic frailty and self-pity. She struggles even harder to move, fighting off the heaviness of her limbs with all the will she can summon. It's as though she's submerged in thick sand, wet and heavy. Small sounds burst from her throat. She finally opens her eyes and rolls off the edge of the bed. She feels herself falling slowly, gracefully, through warm water, and the temptation to stay there, floating, makes her close her eyes again. She fights the stupor and somehow— does it take a minute, or ten?—is on her hands and knees. She pushes her fingers down her throat and retches until she throws up the wine and pills and laudanum in what looks like a bloody swill on her pale carpet; there's nothing solid there.

She collapses, trembling, curled on her side on the floor. She sees herself in the tilted cheval glass near the wardrobe. Her lips are stained burgundy. She tries to lick them, but her tongue is too dry.

There is a tapping on Antonina's locked door, and she hears Lilya's quiet voice: *Madam? Madam?* Her voice grows louder. *Countess Mitlovskiya. Please. Open the door.*

Antonina hears running footsteps, then silence. Within moments the footsteps return, and there is a jangling of keys and the lock turning.

"Tosya," Lilya breathes as she closes the door behind her. She stares at Antonina's mouth and the red pool on the carpet. She moans and crosses herself.

She brings a damp towel and kneels beside Antonina, gently wiping her chin, but the stain has dried there. Lilya's nostrils widen. "It's just the wine?" she says, sniffing, then makes another sign of the cross over Antonina. "Thank God. I thought it was blood."

"I don't know what to do, Lilya," Antonina says faintly. "I can't stand it. The pain."

"Let me help you up," Lilya says, and tucks her hands under Antonina's arms and brings her to her feet.

Once up, Antonina lays her head heavily against Lilya's shoulder. Lilya strokes her back; it's damp. "You are ill, my darling," she says. "You must sleep." She kisses Antonina's hair. "Come, I will put you to bed. Shall we change your gown?"

Antonina shakes her head.

Lilya helps her into the bed, pulling up the bedclothes.

"I need water," Antonina whispers, pushing the blankets away. Lilya rushes to bring her a glass from the pitcher. She holds the glass to Antonina's red lips. When Antonina has drunk her fill, Lilya sets down the glass and sits on the bed, using her thumb to gently wipe at the stain on Antonina's mouth. She rubs her thumb back and forth, slower and slower, until Antonina feebly pushes her hand away.

Lilya says, "You must pray, Ninochka. Pray. It's what I do all day. I never stop praying that God will allow our child to be returned to us."

Antonina blinks. "You mean my child."

"Yes, of course, Tosya. But I miss him too. Every day my arms long to hold him. I want to hear his voice, and his music."

Antonina finds some comfort in sharing this. "You believe that Mikhail is alive? That God has watched over him all this time, and kept him safe? That I will one day see him again?" Her tongue is still awkward, each word a struggle.

She expects—wants and needs—Lilya to say *yes, yes, of course God will return him safely to your arms*. If anyone will believe this, it's Lilya. She's become more and more religious since moving into her new position in the big house. She abstains from all meats and milk and eggs for the five weeks of St. Peter's Fast in May and June. She also fasts for a fortnight of the Assumption in August, for six weeks leading to Christmas Eve and then for the duration of the Great Fast, the seven weeks of Lent. In non-fast times, she abstains on every Wednesday, the day of Judas's treachery, and on every Friday, the day of the Saviour's death. She asks Antonina to take her along when she goes into the city of Pskov, rich with tiny, picturesque churches from the fifteenth and sixteenth centuries, as well as monasteries and convents dating back to the twelfth century. Lilya spends hours on her knees in the Troitsky Sobor—the Trinity Cathedral—and Antonina sees it's difficult for Lilya to leave when she comes to fetch her. For a full day after her prayers at Troitsky or any of the city's other cathedrals, Lilya's face has a look of rapture. Antonina has never forgotten Lilya's childhood wish to be a nun.

But to her surprise, Lilya's face colours, and she swallows before she answers. "It is what we *must* believe, Tosya. We must never stop believing that the right thing will be done."

It is a rather odd thing for Lilya to say, Antonina thinks, although her head is throbbing now. *The right thing.*

"My poor Ninochka," Lilya says, "my poor girl." She leans over and covers Antonina's cheeks with kisses, kisses her forehead and her eyes.

Antonina pulls away. "I want to sleep now," she says, and rolls onto her side, her back to Lilya.

"I will stay with you until you fall asleep," Lilya says. "Perhaps I will sleep here, in your room, from now on. I will have a pallet brought in."

"No," Antonina murmurs. "You must stay with your husband in the servants' quarters."

There is a moment of silence. "Soso is no longer on the estate, Tosya," Lilya says. She tries not to let her relief at her husband leaving come through in her voice. "He left shortly after the serfs were emancipated, to look for something different."

Antonina is so tired. "Will you go to him soon? Will you leave the estate as well, to join him?" Her voice is just above a whisper.

Lilya draws in a breath. How could Antonina think she would ever leave her? "My place is here, with you." And she tries again to embrace Antonina.

"No, Lilya. I want to be alone. Leave me, please."

Lilya's face conveys a mixture of confusion and hurt that Antonina can't see. "But Tosya, I only want to—"

"Lilya"—Antonina's voice is stronger—"I said no, didn't I?"

"As you wish, madam," Lilya says stiffly. She takes the laudanum, the sleeping tablets and what's left of the wine and leaves, shutting the door with a firm click.

19

*A*lthough Dr. Molov has assured Antonina that the amputation was a success and the healing is complete, Konstantin's behaviour becomes more and more troubling. He sits in his room and speaks of nonsensical things. He refuses to come out. Some days he weeps, other days he shouts. He sends for Tania, but when she arrives he thinks she is Irina, come to haunt him, and sends her away. He cries for Irina. He does not call for Antonina.

Some days he talks about his dead son; some days he doesn't remember a son.

At Antonina's request, Grisha has taken over the complete running of the estate. He comes to Konstantin's study to report various incidents to her, or to ask her about paying for repairs, and she looks at him carefully as he speaks, as if it's difficult for her to understand his requests unless she concentrates deeply. At other times she mindlessly doles out a stack of rubles from Konstantin's strongbox without look-ing at the written accounts Grisha hands to her.

Konstantin has always dealt with this. It means nothing to Antonina. She assumes, each time she unlocks the heavy box, that it will continue to contain rubles, even though she has no idea how they get there.

In the first week of June, a man rides into the yard. Antonina has requested that any stranger arriving at the estate be reported to her, hoping it will be news of Misha. A servant runs to tell her of the man's presence.

It's the third time since Mikhail was taken—over two months ago now—that this has happened. The first two times it turned out to be someone stopping to ask directions.

Today, Antonina doesn't react with quite the same alert-ness as previously. She slowly sits up in her bed after the message has been delivered to her bedroom. Lilya opens the window; it's mid-afternoon, and the room, in the grow-ing heat, smells musty.

"Did he come to the house?" Antonina asks. "Did he come specifically to speak to me?"

"No," Lilya tells her. "Apparently he came across the fields, and took the back road to the stables."

"I must go out to him," Antonina says, swinging her bare feet to the floor. "Help me, Lilya." She reaches to the end of the bed for her gauzy robe.

"Tosya," Lilya says, "I will go and see what he wants. You wait here."

"No. No, I must go out. Perhaps he's one of the kid-nappers, with another ransom note." Even as she says the words, Antonina feels no hope. She has given up on hope. She simply waits for each day to pass.

Some days, she drinks tea with lemon, or eats a piece of bread and jam. Mostly she lies on her side, facing the window, watching as the leaves unfurl from the trees. She sits up periodically, to sip from the glass on the table beside the bed. She has grown tired of the thick, heavy wine and now drinks only vodka. Although Konstantin had shut down his distillery the previous year, saying it no longer brought in enough profit, there is a storehouse full of his own special brand, waiting to be sold. There are many, many bottles in the cellar of the manor. The vodka is clear and crisp.

Sometimes a small nightingale comes to the branches of the tree outside her window, calling in a whistling crescendo.

"Antonina Leonidovna," Lilya says, as if speaking to a child who has been ill a long time, "you mustn't overexcite yourself. And if you do choose to go downstairs, please, let me help you dress properly. It isn't good for the servants to see you this way . . . Please, let me help you dress, and . . . your hair." The last word pulses in the air. "Let me attend to your hair."

"There isn't time," Antonina says, but as she stands, she has to shut her eyes and hold on to the bed.

Lilya puts her arm around Antonina's back, feeling her ribs just under her skin. "You must put on a warm gown. And at least cover your head."

⸎

Antonina, with Lilya following, makes her way across the sunny yard, where she sees Grisha talking to a stranger. Unable to wait until she reaches them, Antonina calls out Grisha's name, and he turns, a startled look on his face.

He glances at Antonina's velvet hat, pulled low on her forehead. The collar of her soft wool coat is turned up around her face. It's a warm day, and yet she's dressed as though the air has a chill. Her skin has an unhealthy opaqueness. He hasn't seen her in the last ten days; every time he sent word that he had estate issues to discuss, he was told she was resting and didn't wish to be disturbed, that he should deal with it himself.

"What is it, Grisha?" Antonina says, having closed the gap between them. She looks up into his face, and then into the face of the other man. He is very broad, with a grizzled grey beard. He takes off his cap and bows to her; his grey hair stands up in greasy spikes. "What does he want? Why is he here?" She looks back at Grisha, studying the expression in his dark eyes.

The man lifts his head and stares at her boldly.

"He brings a message," Grisha tells her.

"A message?" Antonina repeats, as if the word is unfamiliar.

"From your son. He brings something from Mikhail."

Antonina doesn't move or speak or even blink. Grisha realizes how ill she is. He wonders if she understood what was just said.

"Madam?" he says softly. "Countess Mitlovskiya? Did you hear? It is a message from Mikhail Konstantinovich."

Antonina straightens and grabs the stranger's arm. "You have him? You have my son?"

"No, no, madam. I only came to give proof. I'm not involved in any way, countess, but simply a messenger. Would I come here, and put myself at risk, if I was involved?" He glances at Grisha.

"Have you seen him?" Antonina's voice is louder than it has been in weeks. "Was he well? Where is he?" She whirls back to Grisha. "Go with him and find him. Get my boy back, Grisha."

Grisha speaks sharply to the man. "Well, Lev? Have you anything more to tell us? Can you tell us where we can find the child?"

When the man Grisha calls Lev doesn't speak, Antonina cries out, "Did you come for money? I can give it to you. Come to the house, and I will give you more money, and then Grisha will go with you to my son. Please, oh, please." She's crying, moving from Grisha to Lev, tugging on their sleeves, the fronts of their jackets, their hands. "Please," she cries again.

Lev looks from Grisha to Antonina. "Yes, I came for more money. Once they have more money, they will return the child. You should know he is alive by what I brought," he says, gesturing to Grisha.

"What did he bring, Grisha?"

"I'll show it to you, madam, but please, calm yourself. We'll go to the house and I'll show you there."

"Show me now," Antonina begs. Demands. "Give it to me, Grisha."

Grisha reaches inside his tunic and pulls out a folded paper. He hands it to Antonina. She studies the music score on one side and then reads the short note on the other. She drops to her knees in the mud and kisses the creased page over and over, rocking back and forth as she holds it to her breast. Her lips move; she is praying. Tears run down her cheeks, and finally she grows still. "He's alive," she whispers. "My Misha is alive."

Lilya helps her to her feet.

Antonina takes a deep breath, wiping her cheeks. She straightens her shoulders and faces the man called Lev again. "You will tell me where you got this." She holds up the page. "You will tell me immediately."

Lilya sees the old flash in Antonina's eyes, a look that hasn't been there for so long. Her voice is once again that of the countess, not a broken, grieving woman. She even appears taller.

Lev glances at Grisha. "Countess, I am not directly involved. I am the messenger," he repeats, "and I receive my instructions by written notes. I do not see anyone."

"I don't believe you. Grisha, do you believe this man? And who is he, anyway? Where has he come from?"

In the silence, a crow croaks from the branches of a linden.

"We have little recourse but to do as he asks, madam," Grisha says. "We will give him the money. I won't let him go until I make sure he has nothing more to tell us. That he speaks the truth. Do you speak the truth?" Grisha asks. Then, his hands flat on the man's chest, he gives him a shove.

Lev falls onto his bottom, looking up, undignified and yet defiant.

"I think I can persuade him to tell us more," Grisha says, and this time he puts a foot on Lev's chest and pushes him flat.

Lev lies in the mud with Grisha's foot on his chest, his eyes narrowed as he stares up at Grisha until the steward hauls him up by one arm. "Don't worry, madam. If there is anything more to learn, I'll beat it out of him."

"What of the money?" Lev says, uncowed.

"What is the demand this time?" she asks him.

"It is the same as the first amount, countess," he answers after a moment's hesitation.

"And when will my son be returned?"

Lev shrugs. "I am only the messenger," he says, strangely calm in spite of Grisha's threats.

At that, Grisha drags him towards the stable. He looks back at Antonina. "Go to the house, madam. I will have him beaten until he tells me what he knows, and then report to you."

Clutching her son's message to her chest, Antonina walks firmly and purposefully back to the house and into Konstantin's study. She takes out his strongbox and fits the key into the lock. She carelessly counts out a stack of rubles, seeing—but not caring—that the box is almost empty. She wraps the pile of bills in her handkerchief and gives it to Lilya, who hurries out to the stable with it.

She hands it to Grisha. He stands in front of Lev, who is leaning against the wall of a stall.

"Leave us, Lilya," Grisha says, and the woman hurries off.

When Lev unexpectedly rode into the yard and produced the letter from Mikhail, written on the back of the Glinka musical score, Grisha had felt an overwhelming sense of relief. The boy wasn't dead. Soso had made him wait all this time, punishing him.

He hadn't expected the countess to come to the yard when Lev was there; she rarely ventures out of the house. It confused matters, her joy at the letter from her son.

"I will hold the money," he tells Lev now. "You don't suppose I will just give it to you."

"But you have proof the boy's alive."

"Yes, but you don't get the money until you bring the child back. Do you understand? There will be no money unless Mikhail Konstantinovich is returned."

Lev looks at him with such venom that Grisha wonders if he has just sealed the child's fate.

"It will take a while," Lev finally says. "If you don't give me the money, it only means you will wait again. Who knows how long this time."

Grisha knows Lev is acting on Soso's commands. "Where is Misha?"

"He's alive, I tell you. That's all that matters, isn't it?"

When Grisha doesn't answer, Lev says, "I'll send word when and where to bring the money, and when you do, I'll exchange it for the boy."

Grisha steps closer. "I'm to believe you?"

"What choice do you have?" Lev asks, and then turns and leaves the stable. Grisha watches him mount his horse and ride away. Surely the boy is becoming a nuisance. How long will they want to keep him?

⌐

Antonina sits behind Konstantin's desk and looks at Mikhail's note again. The page is from Misha's composition notebook, the one he grabbed as he ran from the music salon the day he was taken.

The note is written in charcoal and has some words scratched out in Mikhail's usual style. As she runs her fingers over the writing, Lev, unhurt, is galloping away from the estate through the newly planted fields.

My dear Mama and Papa,

I am sorry for what happened in the forest because I
couldn't turn my horse around. Are you angry with me,
Papa? Will I still get a puppy for my birthday, Mama?
You promised I would get a dog when the weather was
fine. I pray every day that I will come home for my
birthday at the end of this month. This is all I am
allowed to write.

Misha

Mikhail's birthday is June 28.

"June the twenty-eighth," Antonina whispers.

Antonina goes to Konstantin's room and shows her husband
the note.

He swats it away. "It's a ruse. He's dead."

"Konstantin. It's his handwriting, on a page from his own
music notebook."

"It could have been written long ago."

"No. He says—look—*I pray every day that I will come
home for my birthday at the end of this month.* His birthday is
at the end of the month, Kostya. He wrote it in the last few
days. He's coming back to us, Kostya. I gave the man more
money, and now he will be returned."

"Are you an idiot?" Konstantin stands and hits Antonina
across the face with the back of his only hand. He loses his
balance but manages to remain standing.

The unexpected blow is painful, but she says, defiantly,
"He's coming home." Then she leaves her husband, going to
her room to put a cold cloth on her cut and swelling lip.

The day after Antonina received Mikhail's note, she rises from her rumpled bed with purpose. She has hope—real hope—and suddenly wants to go to church. She wants to thank God for listening to her prayers.

She dresses and slips from the house and across the yard; she doesn't want even Lilya to come with her. She walks through the small copse of trees near the estate and arrives at Angelkov's Church of the Redeemer. Behind the church is a cemetery where lilies of the valley flower profusely, and the lilacs are beginning to bloom, their hanging cones of mauve and white blossoms swaying in a soft breeze. There is warbling from the taller oaks. Even with the beautiful weather and the blossoming trees and flowers, the cemetery looks melancholy. There is a sense of disorder, perhaps even chaos. Many of the headstones are listing after the wet spring, the uneven earth humped and dipping, nettles and weedy grass overtaking the graves. It's clear that no one tends to the graveyard anymore. The serf who once looked after it must be one of those who has left the estate; Father Cyril has not come to her to ask that someone else be assigned. Or perhaps he has, on one of the occasions she refused to see him.

Because it's a balmy day, the church door is open. There are only a few benches along the back wall for the oldest or infirm to sit on during the two- to three-hour sermons. All the other worshippers stand or kneel. The stained glass windows of saints and the Madonna and Child, which Konstantin had imported from Italy, glow, throwing their prisms onto the floor. The rows and rows of little red glass candle holders are serenely comforting, although only one candle flickers this morning. Antonina dips a taper into its flame and lights a candle for her son.

The church brings her an immediate comfort. She lights more candles, watching the flames flare briefly and then burn with a steady pulse. Antonina has the small church to herself, apart from a man in dusty overalls above her on some scaffolding, repainting the trim around the edge of the high domed ceiling. The only sound he makes is a slight shuffling as his boots move along the rough board that supports him.

Antonina forgets him once she's prostrate on the floor, arms spread wide and forehead pressed onto the cold stone. She lies there for much of an hour, thanking God for keeping her son alive. And then she has a vision. It may be brought on by her lack of food and proper sleep, but she sees, on the darkness of her closed eyelids, something soft and white.

It is a comforting, floating vision.

Yes, it could be another bird, not like the one she saw when she'd taken too much laudanum and bromide. This is a white bird, its feathers delicate, its eyes kind. It could also be an angel, couldn't it? Antonina wants to think that an angel hovers over her.

The vision is so beautiful that she feels uplifted in tandem with the angel or bird. A warm, lovely calm comes over her. She hasn't felt this sense of calm for so long, not even before Mikhail was taken. When has Antonina ever felt such peace? Maybe not since she was an innocent child on her father's estate. It may be that she is only falling into a natural deep sleep; it's been so long since she slept peacefully. But whatever it is, the clarity of the vision makes her cry. Her tears fall onto the stone floor. In her head she watches the angel, or bird, swoop back and forth, back and forth, in a peaceful rhythm. Finally it comes to rest over her, motionless. It is as if the winged figure is caught on an updraft of fragrant air from the lit candles.

It hangs over her for an indescribable length of time: seconds, minutes, Antonina can't know. Then it slowly, almost languorously, moves its wings.

Antonina doesn't want it to fly away. She wants it to stay over her, blessing her. But the wings move faster and faster, and she hears them fluttering, and strangely, now, it's outside her head, not inside. Without warning, she's pulled back to reality. There's a harsh human cry, which makes Antonina open her eyes, confused, and in the same moment a crash. Something glances off the back of her hand. She winces, her shoulders tensing, and in the silence that follows, lies there, stunned.

"I'm sorry, countess, my deepest apologies," she hears from above her. "A swallow . . . there's a nest here. It startled me, and I almost fell. I grabbed . . . the panel broke off . . . I'm so sorry, countess." The man's voice is threaded with panic.

Antonina pushes herself to her knees. To her right is a pile of white and gold plaster, broken into jagged pieces. Among them is a little golden cherub, perhaps three inches long. Surely it was this that hit her hand. It lies there, undamaged apart from a tiny chip at the end of one gleaming wing.

She picks it up and stands, craning her head to see the man in overalls leaning out over the scaffolding. "I'm so sorry, countess," he calls down again.

Antonina nods at him, but holds the cherub tightly. She knows what it means—this baby angel falling from the skies to her. She's been waiting and watching for any small sign, anything she can cling to. First was the note from Misha, then the vision, and now this. It's more than enough. Her prayers have been answered.

Just as the cherub has fallen to her from out of the skies, one wing only slightly marred, Antonina is now certain that her son will be returned to her.

She passes Olga on the stairs to her room.

"How are you this morning, madam?" Olga asks, peering at Antonina's split lip.

"I'm fine," Antonina says. She keeps her hand with the cherub in it hidden in the folds of her skirt. She wants to go to her room and think about what has happened, but when she gets there, she finds her husband.

"What are you doing?" she asks.

He's hunched over her writing desk. The drawers are opened and papers are strewn on the floor. An inkwell has been spilled. Tinka is quaking behind the chair by the fireplace.

"I'm looking for my money. You're stealing from me," he says harshly. His sleeve is pinned up over the missing arm.

"Konstantin, stop it. Of course I'm not stealing—I'm your wife." She's careful to stay where she is, near the door.

"Everyone is stealing. I dismissed Pavel, the useless bastard. I found him wearing my riding boots."

Antonina glances at his feet; they're bare. "Konstantin," she says softly. "Wait here. I'm going to—"

But he rushes towards her, his face so dark it's almost plum-coloured. She's frozen with shock for a second, and then she runs into the hall, shouting for Pavel, for Lilya, for anyone to help her. Konstantin comes after her, grabbing her by the shoulder. His breath is foul, his pupils huge and black. There is noise and confusion, servants screaming, thundering footsteps on the stairs, Tinka's frantic barking. And then Grisha is there, encircling Konstantin with his arms so that the old man lets go of Antonina, struggling, still trying to kick her with his bare feet.

Grisha, now aided by Pavel, gets Konstantin back to his room. Antonina follows them, her hand over her mouth. As Grisha holds Konstantin tightly, Pavel waves a bottle under Konstantin's nose. "Breathe, count. Come, breathe as usual," Pavel says.

Konstantin inhales deeply, and grows calm enough to be pushed into a chair. He slumps, his mouth open and eyes closed.

"What's wrong with him?" Antonina asks. "What's wrong?"

"I don't know, countess," Pavel tells her. "But it's all right now. I'll keep him from becoming agitated again."

"Come away," Grisha tells her, taking her arm. He leads her to her bedroom. Antonina is trembling violently, and Grisha helps her to her chair by the fireplace. He pours her a glass of water, but when he brings it to her, she shakes her head.

"Vodka," she says, "in my wardrobe."

Grisha's dark, wavy hair is unruly, his cheeks flushed from his tussle with Konstantin. He studies her swollen, scabbed lip for a moment before opening the double doors and looking, with a puzzled expression, at her gowns.

"Reach behind," she says. "There's a shelf with a bottle."

He does as she asks, and pours her a glass.

"Have one," she tells him, but he shakes his head. "What will we do about him, Grisha?"

"I'll send for the doctor." But he doesn't leave. "Countess, I'm sorry for all that's happened. I'm so sorry."

"None of it is your fault." She sips the vodka, mindful of her damaged lip. "I'm grateful to have you to depend on. I couldn't run the estate without you." She takes another sip. "He said he dismissed Pavel. Please, tell Pavel he's to stay, of course."

Lilya appears in the doorway. She looks affronted to find Grisha in the bedroom. "Madam," she says, "I just heard. I was in the hothouse, cutting you some roses. Are you all right?"

"Yes," Antonina says. "Could you clean up the mess? The ink . . . it's stained the rug. But take Tinka outside first—she's terrified."

Lilya scoops up the shivering dog and leaves with her, casting a look behind her at the steward.

"Thank you, Grisha. You may go too," she tells him. "I'm all right now." She finishes the glass of vodka.

Grisha stoops to pick up something from the mess. "Madam?" he says, standing and holding out the cherub. It has only one wing now.

She has forgotten about the angel in all the chaos; she dropped it as Konstantin came at her. She sets down her empty glass and takes it. "But it's broken," she says, and this small fact is enough to bring tears to her eyes.

Grisha looks from the cherub to the floor. "Here, countess. Look. Here's the wing. I'll repair it. Give it to me, and I'll affix the wing right away." He holds out his hand.

Antonina looks up at him, her eyes wet.

"It can be easily fixed, madam," he says. His voice is comforting, and suddenly Antonina wants to rest her cheek on his outstretched palm. She has known Grisha since she first came to Angelkov. Grisha is trustworthy, and capable. As he stands in front of her, there is something in his dark eyes that Antonina hasn't seen before. As if he feels pain. For her?

"Grisha," she says, giving him back the cherub.

He waits.

"Grisha," she repeats, and this time he says, softly, "Yes, madam?"

"I don't know what to do anymore."

Rubbing his thumb over the cherub, he says, "I know, countess."

"Will you help me? You already run Angelkov. But Konstantin . . ." She touches trembling fingers to her forehead. "Finding Misha. I don't know who else . . ."

Grisha moves closer and puts his hand on Antonina's shoulder.

Lilya comes in with Tinka. She clears her throat loudly.

Grisha removes his hand. "I will do all I can, Countess Mitlovskiya." He bows and leaves.

Antonina watches his back, his straight shoulders, as he leaves her.

Lilya watches her mistress.

20

*W*hen he arrived in Moscow in 1844, Grisha was a much different person than the boy who had ridden away from Chita. He was almost two years older, and he had no patience with self-pity or regrets. He had learned that if you face your worst fears and survive, there is never anything to fear again. As a result, he was not afraid of anything. And because he was afraid of nothing, he thought of himself as untouchable.

Nothing made him feel elation or sorrow.

He found a job in a cooperage on the outskirts of Moscow, building perfect barrels as he had learned to do as an apprentice under his father. After a year he heard of a better-paying position and moved on to a cooperage in St. Petersburg. But he was still restless. When another opportunity arose, this one on a private estate in the province of Pskov, he thought it might be what he wanted. With a good recommendation from his employer, wearing new clothing and with a horse he'd managed to buy from his saved wages—he called the horse Felya, as he called every horse he owned from then on—he went to the estate known then as Polnokove and, in 1846, was hired by Count Mitlovsky.

From the start, he despised the count, as he had despised any man—apart from his father—who gave him orders. The count and his pockmarked wife acted as though they were imparting gold to their staff when they lined them up at Christmas and gave them each a flask of vodka—the very vodka Grisha made the barrels for. They were also given a small purse of kopecks, the men a strip of leather for a new vest or belts, and the women a bolt of fabric. At Easter, Grisha stood, his fists clenched, as the staff were again lined up as if they were children and given dyed eggs and *paskhi*, the tall cakes of sweetened curds, butter and raisins. And for this they were to bow gratefully and pretend undying faithfulness. His cake under one arm, Grisha fought memories of Easter in Chita, celebrating the Mass with his father and little brother in the green-domed Decembrist Orthodox Church. It had always been his favourite feast day.

Now it was spoiled.

A year after Grisha arrived, the count's wife died. It took only a few months for the widower to take up with the laundress Tania, who resembled the countess right down to the pockmarks on her cheeks. In another year Mitlovsky remarried. The second wife was little more than a girl, Grisha saw as she stepped out of the carriage holding a tiny dog with a bright pink ribbon around its neck. The house and yard staff of over sixty had been called into the front yard, and lined the walk that led from the oval driveway to the steps of the manor. They all bowed from the waist.

The count led the girl along the drive, the cinders crunching under their feet, to the top step of the manor. "I present the new Countess Mitlovskiya," he announced. "Rise and look upon her."

The staff obeyed.

"To welcome her to her new home, I have changed the name of the estate from Polnokove to Angelkov."

The staff remained still.

The new wife began her greetings by kissing the icon of the Blessed Virgin Mary held by the housekeeper, and smiling and nodding at the servant holding the welcoming bread and salt. And although she appeared outwardly calm as she greeted the staff of the estate, passing in front of each, repeating his or her name and position in a light but respectful tone, Grisha saw, just before he bowed his head and heard her say, *Grisha, cooper*, the uncertainty in her eyes.

He assumed the count would now leave the laundress alone, but he soon realized he was wrong.

The new wife brought freshness to the atmosphere, and when she gave birth to Mitlovsky's son, Grisha's life also changed.

He had talked to the second Countess Mitlovskiya a few times in her first year at Angelkov. Once, she came into the cooperage and asked him to fashion a bed for Tinka, her dog. "She has a velvet bed, but it's quite worn. I thought that perhaps you could fashion a little wooden one. Grisha, isn't it?"

she added. She requested that he make it out of planed, varnished staves, telling him she would line it with padding.

"Yes, countess," he said, bowing, noticing that she was pregnant. Did she really remember his name, or had she asked another servant? "Do you have a particular kind of wood in mind?"

"Whatever wood you think would be best." She looked around at the finished barrels, picking up a planed stave and holding it to her nose. "I like the smell here." She put down the stave and laughed then, as if slightly embarrassed by her statement. She had a high, pretty laugh. Grisha felt strangely pleased, even though he knew, by the way she unconsciously rested a hand on the mound under her flowing gown, that most likely she was simply happy about the expected child.

He made the dog bed and had it delivered to the manor, not expecting to see her again. But a week later she was back. "I came to tell you how much Tinka loves her little bed," she said, the dog held against her. "You love it, don't you, Tinka?" She kissed its nose. "Thank you for your expertise, Grisha," she said, looking from the dog to him.

"It was an honour, Countess Mitlovskiya," he said, bowing.

But she didn't leave immediately, looking around the cooperage, touching various staves and tools as if she didn't have anywhere else to be. She picked up *The Stationmaster's Daughter* he'd left on a stool. "Is this yours?"

Grisha cursed his foolishness at leaving the book in full view. Would she assume he wasn't working when he should be, and have him punished? "Yes. I read when I eat my midday meal."

"Do many of the serfs at Angelkov read?" she asked, looking surprised.

"I am not a serf, madam. I am a free man."

"Oh. I read *The Stationmaster's Daughter* last year," she went on. "It's very sad, isn't it? But I was glad that Dunia defies her father and runs away with the man she loves." She immediately put her hand over her mouth. "I'm sorry. Have I spoiled it for you?"

Grisha shook his head. "I've read it before. I've read all of Pushkin's works at least twice."

"I love that he wrote so many of his books right here, in our province, when he was exiled from St. Petersburg. And I just named my new filly after her—Dunia, the girl in the novel," she added. "You like to read, then?"

"Yes, madam."

"The library at Angelkov is sadly lacking, but I'm trying to fill the shelves. I brought a lot of my own books from home, and I buy more whenever we journey into Pskov city."

Grisha made a polite sound. The countess made him strangely anxious, chattering in such a friendly manner. He hoped Mitlovsky wouldn't come looking for his wife.

She turned away from him then. "Goodbye," she said, "and thank you again." As she left, the sun caught in the intricate weave of her fair hair, and Grisha thought about her and the count. For one moment he tried to imagine the girl laughing her carefree laugh with the old man.

And knew that money truly could buy anything one wanted in this world.

～

The next time he saw her was after the birth of the heir to the Mitlovsky fortune.

The new mother had taken a walk through the yard, the

nanny following with the well-wrapped baby. The countess had come to the stables to see a new foal. But after looking in on the leggy black Arabian, smiling and making encouraging noises to it, she took an unexpected detour. Instead of leaving by the main front doors, she went out the doors at the back into the yard that held the flogging bench.

She appeared at the moment the steward, a bullish man named Gleb, was lifting his knout. He was about to whip a serf who had displeased the count by castrating a bull clumsily. The unfortunate man was shirtless and tied face down on the bench, which was propped vertically against the wall of an outbuilding. Grisha was present in the yard quite by accident, on his way to the blacksmith shed with a broken adze to be soldered.

Grisha was often angry that the count paid no attention to the way Gleb handled his job. The steward was allowed to live in a small but tidy wooden house with a front garden; Grisha sometimes saw Gleb's stout wife bent over the rows of vegetables there. In the two-storey stone servants' house, Grisha shared a room with three men from the cattle sheds and the ever-present smell of manure that seemed ingrained in their skin.

Gleb brought the moistened strap with its strips of leather, each tied with a metal ball on the end, down on the bare back of the serf. The serf shrieked in a high and terrible way, and as his cry died away, those watching heard another cry. They were all shocked to see the new little countess, her face drained of colour, her hand to her throat.

For unknown reasons, she turned to the nanny and snatched the baby from her arms, pressing it against her as if the infant were next in line for punishment. "Stop!" she shouted to Gleb, who had the knout raised over his head for the second blow. "Stop, I said," she repeated. "I demand that you untie that serf."

Gleb lowered the knout and glared at Antonina. "No disrespect, countess, but I don't answer to you. It's your husband who gives me my orders, and it's your husband I've worked for over nine long years. He has never had a complaint with me. My suggestion to you, countess, is that you take care not to come into the flogging yard."

Antonina looked around as if for support. She saw Grisha and opened her mouth.

He gave a small, almost imperceptible shake of his head, and was grateful that she had enough intelligence to understand that it would be wrong to pull him into this altercation. "Fine," she said, looking back at Gleb. "I will report your rudeness towards me to the count. Of that you may be sure." She raised her chin, and then turned abruptly and left.

Grisha saw the baby's small, solemn face over her shoulder.

*

The count was thrilled with the recent arrival of his son. At the child's birth he had provided a celebratory feast for all those on the estate. It lasted for three days, complete with two nights of fireworks. His excitement made him generous, and he also supplied a small flask of vodka and a few kopecks to every one of his souls—over a thousand—who lived in the surrounding villages and worked the land. He carried his son about, showing him to everyone, although not allowing the baby to be touched. The house serfs all agreed they had never witnessed the count smile in this manner.

Mikhail Konstantinovich was only two months old when

Antonina came upon the beating in the flogging yard and reported it to her husband.

"It's perfectly natural," Konstantin said. "Surely you grew up seeing this, or at least knowing of it. How else are we to keep our children working diligently?"

"They're not your children," she said, holding the baby on her lap and thinking of the serf with the scarlet slice on his already scarred back.

Konstantin, on the settee beside her, shook his head, chucking his son under his tiny chin and smiling at him. "You know what I mean," he said, not looking at Antonina but picking up one of Mikhail's hands and gazing at the minute, perfect fingernails. "I must be the father to them, to show them the error of their ways and teach them to never repeat mistakes."

She vividly remembered her own father's similar argument. "I don't like the steward. He's rude and insubordinate. He treated me with no respect whatsoever. I don't want him on the estate any longer." She recalled Gleb's great shaking belly as he brought down the knout, and the spittle shining on his chin as he yelled at her across the yard.

Finally, Konstantin looked away from his son. "What is it you wish me to do, my angel? A good steward is hard to find. They must be able to read and to do accounts. Gleb is not adept at reading—you know I have no patience for it myself—but he is good with numbers. A steward must command authority over the others, and be honest."

"That brute is honest? He doesn't look it to me." The baby still on her lap, she moved onto Konstantin's knee. He looked taken aback, but allowed it. "Please, husband," Antonina said, kissing his cheek, and then Konstantin shifted so that Antonina sat beside him again.

"I *have* been displeased with Gleb for a variety of reasons for quite a while. But it will take some time to find someone to fill his position."

Antonina pressed her mouth against Mikhail's soft scalp, feeling the beat of his pulse under her lips. "What about the cooper? The dark one," she said, without knowing she was going to say it. "Grisha. He's much younger and stronger than Gleb. I know he can read, because I saw him with a book."

"He's good at what he does," her husband said.

"Wouldn't a cooper be easier to replace than a steward?"

"He doesn't say much," Konstantin said. "Still, there is definitely something powerful about him." He stood, impatient to leave—he had made an appointment with Tania. "I can't think it would hurt to at least talk to him."

Antonina smiled at him. He couldn't help but be charmed by her smile.

"Thank you, dear husband," she said, then, "I do believe Misha looks more like you every day. Look at his noble forehead."

Konstantin's chest grew visibly broader.

"You'll speak to Grisha right away?" she asked. Konstantin told her that yes, he would. Then he pulled up his son and held him in the air, beaming.

~

Mikhail had been born with little fuss; it was only long and painful for Antonina in the way of most first deliveries.

She refused to hand her child to a wet nurse. Instead, she fed him herself, to the annoyance of her husband, who felt it was beneath her. As the wife of a landowner, her only duty was to bear her husband's children. The care and upbringing should be left to others: the wet nurses and nannies and governesses and tutors. Parents were only expected to listen to reports of their children's health and, as they grew, observe newly acquired skills: French and German, the first halting musical attempts, horseback riding, archery and shooting for boys, needlework for girls. And yet Antonina was fascinated with her son. Before Mikhail, she had never held a baby. In the first few weeks of his life, while she learned to feed and care for him, she lost all interest in anything else. Was this normal? she asked Lilya.

Lilya didn't know. When she held Mikhail, she did remember the feel of her own babies in her arms, but they had both been sickly and endlessly wailing. She'd had to go back to work in the fields with one strapped to her back and the other to her front when they were only days old. At night she was so exhausted that she wept as she fed them, trying to keep them quiet so their cries didn't wake Soso and anger him. She was grateful to Lyosha; he always helped, holding and jiggling one of the howling infants while she was busy with the other. He also did simple tasks like stirring the kasha on the stove so it didn't burn, and gathering and bringing in small baskets of dried dung to keep the fire going.

Now she felt something almost like sadness as she watched Antonina's joy. She wished she could have known some of this gratification with her babies. She had studied their wee faces and wispy hair. The one who had died last had begun to laugh, and Lilya recalled how that had always given her a small start of pleasure. But it had been so difficult for her to keep up with the work in the fields and in the izba, and to make sure Soso was satisfied. After the second little one was buried, she had had her first full night's sleep in months. She awoke in the morning with a heavy spirit, but also a quiet relief.

It was so different for Antonina, she knew, as she watched the other woman rest in her wide, clean bed with Tinka at her feet, reading and sipping tea with her baby beside her. She watched Antonina instantly put down her book and teacup when the child made the tiniest squeak, picking him up and covering his small face with kisses. Lilya knew what Antonina would like to hear, and so she told her mistress that yes, this was normal, that Antonina had fallen in love with her baby, as nature meant it to be. "Love for a child is perhaps the only real love a woman knows in life, madam, apart from love for God."

Antonina looked at her. "Yes, love for your child and for God." She didn't want to ask Lilya if she thought it possible to feel such deep love for a man.

⤚

Most nights, when Konstantin either was entertaining friends or had gone off, saying he had business on the estate to attend to, Antonina would have Lilya stay with her while she gave Mikhail his last feeding.

Lilya knew, as did all the other staff, that Konstantin spent some of his evenings with the laundress. She wondered if Antonina had any idea what her husband was up to.

One night, when the baby was three months old, Antonina was lying in bed with him in the crook of her arm. He had just been fed and was asleep, his lips still pursed. Antonina was reading, holding a book with her free hand. Lilya sat in a chair nearby, making tiny stitches in a lacy gown of Mikhail's.

Antonina dropped the book onto the bedcover. "My eyes are tired. I want you to read to me, Lilya."

Lilya looked up and shrugged. "You know I can't read."

"I'll teach you," Antonina said. "We will start in a few weeks, when Mishenka is into more of a routine." She kissed his head.

"As you wish, Tosya," Lilya answered, going back to her sewing. "I would be happy to learn to read if you wish me to, although in my life I have never seen the need for it."

"You *should* read, Lilya," Antonina said matter-of-factly, gesturing at a pile of books on her table.

Lilya glanced up from the baby's gown again. "My life leaves no time for such things."

"Then I will give you more time. I'll have one of the other women take over some of the things you do for me, like that— the sewing—and then you could have time to read. You can find out about so many things in the world when you read."

Lilya kept stitching. Finally she said, "There's no need for me to know anything more than what I know." Antonina leaned forward, but before she could respond, Lilya continued, "What good would it do me to know more, when my world is here, Tosya? Would it not bring me unhappiness to know what there is beyond the mud of the villages, beyond the streams and rivers, beyond the boundaries of the estate, when I will never have more than this?" She met Antonina's gaze.

The sleeping baby snuffled, his eyebrows twitching, and Antonina sat back. "But Lilya, there might be a time, some-day, when there are more opportunities. You know of the talk of proposals for emancipation. If this ever comes about—"

Lilya put up her hand and Antonina stopped. "I prefer that you don't speak to me of these things, Tosya. I prefer to live my life as it is. I prefer not to . . ." She frowned as if annoyed with herself, or perhaps with Antonina.

"You prefer not to imagine anything more than what you have today. You have no other dream?" Antonina wondered if Lilya still thought of the convent.

Lilya nipped the thread with her teeth and put the needle back into the pincushion. "*This* is my dream. This is what I dreamed of. And now I have it." Still holding the little gown, she stared at Antonina. "Do you understand? I have everything I want, here, in this room, Tosya."

Antonina was unnerved by the intensity of Lilya's look, but then the baby let out a sudden wail and she turned her attention to him.

～

Grisha knew it was Antonina he should be grateful to for his new life. When the count ordered him to his study and told him there might be an opportunity to take over Gleb's position as steward, Grisha had been astounded. It was the most coveted position for a free man with no title and no land.

"My wife feels you would make a more respectful and even-tempered steward than Gleb," the count said. "Change on the estate is good. The serfs may perform at a higher level with someone new. The salary is much higher than what I pay you as a cooper," he added. "Are you interested?"

"Yes, Count Mitlovsky. I can assure you I would take such responsibilities with the utmost seriousness."

Konstantin nodded. "My wife tells me you read."

"Russian and French."

"French?"

Grisha wondered if he'd taken it too far. "Only a little," he lied. "And I will learn accounting skills, should they be necessary."

"Yes, yes. I won't find another position for Gleb until you've proven you're worthy of the job. We'll try you for two weeks."

Grisha knew the next two weeks would not be easy, with Gleb knowing he and his wife might be moved to another estate in favour of Grisha. Then again, it was Count Mitlovsky who was in charge of Gleb's future, not Grisha.

Grisha quickly proved to the count that not only was he more astute at accounting than Gleb, but he complained less. He handled immediate problems with the serfs on his own, without constantly coming to the count to drone on about small issues and ask for direction.

Two weeks later, he moved into the steward's pleasant house and immediately painted the shutters blue, like the wooden house in Chita where he'd grown up. In place of the vegetables in the garden, he planted cherry and apple trees. He built shelves for the books he had brought with him from Siberia and those he had collected since, as well as others the countess lent to him, believing he would enjoy a particular author. He slept alone at night for the first time in his life apart from those months he'd travelled through Siberia, when the sky was his roof.

And yet he continued to carry a deep sense of restlessness. He believed it was because he was still a slave to another man's whims. He considered Konstantin beneath him in intelligence, and this was hard to bear as well. After Grisha had been steward for a year, the count told him he was weary of sneaking about the manor with Tania and wouldn't lower himself to go to her room in the servants' quarters. He wanted to use Grisha's house once a week. Grisha was aghast and disgusted. But what could he say? The count did not own him, but he owned the house.

Certainly these factors played a part in Grisha's unrest. But a part of it was also loneliness. After working so hard to feel nothing, Grigori Sergeyevich Naryshkin was incapable of recognizing that he was lonely.

~

Antonina gave thanks in her daily prayers for finding Lilya again. But she was sorry their friendship had to remain hidden. Only when they were alone in her bedchamber could she and Lilya talk in the old way. There Lilya could call her Tosya instead of countess or madam, and speak to her with some of her old frankness. Occasionally, when Lilya spontaneously laughed over Misha's antics, Antonina thought she was almost like the girl she had been in the forest.

She wondered about Lilya's life outside her bedchamber, but Lilya made it clear she wouldn't talk about Soso. She did, however, often speak of Lyosha with pride, telling Antonina how strong he was growing, and how he was being given more and more responsibility in the stables.

One morning, as Lilya smiled, smoothing Misha's fair hair with the palm of her hand, Antonina asked, "What of you, Lilya? Do you hope to have more children?"

Lilya stopped smiling, although she continued to run her hand over Misha's hair. "I hope not. I don't want any more."

"Really?" She put her hand on Lilya's arm. "You will always be my maid, even if you have more children. I promise you that. And I want you to feel happiness again, as I do with my Misha."

When Lilya said nothing, Antonina insisted, "Surely you don't mean you don't want any more children. What about Soso? Doesn't he want a son, like all men?"

Lilya shrugged, and the conversation ended.

⌣

Lilya was glad that Antonina needed her to stay with her through the nights while the baby was so small. But as he grew older and Antonina told her she should return to her room with Soso in the servants' quarters, Lilya still found excuses to stay late. She did not like relations with Soso any more than she had when they were first married. She tried to make sure that when she returned to their room Soso was in a deep, snoring sleep, and didn't roll over onto her.

She knew that the fewer times a month she had to submit, the fewer the chances of ever being caught with child again. She despised having to open her legs to him.

Antonina did not know that just as she dreamed of Valentin Vladimirovitch to help her yield to her wifely duty on the nights when her husband moved heavily over her, Lilya envisioned the long, pale neck of the beautiful countess.

21

*I*t's now early September. Mikhail's birthday had passed at the end of June, but there has been no more word. Over and over Antonina questions Grisha. *What did that man Lev say when you beat him for answers? Why didn't you follow him and see where he went? You could have waited, watched his home. He had the ransom money. Someone would have come for it.*

And just as Antonina badgers him with the same questions, Grisha has the same answers: *I couldn't get any more out of him. He moves from village to village; he has no home. He is only the messenger, others are involved. He knows nothing more. We must be patient, countess.*

Patient? How can she be any more patient?

Life at the estate itself has grown even more difficult. Konstantin is a shambling ghost of his former self. He prowls about the house, shouting at the servants, calling them the wrong names, and accusing them of theft and insubordination. They try to stay out of his way, crossing themselves when they see him. None of the women want to go into his room to clean except Tania, and he refuses to be seen by the doctor. Pavel is the only person he will allow near him, but he won't let his faithful manservant help him bathe or change his clothing. His hair has grown long and greasy, his beard matted with food. He swears that his son is dead, and sometimes wanders in the cemetery looking for his grave.

Over the summer, their closest neighbours, Prince and Princess Bakanev, came to Angelkov three times. Each time Antonina made excuses that the count was resting, offering refreshments and trying to keep track of the princess's gossip-filled conversations while hoping Konstantin didn't begin to shout from upstairs during the visit. Other estate owners in the province have sent notes full of sympathy about Mikhail, asked after the count's health and offered invitations to Antonina. She has politely written back that it is a difficult time, and she will look forward to visiting at a later date.

After a while, the invitations become infrequent.

More and more of the former serfs are leaving Angelkov—not only because emancipation has freed them from any legal obligation or responsibility to their former owner, but because their former owner has gone mad. The last of the rubles in the strongbox have run out and Antonina cannot pay them anything. Most would rather try to create new lives for themselves than live on in the disturbing atmosphere of Angelkov.

As each comes to Antonina to say he or she is leaving, Antonina says goodbye and thanks them for their faithful service. She gives them each a small gift: for the girls and women, one of her own pretty shawls or a tortoiseshell comb or bottle of scent; for the men, something of Konstantin's, a pair of monogrammed handkerchiefs or a linen shirt.

She makes the sign of the cross on their foreheads. Some of the women cry, and she holds their hands for a moment, trying to smile, wishing them well.

The house feels larger, emptier and quieter except for Konstantin's sporadic outbursts. In the evening, when the air stills, Antonina can hear the distant sound of the peasants labouring in the fields: their calls and whistles, the steady rhythm of the scythes. The sky is light until quite late, and they work until darkness falls.

Those who remain at Angelkov—the ones who have decided they would rather work for a roof over their heads and the surety of meals—struggle to bring in the garden harvest. Raisa reports to Antonina that they may not get it all in before the first frost. She doesn't have enough help with the kitchen work: salting the cucumbers and putting them into huge brine-filled crocks; picking fruits from the orchard to make jams and compotes or to preserve as conserves; digging up potatoes and other root vegetables and putting them in sacks to be stored in bins in the cool, dark root cellars; curing pork and sides of beef; drying mushrooms—all the work necessary to stock the manor for the winter. Raisa is a tall, solid woman with thick arms and strong hands. She is usually cheerful. Now her face is constantly creased with worry.

As Angelkov starts to crumble without the hundreds of hands needed to keep it running effectively, Antonina hears that the serfs outside the estate are gaining power.

The world she knows is dying. She has no choice but to find a new way to live.

Life has also changed for Lilya.

She and Lyosha are working side by side in the garden, digging out the last turnips. Regardless of their former duties, whoever is available carries out the necessary jobs.

"Lilya," Lyosha says as they both straighten to take a drink of water, "what do you suppose will happen?"

"What do you mean?"

"How long can the count and countess remain at Angelkov?" He gestures towards the manor. "Without enough staff to care for it, soon it will fall into disrepair, and then ruin. They must be making a plan to leave, to go live somewhere else."

Lilya studies him. "The countess hasn't spoken of it to me. As for the count . . ." She shrugs. "He's as useless as dead. Why? Do you know something?"

"No," he says, but Lilya sees his discomfort.

"The countess will find a way to hire back some of the servants, even if it takes time," she says. "Things will be as they once were." Not quite. Not without Misha. Not with the count as he is. But she and Antonina will work together to recreate what they can of the former life at Angelkov. The two of them, together.

Lyosha runs his palm over the handle of the spade, shaking his head. "Things can never be the same, Lilya. You know that."

"They will," Lilya insists. "With you here, as always, and me—"

Lyosha interrupts her. "I plan to marry, sister."

Lilya drops her spade and looks at him, her mouth open. She gives a hoarse croak, as if trying to laugh. Her face is bathed in sweat in the warm fall air. "Marry? Who would *you* marry? What are you talking about?"

"I'm going to marry Anya Fomovna."

Lilya blinks, thinking. "Anya Fomovna?" Not the whey-faced girl from the village? Her?

"Yes."

"Stop speaking nonsense. She's not good enough for you."

Lyosha knew his sister wouldn't take his announcement well, and wasn't looking forward to telling her. He'd been waiting for the last few weeks to find the right time, and finally realized there would be no right time. "Don't speak of her like that," he says. "You don't know her at all."

"I know she's a peasant. I didn't raise you to marry a peasant." Lilya's voice is louder, angry.

"What do you mean? *We're* peasants, Lilya. Who do you expect me to marry?"

Lilya's voice drops, the anger gone as quickly as it had flared up. "I just . . . I haven't thought of you marrying."

"You still think of me as your little brother, but I'm coming twenty. It's time for me to start my own life, my own family."

At that, Lilya grabs hold of him. "I'm your family. *Me*, Lyosha."

Lyosha takes her hands and smiles. "We'll always be family, Lilya. You're my sister, and you know how grateful I am to you. But it's time for me to have a wife. You have Soso. He'll surely send for you soon, won't he?"

Lilya stares back at him. "Soso? Good riddance to him. But . . . have you already set a date? Has the wedding been arranged behind my back?"

Lyosha lets go of her hands. "You won't go to your husband when he's ready for you?"

"I hope never to see that pig again. This is my home. The countess needs me. But I asked you—is the wedding arranged?"

"No. But I've been to visit Anya at her family's izba many times over the last year, and she's happy to have me as a husband, Lilya. I've also spoken to her father about marrying her. All I ask from you now is your blessing, and then I'll speak to the countess, and ask for her permission that Anya come and live with me in the married servants' quarters. Perhaps she can help Raisa in the kitchen for the next little while."

"What do you mean—the next little while?"

"Until we leave."

Lilya swallows. "Leave Angelkov? To go where?"

"We'll go with Grisha."

"Grisha?" Lilya knows she is echoing her brother, but such is her surprise—perhaps shock—that she's having trouble keeping up.

"He's going to have his own place, and I'll be his steward."

"Grisha, a landowner? And how will this happen?"

"He already owns land," Lyosha says calmly. He has no reason not to tell his sister these facts. Grisha has spoken to him about this since February and the announcement of the emancipation.

Lilya's mind races. "He owns land? Where?"

"He bought a small parcel from Prince Bakanev."

"How could he do this?"

"Lilya, you know that Grigori Sergeyevich has worked for the count for many years in a salaried position. He has no wife, no family—he saved what he earned."

Lilya takes Lyosha's hands in her own. "Don't do anything yet, little brother. Please, I beg of you. Don't speak to the countess, and don't talk any more of leaving. Not yet."

Lyosha sees panic in her face, hears it in her voice. And there's something else, something troubling. She's too desperate, her grip on his hands fierce and possessive. He feels sorrow for her. She's been working too hard, he thinks.

Antonina has managed to not fall back into the deep blackness of the first few months after Mikhail disappeared. She never stops thinking about him, but now it's with numbness. She won't believe he's dead, even though there's been no more word from him, no further visit from Lev.

It's also as though she's a widow. Konstantin grows ever more confused, lurching about the dark house at night, his empty nightshirt sleeve swinging. Occasionally she opens her eyes and sees him standing beside her bed, looking down at her. The first time this happened, she cried out, and Pavel came running and led the old man back to his bedroom. The next times it happened, she simply told her husband to go away, and he did.

She has seen Pavel feeding him from a spoon, as if he were a small, weak child. He still needs the chloroform tincture, Pavel insists, although she wonders that he has pain after four months.

Antonina gets through every day as best she can. Because Angelkov now needs her help in a way it didn't when there were serfs—sometimes too many—to do every job, she has something she has never before known: a sense of purpose.

And as long as she has enough vodka, she manages two or three hours of sleep a night, and can carry on.

Antonina receives an invitation to a musical evening at the home of Prince and Princess Bakanev. She plans to decline. They will understand. It's only been five months. To Antonina if feels like five years. She can't remember exactly what her life felt like before, although she can recall so much happiness with Mikhail: hearing the stories he read aloud in both Russian and French, his excitement as he talked of his zoology lessons and the wonderful animals he had discovered on all the continents, his growing understanding of the earth through his geography lessons, his attempts at art with his tutor, and always, always, listening to him play the piano.

There is Lilya to talk to, but Antonina has begun to find her old friend a little tedious. Try as she might, she has not been able to persuade Lilya to go to her own room in the servants' quarters at night. Lilya likes sitting quietly by the fire in Antonina's bedroom, making intricate lace. At Antonina's urging, she learned to read and write when Misha was a baby, although she undertook both slowly and haltingly. Occasionally she reads the Psalter.

She could be a quiet comfort to Antonina, yes, but Antonina doesn't like the way she has to tell Lilya when she wishes to be alone. She doesn't like Lilya's faint but distinct look of betrayal, as if Antonina should never forget what happened so long ago on the Olonov estate.

There is nothing left of that former life. Her father died of heart disease two years after Mikhail's birth, and the estate was sold. Antonina's mother moved to Paris with a French lover shortly afterwards. She wrote infrequently to Antonina, and then the letters stopped altogether; she doesn't know if her mother is still alive. Viktor died after suffering a debilitating injury at the battle of Alma in the Crimean, and her youngest brother, Dimitri, from what she could find out, had disappeared into a haze of alcohol and a life of debauchery. The middle brother, Marik, still lives on his own small estate in northern Pskov with his wife and four children, but he and Konstantin argued a number of years ago at a family celebration. Neither would apologize, and Marik has broken ties with his brother-in-law—and his sister too.

In spite of the loss of her family—or perhaps because of it—before her son was stolen from her, Antonina knew she was fortunate to have her own home, a husband and a child, and berated herself for not being thankful enough. She could fill her hours with the usual pursuits of women of her class: there were endless reasons to visit other estates and stay for a few days or weeks, there was adult company she could invite to Angelkov for afternoons of walks through the gardens, of boating in the summer and troika rides over the shimmering snow in the winter. There could be evenings of whist and musical recitals. But being with crowds of people had never appealed to Antonina. Although she recognized that she had usually been content on her own, or with Misha, she felt a nagging sense of disquiet, as if life was passing by. That she was being swept along in the current, with no real sense of direction or power, looking for something to hold on to. Or perhaps someone.

⁂

Lilya encourages Antonina to accept the Bakanevs' invitation. "You haven't been to a social function since . . ." She pauses. ". . . for some time. Perhaps it would help you to see old friends."

Antonina studies the vanilla-coloured card that has been

delivered to her by Pavel. She is sitting at the piano. "Friends?" she says, looking at Lilya. "They're not my friends. They're Konstantin's friends."

"Still, Tosya," Lilya says, "wouldn't it be lovely to dress in one of your gowns—perhaps the maroon silk? You look so beautiful in it."

Antonina takes another drink of vodka before playing an arpeggio. Her fingers trip on the keys, the arpeggio ruined. She tries it again, then starts a Haydn sonata rondo instead. She thinks of the crush of bodies clad in satin and silk and velvet in an overheated room, bright with candelabras and smoking oil lamps. Of the smell of perfume and cigars. The faces gazing at her with pity, the sighs, the pressing of her hand in sympathy. And then the well-meaning people will turn away from her, relieved to have done their duty with the poor thing, free to go on to their glasses of champagne, the silver trays of hors d'oeuvres of sturgeon and caviar, the anticipation of the music recital.

Then Antonina thinks of the long evening ahead of her at Angelkov. She'll have her light dinner and retire to her bedroom. She will have to tell Lilya she prefers to be alone. She'll read, sipping from her glass until her eyes burn and the vodka has made her drowsy, and then she'll pray for sleep, pray for relief from nightmares about Mikhail.

She doesn't want to think of it anymore. The Haydn doesn't feel right. She stops, and begins Chopin's Prelude in B Minor. After the first ten bars she can't bear it, remembering the pleasure it always brought her to listen to beautiful music, the musical evenings she has loved.

She reaches for her glass but knocks it over. Fortunately, the vodka runs down the side of the piano and not onto the keys. "I'll get Nusha to clean it up," Lilya says, picking up the empty glass.

Antonina looks down at the keys. She knows that what Lilya has said is true: she's alone too much. She needs to get away from Angelkov, away from Konstantin and his distressing behaviour, away from the mindless glasses of vodka.

"Perhaps I'll go after all, Lilya," Antonina calls out. "Not the maroon silk. Take out my black taffeta."

22

*W*ithin the first few minutes in the Bakanevs' drawing room, Antonina knows that it's a mistake to be away from Angelkov.

She has never fit in at such parties, never knowing what to talk about apart from answering questions about her husband or recounting the antics of her son. Now, as she joins each small knot of men and women, it's painfully clear that nobody will mention Konstantin or Mikhail. Evenings of this sort are not the place to bring up such unpleasant topics.

So she smiles and nods, accepting, with as much grace as possible, the comments from all those who tell her that they are glad to see her. She's looking well, she hears over and over, although she knows this isn't true. She is self-conscious in her black taffeta, the black feathers in her hair. She has dressed as if she is really a widow—another mistake.

She answers simple questions about the estate, the flight of the serfs, and agrees about the relief of the fall's coolness after the heat of summer.

She drinks the glasses of champagne she's offered, although she declines the food. Throughout the musical performance she stands at the back of the room. She enjoys the music, watching the eight men without seeing them: they are like a flock of moving black birds making beautiful sounds. But at the end of their last set, when the pianist plays the first chords of Glinka's Separation in F Minor, she feels as though she's been thrown into a pond of icy water.

She sees Mikhail, clutching his little composition booklet as he runs after his father.

Setting down her glass with a shaking hand, she stares at the violinist. She is once more in her father's home, listening to Valentin Vladimirovitch accompany the pianist after he had made love to her mother.

<hr/>

He knows he last saw the woman in black at one of the grand estates that dot the countryside of northern Pskov. When Valentin had been owned by the wealthy Prince Sergius Denisovich Yablonsky, the prince dictated when, what and to whom his carefully chosen orchestra would play. To the audiences in the various opulent salons and ballrooms, the serf orchestra was an evening's pleasant entertainment. To Valentin, it was his life: the soaring freedom of the music combined with the imprisonment of being owned by Yablonsky.

Now, all that is changed. He's a free man, and can choose where he wishes to play, with whom and for whom. Yes, everything in Russia has changed since the emancipation.

And she—the woman—is changed as well. Her face is thinner, almost translucent in its paleness, and there's something about the eyes . . . She looks older, Valentin decides, but not older in the natural way of the passage of time, of the— what is it, a decade or more? since he saw her. No, this is something deeper. He's seen this look before, although not usually on the faces of nobility. He's seen it on the faces of the peasants, those who were so recently serfs, those whose lives have been altered without their control. So something has happened to her, something more than time. All in black, she's a dark shadow in this room of vibrant colour, though the gown sets off her pale skin so that her neck and hands glow.

Valentin shifts his gaze in her direction for brief seconds as the orchestra members lift their instruments and begin. He lowers his bow as the viola picks up and carries the melody, and stares openly at her, finally remembering. It was at the Olonov estate, her name day fete; she stood at the back of the room. It's the same today: she stays back, unlike the other women, who politely fight their way for the best seats in the first rows.

At her own celebration, she'd appeared uninterested while the orchestra played, staring at the baroque border around the high ceiling as if intrigued with the detail of the sumptuous room. And yet he also recalls the occasional movement of her eyebrows, the way her head moved like an animal's that hears an unexpected sound nearby. It had given her away. Unlike the cool, detached exterior she displayed, she was listening with the utmost concentration. He knows music—he has known music all his life—and he recognizes those who also know it. The other young women in their rustling gowns had gazed at the players in front of them with languorous expressions. They kept their heads tilted sweetly to one side, lips wet, slightly parted, as if waiting to hear their names whispered by the strings of the violins and cellos, or blown softly from the mouthpieces of the wind instruments. They thought only of themselves; they weren't part of the music. It didn't enter their blood, rushing through them to create the sensation of a sudden, dizzying fever, too hot and then too cold.

Now, Valentin looks at the woman at the back of the room, trying to remember what he had seen on her face so long ago. Valentin loves women—all women—and has a wonderful memory for them. He has slept with too many to count, but he remembers details about each.

This one he hadn't made love to, but . . . Ah. It had been her mother, the Princess Olonova. The daughter . . . what did he remember about her? There was longing on her face, but not the longing of the beautiful, shallow *devushkas*. Hers wasn't the need for flirtation and an enviable marriage; hers was for something entirely different. There had been no guile there, in spite of the intelligence in her eyes. Were they blue or green? Possibly grey? They were a changeable, irregular colour, which he sensed would shift from one shade to another, depending on whether viewed in candlelight or sunlight, whether she was excited or weary or sad. He had seen eyes like hers before, although only once, in the face of an old woman. He didn't know if she was his grandmother or his *nyanya* or simply a stranger who had cared for him at some point in his childhood. Like so many of his memories from his earliest days, the old woman was like something from a dream.

The last time he had seen this woman, she had, finally,

stared into his eyes as he played, and while he knew he should feel shame for how she had seen him with her mother, he didn't. After that final evening, when they had spoken—he does remember speaking to her—Valentin had lain on a narrow cot in the dank room he shared with the first flautist and the cellist in the servants' quarters, and thought of her.

He liked having a woman to think of when he played. It filled him with desire as he leaned his jaw more deeply onto his violin and shut his eyes. He would feel the desire come through in his playing. The hunger created a passion that ran down his arms and into his fingers and onto the bow. And then it—the bow—slid smoothly, as if slick with lust, over the strings. His blood ran warm through his veins, along his limbs and into his groin, and he grew aroused as he played, but it was an arousal of the emotions, not the body. As he played, thinking of a particular woman, it was as if his heart grew larger, firmer, pulsing as it waited for . . . for what? Fulfillment? Some sort of release? Release from what was never clear to him. Sometimes his closed eyes burned with a yearning for what he didn't recognize.

He had known he would think of her, the Olonova princess. And he did, for the next few weeks, as he closed his eyes and played for rooms of strangers, although she had never again been in the audience.

And after all this time, here she is. What was her name? It was a beautiful name, something elegant, but he can't remember.

Valentin is weary. He travelled for three days in a drafty *britchka* from St. Petersburg to the small capital city of Pskov, where he played with a group at the afternoon birthday celebration of a baroness. Then he had spent another three hours getting here—the home of Prince and Princess Bakanev. He only had time to eat a bowl of fish soup with a piece of dark bread and gulp some bitter, lukewarm tea in the kitchen of the servants' quarters before the two-hour rehearsal, leaving time to change into his evening clothes. The soiree began at eight. Now it was after midnight. Tomorrow, though, he would take up a new position in the household of the prince and princess: he would be music instructor to their two nieces, who were visiting with their parents from Smolensk until at least the New Year.

Is his life much different as a free man than it had been as a serf musician? When the emancipation was announced, Prince Yablonsky had allowed his musicians to take their instruments and musical scores as he dismissed them. Others were not as lucky; many had to leave their beloved instruments and precious scores behind when they were set free from their former owners.

In St. Petersburg, it is easier for Valentin than for some: he has the patronage of Madame Golitsyna, a wealthy émigré from France who had been married to a Russian count. The widow—older than Valentin by twelve years—has taken him under her wing. In exchange for his company and certain favours, she allows him to stay with her when he is in the city, and buys him the clothing he needs for performing.

Valentin learned young—during his first year in Yablonsky's orchestra, when he was fifteen—that he had something to offer to women. That he could use that gift to get some of what he wanted from life. Since the first gloriously dressed and scented woman took him to a curtained carriage after a performance and showed him how to please her, giving him a small purse of rubles afterwards, Valentin has used his charm. It made his life as a serf musician more interesting, and the occasional payments in the form of rubles or a fine piece of clothing or expensive cigars allowed him a more pleasurable existence.

Now a free man, Valentin plays when he can at soirees in St. Petersburg, but when work is scarce, he has to take country jobs. These mean uncomfortable travel and longer hours—all without the comfort of coming home to a warm meal and a warm bed with Madame Golitsyna.

Yes, he is now paid for his work, but it's a pittance.

Nevertheless, he kneels every morning and evening and thanks God that he is a young man in this auspicious time. Now he answers to no one, and no longer lives in fear that his violin will be taken from him on a whim by Prince Yablonsky. He doesn't have to worry that he will be sent to the fields, never again to feel the satin of the chin rest, the lightness of the bow.

Yes, Valentin Vladimirovitch is grateful to God and Tsar Alexander II, but he now has to live entirely by his wits. He is always watching for the next opportunity—or for the next woman—to create a better life for himself.

Tonight, Valentin sees that the woman who was a girl on the Olonov estate comes in after the orchestra has warmed up. She slides into the back of the music salon lightly, as if her bones are porous and fragile, just at the moment when the pianist lifts his fingers over the keys and bows hover over strings. She moves like a feather falling from the breast of a mourning dove. He knows that when she walks, her footsteps make no sound. After all, hadn't she entered her mother's bedroom so noiselessly that her presence startled him?

As before, she doesn't sit but stands, her hands clasped in front of her black taffeta waist as though at any moment she might lift them in prayer. She fixes her gaze on the ornate fringed draperies over the windows, and she stays like this, unmoving but for her eyebrows. He remembers that she requested the orchestra play Separation in F Minor. He can always recall a woman, and a piece of music.

He'll have the orchestra play it for her again tonight, and maybe she'll look at him and recognize him. He wants her to know that he remembers her.

He leans over and sends the message to the rest of the orchestra that they will play the Glinka nocturne as the final number.

"Shall we announce the change in program to the audience?" the pianist asks him.

Valentin shakes his head. He doesn't care if the audience is displeased. He only cares about getting the attention of the Olonova woman, or whatever her name is now: she would have been married for years. Then again, her black attire suggests that she's a widow.

He lifts his bow and waits for the pianist to begin. He watches the woman as the sweet notes of the nocturne build, and when he touches his bow to the strings, she blinks—no, perhaps more of a flinch—then looks straight at him. He feels a surge of pleasure. In the next instant, though, he realizes that it's as if she doesn't see him. Her eyes shine, glittering and too bright. He can see the green even from this distance. But there's no recognition on her face.

In its place is something close to anguish. The song builds slowly, waves of fine notes, the strings of his violin trembling, tense, and her face reflects the poignancy of the music. And then she is gone. She leaves the salon as the last, lingering notes are played.

Antonina wants to go home. She realized it was him, although not until the Glinka piece started. But she doesn't want to speak to anyone; she feels as though she's coming undone. She rushes out into the wide hallway of the Bakanevs' palatial home, looking around for . . . for what? She can't breathe.

A servant sees her running by, one hand to her throat, and comes to her aid. He takes her to the cloakroom, although Antonina can't initially remember what she had worn. When she finally points to the black velvet cape, she asks the servant to summon her barouche. All of this takes an interminable length of time. She goes out onto the veranda, to breathe in the fresh autumn air and cool her burning face.

Setting his violin in its case, Valentin hurries out of the salon, smiling graciously, trying to sidestep those who wish to shake his hand or thank him for a pleasing performance. He doesn't really expect to see the Olonova woman; she had been visibly upset, and has probably left by now. He goes to the veranda to smoke a cigarette. Other men are there, smoking and talking quietly.

And she is there as well.

"Excuse me," he says, stepping up to her and bowing. "We've met. A number of years ago. Your name day celebration, I believe. Madame . . . ?" He waits for her to introduce herself.

"Countess Mitlovskiya," she says, extending her hand. "Yes. I recognized you. I'm sorry—I don't know your surname. But it's Valentin Vladimirovitch, isn't it."

He smiles, bright and pleased, as he lifts his lips from her gloved hand. "What a memory," he says. He's forgotten about the score he'd given her, inscribed with his name.

She puts her hand back at her side. "The playing was beautiful. It's a favourite of mine, Separation in F Minor."

"I know," he says, and Antonina blinks, confused, and fusses with the handle of her small evening bag. Does he remember that night as she does, then?

"I'm waiting for my barouche," she says.

"You live nearby, I assume, if you're not staying the night."

"Yes."

"Ah," he says. She is definitely not forthcoming. "Well, perhaps we will see each other again, then, when you call with your husband. I'll be staying here for the next few months, teaching music to Princess Bakanev's young nieces."

Antonina hears the question in his voice as he says *your husband*, and runs her hand down the full black taffeta skirt. "We don't visit much. My husband is ill."

"I'm sorry."

"Thank you. Oh, here's my carriage. It was very good to see you again," she says, as a barouche with gleaming brass lamps, drawn by two fine dancing Arabians, pulls up to the front of the house. "As I've said, you play as beautifully as before. No, more beautifully, I'm sure," she adds. "Goodbye, Mr. . . ."

"Kropotkin."

"Mr. Kropotkin," she echoes, and then turns and goes down the steps.

He leans over the railing, watching as the driver climbs down and puts out his arm. He's tall, with black, wind-blown, wavy hair, and dressed informally. The woman puts her hand on his arm as he opens the door and helps her inside the barouche. There's something odd about the situation: the man acts too familiar to be a footman.

Valentin turns to one of the guests smoking a cigar near-by. "Excuse me," he says, "but that woman . . . Countess Mitlovskiya . . . do you know her?"

The man takes the cigar from his mouth, emitting a fra-grant stream of smoke from between his lips. "We haven't seen her out for some time. Her husband is very ill. A brain malady now, I've heard. Sad story, the Mitlovskys. Victims of the unrest: the son disappeared in some unresolved crime, and the husband lost his arm. The estate's in a bad way, apparently." The man stops, aware that he has said too much to the musician. He blames the many glasses of champagne. "She lives on the next estate," he says, making it clear the conversation is over. "Angelkov."

23

*T*he next morning, Antonina lies in bed, thinking of the strangeness of seeing Valentin Kropotkin at the Bakanevs'.

Misha had been playing Glinka's nocturne the last time she saw him, and although she's played it many times herself since then, to hear it fully emerge so beautifully from the small orchestra was overwhelming.

It's been over twelve years since she saw the violinist making love to her mother. She doesn't remember the last time she envisioned it—surely many, many years ago. Those fantasies are gone now; in her grief and worry over Misha, her body is more of a burden than anything. It has to stay strong only so that she can run the estate and keep the search for her son alive, somehow.

After Mikhail was born, Konstantin came to her infrequently, perhaps once every few months. She had wanted another child—children, in fact, after she had experienced the deep joy Mikhail brought—but once he had his son, Konstantin appeared uninterested in that part of their marriage. She had not needed to imagine the violinist's embrace to withstand her husband's touch; he didn't touch her.

She has known about Tania for a long time. Walking past Konstantin's bedroom one afternoon a few months after Misha's birth, she had seen him whispering in the laundress's ear, his hand possessively on her waist. She immediately found Lilya and asked her if the count bothered her, or any of the other younger female servants. Lilya had firmly told her no. "It's only Tania, then?" Antonina said, and Lilya nodded.

Antonina doesn't care. In fact, she feels sorry for the laundress. She is old, almost Konstantin's age, her auburn hair threaded with grey and her eyes hooded. Passing the huge laundry room, Antonina has seen her stirring the vats of boiling water and bleach, her face wet with steam and her shoulders rounded. When she occasionally came face to face with Tania as the woman carried a stack of ironed sheets down the hallway, Antonina saw only weariness. How can she blame the woman for what she is forced to do?

Still, there were times when Antonina grew lonely enough to go to Konstantin's bedroom. Usually he reacted as though she were behaving in a wanton fashion by coming to him instead of waiting for him to come to her, and refused her.

In the last three years, they hadn't come together at all. Even when she told him that all she wanted was company, to feel his arms around her as she fell asleep, he wasn't interested.

The decanters of wine and bottles of vodka helped, as they had helped her through many times of her life.

Now she cannot rely on Konstantin for anything. The last times she tried to question him on their financial situation, all he would repeat was that the servants had stolen everything.

After Lilya has helped her dress and done her hair, she writes a letter to Konstantin's lawyer, Yakovlev, in Pskov, asking him to come to the estate. She needs money. As she sends Lyosha off with the letter, she finds herself thinking of the taste of mushrooms, freshly picked, and made into a soup with potatoes. Since the spring she hasn't thought about what she puts into her mouth, just chewed and swallowed without tasting. But on this day she has a desire for mushroom and potato soup.

She goes to the kitchen to ask Raisa to prepare the soup for dinner. Raisa shakes her head, telling her there are no mushrooms.

"But it's September. The woods are full of them."

The older woman nods, bowing slightly. "Yes, countess. But there is no one to fetch them. We are all doing the jobs of three or four."

Antonina looks at her. "I understand. Thank you, Raisa. Do you have a basket?"

"A basket, madam?"

"I'll go and pick them. I did it as a child."

Raisa looks at Antonina's feet as she hands her a woven willow basket and a small, sharp knife. Antonina follows the woman's gaze to her pink silk slippers.

"My boots are under the bench," Raisa says, and then

crosses herself. "I beg your pardon, countess—I know they're old and cracked, but you'll ruin your slippers and hurt your feet."

Antonina sees that the boots will be too big. She could go to the outer room where her riding clothes are kept and put on a pair of fine leather boots, but their heels would make it difficult to walk in the forest. Instead, she smiles her thanks at Raisa. She puts on the woman's boots. As she walks across the yard, they rub the backs of her heels through her thin stockings, and she knows she'll have blisters.

Grisha is on his way to the stable.

"Thank you for driving me to the Bakanevs' last night," she says to him as she walks beside him. She hadn't spoken as he helped her out of the barouche when they arrived back at Angelkov, just run up the veranda steps, dropping her gloves. Grisha had called to her, picking them up and giving them to her. He saw she had been crying.

"But it appears you did not enjoy yourself," he says now, glancing at her basket and knife.

"For mushrooms," she says. "The Bakanevs were very hospitable. But I felt out of place." She stops.

Grisha stops as well. He appears distracted, brushing his hair back over his ears with his fingers time after time. His hair is very thick, and doesn't stay in place. Antonina thinks of brushing back her son's hair from his forehead.

"And still nothing from the man Lev? He took the money and simply disappeared?"

Antonina has asked Grisha this so many times, but she must ask again.

Grisha clears his throat. "You know I continue to do what I can to find your son."

She closes her eyes for a moment, and Grisha berates himself.

He had watched Antonina fall into her state of grieving when the initial planned retrieval of the boy was ruined, and then the situation grew worse daily. After questioning Soso the first time, Grisha had gone to the storeroom to challenge him again, a week later. But Soso was gone. When he asked Lilya about him, she shrugged and told him that he had decided to leave the estate; he was a free man now, wasn't he?

"He told me he would send word when he was settled somewhere, but I doubt that he will." She shrugged a second time, her lips pursed, making it clear to Grisha that she really didn't care.

Grisha had studied her expression. He was very sure she knew nothing about Mikhail's disappearance. Soso had said he wouldn't tell her, and Grisha knew he was right; she was too close to the countess. "You really have no idea where he is?"

"I told you, no. Why do you care?"

Grisha didn't answer, walking away. Lilya was his only thread to Soso, who in turn was his only connection to Mikhail. Lev had disappeared. Grisha had Fyodor and Lyosha follow him the day the man had come to the estate with the letter from Misha, demanding more ransom money. They had watched the village hut he went to, all night, but in the morning discovered he had somehow disappeared.

Grisha had already been to all the villages, looking for Soso. He again searched, this time for Lev, but with no luck. Although he sometimes feared that they'd killed the child and left the province, he also knew the depth of their greed. He told himself they would keep the child as long as they believed they could extort more money.

He had trouble being around Countess Mitlovskiya, and slept little, thinking of it all: the count's worsening health, the countess a ruin, Mikhail's face in the clearing.

He had suffered his own silent remorse until today. Upon awakening, he found a note under his door. He was to bring the second payment to an izba in Tushinsk the next afternoon. Mikhail Konstantinovich would be waiting.

He looks at Antonina in the scuffed servant's boots, the basket on her arm. "I believe today will be a good day, countess," he finally says, wanting to tell her the news but knowing he mustn't, not until he has the boy.

"Will it, Grisha? Will it?"

He smiles, nodding at her basket and knife. "You will have fresh mushrooms."

One side of her mouth lifts in a wry smile. "Yes," she agrees. "I will have fresh mushrooms."

Grisha reaches up one more time, trying to tame his hair.

In the forest, Antonina smells the wet, musty odour of the fallen leaves and remembers the pleasure she had as a child, hunting for mushrooms with one of her brothers or her governess.

She picks her way through swampy thickets, looking for the tiny curve of a cap in the midst of the leaf litter and broken branches and moss that cover the ground. When she spots one, she bends, scraping away damp earth with her fingers, cutting the mushrooms: orange milk mushrooms and perfect red saffron milk caps. From time to time she finds the special *veshenka* mushrooms growing on the base of a tree.

When she returns to the house a few hours later, her basket full, the front door is locked. They no longer have a footman at Angelkov, standing in the vestibule to attend to the door, to usher in guests, accept calling cards, and take wraps and coats. There are no visitors anyway.

She goes around the house and enters the kitchen through the servants' entrance. She leaves the basket of mushrooms on the table. Raisa isn't there, but a large vat of water bubbles on the stove, and there are potatoes cut on a board.

Walking and kneeling and digging have tired her out; she is unused to exercise now. She doesn't even have the energy to unhook and pull off the boots in the hot kitchen. As she slowly climbs the winding staircase, she notices the layer of dust on the edges of each step, as well as a rip in the thick Persian runner. The brass rail of the banister is turning green. There simply aren't enough servants to look after the house. Olga has stayed, although Antonina has recently noticed that Lilya now wears the housekeeper's ring of keys on her belt. She hasn't asked her when this happened, or why.

In her bedroom, Antonina sits in the tufted armchair near the dead fireplace and laboriously unhooks the boots. She kicks them off, leaving them where they drop. Her stockings are stuck to her heels with spots of blood where the skin has been rubbed raw. She lies down, staring at the ceiling. There's no air in the room; it's sultry and smells stale. Everything is as she left it: the bed a rumpled mess, the towel thrown beside the basin of now scummy water, her night-dress on the floor beside the wardrobe.

She gets up and opens the window. The air outside is warmer than in the room—probably the last real heat of fall. She drinks a few mouthfuls of vodka from the flask in her wardrobe and again lies down on the unmade bed. She studies her fingernails: they're broken and rimmed with dirt from picking the mushrooms. One fly then another have come into the bedroom through the open window, and buzz angrily in the hot, still air. After a while she turns onto her side, closing her eyes, hoping for a few moments of sleep. She puts her hand under the lace pillow. She spreads her fingers, savouring that tiny bit of cooler linen. The tip of one finger touches the little velvet bag she keeps there.

She pulls out the bag and opens it, taking out the cherub that fell to her from the church ceiling back in June. She runs her dirty fingers gently over the small gilded body, the wings and tiny feet. Grisha had expertly glued the wing back on; the seam is almost invisible.

Through the long, hot summer, she has kept her hope alive for Mikhail. She goes to the church every day and prays for at least an hour, although never again has she had a vision or received a sign.

There's low thunder in the distance now. Antonina closes both hands around the cherub and presses it to her chest, closing her eyes.

The air changes overnight. The next day is crisp and fresh, although the sun still shines.

Antonina is on the front veranda in the afternoon, looking at the crows in the pines and noticing that the birches have suddenly turned, their yellow leaves twirling on their stems in the slight breeze. She doesn't want to be inside: even though Pavel is attempting to soothe him with the chloroform, Konstantin is shouting.

She sees Grisha mounting his horse, and she calls to him. "Where do you go, Grisha?"

"I have business in Tushinsk." The sun is glinting off his hair. Antonina notices the depth of colour, so black it shines blue in the sunlight.

"Could you wait, please? I'll ride with you." As soon as the words are out of her mouth, Antonina realizes how much she wants to ride. She went out on Dunia just once all summer, and only rode for half an hour. There seemed to be no reason for an aimless ride. But now she wants to be away from Konstantin and the sad decay of the estate.

"Countess, as I said, I have business. I'll ride at top speed, and then turn around and come straight back. It's not meant to be a pleasure ride."

"I will accompany you at any rate," Antonina says, starting back up the steps. "I'll change into my riding clothes, and be back in ten minutes."

"I'd rather you didn't . . ." Grisha's words trail off. He curses under his breath.

He doesn't know how to refuse her.

⹂

"I've heard from the lawyer Yakovlev," Antonina tells Grisha as they ride side by side at a leisurely pace down the wide drive that runs from the house to the main road. "He'll bring all of Konstantin's papers from Pskov in two days, and review them with me. I must find out how to collect Konstantin's funds."

"This is good, madam," Grisha says, and with that Antonina remembers that Grisha needs to be paid. She knows Konstantin paid Grisha his salary every four months; she hasn't given him anything since Mikhail was taken.

"Would you like me to speak to him as well?" Grisha asks. "I often had dealings with him and the count."

"You may be present. Your input will be valuable to me. I have given you too much responsibility. It isn't fair that I've leaned so heavily on you without . . ." She stares straight ahead as she speaks to Grisha. "I know you are past due your salary."

"I am honoured by your trust, madam," is all he says.

"You've been so understanding since the spring. But I'm finding my strength again, and will now take charge. Konstantin Nikolevich, as you know, is unable to be of any use in these matters. In any matters."

Grisha doesn't comment.

"Does your silence mean you think me incapable, Grisha?" Antonina asks, turning slightly in her saddle so she can look into his face. "I can learn. You can be assured that I'll learn how to run the estate."

Grisha nods. "I have no doubt you will understand the financial aspects, once you have ample time to study them. But are you aware, madam, of how many of the serfs have left the estate?"

Antonina looks over at him again. "I do know that many are gone, but they won't all go." She says this with forced confidence.

"The house serfs usually return to family," Grisha goes on. "Those on the land, the former serfs in the villages, are organizing *mirs* now, madam—a form of collective farming. The community will own the land, but individual families will create their own harvests. Everyone works for the good of the community—this is the new law. You will be forced to sell much of your land to them, the former serfs, so that they can farm it in this manner. They'll work it and all share in the profit. As they once gave you their shares, now they'll divide those shares evenly."

Antonina is silent for a moment. Her father and then Konstantin had been completely against the emancipation manifesto. Giving the peasants freedom, they ranted, would leave the landowners without the huge, cheap labour force they needed to maintain their estates. She realizes now that she hasn't asked enough questions; she can hold no one responsible for her lack of knowledge. She had always hated the way she saw her father and husband treat serfs, and had thought no further.

"Wait," she says. "The new law is that I *must* sell my land to them? But . . . is it not my choice?"

"Well, yes, it's partly a choice, but the government will charge you such high taxes for your land that it's unlikely you'll be able to sustain it. Without the peasants, it will be of no use to you anyway. You can't receive the yearly taxes the serfs had to pay you, and with no one to work it, there won't be any harvest to feed yourself and all those you must continue to feed at the estate."

"I'll sell some tracts of my land to them, then. And with the payments I receive, I can continue to run Angelkov, and feed and clothe everyone I'm responsible for, as before," she states.

Grisha utters a sharp laugh that rings in the still autumn air. "That's what the Tsar envisioned."

"What do you mean?"

Grisha pulls his horse to a stop, and Antonina turns Dunia to face him. The horses snicker gently at each other, their noses touching. "Countess Mitlovskiya. Where do you suppose the former serfs will find money to purchase land?"

"Where, Grisha?"

Grisha, for the first time, shows annoyance with her. "They *have* no money, countess." His voice is harsh. "Surely you know this. They have nothing but the rags on their backs. Even the leaking roofs over their heads are not their own. There will be no payment to you—or to any landowners. Not now. There will be forms distributed. Each former soul will put his mark where he is directed. The form ties him to future payment. But he will never be able to pay off the land. Ever. He will never save enough money. And so he will live in the same way as always, except now he works for the good of his village, and not for the good of the landowner."

Antonina cannot meet Grisha's insistent stare. Instead, she looks over his shoulder at a flock of grey-brown curlews with their slender, down-curved bills, making their way south. "So in essence, I receive nothing. I simply lose my serfs and my land."

"Yes, madam," Grisha says. "This is what you face. It's been such for many months."

"Surely Konstantin provided . . ." she says, and then stops. "Yakovlev will tell me what funds I will have. What about you, Grisha? You've always been a free man." As she speaks, she imagines him leaving for the first time. She can't envision Angelkov without him. She can't imagine her life without Grisha in it.

Grisha's face becomes hard, unreadable. "I am not a concern of yours, Countess Mitlovskiya. I have always seen to my best interests."

Something about the way he states the last three words— *my best interests*—chills her. She looks at him, tall and straight on his horse. She realizes she knows nothing of his past. She only knows his house with the blue shutters, the steward's house: books neatly arranged on shelves, a fire crackling.

"You were working for the count as a cooper when I came to the estate," she says.

"Yes."

How much older is he than she? Seven, eight years?

"Are you from one of the nearby villages?"

"No. I came from St. Petersburg, but before that I lived in Moscow."

"Ah, yes," Antonina says. Something about the way Grisha is looking at her is unnerving. It's as though he either wants her to ask him more or wants her to stop asking altogether. She realizes she's deeply uncomfortable, although she has no idea why. She's spent more time with Grisha over the past few months than with anyone, save Lilya. She's never before felt uncomfortable with him.

He's still looking at her, and Antonina grows unexpectedly flustered. She returns his look for what feels like a few seconds too long, and then looks down at her ungloved hands on the reins. A sudden gust of cool wind makes her shiver; gold and orange leaves from the larch trees that line both sides of the road blow in a frantic dance. Clouds pass over the sun, although the sky is still blue.

"Let's continue, madam," Grisha says, pulling slightly on the reins so that his horse faces ahead. Antonina lets out her breath, though she hadn't realized she was holding it.

Antonina turns Dunia as well. "When the lawyer comes, he'll make things clearer."

She touches her horse's flanks with her heels and Dunia walks again, her gait comforting under her. Another gust of wind picks up the edges of Antonina's cloak, and bright leaves rain on them, catching in their hair and clothing and in the manes of the horses.

Grisha looks at the sky. "There will be rain later. Hopefully it will hold off for a few hours." He has one bright copper leaf on his shoulder.

～

Antonina feels the wind ever cooler as they approach the outskirts of Tushinsk. Still, the air is clean, crisp, and she closes her eyes and breathes deeply. She puts a hand into Dunia's mane, feeling its soft thickness.

"Wait for me here, on the edge of the village, madam," Grisha says. He seems oddly agitated. "I'll only be five minutes, and return to you." He stops, and then says, "The ruts are deep, and will be difficult for Dunia to manoeuvre." He's afraid that if she insists on accompanying him, Lev might not hand over the boy.

Antonina settles down to wait. Five minutes pass, then ten. She stares at the central square of bare earth, dominated by the small church and its flaking green-painted dome. Chickens roost on its wooden steps, their feathers ruffling in the wind. A gaunt middle-aged priest with a black and grey beard and long, tangled hair stands listlessly in the doorway, wearing a threadbare cassock and *valenkis*— felt boots. Unlike the higher clergy—the unmarried monks who are eligible for the highest reaches of church life, as bishops and archibishops—simple village priests are obliged to marry before they are ordained. But being one of the poorest in the village—depending on others for handouts and scratching out the most meagre of existences from a tiny garden plot behind the church—makes it difficult for a priest to find a wife. Their only hope is a daughter of another village priest.

She watches men haul carts filled with firewood and sacks of root vegetables as old women sit in doorways, peeling potatoes and onions. Bony dogs lie on their sides against the fronts of izbas, while goats wander past them aimlessly, heads down as they search for something to chew. Younger women with babies carried in shawls on their backs and toddlers at their sides walk slightly bent forward into the wind. A few of the villagers glance in her direction, and in their faces Antonina sees something different than what she's known all her life. Instead of subservience and fear, she senses resentment. Perhaps even hostility.

It's as Grisha said. The serfs are now free, and yet how are their lives different? Antonina studies the miserable hovels with their broken roofs, the half-starved animals, the poverty and despair. What good is this new freedom?

Finally, she grows weary of waiting, and slowly rides down the narrow road that runs through Tushinsk. As Grisha warned, the ruts are deep, and Dunia stumbles more than once.

Antonina stops the horse, afraid of injuring her, and as she does, she looks down a side street, where she sees Grisha. He's standing outside the doorway of a hut, talking to a man who is somehow familiar. Grisha is holding a small package.

She tries to place the man. Did he once work in the cattle sheds or one of the storehouses? Dunia, feeling the reins loosen, slowly begins to walk forward. Antonina notices a woman walking down the road ahead of her. Over her shoulder she's carrying a bundle of sticks. Beside her walks a boy. She stares at their backs.

The boy is Mikhail. He wears his coat. Even from this distance, Antonina can see the blue wool script—her son's name—along the bottom of the back of the coat. She sees his fair hair.

"Mikhail," Antonina says in disbelief, and then she screams, her voice that of a wild woman. "Misha!" In her panic, she yanks hard on the reins. Dunia flings her head up as Antonina leans forward to see the boy more clearly. The horse's head catches Antonina in the face, and she slides from Dunia before the horse has a chance to come to a full stop. She falls to her knees, momentarily stunned by the blow to her face. Then she shakes her head and gets up and runs towards the woman, screaming Mikhail's name. But he doesn't turn. Nor does the woman.

Another woman approaching them points, and when the woman turns and sees Antonina running at her, her mouth opens in a round circle of fear. She drops her sticks and grabs the boy's hand.

Antonina stumbles, her riding boots catching in the deep ruts and oozing mud. Still, she is lighter on her feet than the other woman, or perhaps it is desperation that makes her so swift. As she chases them, screaming Misha's name, peasants come from their huts to stare at her. Women pull their own children close against their sides, and others hide their faces with the edges of their kerchiefs.

"Stop," Antonina shouts. "Stop! You have my son." Still the woman runs, dragging the child, who is stumbling on bare feet, but Antonina soon draws close enough to grab the woman by the shoulder and whirl her around.

The woman—younger than Antonina—falls as she is turned, and looks up, her face a combination of confusion and dread, as though expecting Antonina to strike her. She puts up her arm.

The boy crouches beside her.

Antonina looks at the boy, and then emits a long-drawn-out wail. Her knees weaken, but she keeps her balance. The woman gets up slowly, still looking at her with the same frightened expression.

The fair-haired boy is not Mikhail. A thick stream of mucus runs from his nostrils onto his top lip. He has a pus-filled sty in the corner of one dark, round eye.

Antonina's cry of sorrow ends. She takes a deep breath and closes her eyes, then opens them, licking her lips, her mouth dry as if it is cloaked in something woolly and thick.

"The child's coat," Antonina finally is able to say. "Where did you get it?"

As she speaks, she realizes there is metallic-tasting fluid in her mouth—too much to swallow. She spits it out, seeing frothy scarlet, and reaches up to wipe her nose and lips with a shaking hand. When she pulls her hand away, it's covered in blood. Dunia's tossing head may have broken her nose, or knocked out a tooth. She knows something is wrong with her face, but she has no pain.

The peasant woman continues to stare at her, lips trembling.

Antonina shakes her by the shoulder, ever so slightly. "I asked you where you got the coat. Speak. Answer me." She calms her voice, seeing the other woman's fear. "You're not in trouble. I'm Countess Mitlovskiya. I own . . ." She stops. She no longer owns this village, or this woman. "I . . . I need to know about the child's coat."

The woman's eyes shift to somewhere behind Antonina, and a look of relief comes over her face.

"Please. I beg of you, my lady," a deep voice calls, and Antonina turns to see a young man, axe in hand, running towards them. His face is flushed and he's panting. "My wife—and our son—they're deaf and mute. She doesn't know what you're saying."

Antonina blinks. "The boy's coat," she says, looking from him to the child. "I . . . I need to know where he got it."

The young man is silent for a moment, his chest rising and falling. "She didn't steal it, my lady. We receive many items from the church charity baskets."

Antonina can't answer.

"Countess Mitlovskiya," Grisha says, suddenly beside her. "Countess, you're hurt."

Antonina turns from the young man and looks at Grisha, and her whole face throbs with an unbearable pain, as if she has just at this moment been injured. She shudders, putting out her hand to steady herself on Grisha's arm, closing her eyes against the sudden white heat that wraps around her, blinding her.

"A seat," Grisha says loudly, his other arm around her, holding her up. "Bring the countess a bench, for God's sake."

Antonina momentarily sags against him, then is lowered onto a hard bench. Someone holds a cloth over her nose; she smells soap and leather.

A cock crows, a dog barks, and Antonina opens her eyes. It's Grisha who holds his handkerchief to her face. She reaches up to keep it in place, her fingers over his. He removes his hand.

The peasants gather around her in a wide circle, keeping a respectful distance. As soon as she looks at them, they all bow from the waist.

The young mother has pulled her boy against her; he's between her and the father. She's protecting him. Antonina understands. The boy's legs are long and thin. His mother wipes his nose with her fingers. He can't be more than six or seven; the coat is far too big for him. Her husband tugs on the woman's sleeve, and at his gesture she bows, nudging the boy to bow as well.

"The *talmochka* . . . it's my son's," Antonina says, moving the handkerchief out of the way to speak, although only Grisha is looking at her. To the bowed heads, she says, "That's his name, along the bottom on the back. Mikhail." As Antonina says his name to these strangers, she swallows, and has to draw a deep breath. "He was stolen, taken by Cossacks. He was wearing that coat at the time. Please. You," she says, and all the peasants but the mother and child raise their heads to see to whom she's referring. She's looking at the young husband.

He looks from her to his son, resting his hand on the child's head. At that movement a tiny convulsion goes through Antonina. She knows the man is relieved his child hasn't been stolen. Perhaps, at this moment, he's glad that he's a simple peasant, unable to pay ransom, his child safe from marauding Cossacks.

He touches his wife's sleeve again, and she raises her head. He makes a series of finger motions, and her face softens. She looks at Antonina, holding her gaze for a moment, then nods. She gently draws the boy's arms from the coat and steps forward and hands it to Antonina.

She takes it, pressing her bloodied nose against it, trying to smell her son. But it smells only of grease and smoke. It's filthy, and now it's smeared with her blood.

"Thank you," she says, her voice unsteady, watching the mother wrap her child in her shawl against the cool wind. "My steward," she says, waving weakly in Grisha's direction, "will make sure your child receives another coat." Antonina looks at Grisha, and he nods.

"Come, countess," he says, holding out his arm. "We must have your injuries seen to."

Antonina stands but has to cling to him for support. All the peasants move farther back. "Thank you," she says to the young man, "for my son's coat." She clutches it against her chest. "And tell your wife I'm sorry I frightened her."

"We understand, my lady," he says.

"Thank you," Antonina says again, even more weakly, and then allows Grisha to lead her back to Dunia. His horse waits there as well, its head down. The peasants slowly disperse as she steps into Grisha's joined hands, swinging her leg over the horse's back. The saddle creaks as she settles into it.

"One moment, madam," Grisha says. "I will get the peasant's name so I can send the new coat to him."

Antonina watches numbly as Grisha hurries back to the couple, who are still standing in the middle of the mud road making hand gestures to each other. When Grisha speaks to them, they appear cowed, stepping back. Grisha has his back to her and she can't see his face. The young man says nothing at first, and then begins speaking, putting his arm around his wife's shoulders protectively.

The villager's reaction isn't odd to her. Of course the peasants are fearful of men like Grisha, men who have held a high position.

When Grisha walks back to her, he rubs his hands together as if to clean them of the mud of the village. His face is dark.

He mounts his horse and they slowly make their way back onto the main road. Grisha holds Dunia's reins, and they walk at a slow pace. Antonina clutches Mikhail's coat against her chest with one hand and keeps the sodden handkerchief to her nose with the other.

Grisha glances at her frequently.

Only a verst from the village, there is a low growl of thunder. A few drops are soon followed by a downpour of cold autumn rain.

"Madam," Grisha says, riding close to Antonina as she puts up the hood of her cloak. Because of the noise of the rain, he has to lean close to her. His leg touches hers. "I know a place, a dacha close by. Would you prefer to wait out the rain there, or do you wish to ride home?"

"The dacha," Antonina says, shivering. She is as exhausted as if she's just completed an arduous task.

24

*I*n the dacha's small stable, Grisha helps her dismount, and Mikhail's coat falls to the dusty floor. She cries out. Grisha snatches it up, brushing off the straw, and gives it back to her. She buries her face in the *talmochka*, and a great sob comes from her throat.

As she cries, he hesitantly raises his hands to her shoulders. With her face still in the coat, Antonina leans against his chest. He puts his arms around her then, so lightly Antonina barely feels them at first.

Apart from Lilya's soothing caresses as she bathes her or works on her hair or helps her fall asleep, Antonina has not been touched for a long time. For her to lay her cheek against the rough wool of Grisha's tunic and hear the thudding of a human heart creates in her such a sense of comfort that she finds it difficult to pull herself away.

They stand like this in the stable with dust motes flying

about them, the smell of manure and damp straw heavy in the air. The horses' hooves shift on the wooden floor under the scant cover of old hay. There are quiet whinnies and snickers, the slap of a tail. Rain drums on the wooden roof.

Antonina at last realizes she has remained too long in Grisha's arms, and steps away. She wipes her eyes with her knuckles, sucking in her breath as her fingers brush her bruised nose. This starts a new trickle of blood, and she holds Grisha's handkerchief to her face again on the way to the dacha. Through the trees she sees the glint of water: a small lake.

Grisha steps in front of her to open the door. He ushers Antonina to a small settee near the fireplace, and then kneels and works with kindling and a flint. Within moments the kindling catches and flames leap up the darkened brick cavity. He sits back on his heels and adds small logs to the fire, then shrugs out of his jacket and tosses it onto a nearby rocking chair.

"Soon the dacha will be warm, madam," Grisha says, looking over his shoulder at her. "I'll start the stove as well, and heat water for you to clean your face." He goes into another room, and Antonina hears the splashing of water.

Leaving Mikhail's coat on the settee, Antonina goes down the short hall, where she finds a small, rudimentary lavatory. The wooden dacha is pleasant, well maintained and decorated in a simple but charming country manner, and is the summer home of . . .? Does it belong to the Bakanevs? It's far into the countryside, reachable only by a narrow, almost indiscernible path through the trees, or from the lake.

Looking at herself in the wavy mirror on the wall of the lavatory, she pulls away the handkerchief, wincing. She doesn't recognize herself: there's something wild-looking about her, something that frightens her. The steady throbbing in her nose is making her whole body ache. Her bodice is bloodstained.

Grisha is once more kneeling in front of the fireplace when she returns to the sitting room. "Is the pain great, madam?" he asks, looking up at her.

"Is there anything to drink, Grisha?"

Grisha rises and goes back to the kitchen, returning with a half-full bottle of vodka and a glass. Antonina wonders dully how he knows this place.

"I'm sorry there's no wine or claret, only this vodka, but it's good quality. Not from Angelkov," he says with the ghost of a smile, "but still fine. The water is heating," he adds.

Antonina sits on the settee again, dropping the crumpled, bloody handkerchief beside her, picking up the coat and laying it over her lap. She strokes it, stops, then pulls at a slightly torn inner seam.

Grisha pours the small glass half full. As he does, Antonina utters a cry. "Look! Look," she says, holding up two small squares of the transposed notes to Glinka's music, with writing on the back. They were hidden between the lining and the wool.

As with the note Lev brought, Mikhail has written with charcoal.

I do not like it here. A pig sleeps beside me and I am afraid it will bite me. But I don't cry. I am a soldier for Papa. When I come home I will tell him to punish these bad men.

The charcoal on the second note is so smeared that Antonina has trouble making out the words.

Here is better because there is no pig. I am still a soldier.
But sometimes I almost cry for Mama when I hear the
church bells. It is hot now. I think it is past my birthday
because it is so hot. I am very itchy.

She is weeping. "He was alive in the summer, Grisha, but
why was his coat . . ." She can't finish the sentence.

Grisha says nothing.

She presses the heels of her hands against her eyelids.
What's he wearing now, in the cold autumn? "Why did the
child have my Misha's coat?" she asks, lowering her hands,
still crying as she reaches for the glass Grisha holds.

Grisha knows why. He knows from questioning the villager only an hour earlier. But he can't tell Antonina. He
watches her drink the vodka in one swallow.

"More," she says, and as he's refilling the glass, she looks
up at him. "Drink with me, Grisha."

He hesitates for only a moment, then says, "As you wish,
countess. Excuse me while I bring another glass."

Antonina puts down Misha's notes and her glass and
removes her damp cloak. She picks up her full glass again
and waits for Grisha to return, her other hand on the
smeared pages beside her. The fire is bright, magnified and
dancing through the vodka in her glass, orange and scarlet
and yellow.

Grisha comes back and pours himself a drink, then stands
before the fire.

"To Misha," Antonina says, raising her glass, and at that
Grisha hesitates. Then he steps forward and touches his
glass to hers. The skin of her neck and wrists is pale against
the deep purple wool of her frock.

"To Mikhail Konstantinovich," he says, waiting for Antonina to drink before putting the glass to his own lips.

As with the first glass, she swallows the vodka in one long, smooth gulp. He shouldn't be surprised; he knows the countess likes her drink. Still, he didn't imagine she would drink like a man.

"Another," Antonina says, and Grisha fills her glass again.

"The water will be warm by now," he says, excusing himself. When he returns, he carries a sloshing tin basin and a soft, clean flannel. Her glass is empty. "I'll put this in the lavatory for you," he tells her.

A deep weariness fills Antonina. She shakes her head, the movement setting off the pain again. "I want to stay here."

Grisha sets the basin on the floor and wets the cloth. He squeezes out the excess water and folds it into a neat square, then holds it out to her.

Clutching her empty glass, she turns her face to him.

Grisha sits beside her on the settee and presses the warm, damp cloth under her nose and on her lips. She takes a sudden deep breath.

"It hurts. Give me another drink," she says, sounding like she might have sounded, Grisha thinks, when she was a girl. He knows the power of pure, high-quality vodka. He does as she says.

She swallows half of the next glass and then faces him again, her eyes closed. Grisha continues gently to swab at the dried blood. This time she doesn't flinch.

"May I touch your nose, madam?" he asks.

Antonina nods, and as Grisha's fingertips press lightly on the bridge, she gasps and pushes his hand away. She finishes the vodka and drops the empty glass to the rug at her feet.

"It's broken, as I suspected," he says.

Antonina says, in that same young and unfamiliar voice, "Why don't you drink more with me, Grisha?"

The vodka has calmed her. The dacha is warm, the rain still coming down, although it's no longer the persistent drumming. Grisha knows that if they stay any longer, it will be difficult to see the path through the woods on what will be a moonless evening.

"We should leave soon, madam, to avoid riding in the dark."

Antonina leans forward, resting her head against his shoulder. "I don't want to go. I'm so tired."

Grisha looks at her hands, limp in her lap. Her hair is a soft mass against him. He can smell something sweet, but whether it comes from her hair or her dress or her skin, he doesn't know.

They remain like this, the room dark except for the fire. Logs fall with a thud and crackle. He must add more wood or soon it will go out. "Madam," he says quietly, and she makes a small sound. "I'll stoke the fire, and light a lamp."

As he gently pulls away from her, she picks up the bottle and drinks what is left.

When he turns back to her, she's lying down, one hand holding the empty bottle and the other pillowed under her cheek. He lights the lamp on the round table in one corner. The rain is still soft and steady against the windowpanes. He goes back to the settee and looks down at Antonina, then carefully eases the bottle from her grasp and sets it on the floor. Her nose is swollen and darkening, but she looks serene, her eyes closed and her breathing even. Mikhail's coat has fallen to the floor; he picks it up and sets it on the arm of the settee.

He takes a thick blanket from the back of the rocking chair and lays it over her. A strand of pale hair has fallen across her face, and he wonders what would happen if he brushed it back. He wonders what her hair feels like.

She unexpectedly opens her eyes and looks up at him, not startled to see him so close. She's a different woman here in the dacha. She isn't the woman who gives him orders in the wood-panelled study, who dismisses him abruptly when she's finished with him. In the firelight, he doesn't know her, except to recognize how lovely she is.

"Come nearer," she says, and he kneels beside the settee. She puts her hand into his hair, pushing it back from his temple. "Your hair is so black, as are your eyes. Why, Grisha?"

He doesn't move. "My mother was a Buryat."

"A Buryat?" Antonina blinks. She knows of the Buryats, a race with Asian features who live in the far southeast corner of Siberia, near Mongolia. "How is it your mother was a Buryat, Grisha?"

He doesn't answer, and she drops her hand.

She looks at him for a long time. "I'm lonely, Grisha," she says.

⌒

When he reaches to unloosen the rich weave of thick braids at the back of her neck, she stops him.

She had risen from the settee and taken his hand. She moved with sure-footed elegance in spite of all the vodka she'd consumed. He felt slow, suddenly clumsy, as he followed her. She'd led him to one of the bedrooms and stood before him, looking up into his face, and he knew she wanted him to kiss her.

He cautiously put his arms around her, ready to remove them if she showed even the slightest change of heart. But she didn't. She raised her face, and he pressed his mouth against hers.

Antonina has only known Lilya's one kiss, and Konstantin's. She has never been kissed the way Grisha kisses her. It's the kiss of a man sure of himself, and sure of his desire, but there is no urgency. As they continue to kiss, his mouth growing more insistent, he puts his hand against the small of her back, half lifting her against him.

Then he sets her down. "Are you certain?" he whispers.

It's when she nods that he reaches up to loosen her hair, and "No," she murmurs, covering his hands with hers. "Leave my hair. Please."

He knows he shouldn't be doing this. Can he blame the vodka? Has it affected her, made her susceptible? He didn't plan this, although he has thought about—imagined—having her. He's had many, many women over his lifetime; having a woman has never been difficult for Grisha. For some he has felt genuine fondness, while others simply fulfilled a physical need. He's always been honest with them: he promises nothing, telling them he's not a man made for marriage. Some of the witty ones, the ones who made him laugh, meant more than the ones who were only pretty.

But none of them ever created this disquiet in him; none of them made him confused about his feelings. Since he was fifteen years old, Grisha has taught himself not to fall into anything that could be tenderness, or sympathy. Those emotions could lead to memories that brought back the guilt. Grisha knows that carrying guilt is like having a solid, heavy load strapped onto your chest, a load that is almost impossible to put down. It's difficult to get what you want with a load in your way; it obstructs your view and cripples your stride. Guilt doesn't allow a person to do the things that are necessary in order to live a life where you work towards what you want.

He knows exactly who he is, and what he's done. He sees himself in a hard, unforgiving light. He's a man who will do what has to be done to further himself.

He takes his hands from her hair and cups them around her face. "I will try not to touch your nose, madam," he says, smiling, and she returns the smile with one of her own. It is somehow lazy. No, languorous.

Something within him jumps. He hasn't ever seen this smile.

"But you must call me Tosya," she says softly. "At such a moment, you must call me Tosya." She puts his fingers on the buttons of her bloodied bodice.

. ⌁

When she awakens, the room is dark except for one guttering candle, and Antonina feels ill. Her stomach churns, empty but for the vodka, and her head throbs.

She stares at the low wooden ceiling, feeling the heat of Grisha beside her. She turns her head and studies his profile. The bedclothes cover him to his waist. She looks at his bare chest as it rises and falls and wants to put her hand on it.

She has just seen a boy she thought was her son. Then she had read his written words and held his *talmochka*. She is a mother, a wife—and a hypocrite. That Konstantin would continue to take Tania while married to her had disgusted her; she saw him as weak and immoral. And now . . . She closes her eyes. How has she allowed this to happen?

She crosses herself, praying silently for forgiveness.

Grisha stirs, turning towards her, and she holds her breath. And in spite of her barely finished prayer, she wants him to reach for her again, to feel his hot skin against hers, to put her fingers on his body and trace the play of his ribs, the hollow of his clavicle and the jut of his hip. It shouldn't have happened. But how will she deny to herself how he moved her?

She falls asleep again, but is awakened by Grisha shifting. It's not yet morning, although the room is lightening, the air a soft grey. He's on one elbow, looking down at her, and without allowing herself to think, she puts her arms around his neck and pulls him onto her, arching against him, feeling him ready for her. His desire fills her with more of her own.

Konstantin never desired her. He did what he had to do to produce his heir.

Grisha leans down and kisses her nipple, pulling it into his mouth, and Antonina gasps. His hair falls over his cheek and she brushes it away, cupping the back of his head with her hand, loving the way his dark lashes shadow his cheeks. When he lifts his head to look at her, she puts her mouth on his and he kisses her back, and then in one swift movement he's inside her. He turns her so that they're on their sides, facing each other. He gently manoeuvres her leg up and over his hip, and moves slowly, without the rush of the night before.

"I want you, Grisha," she says, and he says, "Call me Tima. Please. Call me Tima."

Such is Antonina's desire that she doesn't stop to wonder. "Tima," she breathes, putting her mouth to his ear, touching its rim with the tip of her tongue.

When they awaken, a thin sun is streaming through the window. Antonina doesn't know if Grisha woke her or she woke him, but they're looking at each other in that pale sunlight. He opens his mouth to speak, but the full weight of what she's done comes upon Antonina. She sits up, turning from him. Although she had no shame through the night, now she wraps the coverlet around her as she picks up her clothes from the floor. They're damp and cold. She leaves the room without speaking to or looking at Grisha. She goes into the lavatory, where she dresses hurriedly. Then she allows herself to glance in the mirror.

Her nose is swollen and there are darkening bruises under her eyes. There is also a slightly reddened patch where Grisha's chin rubbed against her jaw. Her hair, although still mainly caught in its pins and combs, is snarled and tangled.

More than the sickness in her stomach is the terrible remorse for what she's just done.

She returns to the sitting room and is putting on her cape when Grisha emerges from the bedroom, looking down as he buckles his leather belt over his white tunic. His hair is tousled. His cheeks, beneath the dark overnight stubble, are slightly flushed, and he carries his boots under one arm.

She puts Misha's pages back into the pocket of the *talmochka*. "The roads will be a sea of mud after all the rain," she says, the attempt at keeping her voice matter-of-fact not quite successful. "It will be a difficult ride back."

"Yes," Grisha answers, and looks up from his belt to her. "How is your nose this morning?" He sits on a chair and begins to pull on a boot.

Antonina realizes this is the first time he has sat in her presence without being given permission. Her mouth is dry from the vodka. She longs for a cup of hot tea, and turns away as she ties the ribbons of her cape. "I'll saddle Dunia," she says.

"No, Tosya, let me do that."

The name she'd asked him to call her now sounds wrong in the light of day.

She opens the door. "I'd rather do it myself. And—Grisha?"

He stops, the boot halfway up his leg, and looks at her, expectation of some kind on his face. He's smiling, slightly. He looks pleased.

"I had too much vodka last night, Grisha. I was not . . . After what happened at Tushinsk, and my nose . . . But it was a mistake. Do you understand? I really can't remember . . ."

They both know she needs to lie. He doesn't contradict her.

She can't read his face, but the pleased look is gone.

"We won't speak of it, ever," she says. There's no need to say anything more, but something makes her add, "Do you understand?"

At this, Grisha's face tightens. He is her steward again. She might be ordering him to bring her an account, or chastise a lazy serf. "I understand." There's no tenderness in his voice, nothing to hint at what they've just shared.

"Good," Antonina says firmly. By the time Grisha comes out of the dacha, she's already in the yard on Dunia, who is prancing in the cool autumn air.

⁓

Antonina finds it difficult to ride home beside Grisha.

She knows he didn't force himself on her; it was the other

way around. Grisha would never have taken her if she hadn't initiated it, encouraged him.

She tries to get the name he asked her to call him out of her head.

Tima.

Grisha is remembering the way it sounded coming from her lips. It took him back to a more innocent time, one where he hadn't yet committed his great wrong. It allowed him to forget, for one night, what he has never been able to let go of.

No one has called him Tima—for Timofey, his given name—for twenty years. The last time he heard it, he was fifteen years old, and running away from everything he knew.

25

*T*ima's father was a *polkovnik*—one of a high position—in the Russian army. Senior Officer Colonel Aleksandr Danilovich Kasakov was also one of the notorious Decembrist revolutionaries of 1825. The small group of high-ranking officers had marched to Senate Square in St. Petersburg, trying to force the Senate—and Tsar Nicholas I—to sign a manifesto deposing the autocracy and abolishing serfdom.

Aleksandr Kasakov, like the other officers, had travelled to Europe in the course of previous military campaigns. The exposure to the Western world inspired the well-educated officers to seek change in their own repressed country. But the revolutionary movement these men started was easily crushed, and, in actuality, soured Nicholas I on liberalism for his people. The Decembrists paid dearly for their attempts to abolish serfdom and ensure a better life for the downtrodden peasants. Five of the officers were executed, while most of the others were sentenced to a life of exile in Siberia.

The Tsar, determined to make an example of these men, attempted to wipe out all trace of them. Wives of convicts were usually allowed to follow them to Siberia, but Church and State declared that the Decembrists' wives were now widows and could marry freely, without benefit of a divorce. Some wives refused this edict, and did follow their husbands, but had to give up all their worldly possessions, and, even worse, were not allowed to take their children. Should their husbands die before them, they were told they would have to live out their own lives in Siberia.

Aleksandr Kasakov's wife could not face leaving their two young daughters behind forever. He fully supported her decision to stay, and gave her his blessing from the prison in St. Petersburg's Peter and Paul Fortress. He went further, urging her to marry again so that his children would have a father. He did not want to see those he most loved punished for his crimes.

He served a year of hard labour in a mine in one of the far corners of the Siberian province of Irkutsk. He worked chained to a wheelbarrow, surrounded by atrocities and death. In his mid-thirties, he learned that true oppression works by turning its victims against each other.

After the year of back-breaking labour, he was ordered to live out his banishment in the thinly populated area of eastern Siberia, in Chita. The town was five hundred miles to the east of the largest city in Siberia, Irkutsk, near the crossroads to Mongolia and China. Tiny Chita was inhabited by many Buryats—Buddhists who brought their culture and religion across the nearby border with Mongolia.

Aleksandr was a rag-covered skeleton when he arrived in Chita. He imagined that exile to a windswept village would be easy in comparison with his experiences in the mine. But now he experienced a different kind of pain: loneliness and isolation. As he sat through the endless winter months of near darkness and howling winds, thinking of his lost life, the wife and children he would never see again, his hut so cold that his hair was frozen to his thin pallet in the morning, he knew he had to change his fate. If not, he would die alone and in bitterness.

For a man like Aleksandr, the only way to survive in Siberia would be to find something productive to do. And he needed a woman to keep him warm at night.

The village came to life in the short but warm summer. Aleksandr approached everyone he encountered, asking for work. Most of the villagers knew that well-educated exiles weren't particularly useful with their hands, and were reticent to hire a revolutionist. But one of them took a chance on Aleksandr Danilovich. Temujin, a cooper, taught Aleksandr to cut and plane barrel staves in exchange for food and a better hut than the one he had been given. Temujin had eyed Aleksandr's size and imagined him with some weight on his frame; he was impressed by his dignified manner and tireless work ethic. He didn't care that Aleksandr had been exiled for being a revolutionary. Temujin was a Buryat, a widower who had come from Verkhneudinsk, also known as Upper Vdinsk, a town on the east side of Lake Baikal. Aleksandr liked the smell of the wood shavings and the comforting rhythm of the adze over the strips of timber. Temujin accepted Aleksandr as an honest, hard-working man. In this way, he gave him hope.

After a few months another Decembrist arrived in Chita—someone of his class who had fought the same fight for the same cause—and his friendship brought a quiet relief to Aleksandr. As a few more exiles slowly filtered into Chita, they created their own small social milieu.

Two of his fellow revolutionaries were fortunate enough to still be married. Their wives had made the endless, desperate journey, losing everything to remain with their husbands. Watching the couples, Aleksandr refused to give in to self-pity, but felt an even keener need for his own companionship. There were a few single or widowed Russian women in Chita, but they were of peasant stock. Aleksandr couldn't envision himself marrying anyone but a Russian woman of high standing, as his wife had been.

At first, he hadn't paid much attention to Temujin's daughter, Ula, when she brought her father his noon meal. While he didn't initially find her Mongolian features attractive—the dark, almond-shaped eyes, small, neat nose and lips, and glossy black hair that she clipped at the back of her neck and left hanging to her waist—eventually he became used to her face and shy smile. He also appreciated her demure, respectful nature. She spoke Buryat to her father but addressed the ex-colonel in a formal, lightly accented Russian, which, as he grew more interested, took on a pleasant rhythm.

Ula had been betrothed to a young Buryat who had succumbed to a fever the year Aleksandr arrived in Chita. She found the army man dignified and proper, qualities she had never witnessed among the Russian peasants in Chita. There was something in the direct way he looked at her, studying her respectfully and yet openly—unlike the more modest Buryat men—that both flustered and excited her.

Ula's father wanted to see his daughter married and happy. Aleksandr, at thirty-five, was fifteen years older than Ula, but that wasn't a concern. Temujin worried more about the difference in their culture and religion. Aleksandr attended Mass daily at the small Orthodox church he and his old Decembrist companions had helped to build.

When Aleksandr officially asked Temujin if he would allow him to marry Ula, the father brought up his concern over religion. Aleksandr told him firmly that he had no difficulty in allowing Ula to retain her Buddhism. Should there be children, they could be raised in both faiths.

And so Aleksandr and Ula were married. Aleksandr taught his new wife to write her name in Russian, and read to her at night. He listened to stories of her childhood and learned about Buddhism. Though they had so little in common, Aleksandr was grateful that he had found a quiet, undemanding woman with whom to live out his life, and he experienced true joy when Timofey Aleksandrovitch was born a year after their marriage. It appeared he would be their only child, but seven years later they were surprised and pleased by the birth of Nikolai Aleksandrovitch.

By the time little Tima was old enough to spin a prayer wheel and chant with his mother at the *datsan*—the Buryat Buddhist temple—as well as say his prayers to the icons and cross himself from right to left in the Orthodox way, as his father had taught him, Aleksandr had helped Temujin expand the business. Although originally the new couple had lived with Temujin in the traditional peasant izba, Aleksandr was soon able to build his own cottage. He built it in the style of the small country dachas he had enjoyed over hot summers as a child, and he painted its wooden shutters blue.

In spite of knowing he would never again walk the streets of a thriving, exciting city, never again ride a tall military horse, never again mingle with St. Petersburg or Moscow's social elite, and never again effect any change in Russia's politics, Aleksandr Kasakov nonetheless found a strange happiness.

He had lost the energy to fight for anything. He was finished with conflict.

When he made the sign of the cross over his sleeping sons or held his wife in the dark of the night, his face in her thick, fragrant hair, he felt he had been given a new life. His wife and two daughters in St. Petersburg could not be replaced, but with Ula and his sons he could let go of the pain.

Timofey inherited his mother's eyes and high cheekbones, but from his father he possessed fair skin and the soft waves in his black hair. His younger brother Nikolai—Kolya— had the fair hair and deep blue eyes of their father. He was also built more delicately than his brother.

Aleksandr made sure his sons knew how to read and write in both Russian and French. He also discussed the political situation in Russia in simple terms with Tima as soon as he thought the boy could understand; he talked openly about his past life in the army, his role in the uprising and the reason for his exile. He stressed the idea of freedom, and how he had fought for this for the peasants who made up over eighty percent of Russia's population. "To live freely, to own your own land—and your own soul—is what is important to a man," he told his son. "In other places in the world there is freedom for all. Remember that, and don't ever find yourself in the possession of another man. To be free is a God-given right."

Tima was not always a willing audience, but he eagerly devoured the books his father owned. And soon Aleksandr had borrowed all of his friends' books to feed the passion of his older son. Kolya, on the other hand, wasn't as interested in reading, or learning sums, or hearing his father's recitations about their country. He preferred to spend time sitting quietly in front of the fire or the stove, his head tilted slightly as if he was listening to something no one else could hear. As a very small child he hummed and made simple melodies with little Tibetan chimes and blocks of wood. From a young age, he loved going to worship with both his parents, growing rigid with concentration when the Orthodox priest chanted rhythmically or when the Tibetan monks hit their gongs and rang their bells. He would always stop what he was doing when the Russian church bells rang, both morning and evening, nodding his head with the beat.

Ula protected Kolya in all ways, neither pushing him nor having many expectations of him, as she did of Tima. Aleksandr felt she babied the child, and in his heart wished his second son were more like Tima, so interested in the world around him, so candid and inquisitive.

Temujin owned an ancient squeezebox, and occasionally played it for his grandsons. When Kolya was four, he took it from his grandfather's hands and pushed and pulled it with a strange attentiveness, placing his little fingers on the buttons. Within a week he had taught himself to play, creating music that none of them had heard before. They were not the Buryat melodies his mother sang to him, nor the lively military or Russian folk tunes his father whistled. None of them understood how he knew how to do this, but Aleksandr at last concluded that Kolya was a natural musician. With hard-earned kopecks, he paid an elderly exile who played the violin with aching sweetness to teach his son. The old man had a finely made small violin and taught the young Kolya on this instrument.

Oh, the boy can most certainly play, the old music teacher told Aleksandr after three lessons. Within a year the teacher reported that it was pointless for Aleksandr to spend any more money on the tutoring. *I can't teach the boy anything more,* the old man said. *He so quickly learned to read music. And once he has listened to a tune, he can play it perfectly. He makes up his own melodies, and can harmonize with me to any-thing I play.* The music teacher went on to say that he had rarely witnessed such early talent.

Aleksandr bought the small violin from the old man, and handed it to Kolya. The boy played for hours every day, showing little interest in anything else. He told his family that when he played, the world turned a beautiful colour—gold, the colour of the leaves in the fall when the sun shone through them.

As Kolya learned the language of his violin, Timofey grew tall and strong, and spent much time competing in games of strength with the other boys in Chita. It was clear to his parents that he had the qualities of a leader, and they observed how the others regarded him with respect and a certain cau-tion, always deferring to him.

Kolya, on the other hand, was sensitive and physically slight. His mother was glad that he would rather stay inside with her and play his little violin than be outside in the cold wind. And besides, Kolya's long, curly hair and wide eyes and delicate features made him a target for the other boys, and he was taunted when he went out into the muddy road that ran down the middle of the village.

If he did go out, it was up to Tima to keep him safe. Tima was angered at being forced into looking after his little brother. "Hurry, Kolya. Can't you go any faster?" he'd badger the smaller boy, who trotted behind him as he walked with long steps to keep up with his friends. "Put your hands in your pockets if they're cold—stop bothering me."

When Kolya tripped and scraped his knees, and cried to go home, Tima shook his head. "You have to be braver, Kolya. You can't always run home to Mama when something happens," he said, and then, looking over his shoulder to make sure the other boys didn't see, used his sleeve to wipe Kolya's running nose. "Don't cry to Mama about this," he said, pointing at Kolya's knees, "or I'll get in trouble for not watching you carefully enough. Promise," he said, and Kolya, sniffling, nodded at his big brother.

Aleksandr and Ula gave all their attention to Kolya, because Kolya needed it. Timofey was resourceful from an early age. By the time he was twelve, he was working alongside his father. Temujin had died earlier in the year, and Aleksandr had taken over the older man's job of creating wooden barrel hoops. Aleksandr brought Tima into the cooperage and instructed him on the intricacies of stave making, just as Temujin had instructed him years earlier: riving the pieces of wood to taper the staves at the ends while making sure they were left wide in the middle, allowing for the creation of the cylindrical bulge in the barrel.

It required a keen eye, not only for judging the taper but to spot weak grains or knots in the wood. Tima caught on immediately. Aleksandr then introduced Tima to the tools of the trade: the adze, drawknife, scorp, mallet and a variety of chisels, and Tima learned to plane the outside of each stave for smoothness, and slightly cup the inside. The staves were then soaked so they could be curved properly. Once the hoops were secured around the barrels, Tima sealed the staves with pitch.

Aleksandr hired another man, Antip, as the business prospered and he and Tima could no longer keep up with the orders. His barrels were used for storage not only in Chita but by many of the surrounding villages and hamlets.

When Tima had finished for the day—his father let him leave two hours earlier than himself and Antip—he then had to watch his brother. This was to give his mother time for her errands without the boy clinging to her. Timofey was instructed to take Kolya outside for fresh air in the good weather, and to make sure the younger boy didn't get bullied or hurt himself. But after he'd put in a man's day of work, Tima wanted to go off with his friends for a few hours, not look after his little brother. While he did feel protective, he grew more annoyed the longer he was forced to play the protector—as Kolya got older and yet no tougher.

One afternoon, while Tima knelt on the hard dirt playing a gambling game of stones with three of his friends, he heard Kolya's cries from down the road—though he'd told him to stay put until he was done.

"Tima! Tima, help me!"

Tima glanced over his shoulder. A boy, older and much bigger than Kolya, was pushing him along, holding on to

Kolya's hair. "Are you a girl or a boy, with all these curls?" the boy taunted, yanking and laughing.

"Tima!" Kolya howled.

Tima tried to keep playing, but Kolya's cries escalated until finally—silence.

One of his friends nudged him. "Look at your brother."

He dropped his stone and looked behind him. Kolya lay motionless on the ground. Tima jumped to his feet and ran to him. "Kolya," he said, shaking the boy's shoulder. "Kolya, wake up."

After a moment, Kolya opened his eyes. "He pushed me down, Tima." He took deep breaths, holding in his sobs. "Don't worry, Tima, I won't tell Mama."

Tima hauled him up by his jacket. There was a thin trickle of blood on Kolya's cheek where he'd fallen on a sharp stone. "You're all right." He spit on his fingers and wiped the blood from Kolya's cheek. It was only a small cut.

"I called you, Tima. You didn't come." Kolya was staring at him, his expression sad. "You didn't come."

Timofey shrugged. "It's time to go home. And remember, don't tell Mama or Papa."

Kolya tried to take Tima's hand, but Tima pulled free and walked home in front of his brother.

In years to come, he never forgot that look on Kolya's face, nor the sound of Kolya's voice, nor how he'd jerked his hand away from his little brother.

Although he came to accept the solid, uneventful life for himself in Chita, Aleksandr Kasakov wished he could give his sons more. He knew what the future held for them in the isolated

Siberian town, and often envisioned the career Timofey could have in the army or imagined Nikolai as a musician, playing in an orchestra for appreciative audiences in St. Petersburg or Moscow. He also knew they were only dreams.

When Tima was fourteen and Kolya seven, Aleksandr had been chilled by the first spots of blood coughed into his handkerchief. He hid it from his wife and sons as long as he could. Eventually the deep, endless coughing, followed by a sudden small hemorrhage, terrified his wife and frightened him into action.

Aleksandr expected Timofey to take over the business. From the first day he had put a strip of wood into his son's hands and demonstrated what to do, the boy had tackled the work with skill and dexterity. On top of that, he was good with figures—quicker, Aleksandr had realized for the last year, than he himself at writing out the orders and making sure the rubles were collected.

"I am proud to have a son to carry on the business," he often told Timofey. "You'll never go hungry, because people will always need barrels. And when it's time to marry and have your own family, you'll be able to offer them a good life. As for your brother . . . well, he's lucky that you'll always be here to look after him. He'll need you, Tima. Once your mother and I are no longer alive, you will be his only family." Still, he worried whether Tima would really take his duty to his brother seriously. In the boy he recognized a sense of adventure, a dislike of being told what to do. Aleksandr felt his older son's restlessness, and yet he assumed that Timofey was pleased to be heir to the family business.

Timofey did not appreciate his father's descriptions of his future. The stories of Aleksandr's former grand life in both

Russia and Europe had awakened in Timofey a desire for exploration and challenges. Tima gave little thought to the issue of serfdom, in spite of his father's explanations. The land here was as unforgiving and brutal as a cruel master. There was little hope of furthering oneself in the isolated steppes and wintry taigas of Asiatic Russia.

"You've never asked whether I like the work," Timofey said to him. "You expect me to be satisfied with the monotony of planing for the rest of my life?" Tima hated the endless slivers embedded in his palms, the smell of the black pitch and the way it looked under his fingernails. "I don't want to be a cooper forever." His voice was bold.

Aleksandr sat silently while Tima paced in front of him, then asked, "What is it you would like to do, then?"

"I don't know. But I don't want to stay here."

Timofey visualized a far more exciting future for himself, possibly in Irkutsk. It was much more civilized than Chita and, Tima had heard, quite a splendid town with its own theatre, a museum, municipal gardens where orchestras played concerts on warm evenings, and walkways made of wood over the mud streets. Although he had never been outside Chita, Timofey knew the village wasn't enough for him.

When Timofey at last understood that his father was desperately ill, and that he was expected to not only take over the business but be responsible for the rest of his life—in Chita—for his younger brother, a huge, dark cloud descended on him.

Timofey did not want to be held back. He began to think further than Irkutsk, of the world outside Siberia, perhaps in one of the capital cities of Russia. If he was forced to follow the map his father had drawn for him, he felt his life would stall before it had even started.

But Aleksandr heard Tima's rebellious words as simply the posturing of a headstrong young man. He felt that he had set him up for life. Nikolai—little Kolya—was his concern.

And Aleksandr, tasting the metallic tang of his own blood in his throat, sent out all the prayers he could, begging for a sign as to what to do about his younger son. Shouldn't something be made of the boy's musical ability? Shouldn't there be a better life for him than sitting in a village, creating astoundingly beautiful music on his violin?

He told Ula of his deep concern, but she refused to believe that her husband would soon die. And even if he did, well, she imagined she would be around for many, many years to look after her younger son and make his life as happy as possible. She knew little about the world beyond Chita, and had no interest in it. Nevertheless, when Aleksandr asked her to pray, she obligingly took out her prayer wheels and visited the *datsan* twice daily, lighting incense and chanting to the small replicas of stupas, tying strips of blue cloth—prayer flags—to the good luck trees that framed the Buddhist temple.

Then something happened which made Aleksandr believe that the combination of Orthodox and Buddhist prayers had brought the longed-for sign.

26

*I*t was announced, in May 1842, that for the first time in Chita there would be a recital put on by a small group of musicians from Irkutsk. They would play in the tiny town hall for four evenings. Aleksandr sent his wife and sons to the first concert. When they returned, Kolya's eyes were shining; he told his father that it was the most beautiful music he had ever heard. He was only eight, and yet he spoke with adult passion.

And then Kolya took out his violin and played some of the melodies of the repertoire he had just heard, his eyes closed. He moved as though possessed by a spirit, his body swaying as he passed the bow over the strings, and Aleksandr was both overwhelmed by the depth of his son's abilities and frightened at the prospect of what would become of him in a place like Chita.

When Ula and his sons had gone to bed, Aleksandr wrote a

letter. The next morning he gave it to Timofey to deliver to the maestro of the orchestra. It was an invitation for the maestro to come to their home for dinner. Aleksandr had written that he, Senior Officer Colonel Aleksandr Danilovich Kasakov, knew how far and long the maestro and his orchestra had travelled from Irkutsk, and now wanted to offer him his best Russian hospitality in a village so primitive and uncultured.

. While Aleksandr knew that the maestro would be fully aware that a former member of the Russian army in Irkutsk had to be a political exile, he hoped he wouldn't hold it against him. Fortunately for him, the maestro was down on his luck; he had incurred debts and couldn't find enough steady work in Irkutsk to pay them off. He had been forced to travel for months throughout eastern Siberia, playing in towns and villages. He hated the uncomfortable travel, the musically ignorant audiences and the poor wages he was paid for his talent. He was flattered to be invited to the home of a Russian former colonel. He didn't care what the man—this *polkovnik*—had done in a former life; all he knew was that he would welcome a good meal and a brief respite from the drafty rooms over the miserable hall where he and his musicians were billeted.

He wrote back that he would be happy to come the following evening, and gave the note to the young man who stood waiting for an answer.

When the maestro arrived the next night, Aleksandr rose carefully to greet his guest. He didn't want to set off a bout of coughing. He was pleased at the maestro's comments on the pleasantness of his home and the appetizing smells of the meal his wife was preparing. Aleksandr introduced himself— *please, call me Sasha*, implying an immediate friendship with the maestro—and his wife and sons.

Ula was an excellent cook, and the rich, tasty food, combined with an endless supply of the finest vodka Chita could offer, kept the conversation lively. After Ula had cleared the table, Aleksandr instructed little Kolya to perform.

"What shall I play, Papa?" the boy asked as he readied his violin.

"One of your own compositions, Kolya," Aleksandr instructed him, glancing at the maestro. He watched the man's face as his son played. When the child finished, the maestro slowly nodded. Aleksandr sent Kolya to the bedroom to put away his violin, and told Tima he could leave to meet his friends. Then he asked his wife to go to the kitchen to prepare the samovar and bring tea and cakes.

"Well?" Aleksandr said. "What do you think?"

The maestro nodded again, studying Aleksandr's pallor, the skin stretched tight over his gaunt face. He saw how the man tried to stifle the deep, wet cough in his handkerchief, and knew that the consumption would claim him before the month was out. "He has a considerable talent."

"I propose a situation to you," Aleksandr said, and the maestro nodded a third time. He understood there was a situation. "I wish my boy to have the best life he can. There is little possibility for one of his talent here in Chita. I know he is only a child—he is just past eight—but is it not better to start with professional training when young?"

"You wish to send your son to Irkutsk with me?" the maestro asked, not wanting to waste time when he knew the eventual question.

"I wish him to be able to make the most of his talent," Aleksandr said. It was growing harder to control the coughing, and he had already gone through three handkerchiefs, immediately folding them in his lap so the maestro wouldn't see the blood. "He wants nothing more than to play, and his disposition is such that it's clear this is what he is meant to do. You would find him an attentive and obedient student. If you could tutor him, perhaps . . . I really don't expect that he would ever reach Moscow or St. Petersburg, but surely he could find an appreciative audience—and a life—in Irkutsk. As you have."

The maestro gave him a glance then that was hard to decipher. Aleksandr pressed on.

"Should he remain in Chita, he will spend his life playing alone in his home, or for the occasional peasant wedding. I want more than this for him." His face contorted, and he coughed so hard into his handkerchief that it sounded like retching.

The maestro brought out his own handkerchief, shielding his nose and mouth. Ula hurried from the kitchen and stood over her husband, her fist pressed against her own mouth as if she too were fighting not to cough. She patted his shoulder with her other hand, murmuring *Sasha, Sasha.*

The coughing fit subsided and Ula again retreated to the kitchen.

The maestro said, "I understand. But the child is very young, and we must be honest and clear here. To take him from his mother . . . how will he cope? Even to travel with us to Irkutsk—you believe your son can do this?"

The maestro, however, was already envisioning the money he could make with a child of this ability. Within a few short years, the boy could be sold for the highest price to a landowner in the western Russian provinces, as a violinist for his serf orchestra. They were always competing with each other, these wealthy aristocrats who had nothing better to do than entertain themselves and their guests.

Aleksandr hadn't responded to the questions.

"I leave in two days," the maestro said then, slowly. "Could the boy be ready to go by then?"

Aleksandr's face shone with perspiration. He couldn't envision Kolya away from his mother and his home, in the care of this stranger. "He will be ready," he said, fighting his instinct. "And I know he'll manage the travel. He's a resilient boy." It was an outright lie to call Kolya resilient, but he was desperate enough to do this for his son.

Ula came in, carrying the samovar. As she set it in the middle of the table and turned to go back to the kitchen to fetch the cakes, the maestro asked her, "What did you say the boy's name is?"

"Timofey Aleksandrovitch," she answered. "He's past fifteen now. And you can see he's already a man."

"No, the other one."

"Oh. My little one is Nikolai Aleksandrovitch, *moy mal-ishka*. Kolya," she answered, smiling proudly.

Aleksandr closed his eyes, unable to bear what he was about to do to her. To Kolya. To all of them.

It's for the best, he told himself, reaching for the bottle of vodka, unaware that flecks of blood dotted his chin.

꙰

After the maestro left, he tried to think of a way to tell Ula about his plan for Kolya, to prepare her and make her understand that he was doing it for their child's future. That she would be able to visit him in Irkustsk: Timofey would make the journey with her at least every summer.

When she came out of the bedroom in the middle of the night to where Aleksandr now slept, propped on the cushioned bench, so as not to cough into her face, he was sitting upright. In the light of the candle she carried he saw concern on her face, but the flame also accentuated the hollows under her eyes and the lines around her mouth. She was suddenly older.

"You're not coughing, Sasha," she said. "Why can't you sleep?"

He looked up at her, her long black braid, now threaded with white, hanging over one shoulder.

"You're crying," she said, kneeling beside the bench. "I have never . . . What is it?"

He couldn't speak.

"I'll make some tea," she said, rising, but he caught her wrist. He took a deep breath and passed his other hand over his eyes, wiping his cheeks.

"It's the future, Ula," he said. "I'm worried about what will happen to you and the boys when I'm gone."

"I don't want to talk about it," Ula said, pulling her wrist free.

"We must talk about it. You know it will come. Soon," he added, and Ula clenched her lips and closed her eyes. "You can't pretend it isn't happening," he said, and at that she also wept, kneeling to lay her head on his knees.

"I have a plan," he told her, and she raised her face to study his. "For Kolya." But he couldn't go on. He knew what it would mean to her to lose Kolya. It would be like a death right before his own. What was he thinking? How could he have imagined it to be a good idea? No. He would write another letter to the maestro, telling him he'd changed his mind, and send it with Tima tomorrow. He had been impetuous, and foolish.

"It's Kolya I'm most worried about," he finished.

Ula nodded. "I know. Tima will be successful with the business. Already I can see this. He works like two men, and is smart with figures. So Kolya can work with him."

They both knew the last part wasn't true.

"Don't you want more for him?"

At this, Ula's face grew more composed. "It was good enough for my father, and for you. Why shouldn't it be good enough for the boys? It's honest work."

Aleksandr saw that she was pretending not to understand the question. His throat constricted and he fought the first cough, which would lead to prolonged, harsh and harsher coughing, and the eventual hemorrhage. But he was powerless to stop it. As he coughed, bending over, a handkerchief pressed to his mouth to absorb the flood of crimson, Ula hurried to make tea. No more was said about Kolya's future.

The next morning—a calm spring day, the sky cloudless—the maestro stood in the doorway of Aleksandr's home.

Tima was working at the cooperage and Kolya was in the boys' bedroom playing his violin. Aleksandr lay on the padded bench. Ula had taken her basket and gone to the shops. Before she left, Aleksandr had her set out pen and paper and ink. When he had a bit more strength, he would write the letter and have Tima deliver it later in the day.

The sight of the maestro standing in the open doorway sent a chill through Aleksandr's heated body. His throat was raw from coughing, his whole body feverish and aching. He could barely pull himself to a sitting position, but he did, shakily smoothing back his hair with one pale hand.

Behind the maestro were the other musicians in an open *tarantass* pulled by three horses.

"Good day, Kasakov," the maestro said. "I know I'm a day early, but last night the audience was so small and unreceptive—so unappreciative—that I've decided it's not worth our time to play the final concert. Can you make your son ready now?"

Aleksandr didn't answer, licking his lips. The music in the bedroom stopped.

"Come, now. We had an agreement," the maestro said, still in the doorway. "I'm leaving Chita immediately, and we need to arrive in the next village before dark."

Still Aleksandr didn't speak. As the maestro came into the room to stand in front of him, Kolya stepped out of the bedroom, his violin in one hand and the bow in the other. He was barefoot in the warm weather, and wore a clean white tunic and a pair of dark trousers. Aleksandr noticed—was it for the first time?—the delicacy of his son's ankles.

Nikolai looked at the maestro and his lips parted in his sweet smile. "Hello, maestro," he said.

Aleksandr's chest constricted painfully, and in that moment he knew he had to go through with what he had originally planned—quickly, before he changed his mind again. "Kolya," he said, "I want you to put on your boots. Then gather your clothes—all of them—and put them in a flour sack. Take one from the kitchen. Also put your violin in its case."

The boy nodded, going to the kitchen and then back through the sitting room and into his bedroom, the empty sack under one arm. Aleksandr knew his son wouldn't question him. He always did what he was told without reservation or hesitation.

While they waited in silence, Aleksandr's mind raced along with the pounding in his chest. He could feel the burning weight of blood collecting in his lungs. "You'll be good to the boy," he said to the maestro. "You can see that he listens well, and obeys. He is . . ." He stopped. "He is my son. You understand." He pulled the sheet of blank paper towards him, and shakily and quickly wrote a number of scrawling lines, dotted with falling ink. "He can read, although he may not fully make sense of what this says until he is older. It's important to me that he understands why this has happened to him. Will you make sure that he doesn't lose the letter I give him?"

The maestro nodded, but his expression was one of impatience, and Aleksandr didn't wish him to take the boy while feeling annoyed. "Kolya!" he called, finding sudden strength. "Come. Come here, now."

The boy came from his room, the bulging sack in one hand and the little leather violin case in the other. He looked at his father, his eyes wide. Aleksandr realized he had frightened him by calling to him in the unfamiliar, loud voice.

"It's all right, Kolya," he said quietly. "It's all right—you've done nothing wrong." Kolya's shoulders lowered and he smiled at his father. "Kolya," Aleksandr said then, fighting the dreaded feeling in his chest, "you will go with the maestro."

Kolya looked at him, his head tilted slightly.

"You will play your violin with the others. It's what you want, isn't it? You want to play your violin every day, and make wonderful harmonies."

Kolya smiled and nodded. "Yes, Papa, I will play my violin with them today, and come home tonight and tell Mama about it."

Aleksandr closed his eyes. His beautiful, musical Kolya. He put the folded paper into the boy's tunic pocket. "This you must always keep. Do you understand?" He put Kolya's hand on the pocket. "It's very, very important. It says your name, and where you live. It tells my name, and your mother's, and Tima's. It also says . . . It's a letter, for you to read. You don't have to read it now. Read it when you are a bigger boy, Kolya. You mustn't ever lose it."

Kolya patted the paper, smiling at the rustle, and nodded at his father. "Mama is making *shuba* for supper today. I love chopped herring and egg."

Aleksandr pulled the boy against his chest. He felt the child's bones, barely covered with flesh. Then he looked into his narrow face and brushed his hair back from his forehead. "You are a good boy. Always remember that your father and mother know you are a good boy. And you are a brilliant musician. Brilliant."

Again Kolya nodded.

"Go with the maestro now," Aleksandr said, the cough bubbling up again. "Say goodbye to your papa." He kissed the boy's forehead and cheeks, not wanting to touch Kolya's lips with his own because of his disease.

"Go now," he urged, wanting his son to leave before the coughing began, knowing too that he was about to cry.

27

*U*la arrived home as the tarantass was rumbling away from the house.

"Whose carriage is that?" she asked as she set down her basket. "Are you feeling any better?" But as she looked at her husband, some odd, unreadable expression on his face made her legs unexpectedly weak. She swallowed and went to him. "What is it, Sasha?"

"Ula," he started, unable to find the right words. "Our boy, I . . . I thought . . ." He looked towards the boys' bedroom.

She followed his gaze. "Was Tima hurt at work? Tima?" she called. When there was no answer, she hurried across the room, her boots staccato on the uncarpeted floor. "Kolyenka?" she said, looking into the tidy, empty room. She whirled round to face Aleksandr. "What's happened? Kolya—where is he?"

Aleksandr was so pale—apart from two high, hectic

spots of fever on his cheeks—that in that instant Ula knew what he would look like when he was dead.

"This is better, Ula. He will have a future—"

"Who?"

"Kolya."

"A future?" Ula's voice was low with confusion. "Kolya's future is here, with us." She cocked her head. "With me. This is his home. He can't be anywhere but here, with me." Her voice had risen. "What have you done?" She looked towards the open front door, blinking as she tried to make sense of what her husband was saying.

Aleksandr rubbed his eyes as if awakening from some deep, confusing dream.

Ula crossed the room to him in a strange sliding run, her arms out at her sides as if the room were tilting. "Tell me what you've done," she insisted, so low that her voice was almost a growl. She glanced at the open door again. "What have you done, Aleksandr Danilovich?"

What *had* he done? Aleksandr was overcome with panic, the cough rumbling. He remembered the boy's fragile body against his, the shoulder blades sharp. "His music," he said. "His talent. The maestro can . . ."

In that instant, an animal howl came from Ula's throat. Aleksandr had never heard this sound, not even when she was giving birth. She ran from the house and down the road, the howl echoing.

※

Only Timofey carries the secret of what happened next.

He heard his mother's screams from the cooperage at the end of their road, and thought, *It's happened, Papa is dead.*

Nothing else would make his mother shriek so. He ran out to see her coming towards him, her shawl trailing behind her, her skirt held high in both hands, showing so much of her legs that he was embarrassed in spite of the cold fear in his belly.

"Papa?" he called, rushing to meet her. "It's Papa?"

She shook her head, gasping, her mouth open, her lips edged with white spittle, an odd ashy sheen to her skin. "Go!" she shouted, pushing his shoulder. "It's Kolya. Go after him." She was panting, trying to speak around the gasping breaths.

"What's happened? Go where? Has he wandered off?"

She slapped him then, slapped his cheek hard, and he reached up to grab her wrist. His mother was so gentle. She never screamed, had never slapped him, or even kicked at one of the dogs they'd owned. She was unlike his friends' mothers, who beat their sons regularly. He was so confused he didn't know what to think.

"I told you to *go*. Run! Get a horse. Go after them," she panted through her sobs, her body trembling violently.

"Yes, yes, I will. But you have to tell me who. Who am I going after? What's happened to Kolya?" He put his hands on her shoulders. "Mama?"

At the last word, Ula drew a deep, shaky breath and struggled to compose herself. She wiped her lips. "I'm sorry, Tima. I'm sorry. It's the maestro. Your papa—he let him go with that man. He *gave* him to him. He's taking him away."

"Gave him away?" Tima wondered if his mother had gone mad. His father couldn't have done what she was saying.

"Music—for the music. He's taken my baby, my Kolyenka." She started to sob again, dropping to her knees on the road, pulling at Timofey's callused hands. People had come out of doorways to watch them.

"Timofey Aleksandrovitch!" someone called. "Do you need help?"

Tima didn't answer. He turned from his mother and ran down the road, the dust kicked up in a long grey plume behind him.

He had run for perhaps five minutes down the twisting road when a horse plodded up behind him. It was just an old nag, an unsaddled Mongolian pony, but the man who had called out to him had heard Ula's pleas. He'd taken the horse from his yard and come after Timofey. He slid off and Timofey used the horse's mane to pull himself onto her bare back.

His fingers in her mane, he urged her on with a series of kicks to her bony sides. The old mare did as well as she could, hobbling in a painful, unrhythmic trot, and within another ten minutes Timofey spotted, in a cloud of dust, the back of the musicians' open carriage.

He kicked the horse harder, and she managed to break into a canter, and Timofey saw that he was gaining. In another few moments he would reach the carriage. He would ride alongside and call to the maestro to give his brother back. It was all a mistake—he wasn't to take Kolya after all.

He envisioned Kolya crying. Did Kolya understand what was happening? Perhaps his little brother was smiling, thinking he was out for a carriage ride.

No. Kolya would be crying.

Even though the maestro would argue, Timofey would threaten him. His work had defined his chest and created well-muscled arms. He knew his own strength, and envisioned pulling the man out of the tarantass and drawing back his fist. The others were weedy young musicians. They would be afraid of him, and concerned about hurting their hands—their livelihood. It would be easy to scoop up Kolya and put him in front of him on the nag.

Tima envisioned Kolya smiling with relief the way he did the other times Tima had come to his rescue. He also imagined his mother's face, her own relief and swooping joy when he rode up to their home with Kolya. He couldn't envision his father's face; Timofey didn't know how he'd let this happen.

All this went through his head as he rode towards the back of the carriage. The dust stung his eyes and coated his lips. Even with his mouth closed, he tasted the grit of the road.

He was soon close enough to hear the jingling of the harness bells on the horses pulling the tarantass.

And then, like a small explosion with an accompanying burst of light, Tima saw something else. He saw himself on a horse—not this broken, sway-backed old creature, but a sturdy, high-spirited horse—riding away from Chita, down this same road. Without his brother to care for, to weigh him down for the rest of his life, he would be free to go when his mother no longer needed him. He would not be tied to the business—or to Kolya.

Tima would be free to live the life he wanted, fettered by nothing and no one.

As if hearing his thoughts, the horse's gait slowed, and she made a coughing snort, shaking her head.

He kicked her again, close enough to the carriage now to think—he couldn't be sure—that he saw the back of Kolya's head. The head turned. Was it Kolya, calling out? *Tima. Tima, help me.*

The tarantass was coming to a fork in the road. He squinted, peering through the dust, trying to make out the jumble of bodies crowded onto the wooden seats. But the vision was clear: his brother's face wet with tears, crying for him as he had so many times, depending on him for rescue. Needing him, today and forever.

And just like that, in a moment he would relive for the rest of his life, Timofey lifted his heels. At the signal, the horse slowed further, and then stopped. Her head drooped, a great shudder of relief going through her.

Timofey sat in the warm May sunshine on the wheezing horse until the carriage turned down the left fork in the rutted, dusty road and was gone.

He rode slowly back into Chita, returning the horse to the kindly neighbour. He entered the house alone. His mother stood for a long moment, looking at him. When he shook his head, she ran to the bedroom, wailing.

Tima kept his face tight, unable to speak, afraid that what he had done could be read on his features.

His father explained his thinking, looking for the understanding from Timofey that he couldn't get from his wife. "You must know why I thought it best, son," he stated weakly, taking deep, painful draws of breath and wiping his mouth. "You know Kolya, perhaps better than anyone. I did the right thing." He stared down at the blood-soaked handkerchief in his hand.

Timofey came close to his father. "No. You didn't do the right thing. Look what you've done to Mama. And Kolya . . . he can't survive away from home. From us, from me. I'll never forgive you. Do you hear me? Never!" Then he ran outside.

Even as he ran, Tima knew he had treated Kolya far worse than his father had. His father had acted out of misguided love; Tima had failed to act out of selfishness.

Timofey knew he would never be forgiven, even if he confessed to the priest. It didn't matter what absolution the priest might give. It didn't matter that he could also go to the *datsan* and spin prayer wheels and tie blue prayer flags on all the branches he could. He was caught between religions, aware of both the flames of everlasting hell and the power of karma. In one religion he would suffer an eternity after his death, and in the other be reborn as a lowly dung beetle.

He knew he would never forgive himself. Yet he also knew that, given the choice a second time, he would do the same thing.

The day following the commission of his great sin, Timofey's mother came into his bedroom as he was getting ready for work. She urged him to set out for Irkutsk instead. The maestro would be travelling for many days, stopping in villages overnight. Timofey could go to each village until he found Kolya, and bring him back. "Shut the cooperage, and go," she said dully, her face blotchy and her eyes swollen nearly shut from a night of weeping.

"But Papa is . . ." He caught himself. "Mama, how can I go away when Papa is so ill?" He glanced through the doorway to the sitting room, where his father lay on the bench.

But Ula shook her head. "Don't worry about your father." Her voice took on a hardness that shocked Timofey. He thought he understood the depth of her anger, but to see her react so stonily was as much a surprise as her slap across his face the day before. Had he ever really known her, or was this what grief did to people?

"There's enough money to take from the business—you can travel all the way to Irkutsk if you must," she said. She made no attempt to lower her voice. "You have to search until you find Kolya, and then bring him back to me."

"What makes you so sure I will find Kolya?" Tima dared to say, a slow anger towards his mother inexplicably building. He knew it would hurt her to hear his doubt, but feeling anger took away some of the guilt. "It's a big place, isn't it?"

"There can only be so many maestros, and so many little boys who play the violin and are new to the city. You'll find him," she said with such certainty that there was nothing for Timofey to do but nod. He said, *Yes, yes I'll go, once Papa*... He turned away before he finished the sentence. But Ula said, even more loudly, as if making sure Aleksandr could hear, "Yes, once your father doesn't need you, you'll go and bring my son back."

⁂

Aleksandr Danilovich Kasakov died three days after Timofey watched the carriage carrying Kolya rumble away.

Those three silent days were filled with grief: Timofey left for the shop early and stayed as long as possible. He didn't wish to be in the house, with his father's endless choking and bloody retching and his mother's quiet, steady weeping.

The last words he had spoken to his father haunted him.

⁂

The house was eerily quiet without Aleksandr's coughing.

His body lay in the open, rough-hewn coffin supported by chairs in the sitting room and surrounded by flickering candles. His stiff hands had been placed on his chest and curled around one candle that illuminated his face. Timofey sat on a bench. He tensed for a cough from the casket.

Some of Aleksandr's friends had come by earlier in the day, but Ula didn't welcome them, didn't offer them tea or a chair. They stood in the small, low-ceilinged room for a few moments, in awkward silence, and left.

When they were alone again, Ula had gone into her bedroom, choosing not to sit with Timofey, not to cry and pray and mourn for her husband's soul in the Russian way, nor chant and burn incense in the Buddhist way. Timofey remembered the death of his grandfather, and how his mother had told him not to be sad, although it was all right if he must cry. Temujin's death, she told him, was simply another turning of the Wheel of Life, and it was important to remain calm and think good thoughts. "Temujin is going through a change," she'd said, "preparing for his rebirth. My father was always a good man, and will be reborn into a positive form." For three days there were Buddhist monks and visitors to their home, and texts chanted in unison, with ringing bells and beating drums and horns sounding at various intervals. There were burning oil lamps and incense in front of an image of Buddha that sat beside Temujin's body until it was removed for the cremation at the *datsan*. Many of Temujin's friends came quietly to pay their respects. Everything felt graceful and slow, almost dreamlike.

In contrast, the funerals he had attended with his father at the Decembrist Orthodox church took on a showy and chaotic frenzy, pleading for God to have mercy on the sin-riddled souls of the dead. To Timofey the Orthodox rituals created a certain hopelessness about death, which was a necessary consequence of human life, due to original sin—unlike the Buddhists, who believed that death was necessary to achieve everlasting life.

To see his mother refuse to treat his dead father respectfully in either religion upset Timofey. He was unable to understand the depth of Ula's anger. Even with his death, she couldn't forgive what Aleksandr had done, couldn't mourn him. He realized, as he sat through the long, dark night, that it was because she was already in mourning for Kolya.

In the wavering light of the candles, Timofey grieved alone for his father, looking at Aleksandr's waxy profile and thinking of all the time he had spent with him, learning to read and write in two languages, discussing world history and politics and life outside Chita, as well as learning his trade. He thought of the times his father had patted his back and smiled proudly at him, and felt true sadness.

He cried then, on his knees beside the coffin, kissing his crucifix. But even as he wept, he knew he cried partly for himself.

He recognized the selfishness of his act, and knew that what he would do next was as bad, or worse.

The day after the funeral—Aleksandr was buried with the Russian rites, in the cemetery behind the timbered, green-domed Decembrist church—Ula told Tima he had to go to Irkutsk. "Your father is dead. There's no reason to linger. The longer Kolya is away from me, the harder it is on him."

"You want me to leave right now? Shouldn't I stay for the nine-day ceremony marking Papa's death? It doesn't feel right to——" Timofey said, but Ula shook her head impatiently.

"You must go." At that her face crumpled, and Timofey realized she hadn't cried during Aleksandr's funeral, standing as if deep in thought, looking at the budding trees behind the church. "It's only Kolya who can make me feel better, only my baby. He must be here, with me. He's all that I want, and need." She turned away from him then, and something cold settled in Timofey's chest.

"All right," he said to her back, his voice unemotional. "I'll go as soon as I've finished the last order, in two or three days." He would have to lock up the cooperage. Antip, ten years older than Timofey and adept at the physical work, couldn't read. He amiably took his orders from the younger man, but had absolutely no ambition. "I'll buy a horse and go."

Over the next two days, Timofey worked tirelessly to finish the order. The rhythm and monotony of the movement—the rasp of adze on wood—calmed him, and allowed him to devise his plan.

It was easier than he thought. He told Antip the cooperage would be closed for an indefinite period, and gave him an extra week's salary, apologizing for putting the man out of work. Then he drew up a paper making sure his mother would receive the proceeds from the eventual sale of the business. He had it witnessed and signed by his father's faithful friend Georgi, the only remaining exile in Chita. The rest of the Decembrists had died; many were older than

Aleksandr, and all had been physically weakened by their brutal penal service.

"This is to protect my mother," Timofey told Georgi, "if something should happen to me."

Georgi shook his head. "A strong young man like you will be running the cooperage for many years longer than your mother will be on this earth."

Timofey nodded, but asked the man to keep the paper for him.

With cash from the business, he bought Felya, a fine young Don horse, and a pair of new boots. His mother made him as much food as could be packed into the woven saddle-bags, and handed him two warm Mongolian blankets, spun from yak wool.

He took his father's crucifix and books, and a prayer wheel. He also took the small *svirel* Kolya had given him on his last name day. Kolya had clumsily carved Tima's name into it, and proudly presented it to his big brother at the family celebration.

"You'll find him, and come right back," Ula said as Timofey stood beside his horse. It was morning, and the bells were ringing for late Mass.

Timofey couldn't meet her eye. He ran his hands over Felya's high honey-coloured withers, the sun gilding them.

"How many days will it take you to get there?" his mother asked.

"Many. It will depend on the weather and the roads." Tima wanted to ride away from his mother's sad yet hopeful face as quickly as possible.

"It's June now. That's a good thing," she called to him as he mounted. She hadn't embraced him.

He pulled on Felya's reins, turning him towards the open road. "Goodbye, *Mamasha*. Blessings upon you with both hands," he said. He suddenly remembered how she used to sing to him when she tucked him into bed as a child, her smile as she set his favourite dishes in front of him, her gentle touch.

"I will watch for your return with your brother," she said. "I know I can trust you. You are a good son, Timofey Aleksandrovitch. A good man." She added her own blessing in Buryat, and Timofey kicked his heels and rode out of Chita.

28

*G*risha tried to forget his mother's final words to him.
He knows, as he and Antonina ride back to Angelkov
from the dacha, that his mother was wrong. He was not a
good son, and he is not a good man.

Antonina's smell is on his skin. When Antonina allowed
herself to stop being a countess and simply be a woman, he
lost the tight control he'd maintained for most of his life.
Watching her sleeping, he felt a desire to protect her, to take
away the pain.

The pain of a betrayal that is his own doing.

And in spite of the way she had spoken to him before she
turned and walked from the dacha an hour earlier, his feelings for her haven't changed. As they ride side by side in
silence save for the sucking of the horses' hooves in the mud,
the cawing of crows, he wants her to smile at him the way
she did in the candlelight in the dacha.

Seeing her now, clutching Mikhail's coat—all she has of him—he remembers her ten years younger, in the flogging yard holding her baby with such fierce protectiveness.

Grisha knows she trusts him implicitly. It pains him to think back to the previous day in Tushinsk. He had hoped— prayed—that he would go to the door Lev had described, hand Lev the stack of rubles, and Mikhail would come out of the hut. But that wasn't what happened. Lev didn't have the boy. He said the Mitlovsky brat was waiting for Grisha in another village, farther down the road. He would take the money Grisha had brought and give him instructions on how to find the boy. Go with me now, Grisha had said, take me to him, but Lev shook his head. Grisha was furious, arguing with Lev as he held the rubles, telling him it was another ruse. He would keep the rubles until he knew with certainty the boy was alive. Give me proof, then take me to him, and once I have him, you will get your money. And as he stood arguing, he heard the countess's screams. He shoved the money back into his tunic and ran to find her face covered in blood, and her pointing at the village child in Mikhail's *talmochka*.

When he went back to question the father of the deaf child, he'd said, "Tell me the truth." He knew, by the younger man's blinking and swallowing, that he was hiding something. "Do you remember when I came to Tushinsk in the spring, looking for the landowner's child?"

The man nodded.

"So you know who I am."

The man nodded again.

"Then you have nothing to fear. All I want is to find the child and return him to his mother."

The man looked over Grisha's shoulder at Antonina.

"You will not be punished. You have my word. Tell me what you know."

At this, the younger man, his arm around his wife, told him that they had been forced to hide the boy during the summer, a few months after Grisha had come to Tushinsk looking for him. The boy was brought by three men. This was sometime in early July; the barley was already high. They had come to his door in the night. He remembered that it was a hot night, and the boy carried his coat. He held it tightly—it was all he had. The man told Grisha he had been chosen to hide the boy because his wife and son were deaf and mute; they could communicate with no one except him, and no one paid them any heed. He was told that should he disclose that he was hiding the boy, or allow the child to leave their izba, his own child would be killed.

"I knew he was the landowner's kidnapped son. But what was I to do?" he said to Grisha. "I wouldn't risk my own son's life for another's."

Grisha looked at the deaf boy, his head pressed against his mother's arm. "Was Mikhail—was the boy in good health?"

"He was thin and dirty, his clothes tattered and his hair long. He had a few bruises on his arms and legs. He didn't talk except to ask me to help him escape. He told me his father would pay me hundreds of rubles." The villager took a deep breath. "I told him his father was powerless now, and the boy tried to hit me. I saw he was scared, but I knew he wouldn't be easy to keep. I had to make sure he didn't do something to get my own boy killed." He put his hand on his son's head, and his voice grew bolder. "I taught him a lesson, and he quieted down. I had to keep him tied, because I was afraid he'd still try to escape, even after the beating. And then a week later the men took him away, again in the middle of the night. He had been asleep when they untied him and dragged him out, and he left his coat behind." The man looked closely at Grisha. "Are you a father?"

Grisha shook his head. There was a steady tick in his right cheek.

"If you were, you'd know why I did what I did." The younger man's expression was defiant.

Grisha looked at the man's dirty child. "As the countess said, a new coat will be sent for your son. And also a small reward—for your honesty." He turned and went back to Antonina, slumped on her horse.

Now, riding back to Angelkov, Grisha thinks of the villager's casual mention of beating the boy and keeping him tied up. He wonders how Mikhail is surviving. If he's surviving.

In Mikhail's favour is that he is his mother's son. The boy takes after her in all ways: bright and curious, with sensitivity as well as a mischievous side. He is winning, like she is. Should he have been like his father, imperious and self-absorbed, it might go worse for him. Grisha tries to comfort himself by remembering his own youth: he was less than five years older than Mikhail when he set out on his own, and he'd survived.

But the boy is not like Grisha. No, with his fine bones and clever fingers and instincts, he is more like another boy Grisha once knew. Mikhail reminds him, he has to admit, of the little brother he hasn't seen in twenty years. Kolya.

Since the kidnapping, Grisha has berated himself daily for putting Mikhail into danger and nearly destroying the countess, all because of his contempt for the count. He hadn't prayed since he left his home in Chita, but after Mikhail was not returned as promised, he needed to pray. And so he went to the church on the estate, late at night when Father Cyril slept, and prayed that the child not be harmed.

But prayer does not assuage his old guilt. He has betrayed a second boy.

⁓

As they ride into Angelkov, Lilya runs from the house. She gasps and covers her mouth as she looks up at Antonina's bruised face, the bloodied bodice under her open cloak. She glares at Grisha as if he is responsible.

"Hurry, madam," Lilya says then, still looking at Grisha. "It's the count. He . . . It's bad."

Antonina slides off her horse, clutching Mikhail's coat. "What happened?"

Lilya touches the sleeve of the *talmochka*. "Where were you last night? What happened to your face? And where did you find Misha's—"

Antonina walks towards the house. "Tell me about the count." She doesn't look back at Grisha.

But Lilya does, and sees that he is watching Antonina intently.

"After the count had his chloroform last night, Pavel fell asleep," Lilya tells her. "Then, just before dawn, when Pavel awoke, he saw that the count's bed was empty. He thought maybe he had gone to your room. So he went there, but . . . there was only me, sitting up waiting for you. How could I sleep when you hadn't come home?"

Antonina is crossing the veranda, Lilya following, talking quickly. "Pavel told me your husband was missing. I went to the servants' quarters and woke Lyosha and he got all the servants up to search for you both. We thought the count might have done something to you. We were all so worried, Tosya." She bumps into Antonina as the other woman stops and turns to her.

"So he was found?"

"Yes. Yes, Lyosha found him in the cemetery, soaked through and shivering, lying on an old grave. When he was brought home, he said he was sleeping with his son. He's very ill, Tosya, even worse than before."

Tinka is dancing about Antonina's feet as she goes down the long hall and into Konstantin's bedroom. Pavel, sitting beside the bed, jumps up as she enters.

"How is he?" she asks. Her husband's breathing is laboured.

"It appears he has succumbed to fever again, madam. I don't know how long he was out in the rain and cold. Madam, I'm sorry, I thought he would sleep all night, I—"

"It's not your fault, Pavel. Has the doctor been sent for?"

"No, madam. There was no one to give the order. You were not here. We went to Grisha's house. He was also not at Angelkov." Pavel looks at her for a few seconds too long.

"Send Lyosha for Dr. Molov. I am back, and I am ordering it."

Already God is punishing her for her behaviour in the dacha. Already He is letting her know that for her sin, there must be a reckoning.

Lilya follows her to her room, but Antonina picks up Tinka and tells her she wants to be alone. She locks her door and sets Misha's coat on the window seat. She washes herself and puts on fresh clothing. She sits with the coat in her lap, stroking it, Tinka falling asleep beside her.

Antonina finally leaves the window seat and looks in the

mirror at her blackened eyes and swollen nose. Full of shame for sharing her body while her husband wandered in the night—while she should have been thinking only of finding her son—she kneels in her prayer corner. In front of the table decorated with her icons, she confesses to God and the Holy Mother that she is guilty of breaking one of the commandments, and of committing one of the deadly sins. She begs for forgiveness for her adultery and lust.

That evening, Antonina is again sitting on the window seat when Lilya comes in.

"Good evening, Tosya," she says, glancing at Mikhail's coat, still smeared with grease and soot and dried blood, in Antonina's lap. "I've brought your hot chocolate." She sets down the silver tray with its tall, steaming mug, and then goes to the bed to turn down the coverlet. "Did the doctor give you something to help with the pain from your nose?"

"How do I appear to you, Lilya?" Antonina asks, ignoring the question.

"Why, you will soon look fine, Tosya." Lilya is straightening the pillows on the bed. "Your nose will heal well. The plaster the doctor put on it will hold it in place so that it retains its shape, and . . ." She stops as she finally turns to face Antonina. She draws in a breath. "Tosya, what is it? You look . . . different."

In spite of the thin strips of plaster over the bridge of Antonina's nose and the evidence of trauma to her face, there's something else. It's similar, Lilya realizes, to the way Antonina looked the first few days after Mikhail was taken—as if she's had some sort of shock.

"Different?" Antonina says. She covers her face with her hands.

Lilya is confused. She had been sick with worry when Antonina hadn't come home the night before. When the doctor was with Konstantin, Antonina told her about seeing the child wearing Misha's coat, and how she had hurt her nose. She told Lilya that because they were nearer to the home of the Prince and Princess Bakanev, she had asked Grisha to take her there. The rain started and the Bakanevs persuaded her to stay for the night.

"Tosya," Lilya persists, "what is it? What are you not telling me?"

Antonina lifts her face from her hands but doesn't speak.

Lilya drops to her knees and grabs Antonina's hands. "Is it about Misha?" she breathes. "Is there something more, more than his coat, and his notes?" Only fresh distress over her son, Lilya thinks, could give Antonina this odd expression of fear. And there's something else.

Antonina's face closes, and she pulls her hands from Lilya's. "No. There's nothing more about Misha." She turns to the window to stare out at the blackness beyond.

Lilya is still kneeling. "Would you like me to take Misha's coat and clean it?" she asks.

Antonina murmurs her consent.

Lilya knows something important has happened, but she can't figure out what it is.

⌒

Early the next morning, Antonina is still in bed when Olga knocks quietly, announcing that Fyodor must speak to her.

Antonina hasn't been able to sleep, thinking of what

happened in the village and what happened in the dacha. The doctor told her Konstantin had been badly affected by his night outside, and that he would return today to see how he was faring.

There's so much guilt.

She throws a shawl over her nightdress and shuts Tinka in the bedroom. She goes down the stairs, her feet bare. Her hair is in one long plait she's pinned loosely around her head, her face a darkened horror. She no longer cares that the servants see her like this. What does it matter?

As she descends the staircase, she's aware of stiffness in her inner thighs—another reminder of what she's done with Grisha.

In the vestibule, Fyodor turns his cap in his hands. His face is pale and drawn. Antonina doesn't understand his expression.

"Countess," he says. "There is . . . It is bad news, I'm afraid."

What more could go wrong? "Mother of God," she murmurs. "Please. It isn't . . . Is it Mikhail? What is it? Tell me, Fyodor," she says, panic in her voice.

He looks at the floor, turning his cap more quickly. "I'm sorry, countess. One of the horses . . ."

Antonina draws in a deep breath of relief. It's not Mikhail. "Dunia? Is she ill?"

"No. It's Felya, Grisha's horse. It's dead. I'm sorry, madam."

She takes a moment to absorb this. She knows Grisha loves the horse. "But there was nothing wrong with him. Grisha rode him yesterday." She brushes past Fyodor to go to the stables, to see for herself what's happened, but the man reaches out and catches her arm. She looks down at his thick fingers on the delicate cambric of her sleeve. His knuckles are dark, as if slightly bruised. There is a deep, freshly scabbed scratch on the back of his hand, running to his wrist. He looks at Antonina and removes his hand.

"It's better if you don't, countess. You shouldn't see the horse in this . . ." He stops, and something heavy drops in Antonina's stomach. "It is very unpleasant, madam, but you had to be informed. The carcass will be removed shortly."

Antonina pushes past him, hurrying out of the house to the stables in her nightdress. Her feet are still bare, but she doesn't feel the cold packed earth, damp and sticky from yesterday's rain, as she crosses the yard. She hears Fyodor's footsteps behind her. Her breath streams in the cool autumn air. A handful of men stand in the doorway of the stable. They all look down when they see her approach, and part for her as she hurries to Felya's stall.

The stable is near to empty. In the last few weeks Grisha has sold off most of the Orlov Trotters—considered the equine royalty of Russia—for a good price. The countess was pleased when he came to her with the rubles from the sale. There were only six horses left: three of the Orlovs for pulling the troika, Dunia and one Arabian. As well as Felya.

Lyosha stands with legs wide as if on guard, his face contorted in grief, his cheeks wet. He shakes his head, saying, *No, countess*, but she pushes past him.

Antonina stares into the stall, her brain trying to understand what she's seeing. She clamps her lips to hold back a cry at what is left of Felya. She puts one hand over her mouth and nose. There is a frenzy of flies gathering over the animal, and the stink of blood and the exposed organs is strong.

Antonina gags, not only at the smell, but at the brutality.

Felya, noble, high-spirited Felya, has been ripped open from the base of his neck to his tail. Cut, sliced down the belly as one slices a fish, and gutted, his entrails spilled onto the straw of the stall. The eyes are still open.

Around the horse's slender black neck hangs a rough rope, and on it a jagged piece of wood. Misspelled in charcoal are two sentences: *This is what happens. You don't do what we say.*

"Where is Grisha?" she asks.

"I went to his house, countess," Lyosha says, wiping his eyes with his sleeve. "But he isn't there. Do you know where he is?"

There are hard, fast footsteps and suddenly Grisha is standing beside her. He grips the top rail of the stall as he looks at the horse. The skin around his lips is white with shock.

Antonina doesn't want to witness his grief. "I'm sorry, Grisha," she says, her voice low as she looks away from him.

"We will bury him, Fyodor," he says, his voice hard.

"But we burn the dead animals. It will be difficult to dig such a large—"

"There are enough of us. He won't be burned. Do you understand?"

"All right, Grisha," Fyodor says. "If the countess gives her permission," he adds, turning to her.

She sees that his gaze is on her bare feet.

Having a stable serf—former serf, she has to keep telling herself—see her naked feet reminds her of who she is. "Of course. It will be as Grisha wishes. Thank you, Fyodor," she says, and he lifts his eyes from her feet to her face. She doesn't know if Fyodor truly does look at her with something slightly less than respect. But then he nods to the men behind him, and Antonina steps aside, closer to Grisha, as they move into the stall and spread a large sheet of canvas. With grunts and muttered curses they start to haul Felya's remains out of the stable.

Antonina watches them, seeing that Lyosha is still struggling for control. He's a gentle boy. Man, she corrects herself. He must be past nineteen by now. He has no violence in him.

She thinks of Fyodor's bruised knuckles, the deep scratch on the back of his hand. Is he one of the men who butchered Felya, putting on an act of dismay so as not to arouse suspicion?

In the next instant, Antonina tells herself that her imagination is running wild. All of the yard servants carry fresh bruises and scrapes on top of old scars from the hard work they do. Fyodor and Raisa laboured for Konstantin for many years before she arrived at Angelkov as a bride, and Fyodor has always been a respectful and hard-working head stableman.

"Wait," she calls out, and the men stop. "Cut the board from the horse's neck and give it to me," she orders. Grisha watches her as Lyosha hands it over.

"It's a warning," Grisha says.

She studies the splintered board. "A warning? Of what, Grisha?"

Grisha hadn't given Lev the money. Now his beloved horse is dead. They are becoming bolder. "You're meeting with the lawyer this afternoon?" he asks, avoiding her question.

She has forgotten about Yakovlev's visit. "Oh. With all of this, and Konstantin deathly ill . . ." She wants Grisha's comfort. "I wish I could cancel the appointment, but Yakovlev will already be on his way. Do you still wish . . . Shall I call for you when he arrives?"

He nods—little more than a dip of his head—and leaves her, standing with her bare feet suddenly cold, the board hanging from one hand.

*

Back in her room, Antonina shudders, holding Tinka to her chest as she leans her forehead on the window. The splintered board sits on the table near the fireplace. *This is what happens. You don't do what we say.* Don't do what who says? It was Grisha's horse. Is it Grisha they're warning?

Her son is gone, her husband . . . Who knows what will happen to him? The servants are all leaving. She has committed a terrible sin. Now a beautiful horse is slaughtered.

From the window, Antonina can see Olga in the wide flower garden, cutting the last of the hardy bronze and gold chrysanthemums and orange gerberas. Olga has no family, and nowhere to go. She counts on Antonina to support her in her old age.

How many of the servants will continue to depend on her? Without them, she cannot run Angelkov. How can she keep up the magnificent house, the small orchard, the vegetable and flower gardens and the hothouse of exotics, as well as the granaries and cattle barns and stables? She needs money. Even though the last thing she wants to do today is speak of finances and the estate to the lawyer, she must. It's bewildering at the best of times. After all that has happened in the last two days . . . Again she thinks of Grisha's unreadable expression as she stood beside him in the stable, and that makes her put down Tinka and cross to the wardrobe to take out her vodka.

There are streaks of blood on the pale carpet. She must have cut her foot on something, a splinter in the stables or a sharp stone in the yard. She stares at the blood, remembering the stains from Konstantin's hand on the green silk settee.

She retrieves the bottle and puts it to her lips. At the first taste she thinks of drinking with Grisha in the dacha, the way his lips curved on the rim of the glass. The way they'd felt on hers.

She covers her mouth with her hand and swallows. She is still a wife. She returns the bottle and goes to see Konstantin. His breath rattles the quietness of the bedroom.

"Please let me know when the doctor returns," she tells Pavel, then goes into the hall. "Lilya!" she calls, but Lilya doesn't appear. She calls for her again, and finally a young girl comes out of another bedroom carrying a rag and a pail. "Nusha," Antonina says, "find Lilya and have her come to my room."

The girl ducks her head and scampers down the stairs.

Lilya arrives a few minutes later. "Where were you?" Antonina asks. "I called for you a number of times. I wish you to bring me warm water to clean my feet. But . . . what's wrong, Lilya?"

"The horse. I saw it."

"Who could do such a brutal thing?"

Lilya doesn't respond. She is twisting her hands in front of her.

"Do you care so much about it?" Antonina asks. She hadn't thought that Lilya would show emotion over the dead animal. Lilya has never shown any interest in animals apart from Tinka.

Lilya still doesn't answer, shaking her head as she continues to wring her hands.

A thought comes to Antonina. Surely she's wrong, she

thinks, as she glances at the splintered board with its bloody warning.

Lilya's writing has never progressed beyond a very rudimentary style. She always wrote the letter *h* backwards in the psalms she printed out. No matter how many times Antonina pointed out the inverted letter, Lilya continued to form it incorrectly.

Lilya leaves to fetch the water and Antonina picks up the splintered board. As she studies the crudely printed letters, she knows it isn't Lilya's hand; there are too many other errors. Still, the letter *h* troubles Antonina—one letter, yet she can't stop thinking about it.

She recalls Lyosha's face: thoughtful, a little wistful. Did Lilya teach her brother to write? Please, not Lyosha, she prays.

Not Lyosha.

29

"*It* sounds like the beginning of pneumonia," Dr. Molov says, his eyes closed as he presses his ear to Konstantin's lungs. He straightens, taking a small rubber hammer from his bag and tapping on Konstantin's chest, producing a dull thud. "Yes, there is fluid collecting."

Konstantin moans, and Pavel steps beside him with a bottle and a glass.

The doctor looks at it. "What's this?"

"Chloroform, doctor," Pavel says, "as you instructed."

"As I instructed? When? Do you mean after the surgery to his arm?"

Pavel swallows, then nods.

"You allow him to regularly breathe chloroform?"

"This is a tincture, mixed with alcohol. He drinks it. When . . ." Pavel knows, by the doctor's expression, that something is very wrong. "When the bottle you left him was finished, it was arranged to have someone bring a supply of it to the estate."

The doctor sits heavily in the chair beside the bed. "Holy Mother of God."

"What is it, Dr. Molov?" Antonina asks.

"His behaviour—the spells of shouting and confusion, his irrational suspiciousness and threats."

"Yes. He's grown worse steadily since the amputation."

The doctor stands. "Chloroform is a poison to the brain. It's only to be used in the smallest quantities, to put a patient to sleep temporarily, to allow him or her to withstand great trauma to the body." He looks from Pavel to Antonina. "The chloroform has caused his madness."

"But you told Pavel that—"

"For the first two or three days. That's all. Not daily, not for months." He makes a sound of disgust. "Can nobody follow a simple order?" He snaps his bag closed and gestures for Antonina to follow him away from the bed. They stop at the door. "His sputum is discoloured. If he can't clear it, in a few days he'll drown from the fluid in his lungs. I'm sorry to have to speak so bluntly, countess."

"But there's a chance he'll live?" Antonina asks.

"There is little chance of a full recovery. There's nothing to be done. You should also know"—the doctor glances back at Konstantin—"that should he rally physically, his mental condition will not improve. The damage cannot be reversed." He opens the door. "I suggest, Countess Mitlovskiya, that whatever the outcome, you will need to prepare for a very difficult time ahead."

The lawyer, short, heavy Yakovlev, arrives at two o'clock.

Antonina's head is pounding over all that's happened, but she forces herself not to drink any more from the bottle in her wardrobe. She needs to be as clear as possible when she speaks with Yakovlev. For the same reason, she also makes the decision not to have Grisha present. Even though she had told him earlier that it would be helpful to have him there, she knows how distracted having him near will make her.

Standing behind Konstantin's desk, she finds Yakovlev annoying with his endless fiddling with his moustache and the spastic blinking of his right eye. He has his nostrils stuffed with cloves. As he greets her, he apologizes, saying he has a head cold and the cloves alleviate the clogged sensation.

Yakovlev studies her face. His breeding does not permit him to inquire about her injuries, but he does ask after Mikhail. "Your son . . . there is still no word?"

Antonina shakes her head.

"And the count? How is his health?"

"He's taken a turn for the worse."

Yakovlev makes a sound of sympathy, but begins to spread his papers over Konstantin's desk. "Madam," he says, looking across the desk at her. "The situation is very grave indeed." His voice is nasal because of the cloves in his nose.

For a horrible moment, Antonina has to fight an almost hysterical laughter. The doctor has told her, only hours earlier, to prepare for difficulties. Now the lawyer is telling her the situation is very grave. Under what conditions do these men suppose she's been living for the last months? She covers her trembling, involuntary smile, turning away.

"Are you all right, countess?"

In the next moment, she looks back at him, composed.

She sits in Konstantin's chair, nodding to indicate he should sit as well. "Yes. Tell me about the situation," she says, refusing to give in to alarm. Yakovlev's idea of gravity may be different than hers.

"For the last few years, your husband has been rather remiss in handling his finances," Yakovlev says. "Specifically, he's incurred debt and neglected to pay the estate taxes. Although I spoke to him on both matters frequently, as I know your steward also did, he chose to ignore our advice. There is a great amount owed, countess."

"I see. We owe the government taxes. I must pay them, then. What resources does the count have?"

Yakovlev frowns, leaning forward. "Resources? What do you mean, my dear lady?"

Antonina feels something flutter against her ribs. "I mean, Attorney Yakovlev, from where shall I take the money necessary to pay the government what they—you"—she nods at the papers between them—"say I owe?"

Yakovlev plays with the waxed ends of his moustache. Antonina sees that one side is thicker than the other.

"But Countess Mitlovskiya," the man continues, and Antonina knows what he will say before he says it. She grips her hands in her lap, where Yakovlev can't see them behind the desk. "There are no resources. There is nothing but what you have here in the house. The count has been selling his businesses for the last few years, just to keep Angelkov afloat." He leans back again.

Antonina's eyes go to the bureau-bookcase—a lovely, hundred-year-old piece Konstantin inherited from his father. It has a flap front that becomes a writing table. In the locked bottom drawer sits Konstantin's padlocked box, which had once contained piles and piles of rubles. It is now empty, as is the smaller safe in his bedroom.

She swallows. "I knew, of course, that he shut down the distillery. Other than that, my husband did not keep me informed about business matters. But the government . . . if one can't pay the taxes—and certainly I'm in a category with many other landowners," she adds, remembering Grisha's words, "—if I can't pay the taxes, what can the government do about it?"

Yakovlev's stomach grumbles, and Antonina knows she's remiss in not offering him a meal or even tea after his ride from Pskov. But she wants him to give her the facts and then leave. This is not a social call.

Yakovlev clears his throat. "For all of those deeply in debt, as is the case with Angelkov, the government will take ownership. Or . . ." He stops.

"Take ownership? I could lose Angelkov?" She's shocked by Yakovlev's casual pronouncement. His silence is the answer. Finally she says, "Or? You said 'or'—there is another possibility, Attorney Yakovlev?"

"You could sell off the land not owed to your former serfs. Sell your livestock, furniture, anything that you can, in order to raise the funds to give a deposit. If the government sees that you are attempting to pay your debt, there is the hope they will be lenient, and allow you to stay on your land. You must be able to meet a minimal sum each year. I would suggest you begin some form of payment immediately—at least by the start of next month."

"You're suggesting my neighbours would buy what's left of my land?" She thinks for a moment. "What *is* left of my land?"

Yakovlev nods. "It's calculated on the number of souls your husband owned. In this case, a great many—thousands. So once the land is divided into *mirs*, there would be enough for a small harvest to support you, if you could get your unpaid servants to work it, and perhaps another fifteen versts of forest. That's all. It's a difficult time for everyone, Countess Mitlovskiya," he finishes, and Antonina knows her distress is visible on her face, in her voice.

They sit in silence for a long moment. Outside, one of the dogs barks, but is silenced by a man's shout.

"Do you know . . . have any of the other landowners been threatened?" she asks, Felya's grisly image still so vivid.

Yakovlev's eyebrows rise. "There is definitely unrest, countess, unrest and dissension in many areas. Things will settle when the former serfs understand that protests will get them nowhere, when they remember they should be grateful to God and the Tsar for the great blessings bestowed on them."

Antonina thinks of the misery of Tushinsk. "Blessings?"

"Their freedom, of course. There has been too much bloodshed for decades, starting with the Decembrists in '25. Now the serfs have freedom, yet they act like ungrateful children." He shakes his head. "They depended on their little fathers—the landowners—for everything, doing nothing but complaining. Then we give them freedom, and what do we have? More discontent." He sighs, pressing his fingers against his middle, and Antonina hears his stomach groan again.

She stands, extending her hand. "Thank you, Attorney Yakovlev. We all have much to do now." A shadow of disappointment crosses the man's face as he realizes he won't be fed.

He bows over her hand. Antonina grimaces at the eczema on his scalp. "I will leave my bill," he says, looking up. "Although, in order not to cause you any further time, you may choose to . . ."—he hesitates, searching for the right phrase—"save us both the bother of me having to return for the payment. You understand." He is still holding her hand.

"I do," she says, pulling her hand away. "But please don't leave without a meal. I'm afraid I can't join you, but I'll have the table set up for you in the smaller dining room. And I'm certain there are some wonderful vintage wines in the cellar. You might enjoy a glass with your meal, and . . . would you honour me by taking two—perhaps three—as a small gift?"

Antonina isn't fooling him, but Yakovlev is willing to play the game. He bows again. "It would indeed be my honour, countess," he says.

"I'll have some brought up immediately," she adds, and he smiles.

It's more than many of his clients can offer these days.

Antonina summons Lyosha as soon as Yakovlev is settled in the dining room, eating boiled beetroot salad with onions and sunflower oil with undisguised pleasure. A nice piece of fish sits in a chafing dish in front of him.

The young man comes into the study, his hat in his hand. He has removed his boots and someone has given him a pair of felt slippers to wear in the house. They're too small and his toes push against the soft fabric.

"Can you read and write, Lyosha?" She wants him to say no.

"Yes, madam."

"Then please, sit here," she says, gesturing at the desk,

where there is paper, a pen and an inkwell. "I want you to write something for me," she says, keeping her voice non-committal but firm.

Lyosha's Adam's apple bobs as he swallows and sits down. When he's dipped the pen into the ink and has it poised over the paper, he looks up at Antonina.

"What shall I write, Countess Mitlovskiya?" Something in his expression reminds Antonina of the little boy with the wet cough, hiding behind his mother's skirt so long ago. Surely he couldn't have been part of such brutality.

"Let joyous angels receive him."

"Yes, countess," he says, and the pen moves across the paper quickly.

She watches over his shoulder. His letters are firm and well formed; he writes far more quickly than she would have expected. The *h* is perfect. Antonina closes her eyes, relieved. She exhales and puts her hand on Lyosha's shoulder. "You write very well. Lilya taught you?"

He looks up at her. "No, countess."

"Who, then?" Antonina asks, surprised.

"Grisha, the year I came to the stables."

"Why did he teach you?"

Finally Lyosha smiles. "He said I showed promise, and that someday I might be able to move out of the stables. But Lilya taught Soso."

"Soso?"

"Yes."

"Thank you," Antonina says after a moment. "You may leave now."

Lyosha stands and bows from the waist, and then turns and leaves, walking awkwardly in the tight slippers.

That evening, alone in the study, Antonina sits at Konstantin's desk and thinks of Soso. She'd learned from Lilya that he had left Angelkov after the kidnapping. Many of the servants had gone; why should Soso's disappearance have struck her as strange?

Exhausted, she shuts her eyes and recalls her conversation with Yakovlev. Could it be possible that she might lose Angelkov? Where would they go, she and Konstantin—if Konstantin lives? And if he doesn't? She sees herself a widow with nothing. Abruptly, she opens her eyes. "How would I survive?" she speaks aloud.

The thought of being a *prizhivalet*—a noble down on his or her luck who begs to move in with a wealthy neighbour or distant relative—is despicable to her. Those with riches of their own don't want to be seen as miserly, and almost always provide a permanent room for the uninvited guest. But life in someone else's home makes the displaced noble's position vulnerable, and humiliating. *Prizhivalet.* The word itself is undignified, indicating something hanging on to something else, little better than a parasite.

She thinks of her brother Marik. They haven't spoken in years, but the long-ago fight was between him and Konstantin. She could ask him for money, but in the next instant she realizes it's very unlikely that Marik would pay huge sums—which he might not even have—to help keep her estate running.

No. If she came to him as a penniless widow—if that's what it comes to—he would offer her a place to live. She imagines herself growing old in his home, the widowed sister, her hair fading and her skin thinning, the fine tracery of lines around her eyes deepening. As a form of repayment she would help with his children, perhaps giving them music lessons. She thinks of Marik's wife, pleasant enough when she last saw her. But how long would her patience last with another woman—her sister-in-law—living with them for the rest of their lives?

Not yet, she persuades herself. I'm not ready for that yet. I will not give up Angelkov. Not until it is absolutely necessary. "Not yet," she says aloud.

And what of Mikhail? What if she's forced to leave this place while he's still missing? What if he eventually finds his way back to Angelkov but she isn't here?

She can't think about it—any of it. She crosses to the cabinet holding bottles and glasses as there's a knock on the door.

"Enter," she calls, still beside the cabinet.

It's Grisha. He looks at her from the doorway before stepping in. "There is no one to answer the door, madam. I came through the back servants' entrance."

"Please come in, Grisha." She feels uncomfortable saying his name. In the private world of the study, it feels too intimate.

He walks towards her, but stops a few feet away.

"What is it you come to see me about, Grisha?" she asks, forcing herself to say his name again.

"First of all, I wanted to ask after the count."

"It's pneumonia. The doctor is not hopeful."

He nods respectfully. Neither of them has anything more to say about Konstantin. "Your meeting with the lawyer—did you get the answers you seek?"

Antonina sighs, her shoulders falling. "I'm sorry I didn't summon you. I know I said I would, but after the doctor's visit . . ." She swallows and her top lip moves, a tiny, almost imperceptible tremble. "I thought it best to deal with Yakovlev on my own. The problems are my husband's doing, and now my responsibility. What I learned was highly disturbing. I would like to speak with you about the estate, frankly, as before."

His jaw tightens. Antonina sees the firmness of his chin, and she remembers the way he looked down at her in the rumpled bed, the smooth curve of his cheekbone. She knows what his hair feels like. The muscles in his arms. His breath in her ear.

He knows the contours and hidden places of her body, the texture of her skin.

She feels heat in her face, and has to look away.

"I am honoured that you would ask my opinion," Grisha says, bowing. He acts as though nothing happened between them less than forty-eight hours earlier. "What is it you would like to discuss?"

Antonina again runs her hand over her forehead, as though a strand of hair bothers her. She doesn't want to tell him that she doesn't know what to do. She takes a deep breath. "We don't have anything left to run the estate, Grisha. The count is deeply in debt. I have to figure out a way to . . ." She panics. *A way to live.* "I need your help, Grisha." She comes close to him then, and despite all her resolutions, she leans her head against his chest. He puts his arms around her.

She looks up at him, fighting the panic about losing the estate. About wanting him so much. Vodka will help. "Have a drink with me."

He goes to the cabinet and pours them each a glass of vodka. He comes back to her and hands her a glass, then steps back.

"How will I find money to pay the government and to continue to run the estate?" Antonina asks after a sip. "Without servants, how will I . . ." She stops, not wanting to sound helpless. "A place as vast as Angelkov will fall to ruin quickly without care. What will we do, Grisha?"

"We?" Grisha echoes. "This is *your* estate."

Antonina straightens her shoulders. "Yes. You're right."

Grisha waits for her to continue, studying the painting behind her head.

"Will you be like so many of the others, then, Grisha? Will you leave me as well?" Her chest rises and falls as she waits for his answer. She knows what she wants—what she needs—to hear.

Grisha steps closer to her once more. "Do you wish me to stay and help you run the estate? To continue as I always have?"

Antonina swallows. She draws a deep breath and straightens her shoulders. "Yes. I would like you to stay. But . . . but I can't pay you. I have nothing left. Would you agree to stay, even in this situation? It means you will continue to live in your house as always, eat whatever we can raise on the estate, from the gardens and animals. Surely we can sustain ourselves for a while in that regard—now that so many servants have left and we no longer have as many to feed. The storehouses . . ." She stops. "Are the storehouses well stocked?"

Grisha drinks. "They've been looted. There's little left in the storehouses or the distillery."

"What? Why wasn't I informed? Was there no one guarding them?"

"Yes. But the guards, like so many men, were weak. After the count was injured, they took what they could, over many nights, sack by sack, bag by bag, to sell. They were eventually caught and punished. But most of the goods are gone."

"How did I not know?"

"Some days, madam . . . no, many days, you refused to see me, or anyone. Lilya reported to me that you . . ." He stops.

What has Lilya told him? Does he know of the days she slept away, aided by the bottles in her wardrobe? She drains her glass and holds it out for more.

He ignores it. "To be honest, madam, I didn't insist on reporting all of this to you because I felt you had too much to worry about. For a while I thought the count might recover. But then, when I saw his mind was affected, I made the decision to talk to you about it when I felt you were stronger." Finally he takes her glass, but he sets it and his on the cabinet. "Come. We need fresh air." Holding her arm, he leads her to the tall French doors. He flings them open and puts his hand on the small of her back, directing her out onto the wide veranda as if he is the master of the estate.

It's she who has initiated the confusion between them, by what she allowed to happen at the dacha—partially out of sadness and loneliness and, of course, the vodka. The simple, understandable role of mistress and servant will no longer work. Grisha is a free man, and can leave her at any time.

"I will stay, Antonina," Grisha says. They are both aware of his use of her name. They stand at the railing, looking at the land spread before them. The railing needs care; the paint is peeling. "And I accept that you do not have the means to pay me a salary. In return, I will accept a few versts of land."

He should be compensated, of course. "Yes, yes, take the versts—two or three?—that you wish."

"We shall say six," Grisha tells her. "There's a good tract close to your boundary with Prince Bakanev's estate." He pauses. "It will help secure my future."

She feels a surge of disappointment, and then tries to understand her reaction. Isn't his future here? She has never thought of him in any other life but in the house with the blue shutters. And yet . . . he now has every right to his own home. To land, and a house he can build to his liking. To a wife, she thinks then. Children. "Oh," is all she can say.

Grisha smiles, but it isn't exactly a smile; it is more of a reaction, a showing of teeth. "It won't be for some time, Antonina. You—and Angelkov—are my concern for now. But I'm simply thinking of my future," he says, as if needing to stress this a second time. "As we all must. It's a new Russia."

Antonina is tense, and her mouth trembles. It's as if he's read her thoughts.

"We'll walk," Grisha states, in that same confident tone. He doesn't touch her as they go down the steps and across the yard.

Antonina shivers; the early evening is cool. "Yes. It is a new era, Grisha. Grigori . . ." She stops. "What is your patronymic?" In a flash she recalls his desire that she call him Tima. This isn't the time to ask why. No, she corrects herself, there will never be another such time. She will never know, and she can't allow herself to wonder about it.

"Sergeyevich."

"Yes, it's a new era, Grigori Sergeyevich," she repeats. If she is going to depend on him so completely, she should respectfully call him by his given name and patronymic, instead of the short form used for all servants. It's a new era, indeed.

As the stable comes into view, Antonina's mouth fills with saliva as she tries not to let the image of the gutted horse fill her mind, picturing the bloodied board with the inverted letter *h*. She thinks of Mikhail.

"I am shaken by what happened to Felya. Could it be that whoever did this also played a role in Mikhail's kidnapping?"

How to answer her? "The country is full of dangerous people now."

"Do you believe I'm in danger here, in my own home?" Antonina prods.

"I am at your service, Countess Mitlovskiya," he says, reverting to her title as he stops and turns to face her. "With me, you are safe. No harm will come to you," he says, and his face softens, as when they had looked at each other in bed.

Antonina finds it difficult to breathe, having him so close, looking at her that way. *With me, you are safe.* Is that what she had felt in the dacha? Is that why she weakened— because, for the first time in so long, she felt safe?

"Thank you," she says, making the sign of the cross in the air in front of him. It's an automatic gesture, the usual blessing of a landowner, even though the rules of the game are now different. But as she does this, she knows she wants to touch her fingers to his forehead, and move them across his wind-darkened skin to his temple, and down his cheek-bone to his mouth.

She drops her hand to her side, and Grisha bows his head. "You are cold. I will take you back to the manor."

He leaves her on the veranda steps. She notices that one of the long shutters over the front windows hangs crookedly, a hinge missing.

30

*A*t daybreak, Pavel stands outside Antonina's room. When she doesn't respond to his quiet knock, he opens the door hesitantly. "Countess Mitlovskiya," he calls. "Please. You must come to the count's room."

"Yes," she answers groggily, and sits up. When she goes into the hall, Lilya is there, rising from a pallet on the floor beside her door. Antonina had told her to leave last night, when she came in from being with Grisha and wanted to be alone with her thoughts. She assumed the woman had returned to her own room in the servants' quarters.

In Konstantin's room, she immediately sees that he has worsened. His skin is clammy, his lips and nail beds blue. He struggles to breathe. Pavel must have sent for Father Cyril; he sits on a low chair beside the bed praying over him, his incantations no more than the buzz of a fly to Antonina, his long black robes and tall mitre appearing outlandish.

At one point, Father Cyril rises and speaks quietly to Olga, who nods, weeping. Antonina watches her set up a small table covered with a white cloth. On it Father Cyril puts a crucifix, two candles, a bottle and a small wrapped packet. Olga weeps more loudly, covering her face with her shawl and rocking back and forth.

The priest is ready for extreme unction should Konstantin ask to be anointed, to speak his confession. All here is in preparation for her husband's death.

The dark, early morning sky lets little light into the bedroom. Antonina looks at the priest's profile in his tall hat, and then at Konstantin.

His crackling breathing is terrible to hear.

"Shall I send for the doctor, madam?" Pavel asks, and she shakes her head.

"There is nothing to be done. He predicted this."

Pavel crosses himself.

Antonina stands beside the priest. His prayers grow in intensity as he swings his censer of incense in wide arcs over the bed. Konstantin is motionless but for the rise and fall of his chest. Only the priest's voice and Konstantin's laboured breathing break the silence of the room as the count slowly suffocates.

She will not grieve for him when he dies. There has never been love. Her husband has never really been a husband. But she knows this is God's punishment for her wanton behaviour with Grisha. He is punishing her, leaving her a widow. This forces her to think what she hasn't allowed before: if Mikhail is already dead, Konstantin will be reunited with him in heaven.

And he doesn't deserve to see his son again so quickly.

Studying his face at this last thought, rage rises in her. At first it's only a flicker, but then it crescendoes to a hard beat until her own breathing grows louder, heavier. She puts her hands to her chest, fighting for composure.

"Leave us for a moment, please, Father Cyril," she says when she has controlled her visible agitation. "I wish to spend a few moments alone with my husband." Olga and Pavel immediately bow and go out the door.

The priest sets the smoking censer on the floor at the side of the bed and steps into the hall.

Antonina drops to her knees, her face only inches from her husband's.

"Konstantin," she hisses, mindful of the open door, the edge of the priest's robe. Konstantin's eyes remain closed. "Konstantin. Can you not speak one more word to me? Is this how you wish it to be, then?" She's so full of bitterness that she chokes on the heavy, smoky incense, and as her coughing gives way to weeping, Konstantin's eyes open.

Antonina sees that they are clear for the first time in weeks. She draws a quavering breath. "Konstantin?" she says, but his gaze moves from her to the doorway. He blinks heavily, and the priest, who also turned at the sound of Antonina's cry, returns and leans over her husband. He treads on the edge of Antonina's skirt so that it pulls tight at her waist.

He has his ear to her husband's mouth. The priest's long, wiry grey beard obliterates her view of Konstantin's lips, but she hears something, little more than the slightest sighing whisper. The priest turns back to her. "He asks for Tania."

Antonina says nothing, her back teeth aching as she clenches her jaw and shakes her head.

The priest again lowers his head to hear Konstantin's whisper, then nods and turns to the table, blessing the candles and lighting them, uncorking the bottle of holy water, and at that Antonina feels such fury—even stronger than the wave she experienced moments earlier—that her hands curl into fists at her sides.

Konstantin has found his voice. He has asked, with his last words, to see Tania. He has requested extreme unction and Communion from Father Cyril. He will confess his sins, and in this way will go to his death absolved of all guilt. He will go to meet the Saviour clean and whole.

He has chosen not to say goodbye to her.

Konstantin dies an hour later. His eyes are sunken, the skin on his face like roughened vellum, as deeply grooved as the hide of some exotic foreign beast—an elephant or a rhinoceros.

Olga comes in with a tray of glasses and a small silver teapot. She looks from the priest to her mistress. Setting the tray on the nearest table with a clang, she hurries to the bed. She stares at Konstantin, crossing herself over and over, then begins to wail. Within moments the house, so unnaturally silent for the last few days without Konstantin's usual raving, comes alive with crying and moaning. Footsteps sound on the stairs and along the hallway, and the doorway fills with the last of the servants—both from the house and from outside—crowding to look at their dead master.

Antonina can't bear to remain near her husband's body, with the servants pulling their hair and falling to their knees, kissing their crucifixes and crying out to God. She pushes through them and goes to her own room. She finds Lilya changing the linens. Tinka sits quivering on the window seat, her ears pricked forward at the cries from the hall.

Antonina knows Lilya hears the wailing and prayers, and understands that Konstantin is dead. But Lilya hasn't rushed to Konstantin's room like the others. Instead, she continues her work.

"He's dead, Lilya," Antonina says, unnecessarily. "Konstantin Nikolevich is dead." Said aloud, the words sound odd. "The master—my husband—is dead," she says a third time.

Lilya simply looks at her, a pillow half into a fresh case.

Antonina notices the intricate lace edging the case. She bought the bed linens in St. Petersburg over twelve years ago, for her trousseau. "My husband is dead, and my child . . . my child . . ." Antonina isn't able to finish the sentence.

Lilya sets the pillow on the bed and comes to her, putting her arms around Antonina. "Sit down, Tosya." Her voice is barely above a whisper.

Antonina lowers herself into the tufted chair near the fireplace, cautiously, as if a sack of flour has been strapped to her back and she's unsure how to cope with its new and unexpected weight. As if it might throw her off balance if she doesn't judge every movement. She closes her eyes and grips the arms of the chair; she's overcome with vertigo even as she sits.

Lilya kneels in front of her. "Now it is just us, Tosya. Just you, and me."

Antonina opens her eyes and looks down at her. She knows Lilya isn't sorry for the loss of her master. She knows how Lilya feels about Konstantin Nikolevich. She sees that Lilya's eyes are bright, her face calm.

Looking at her, Antonina knows there is something else she must speak to Lilya about. Soso. Yes, she must speak to Lilya about Soso. About the board around the horse's neck. But not now.

⁓

Konstantin is buried on the third day after his death. The funeral is well attended, with more than three hundred people from across the province present for the service and Mass at the Church of the Resurrection. Antonina sees many familiar faces, including the violinist, Valentin Vladimirovitch Kropotkin, with others from the Bakanev estate. As well as all the servants, the yard outside the church is filled with Konstantin's former serfs.

After the Mass, the procession follows the casket to the plot in the cemetery behind the church, the cemetery where Konstantin thought he slept on the grave of his son. The older women servants and villagers wail.

Tania is with the other house servants. Unlike many of them, her eyes are dry, her face emotionless. Antonina looks at her; the woman returns her stare.

The violinist is suddenly beside her, pressing Antonina's hand between his. "My deepest condolences, Countess Mitlovskiya," he says.

"Thank you," she says, looking away from Tania as the priest's prayers begin. The violinist bows and moves back into the crowd.

She hears the priest's familiar words, but cannot think of Konstantin. It is Misha who is in her thoughts. Then, unbidden, the image of Felya comes again, and the board around his neck. She is aware of Grisha, standing behind her.

He takes her elbow, once, as she stumbles on a clod of earth.

When the prayers are over, she sees Lilya go to Tania. She watches, slightly unfocused, as Tania shakes her head, her mouth moving. Finally she turns and walks away from Lilya.

As the mourners slowly depart and the grave is covered with soil, Grisha and Lilya stay with Antonina. Finally, when the three men with shovels bow to Antonina and leave, she turns to Grisha and Lilya. "I'd like to be alone, please," she tells them, and they do as she asks.

Amidst the cracked and moss-covered headstones, Konstantin's grave is a hump of newly turned earth. Antonina knows she should have a headstone carved for him. And yet there isn't money for even this.

Father Cyril comes to stand beside her. "Perhaps, Countess Mitlovskiya, it would comfort you to also have a place to pray for your son as you pray for your husband."

Antonina looks at him. "What do you mean, Father?"

"I'm suggesting a marker for Mikhail Konstantinovich. When you have a stone carved and erected for Count Mitlovsky, you can also have one made for your son."

Hadn't Konstantin, in his madness, once suggested the same thing? A look of horror crosses Antonina's face. "No," she says loudly. "What are you talking about?" Her voice rings in the still air. "My son isn't dead. He doesn't need a marker."

"Of course, of course, my child," the priest says in a soothing voice. "I simply meant it might bring you comfort to have something tangible to pray to."

She hates Father Cyril at that moment, and decides she won't return to the church. She will pray to her own icons in her bedroom.

The morning after the funeral, Grisha's presence in the kitchen surprises Lilya. She ignores him, arranging a breakfast tray to take to Antonina's bedroom.

"Tania told me that yesterday you said she was to leave Angelkov," he says. "You don't have that authority."

Grisha doesn't like Lilya's boldness. He has always felt sorry for Tania. He gave her a small packet of his own rubles when she came to his door to say goodbye, carrying her belongings. She told him she was glad to leave Angelkov with all its misery; she had planned on moving to her old village right after the funeral. Lilya had nothing to do with her decision. "I wouldn't take orders from her anyway," she added. "Tell the countess . . . tell her goodbye from me. That I wish her well."

Now Lilya shrugs. "We all know there's no reason for her to stay, with the count dead. I wanted to save the countess the distress of having to speak to her." She fusses with the cutlery on the tray. "Don't we both want as little anxiety as possible for her? Besides, Nusha can look after the laundry now. There is so little, with only the countess to attend to."

"How is her mood today?" he asks Lilya.

"Her mood? What do you suppose? Besides, why are you asking me?"

"You know her better than anyone," Grisha says.

"What do you mean?"

"She shares her thoughts with you, doesn't she?"

"Maybe," says Lilya cautiously.

Grisha picks a brown, speckled egg from a bowl on the table, tossing it in his hand. If Lilya didn't know better, she would think he was nervous. Grisha is never anxious, or even excitable. In fact, he usually has a strange, unnatural calm. "Has she spoken of anything out of the ordinary? Acted . . . I don't know . . . differently in some way?"

He can't stop thinking about her, about what they shared in the dacha. He doesn't know what she's feeling. What she's thinking about him. He offered to stay and help her at Angelkov. She accepted his offer, but has anything changed?

Lilya tilts her head. "Naturally, she's in a terrible state what with the old man's death, and her son still missing. You really need to ask me about her mood?"

He can tell that Lilya knows nothing more. She can't hide things from him the way she can from Antonina.

"All right," he says, and leaves, the egg still in his hand. He has forgotten he's holding it.

Lilya has never been sure how she feels about Grisha. Lyosha adores him, and looks upon him as a big brother. And she must admit, Grisha has been good to the boy. There is a special patience in him she sees only when he deals with her brother. Grisha has been more of a protector to him than Soso ever was.

A few minutes later, as she stands outside Antonina's bedroom, she thinks of Grisha again, and of the way Antonina had returned after the night of the thunderstorm, when old Mitlovsky had spent hours in the cemetery. At the time, Lilya couldn't put her finger on it, but something didn't feel right about Antonina's story. Now Grisha comes poking around about how her mistress is feeling. Never before has he asked her about the countess in a personal manner.

Lilya doesn't like it. She takes a deep breath and calls, quietly, through the door. "Tosya, your breakfast."

At the low, answering murmur, she manoeuvres the tray against her hip and turns the crystal doorknob.

⚶

A few minutes later, her breakfast untouched, Antonina asks Lilya to sit down.

Lilya turns from the bed, the coverlet still in her hand.

"I want to ask you something," Antonina says from her chair near the fireplace, Tinka on her lap. "Please, sit with me."

Lilya drops the bedding and lowers herself into the chair on the other side of the fireplace.

"Have you heard from Soso?" Antonina asks.

"Why do you ask about my husband now, Tosya? Is it that you just lost your own?"

"I want to know if you know where he is, or what he's doing."

First Grisha's questions in the kitchen and now this. "No. I don't know where he is, and I don't care. I told you that. I told you I don't feel anything for Iosef Igorovitch."

"All right," Antonina says. "But if you do hear from him or anything about him, maybe from one of the other servants, will you tell me?"

"Why don't you ask Grisha?" Lilya says.

Antonina frowns. "Would Grisha know his whereabouts?"

Lilya shrugs, picking at a loose thread on the brocade of the cushion on the chair. "Grisha thinks he knows everything about everyone," she says, and Antonina hears an undertone. "And maybe he does. At least for now."

The last two words make Antonina uneasy. "What do you mean—for now?"

"For as long as he's at Angelkov. Which might not be long."

"You're mistaken, Lilya. He hasn't spoken of leaving any time soon."

Lilya is thinking of what Lyosha told her, about Grisha becoming a landowner, and he his steward. "He might say that to please you. But now that he has his own land, do you really think he'll stay on?"

Antonina studies Lilya. "How do you know this?" Antonina can't imagine Grisha—private, discreet Grisha—talking to any of the other servants about the six versts she and he had discussed just before Konstantin died.

Lilya's face is composed. "One hears things."

Antonina sees that Lilya is being purposefully cryptic. But why? "That's all, then, Lilya."

Lilya gets up and walks to the door. As she opens it, she glances over her shoulder at Antonina, and in that instant something in her face unsettles Antonina even further.

⁓

Antonina knows sleep will be impossible that night. She drinks three glasses of vodka, which calm her enough so her teeth don't ache from holding her jaw so tightly. She lies on her bed, but images—Misha without his warm coat, Konstantin's dead, bluish face, Father Cyril suggesting a marker for Mikhail, the butchered horse—distress her so much that she has to sit up, staring into the darkness. She needs to think of something else.

She opens the tiny corner of thought she tries to keep locked: Grisha in the dacha.

But as she remembers she and Grisha together, something crosses her mind. She had been so distraught in Tushinsk, seeing the child in Mikhail's *talmochka*, and as she untangles the thoughts from that day, she thinks about the man—what was his name? Lev?—who brought the letter from Misha. Was he the man she'd seen Grisha talking to? Surely not, or Grisha would have told her.

But she also remembers seeing Grisha holding a package out to the man. What was it?

She leaves Tinka on the bed and pulls a shawl over her nightdress and opens her door. Lilya is asleep on the pallet, her mouth open and one hand flung up beside her head.

Antonina is annoyed. Tomorrow she will tell Lilya she doesn't want her sleeping outside her door as if she's a child who might wander in the night and get into trouble. But as she silently goes down the stairs, she asks herself if this isn't what she's doing. She knows she's had too much vodka.

There are so few servants left that she has no fear of running into any of them. Two dogs—piebald harriers, once used for hunting but now simply hanging about waiting to be fed, since there is no hunting at Angelkov this fall—jump up from the veranda as she comes out the front door. She snaps her fingers once and they drop back down, their chins on their paws. Her steps uneven, she walks through the still, chilled night, past the stables and outbuildings, past the servants' quarters, down the winding road lined with bare linden trees. Her heart lifts when she sees lights in the house with the blue shutters. She imagines Grisha sitting by the fire, reading. She just wants to ask him about the man in Tushinsk.

Is this all?

Or does she want to be in his presence because she wants to feel like a woman? She knows she wants to feel his arms around her, strong, capable arms, his voice telling her it will be all right. That she needn't be afraid, that her son will come back. That she won't lose Angelkov. That he won't leave her.

She wants to go to his bed.

Already unsteady, she trips over something on the road—a stone, a branch—and comes down hard on her knees, skinning her palms as she reaches forward to break her fall. She sits back on her heels. An owl hoots, and she shivers. At that moment Grisha's lights go out.

She stands and slowly walks back to her own house. Her footsteps are loud on the cinder drive. Surrounded by the bare trees, in complete darkness, the manor is suddenly ominous. It no longer feels like home.

31

few afternoons later, she tries to distract herself in her bedroom by reading, but after some time she comes to the conclusion she's already read the passage she's attempting to concentrate on. She realizes she finished the book before Konstantin died. As she descends the staircase to go to the library to fetch another, she pauses at the landing window. It looks onto the front grounds of the estate and the long drive leading to the road. The sun is shining in a deep blue sky, and Antonina sees Grisha speaking with a man. She can only see the top of the man's hat, black, with a brim, his shoulders in a fine black coat with a grey lamb collar, and the toes of polished black boots.

Grisha does not wear a hat, and even from this distance Antonina sees the sunlight gleaming off his hair.

As Grisha shakes his head, the other man tilts his face,

glancing at the house. Antonina steps behind the curtain, but not before she has a glimpse of the man's features.

He walks back to his horse, its bridle held by Lyosha.

After the man has ridden away, she sends for Grisha. He stands in front of her in the study. The cold fall air has ruddied his cheeks.

"You are well, Antonina?" he asks.

"The man you were speaking to. What did he want?"

Grisha doesn't answer for a moment. "It was the music teacher from the Bakanev estate."

"The violinist," she states.

"He said he was the music teacher."

Antonina waits a beat. "What did he want?" she asks again.

Something shifts in Grisha's face. "He came to pay a call of condolence."

Antonina thinks of her gloved hand between Valentin's at the funeral.

"I told him it was impossible, you weren't receiving. I am correct in this, am I not"—he glances at Pavel passing the open door—"Countess Mitlovskiya?"

"I suppose so."

"I asked why he thought he could simply arrive only a week after the funeral, without a social appointment or at least a calling card in advance, and expect to be received. He hasn't the manners you are due."

"But you sent him off without speaking to me first?"

Grisha's eyes move from her eyes to her mouth, back to her eyes. "You wanted to see him?" When she doesn't answer immediately, something makes him asks, "You know this man?"

Why does she feel guilty? She's done nothing wrong.
"He played at my father's estate, a long time ago, before I
was married. And then I saw him again, at the musical evening at the Bakanevs'."

"And you recall him from all those years ago?" Grisha
pictures the other man's face. It's manly and yet somehow—
he wants to use the word pretty, although that's not it exactly.
It's the kind of face that would appeal to some women. But
far too delicate for a woman like Antonina, he thinks.

"Did you not consider asking me if I would receive him?"
she asks again. "Is it not my choice whom I see, even if they
appear in an unconventional manner?"

Grisha feels scolded. "I was simply protecting you,
Antonina," he says, holding back sudden anger. "It's not as
though you generally welcome visitors, even those you
know. I assumed you wouldn't wish to be called upon by a
near stranger."

Antonina is oddly flustered. She shakes her head, her lips
tight. "The point is, you can't make decisions for me."

"I can't?" Grisha says, his voice cold, and Antonina swallows. "Isn't that what you've asked me to do with the estate?
Make decisions?"

"Well, yes, with the estate," she answers, emphasizing the
last word. "Not with my personal life."

The air is heavy, as though loud, harsh words have been
exchanged, though neither voice has been raised.

"As you wish," Grisha finally says, reaching into his coat
pocket and pulling out a small square. "Here's his calling card.
Should you wish to receive him, you may send word to him."

"Thank you," Antonina says, taking the card by the very
tip of one corner, so that there is no chance her fingers will

touch Grisha's. She is afraid of what will happen should she come in contact with him, afraid of what she might do. The small square vibrates, just a little, as they both hold the card for those few seconds. Are her fingers trembling, or his? He lets go of the card, and she tucks it under her belt. "Thank you," she says again. "I'll look at my calendar." They both know this is a ridiculous statement. What would Antonina have on her calendar? "And if I wish to have him call, I'll decide on a day, and pass it on to you."

Grisha hasn't moved.

"That's all, Grigori Sergeyevich," Antonina says. She fights not to thank him again, simply to prolong the conversation, and moves to the desk as if searching for something in a small pile of papers. "Oh. No, wait." She turns back to him, remembering. "The peasant in Tushinsk. The one you were talking to."

Grisha nods. "I sent a coat for the child, as well as a basket of new clothing as a reward."

"Not him. The man in the doorway I saw you with just moments before I saw the child in Misha's coat."

Grisha waits.

"Who was he? Did he work for me at one time?"

Grisha's face is immobile. "Yes," he finally says.

"I thought he was familiar." So it wasn't Lev. "Have you made any further discoveries about what happened with Felya?" She wants to ask him if he has any suspicions, if he thinks it could have been Soso. If he is worried about further threats at Angelkov.

"No," Grisha says, his face expressionless.

As the silence stretches, she again looks at papers on the desk, glad she hadn't knocked on Grisha's door a few nights earlier, glad she came to her senses before she embarrassed herself. I am not like my mother, she thinks, the picture of Galina Maximova and the violinist—Valentin—once more vivid in her mind.

What she did with Grisha was a mistake. Everyone is allowed one mistake.

When she finally looks up and sees she is alone, there is a moment of disappointment. She sits, heavily, in Konstantin's chair behind the desk. But the air is chilled, the fire dying. She shivers in the room filled with the memory of her husband. She rises to go to her bedroom. Lilya always keeps a fire lit for her. She looks down at the card in her hand, and reads the name, written in curling cursive.

⌁

Three days later, Valentin Vladimirovitch Kropotkin is ushered into the library. Antonina is waiting. The moment he arrives, she's sorry she invited him to call. What was she hoping for? What will she say to him? Will the ghost of her mother stand in the corner, smirking?

Antonina told herself, when she sent the note to the Bakanevs', that she was instigating this social call to distract herself from her ongoing grief over Mikhail, from her new widowhood, from her worries about Angelkov. She knows this is partly true. She also doesn't want the complicated thoughts of Grisha.

It's Grisha who greets Valentin in the yard, speaking to him as they walk towards the front door.

"I hope you're aware of the grief that has been visited upon Angelkov, apart from the count's death," he says, glancing at Valentin. He's taller than the musician by a few inches.

"I heard about the kidnapping of the Mitlovsky child at the funeral."

"It's been six months of hell for the countess. She is not herself. And now her husband's death, so recent . . ." He glances at the musician again. "Do you understand what I'm saying, Kropotkin?"

"Have you appointed yourself the countess's bodyguard?" Valentin doesn't have to explain himself. He's a free man now. He realized when he came to Angelkov to try to see the countess the first time that Naryshkin was the man he had seen helping Countess Mitlovskiya into the barouche after the musical evening. "I am here to offer my sympathies." He looks at Grisha. "And you, Naryshkin?"

"What?"

"Why are you here?"

Grisha stops, forcing Valentin to stop as well. "You know I'm the steward. I help her run the estate, as I helped her late husband."

"I see," Valentin says.

To Grisha, the two words sound condescending, perhaps even suggestive, or insulting. He watches as Kropotkin puts his hands together and squeezes, as if releasing some tension in his fingers. They're long and delicate. Something about the unexpected movement reminds Grisha of Mikhail.

It's because they're both musicians, Grisha tells himself.

Valentin notices, as Grisha ushers him through the tall front doors, that there are few servants apparent in such a large house. There is none of the usual bustle of the Bakanev manor, with endless staff cleaning and moving about on all the floors. There's an elderly man in a house servant's uni-form standing in the entrance hall, but that's all. Valentin also finds it odd that the steward is the one to bring him inside. When he'd arrived, the steward whistled, and a young man ran from the stable and led his horse away.

Grisha stays where he is while Pavel steps up and takes Valentin's coat and hat and then, with a short bow, extends his hand down the hall towards the library. Antonina has chosen the cozy, book-lined room to receive this guest.

Grisha hears stealthy footsteps on the staircase and looks up to see Lilya, who is staring after Valentin. Then she glances at Grisha, and Grisha sees the disapproval on her face.

When Valentin walks towards the carved doors without another word to Grisha, he feels fresh anger. The man has forgotten that less than a year ago he was a serf. That a year ago Grisha, as a free man, would have been above him, and the musician would have had to bow from the waist to him, or be reprimanded. Or perhaps the musician hasn't forgotten—how can one so quickly forget the pat-terns of a lifetime?—but is making it clear to Grisha that he doesn't owe him any courtesies. That they are of the same class now: free men.

Grisha waits, listening, as Pavel opens the doors and ushers Valentin in. He can't believe that Antonina has allowed this simpering, effeminate man to call on her. Grisha hears Antonina's voice—although he can't make out what she's saying—and then Kropotkin's in response. And then Pavel shuts the doors and takes his place outside the library. Lilya is still on the stairs.

Antonina has chosen to be unchaperoned during her visit with Kropotkin.

Grisha is made uncomfortable—more than that, is troubled—by Kropotkin's presence in the manor. Something about the man gets under his skin. But he can't stay without a reason. He turns and leaves, not wanting Pavel or Lilya to see his expression.

Valentin Vladimirovitch is used to being adored by women but has no room in his heart for the complexities of their feelings. It's the same every time: the exaggerated sighs and lingering looks, the first tentative and then bolder touches, the melodrama at the beginning of the affair, and then at the end. It is as steady and tiresome as the dripping of rain off a roof. And yet he still enjoys the game, and has long understood the rewards. He gives women what they want—whatever form of adulation or respect or romance or sensuality they require—and in return he gets what he needs.

When he saw the Olonova princess—now a countess—at the Bakanevs', he recognized that she was distraught. Now, knowing of the disappearance of her child and the death of her husband, Valentin imagines that she is very vulnerable. It may be that the Countess Mitlovskiya, alone and bereft, could benefit from his company. It might be that he could benefit from hers.

Her edginess and uncertainty are apparent as she greets him, tightly holding a little lapdog with one arm. He offers expressions of sympathy regarding her husband's death. From her rather unemotional reaction both at the funeral and today, he assumes that there was little affection between her and what he knows was a much older man. A typical situation: how often he has offered companionship to a bored young wife, too passionate and enthusiastic for a husband decades older and no longer interested in youthful pursuits.

Valentin fills the visit with clever and droll stories of situations he has encountered at some of the estates he has worked on. He accepts two cups of tea and three small cakes, complimenting her on their delicacy: *A cook who can create such light pastry is difficult to find in the provinces.* He answers Antonina's questions about his favourite composers and what he is teaching the Bakanev nieces. He and Antonina agree that this October seems cooler than last. He comments on Tinka's devotion to her mistress, and the pleasure of canine affection. He is aware of the time, and leaves after exactly an hour.

He made certain that the conversation was light and effortless. And yet, Antonina realizes once he's gone, in no way is Valentin Vladimirovitch an uncomplicated man. She also recognizes how hard he must have worked to create such sociable conversation. She knows fully how painfully awkward she is. He offered her opportunities to speak of her deceased husband, but he hadn't asked her about her son, even though the Bakanevs would have no doubt recounted the terrible story. Proof that he is thoughtful and sensitive.

She doesn't expect that he will wish to see her again, as the visit couldn't have been particularly pleasurable for him.

When she receives a note from him the next day, telling her how much he enjoyed his time with her, she is surprised. After some thought she sends a note back, telling Valentin Vladimirovitch he is welcome to pay her another call the following week.

When he comes to Angelkov the second time, he brings his violin. "I thought we might play together."

"Oh, I don't think so, Mr. Kropotkin."

He sets down his violin case. "I understand. And I apologize for my forwardness."

"I simply don't feel prepared to accompany you. But I would love for you to play," she adds with a kind of anxiety, or perhaps it's relief. It may just be that if he plays, she won't have to make conversation.

He sees, as he did on his first visit, that she's uncomfortable with a man calling on her, and yet she hasn't turned him away. Though it's really too early after her husband's death for him to be here.

They go into the music salon, and she sits on the settee while he stands near the bay window. "Do you have a request, countess?" he asks, taking his violin from its case. The instrument has a beautiful red-brown veneer, and a gold fleur-de-lys on the tailpiece. "I have a large repertoire," he says, with no attempt at modesty. He's a musician, and this is what he does: he plays for people. "Is there a composer you favour?"

He knows what the Glinka piece did to her the evening at the Bakanevs', and worries that certain other pieces or composers might affect her as deeply. She is, he's realizing, in a fairly unstable mood, and he recalls the steward and his warning. He doesn't like the man.

"Perhaps Bach?" he asks when she doesn't answer. "The Partita in D Minor? I would play the first and second movements."

She nods, folding her hands in her lap and sitting back.

Valentin steps closer to the square Érard and lifts the key lid. He plays the A of the middle octave.

The piano is slightly out of tune. As with the rest of the estate, there has been no upkeep. What a pity that the beautiful

French piano is neglected. What concerts Valentin could give in a salon like this. He sees a stack of sheet music and looks closer: it's Glinka. And it's from him, to the Princess Olonova. He had forgotten about giving this to her on her name day so long ago. The top sheet of Separation in F Minor is slightly torn and streaked with fading red marks.

"Countess," he says, looking at her. "You still have it. The music I gave you."

Her face flushes. "Yes. I have so enjoyed it. I transposed some of Glinka's more complex works for my son when he was younger. But now he is able to play it as it is written, with ease. Of course, you understand the underlying difficulty of perfecting Glinka's compositions: they require a sense of simplicity and naturalness that is actually very arduous to achieve. My Misha was playing that—Separation in F Minor—the last time I . . . when we were together last . . ."

Now he understands why the Glinka nocturne distressed her so.

"I'm sorry, countess," Valentin says, stepping away from the piano. He pulls a small tuner from his case and uses this to tune his A string, turning the tapered pegs in the peg box a fraction and plucking the string. When he's satisfied, he tunes the other three strings to the A. Then he settles his violin under his chin and lifts his bow, and the rich notes of the first movement sing into the quiet room.

After Valentin is gone, Antonina brings to memory the image of his bare arms and legs as he lay in her mother's tumbled satin bedclothes. His limbs were well formed, and yet there was something delicate about him. And now he's older, yes, as she is, but still slender and somehow boyish. He's like a horse bred for speed, Antonina thinks, with a strong and yet lithe body, perhaps a vulnerability about the mouth. He gives the impression of the perfect fusion of strength and gentleness.

He's not like Grisha, hard and restrained, confusing her. Valentin wears his emotions on his face, while Grisha . . . the man is unreadable.

In spite of what Grisha has said about Valentin's manners over arriving without sending a calling card, Antonina observes that he is indeed cultured. She knows that in his former life as a serf musician he was taught the behaviours necessary for mingling with royalty and nobility as he played in their music salons and theatres and ballrooms. He's also well educated: he drops French phrases with nonchalance, and mentioned that he is currently reading Musset's *La Confessions d'un Enfant du Siècle*.

When he plays, a lock of soft blond hair falls over his high, pale forehead. He touches his violin as though it is a beloved child. No, his grip is too firm—as if it is a secret lover.

But this leads her back to Grisha, and the way he so easily lifted and held her against him, the way he led her with confidence, and yet also let her take the lead.

Grisha. If not for him, Antonina wouldn't suddenly and unexpectedly have this disturbing ache for the sweetness of skin on skin, the sensuous remembrance of the weight of a man atop her, the push and pull of desire.

She falls to her knees and prays to try to drive away the images.

At the end of that second visit, Valentin had asked if he might call on her with regularity. "It's so tedious, the back and forth of cards between the estates, don't you think?" he asked. "I teach only in the mornings," he continued. "My afternoons are free to do as I please. And you, countess, do you have any time you may call your own? I can understand how the running of an estate such as Angelkov could take great effort."

She had nodded uncertainly. She's not sure if she really wants this, and yet she doesn't know how to politely deflect Valentin. He's so full of life, and even after two visits she sees how he brings colour and music into her dull days. How he takes her away, briefly, from the thoughts that plague her: her own remorse over her behaviour while her son suffers away from his home, the financial troubles of the estate.

Antonina sends for the piano tuner from Pskov, and pays him with a heavy silver snuff box of Konstantin's. The silver is badly tarnished; none of the Angelkov silver sparkles any longer. The man turns it over in his hands, and Antonina knows he'll clean it and sell it for far more than he could have charged for the job.

Valentin continues to bring his violin, wrapped in wool and a sheepskin to protect it during the ride from the Bakanev estate to Angelkov. Now, upon arriving, Pavel takes him directly to the music salon, where Valentin unwraps the violin and takes it out of its case. He sets it on an ottoman in the warmth from one of the stoves in the corners of the room before tuning it and applying resin to his bow. While he waits for the instrument to adjust to room temperature, he and Antonina talk. It's easier now; she grows more open each time he comes.

For Antonina, it's good to be in the music salon again. The way Valentin moves his bow over the strings, evoking and shaping and colouring the sounds so that her heart expands to fill her chest, gives her a deep sense of gratitude for the happiness she knew with her son in this room. She remembers so many lovely hours, so many weeks and months and years as he sat at the piano and played with such commitment and expression. When he turned on the padded bench, his eyes bright, asking, "How did I do with that last movement, Mama? Were the trills light enough? What shall I play now?"

Misha. She glances at the rain-streaked windows. The weather is definitely turning; winter is so close. Is he warm?

Long before dusk, Lilya always comes in to light the candles and lamps, a subtle clue that it's time for Kropotkin to be on his way. She is unusually slow in these simple tasks, lingering too long at each one, watching the violinist with an almost petulant expression.

Antonina wonders what's got into the woman. Why does she appear so sour? It's quite evident that Lilya doesn't like having Valentin at Angelkov, and surely it isn't because it means she has the simple extra job of serving them afternoon tea.

It's only after the third or fourth time Lilya has made a big show out of lighting the lamps that a thought crosses Antonina's mind: could Lilya be jealous?

Almost as soon as the idea comes to her, she dismisses it. Why would Lilya be jealous?

Lilya thinks she understands what's happening: Valentin is falling in love with Antonina. It is natural for Lilya to think this; she assumes that no one could be around Antonina for any length of time and not fall in love with her.

She can't tell what Antonina feels for Valentin, although she does try to gauge her in a breezy, conversational way. *How long will Mr. Kropotkin stay at the estate of the prince and princess? Is he married? Where is his home? Will he return to St. Petersburg when the Bakanev nieces leave, or might he stay in the area, teaching other landowners' children?*

Antonina is straightforward in her answers to Lilya's casual questions as the woman straightens the bed or hangs up a gown after one of Valentin's visits. But when Lilya makes small criticisms of him, saying, *He certainly eats a great many cakes every time he comes, and did you see? He held a piece of sugar in his teeth and drank his tea through it—a sure sign of his peasant roots*, she expects—hopes—that Antonina will laugh and agree with her.

Instead, Antonina speaks to her sharply. "Your job is to serve the cakes, Lilya, not count how many are consumed." Lilya thinks, then, that Antonina cares for Valentin Vladimirovitch in a way that has nothing to do with how he plays the violin.

~

Lilya knows that Grisha too is angered by Kropotkin's visits. Each time the violinist arrives in the yard, Grisha escorts him to the front door, watching as he is led to the music salon by Pavel.

She watches Grisha's face when he brings Kropotkin to the door, and she now believes that what she had begun to suspect a few weeks earlier is true. Grisha has strong feelings for the countess. But she knows the countess can't possibly care about Grisha; he is only her steward. So she will use Grisha to derail Valentin.

Nobody will come between her and Antonina.

32

*O*n the afternoon of one of Valentin's visits, Grisha has, as usual, escorted him to the front door. But as he's going back down the veranda steps, Lilya calls his name. She's right behind him: where did she come from?

"Lilya! Why are you creeping up behind me?"

"I must talk to you."

He can almost swear she's being coy. "What do you want?"

"Not here. We have to speak privately. I'll come to your house."

"No. Say what you wish right here."

Lilya looks over her shoulder. "Tonight, after she's in bed, then. Come to the kitchen."

He's annoyed with her heavy-handed attempt at intrigue. "What is it, Lilya?"

"It's about Misha," she says, and his annoyance falls away. He thought she knew nothing about the kidnapping, nothing about Soso's or his own involvement. And yet looking at her now, he wonders if he was wrong.

"What do you mean?"

She lowers her eyelids, still staring at him in that odd, sly way. "We'll talk about Misha later, in the kitchen."

Since the violinist had started coming to visit the countess, and Lilya had seen Grisha's reaction, she had acted quickly. She is now ready to talk to Grisha.

Because she recognized Soso's writing on the wood around the horse's neck, Lilya knew that he had to be somewhere in the vicinity of Angelkov. While the realization of what he had done to the horse chilled her, it brought back old thoughts. For a few troubling days last April, Lilya wondered if Soso had, in some way, been involved in the kidnapping of Mikhail. When he'd left the estate shortly after the boy had been taken, she'd been glad to be rid of him, and convinced herself it wouldn't have been him. Everyone had called the kidnappers Cossacks, and Soso wasn't a Cossack.

But after Felya's murder, she thought about it again: just because the men were dressed as Cossacks, and carrying Cossack sabres, it didn't mean they actually *were* Cossacks.

She turned it over and over in her mind. Why did Soso brutally kill the horse Grisha loved? Why? Lilya thought long and hard about why he would want to anger Grisha. The more she thought about what was written on the board—*This is what happens. You don't do what we say*— the more she thought that if Soso had been involved in the kidnapping, maybe Grisha was involved as well.

She needed to find Soso, and confront him.

It didn't take her long. Soso was clever in some ways, but not quite clever enough for her.

She had Lyosha hitch up one of the Orlov Trotters to a cart, and drove, alone, to the village of Borzik, halfway between the Angelkov estate and the city of Pskov. Borzik wasn't the village where Soso and Lilya had lived before moving to the estate, but the village of Soso's grandmother. Although she was long dead, he had loved his grandmother, and had often spoken to Lilya of visiting her in her izba on the edge of town. He had also fairly regularly visited cousins who lived there after he and Lilya were married. He told her he was always welcome: whenever he stopped by, there was a bed and vodka waiting for him.

As she entered Borzik, Lilya almost immediately spotted Soso, lumbering down the muddy street in his bearskin coat. She knew he liked to wear it because it made him look bigger. She called his name, and he didn't look either happy or displeased to see her, merely surprised. "What are you doing in Borzik, Lilya?"

"I thought you might be here. I want to talk to you, Soso."

"I'm not coming back to Angelkov."

"That's not what I want to talk about. Where are you living?"

Soso gestured to an izba down the street. A downcast donkey was tethered at one side. "At my cousin Max's."

"Take me there so the street doesn't hear our business," Lilya told him, and he walked ahead of her, dipping his head under the low lintel as he went inside.

Holding the sack she'd brought, Lilya glanced at the dirty knife and spoon on the table, the pot stuck with dried buckwheat porridge, the scattered blankets on pallets on the floor. She heard the rustle of cockroaches in the filthy straw packed between the walls and the floor to keep out the draft. The donkey brayed outside the door. "Just you and Max are here?"

"His wife is tending her mother in the next village."

"Holy Mother of God, Soso, what a swine you've become."

He laughed and looked pleased, as if she'd given him a compliment.

"I've brought you something," she said then, pulling out the bottle of good vodka she'd taken from the cellar at Angelkov. "And sausage and bread. Salted milk mushrooms, too." The mushrooms were a favourite of Soso's to eat while drinking vodka. "Sit down," she told him, and he threw his coat on the floor and sat on the bench on one side of the table. She sat on the other side, wiped the knife on her skirt, and sliced the sausage and put it between thick slabs of Raisa's high, light bread. She handed it to him along with the open jar of mushrooms, then pulled the stopper out of the vodka with her teeth and pushed the bottle across the table. He looked at her and she smiled.

"What do you want?" he asked, taking a big bite.

"I've missed you, Soso. My bed is cold," she said, then was quiet as he ate. He turned away once, to spit something onto the floor. She took one mouthful of the vodka but let him drink the rest of it. She had time.

When the bottle was empty and the mushrooms were gone and he looked at her across the table with the bleary look she knew so well, she went to him and took his hand. "I missed you, Soselo," she again said, nodding at the pile of blankets. "Come."

He followed her. Lilya murmured encouragement, pulling up her skirt as she lay down. Although Soso was drunk, he wasn't too drunk. Later, she rested her head on his chest and let him fall into a snoring sleep for half an hour. Then she gently shook him out of his stupor, her head still on his chest.

"You should hear how the countess still cries over the boy," she said. "It's hard to be near her."

Soso breathed loudly through his mouth, then smacked his lips and swallowed.

"Whoever took Mikhail Konstantinovich—those Cossacks—are real men, afraid of nothing. And they taught Grisha a lesson when they beat him," she said, hearing Soso's stomach digesting the food. "It serves him right. You'd think he owns the estate, the way he swaggers around, so boastful."

She waited for Soso to speak. When he didn't, she gave a low laugh. "The countess has turned into a stuck-up tsarina now that she's the landowner. She and Grisha are making life impossible for those of us left. I hope God punishes them." She crossed herself.

"If not God, we'll do it," Soso said, and Lilya waited a heartbeat. "Just like we showed the old bastard."

"What do you mean?" she asked, her hand on Soso's chest. "Don't tell me . . . Soso," she breathed, "was it really you? Did you have something to do with the kidnapping?" She leaned on her elbow and widened her eyes at him, a proud wife.

Soso's chest expanded under Lilya's hand as he nodded.

"Now what, my darling, my brave man? Now what?" she asked.

"We'll get more money for the boy."

"Were the other two really Cossacks?"

"You don't know them."

"Not from Angelkov?"

"No."

Lilya ran her fingers through Soso's beard. "He's still alive, then? Mikhail?" she asked casually.

"He's alive," he agreed. "Until we get more money, he stays alive."

"You'll go to the countess again?"

"No. We're waiting on Grisha to bring it to us. He's taking too long."

"Grisha?"

"He was in on it."

Lilya jumped to her knees, putting her hands on Soso's shoulders. "Grisha was part of the kidnapping?"

Soso pushed her hands away. His eyes were closing, and he verged on sleep.

"Soso, sweetheart. Stay awake. I can't stay long. Talk to me. What has it to do with Grisha?"

Soso rubbed his eyes as he struggled to a half-sitting position, leaning against the rough wooden wall behind him. He looked at her, his eyelids heavy. "You want to help?"

Lilya licked her lips. "I see him—the bastard—every day. There might be some way. As long as I get some of the ransom."

Soso shrugged. "Lev—one of the Cossacks—and I have decided Grisha must now provide even more money than what he holds from the countess. We want more— much more." His eyes closed. "The first ransom has already been spent. We need him to get us more now." The last words faded.

"But Soso," Lilya said, a little louder, and he opened his eyes again, "if Grisha was in on it, why is he paying you?"

"We just used him as we needed him. But I showed him

I meant business with the horse. He didn't even get his share from the ransom he brought to us in the forest." He snorted. "I never thought he was such a fool."

Grisha is not a fool. Her suspicions were right, then. She knew with certainty, at that moment, why he was trying so hard to get Misha back for Antonina.

"But it better be soon. The priest doesn't want the boy much longer. He's hard to control, and stirs up the other boys."

"Yes," she agreed, her thoughts tumbling. "Mikhail Konstantinovich is too strong-willed." *He is in a church, then, or some sort of monastery.* "What priest?"

Soso burped. "Remember Slava Saavich, from our village?"

"Yes," Lilya said again. Slava Saavich was little more than a wandering pilgrim, his burlap robe tied with string, everything he owned in a sack on his shoulder, begging across the province. He had stopped in their village, where their priest had recently succumbed to typhus and the church needed someone. Soso appealed to the count and Father Saavich had stayed.

"But Saavich left the village, didn't he?"

Soso spoke slowly, pausing a long time between sentences. "He's taken over a monastery, training orphaned boys to be village priests. He owes me—I saved his neck more than once. He was persuaded to help me with flasks of vodka and sacks of dried beef and sunflower seeds I took from the Angelkov stores." He rubbed one hand over his eyes. "Right now, Misha is just another village boy in a poor hermitage. But Saavich knows that if the boy escapes and tells where he's been, it will be on his head. So he's very careful. But he's sick of the Mitlovsky brat now. So are we. With

one more payment—and Grisha must provide a big one—
that'll be the end of it. We'll all have it good, Lilya."

"You're so clever, my sweet," Lilya murmured. "So with
the final payment Misha will be returned?"

Soso made a sound that was almost a laugh. "And tell his
mama all about the bad men who took him? He's seen me,
Lilya, and of course he knows Saavich. No, once Grisha
brings the last of the money, the boy is gone. For good." He
reached out and touched his bearskin coat, in a heap near the
bed. He dragged it closer and fumbled in it for a moment, and
then pulled out a pistol. "He's gone, and the same for Grisha.
The finest of Cossack pistols," he said, waving the weapon
about. "Lev gave it to me. Look at the leather on the stock,"
he boasted, more awake now, running his hand over it. "So
then we'll all have what we want." He cocked the hammer
and aimed the pistol at the stove. "Boom," he said, and then
clicked the hammer back in place. "I always keep it loaded
and ready."

Lilya looked at the pistol and smiled at Soso, but her
mouth was dry. She wouldn't let Misha be killed; he was a
sweet boy, so like his mother. And it would destroy Antonina
further. She wanted it to be like before—Misha, the countess, and her. With Konstantin dead and the violinist driven
away by Grisha—and Grisha himself dead, as Soso promised—it would be perfect. Perfect. "Put it away, Soso," she
said. "You're scaring me."

He smiled proudly and stuck the pistol back in the pocket
of the coat.

"How can I help you, sweetheart?" Lilya asked. "I want
to be part of this, with you. Let me help you punish that
bitch," she said slowly. "I hate the way she treats me now."

"Work on Grisha, then. Tell him to hurry up and get the money. Not just what he holds from the countess. It must be hundreds of rubles more. You tell him that."

"Yes. Yes. I'll bring him to you with the money, all right?"

Soso pointed a dirty finger at the icon over the stove. "Behind there is a letter from the boy. I got him to write it last week. Lev told me I had to get proof for Naryshkin or he won't give us any more money. It's there," he repeated, pointing at the icon.

Lilya nodded. "I'll show it to Grisha, and he'll trust me. And then, Soso, we'll have enough money to do whatever we want. Where is the boy, then, my darling? He must be nearby, if you saw him last week."

Soso's eyelids were heavy again. "You and me, eh, Lilya?" he said finally. "We're worth more than them up at the estate."

"Yes. Where is Saavich's monastery?" Lilya repeated, but gently, in a soothing tone. "Far from here?"

Soso's eyes were closed. "No. It's on the outskirts of Pskov city. Ubenovo Monastyr, a godforsaken place."

Lilya looked down at Soso. It was so easy to see into his mind, especially when he was drunk. She knew she might as well put the pistol to her own head once Soso had the money. Of course he wasn't going to share it with her.

Soso unexpectedly opened his eyes and gave her a wink. His teeth were mossy. In the next moment he was snoring.

"This way," Lilya orders Grisha when he comes into the kitchen that evening. She leads him past Raisa and Olga and Nusha, cleaning up from dinner and preparing for the morning.

She takes him into the pantry. It's a long, high room lined with shelves containing foodstuffs: jars of pickled cucumbers and mushrooms and tomatoes stewed with herbs, bags of flour and oats and bran, sacks of potatoes and onions, sugar cones wrapped in gauze, and canisters of tea.

With no preamble, she says, "I've seen Soso. I know he killed Felya—as you do. And I know why. He told me about waiting for the money from you."

She's glad to see Grisha swallow, although that's his only reaction.

"You know where he is, then?"

"Yes," she says firmly.

"Does he have Mikhail with him?"

"No. But he knows where he's being kept. And they're ready to return him, Grisha. They don't want to keep him through the winter. He's become nasty and hard to control."

Grisha doesn't want Lilya to see how keen he is for her to tell him more. There's something about her, lately, that troubles him. "How do we get the boy back?"

"You know it's all about money. But because you've held them up, now they want more—a lot more. Soso says, if we bring him enough, he'll take us to Mikhail."

Grisha slams his fist onto a shelf so hard the jars rattle. "No. It's the same story. I've attempted to follow their orders, but they don't hold up their end. Do you even know with certainty that Mikhail is alive?"

"He's alive."

"Because the husband you despise says so? And you believe him?"

Lilya pulls the folded note from the boy from within her blouse. She hands it to Grisha. He opens it. Like the others, it's in charcoal on the back of a page of music Antonina has transposed.

Mama, I miss you so. They told me Papa is dead. I'm sad.
I pray every day. I still have the rest of my notes to
Glinka. Please keep this one for me until I return to you,
dear Mamushka. I will look after you now. Misha.

"Have you shown this to Anto—to the countess?" he asks.

"No. I don't think it's wise, just yet."

Grisha studies the woman's face. "You don't think it will bring her comfort to know that her child is alive?"

"And how would I explain that I have it, Grisha? Anyway, it's just one more payment. Soso has promised me."

"I've been promised the same thing before."

"But like I told you, Soso says they're sick of keeping the boy. And they want to leave Pskov for another province. Perhaps to Voronezh, or farther, where they can start new lives." Soso hasn't said any of this, but she feels it makes the story stronger. She takes the note back from Grisha, refolding it and putting it inside her blouse. "Apparently Misha isn't well."

"What do you mean?"

"Soso says he's fallen ill." She's deep into the lie, trying to make Grisha more desperate to get the boy back. "He can't survive much longer under harsh conditions, not a delicate boy like Mikhail Konstantinovich." She watches his face. "Misha didn't see you, did he? When he was taken from the count?"

Grisha shakes his head. The boy had only seen him as his rescuer.

"Then you will be his hero, his and the countess's. You will bring the boy back to his mother. She will be forever grateful to you."

Grisha doesn't trust Lilya. "What do you mean?"

Lilya smiles, an odd, dark smile, and as she lifts her hand to scratch her neck, he smells attar of roses. Antonina's scent. "She'll be so grateful she may even decide she doesn't have to hide what's happened between her and you. She may invite you into the manor to stay with her." This is a long shot, but Lilya is willing to take it. She's convinced herself that something occurred between Grisha and Antonina the September night they were away together; it was after that night that Grisha's attitude towards the countess changed slightly. But nothing further has happened between them. Lilya has made sure of it: she knows where Antonina is night and day.

She's rewarded by Grisha's reaction. "She told you?" he asks, looking startled.

Lilya ignores his question. "So you must get more money quickly, Grisha. And then I'll take you to Soso. He'll lead us to Misha. And if you have to sell your land to get the money, then do it. Do it for the countess."

"What do you know of land?" His voice is sharp.

"Lyosha told me that soon you will leave here to be a landowner, and he your steward. He and his *wife*." She says the word with venom.

Grisha hadn't put Lyosha under a vow of secrecy, and yet he was somehow surprised he'd told his sister the plan. "Have you spoken of this to the countess?"

"Do you think I share servant news with her? Do you think she begs me, *Oh Lilya, sit and talk with me, tell me of your brother, and of yourself. Tell me what you know of Grisha and his plans.*" There is bitterness in her voice. "Or is the countess too wrapped up in her own thoughts to care about us? Tell me, Grisha, which do you think it is?"

He doesn't answer. "And you, Lilya? If I agree to what you suggest, what do you get out of this?"

"What do you think? Do you think I'll help Soso for nothing? I can't wait to get away from here." Lilya shrugs one shoulder. "I'm sick of this life. I can have a better one somewhere else, where I'm more appreciated. A clean start, like Soso says. We'll all benefit. The countess will have her son back. You will have the countess. And for once I will live my own life, without *her* controlling it."

Now Lilya scratches her shoulder. She was bitten by fleas while in bed with Soso. The note within her blouse rustles at her movement.

Grisha hears it, thinking of the boy, and of Antonina. He doesn't trust Lilya, or Soso, but he is out of options.

$\approx$

Later that day, when Valentin has once again arrived at Angelkov to visit Antonina, Grisha rides to the Bakanev estate to speak with the prince's steward about the land he purchased—twelve versts that adjoin Angelkov—over a year ago.

He reasons, as he rides, that if the prince is willing to negotiate—what are a dozen versts to one who owns thousands?—and the money isn't too slow in coming, Mikhail could be with his mother before the first snow. He knows that even if the prince agrees to buy back the land, he can't be assured of getting the full amount he paid. But it will have to be enough for the greedy bastards. Any amount is better than nothing.

33

The following day—it is the eve of the two-hundredth day since Mikhail's abduction—Lilya sends words to Grisha that she wishes to speak with him again.

Grisha comes in the back door and stamps the mud from his boots. "What do you want this time?" he asks, eyeing the full bottle of vodka on the table. The woman is getting bold, he thinks, helping herself from the countess's stores.

"Sit down," Lilya says, pouring them both a glass, then pushing a crystal dish of pickled, salted pearl onions and cubes of beetroot towards him. "So? Did you get the money?"

"Soon—a week at the longest. There's paperwork to be done, and the prince is away for a few days. I can't get the money until he returns."

"Hmm. What about Kropotkin, eh?" she says then, taking a drink.

Grisha holds his glass, watching her.

"He's charming the countess with his music and his sweet talk. I hear him," she says, "and see the way she looks at him."

Grisha's hand grips the glass more tightly.

Lilya notices that his knuckles have whitened. "I think if this goes on long enough, he's going to try to marry her."

Grisha half stands, the chair sliding back on the wooden floor with a long screech. "What are you talking about? He's only been here a few times."

"Six," Lilya says. "He's been here six afternoons over the last few weeks, and today she told me he would be staying for dinner tomorrow night."

Grisha gives her a wild look, lifts his glass and drains it in one gulp. "Her husband is hardly cold. You're mad to suggest there is anything between them."

"Stranger things have happened. We have to protect her from him, Grisha. Maybe from herself." Lilya motions with her hand for Grisha to sit again. "The countess has ordered Raisa to use the last of the salted beef for soup, and to have a chicken killed. No doubt she'll call up one of the last bottles of wine for her guest. And if he stays for dinner, do you suppose he'll saddle up later, in this cold, and ride home in the darkness? Do you really suppose that's what he'll do? Surely he'll stay." She stops to let her words sink in. "It's not good, Grisha. He's not good for her."

"What does she see in him?" Grisha asks, filling his glass again. "He's a serf."

Casually, Lilya says, "He *was* a serf. He could easily work his way into her heart. She's lonely, Grisha."

At that, Grisha grows too hot, still wearing his heavy quilted coat in the kitchen, which is overheated by the roaring stove. He throws it off and takes another drink. He thinks of the way Antonina had tipped her head to swallow her vodka in one mouthful in the dacha, her long pale throat exposed, vulnerable. That was what she'd said to him before she led him to the bedroom. *I'm lonely, Grisha.* Is she using the same words with the violinist?

"You're right. We must protect the countess from him."

Lilya pushes the bottle closer to Grisha. "As a widow, Angelkov is hers to do with as she wants." She shakes her head, picks up a piece of beetroot and takes a delicate bite. "But should she marry Kropotkin, the estate and what versts are left after the final division and dispersing to the local *mirs* would become his."

Grisha is surprised Lilya is aware of the law—that the only thing a single or widowed woman in Russia can own is land—and therefore what's at stake should Antonina marry. He'd thought the music teacher would be gone from the Bakanevs' by now, that it would be a simple matter of a visit or two.

Lilya shakes her head and takes another bite of the beetroot. "I'm surprised at madam's behaviour. What I've seen . . . well, it's quite unbecoming for a woman of her class." She finishes the beetroot and lifts her apron to wipe the corners of her mouth. She knows Grisha wants to ask what she's referring to exactly, but won't. It's better this way. Lilya knows the power of imagination. "I just thought you should know." She stands. "Since you're as concerned about madam's well-being as I am."

Grisha studies her. He stands as well, finishing his drink and picking up his coat. As he shrugs his arms back into it and opens the door, Lilya speaks once more.

"I'll let you know what happens tomorrow. When he comes for dinner."

As he walks back to his house, Grisha remembers how Antonina kissed him, how hungry she had been, how unafraid to show her heat. Certainly she was loosened by the vodka, but Grisha knows that Antonina wasn't putting on an act when she made love to him.

The musician could never handle a woman like her.

"The violinist is wrong for her," he says into the darkness.

⁓

Valentin and Antonina have had their *solyanka*, the thick, piquant beef soup, followed by a main course of baked fowl with gravy and a potato salad with capers, olives, hard-boiled eggs and peas. In the kitchen waits a platter of cheese and pickled beets, as well as a cake, which Antonina knows has taken far too much of what's left of their sugar.

Valentin notices that they are served dinner by the same man—Pavel—who ushers him into the house and takes his coat. Obviously, there is no longer any specific serving staff. It's clear that the countess and the estate have been adversely affected by the serf emancipation.

Antonina eats little but drinks her wine steadily. Pavel soundlessly opens the second bottle and replenishes Antonina's empty glass. He then moves towards Valentin, the bottle poised, but Valentin shakes his head. Pavel sets the bottle back on the sideboard and returns to his position at the door.

"It's rather simple fare," Antonina says. "I apologize."

"Do you know why I remembered you all these years, countess?" Valentin asks, ignoring her comment about the food. "And why you made such an impression on me when I first saw you at your name day celebration?"

Antonina looks directly into his eyes. She doesn't want what happened with her mother to have anything to do with the answer.

"I saw you the first day as we rehearsed. You thought you were hidden behind a pillar. What I noticed was something free about you. You had a wildness—I know of no other way to describe it. It was subtle but apparent: the way you moved, the way you impatiently brushed back your hair as if it was put on your head to annoy you. And you were so unaware of it. That was part of the intrigue—that you had no idea of your uniqueness. I saw even then that you had the ability to break the hearts of men, if you would but recognize it."

Antonina wonders if he is certain it was her. No one has ever described her like this: a desirable woman.

The candlelight wavers across Antonina's face. She's very good at masking her emotions. Valentin sees through this, though. He's more than a musician. He knows what women like to hear, what they desire men to see in them. And so he continues.

"And when I saw you recently at the Bakanevs', your girlish prettiness had evolved into beauty." He lets her absorb the compliment. "But there was no longer any wildness in you. You looked bewildered, as though you had been trapped. Countess, you look lost." His voice, so soft, is full of sympathy.

Antonina takes another sip of wine. It's a French burgundy that warms the inside of her mouth. Tonight she's enjoying wine more than the crisp burn of vodka at the back of her throat.

"May I be so bold as to inquire why you don't wish to

accompany me when I play?" Valentin asks, and Antonina looks away.

"Why won't I play?" she asks, feeling slow-witted.

Valentin nods encouragingly. His compliments and empathy don't appear to move her, so he is trying a different tactic.

Antonina moves from the table. "Please, bring your wine. Let us go to the music salon." They walk out of the dining room, and she tells him, "It relaxes me to be near my piano. My son and I . . ." She stops to take a drink. "Mikhail insisted I play with him daily," she says after she swallows. "I haven't played for anyone—with anyone—since he was taken." The words catch in her throat. She wets her lips with her tongue. They are at the music salon door.

Valentin opens it for her, then follows as she goes to the piano and sits on the bench. "It's quite different for you, Mr. Kropotkin. You are able to use your ability—the talent you were born with—to bring enjoyment to wide audiences." Valentin sits beside her. "It's taken you somewhere—look at your life now." She puts her wineglass on the top of the piano and looks at him. "I know you must have once been a village child."

Valentin drinks the rest of his wine and sets his glass beside hers.

"And now . . . here you are, a fine gentleman in a tailored suit, dining with a countess." Her hands rest on the keys, and she appears relaxed with him for the first time. "Dining with a countess."

Valentin glides his fingers over hers on the keys.

"While your music took you into a different world," she went on, still looking at him, "for me it was forever trapped within the walls of home. Like every other woman of my class, I am only allowed to play for the enjoyment of my family."

Valentin realizes she's intoxicated. She tries to hide it, but is not quite successful.

"Because, as you know, Valentin Vladimirovitch," she says, using his Christian name and patronymic for the first time, "no matter how talented, no woman of the noble class in Russia can hope for anything more."

There is a loud, booming crack, and they both jump. "What the cold does to the old timbers," Valentin says, glad for the interruption of the countess's monologue. "Always snapping as they contract."

Antonina is suddenly aware that she has embarrassed herself, and surely her guest. She moves her hands from under Valentin's and stands.

Valentin stands as well. "Countess," he says, but her face has lost its slight daze. Her eyes are focused on his, and he knows he must not rush her. "Certainly this situation—the life you speak of—is changing since the manifesto was declared. It may not be as apparent in the provinces, but in the capitals the nihilists are truly creating a new Russia for both men and women. There is talk of emerging conservatories in St. Petersburg and Moscow which will welcome both men and women to be instructed in a professional music career."

She hasn't moved away from him. "It's been some time since I've been to St. Petersburg. Not since . . . well over a year. Yes, before the emancipation was announced." She wants her wine, but Valentin is between her and her glass.

"I think you would find it very different," he goes on. "Things are opening up in surprising ways. The Russian Musical Society that came into being a few years ago is intent on raising the standard of music in the country, and on allowing musical education to be available." He stops, but when she doesn't respond, continues. "The diversity of the students is astounding—from bureaucrats and merchants to university students. Even young women who cannot afford to study privately are attending. There are wonderful fresh options and opportunities."

Antonina can see her half-full glass over his shoulder. "I wasn't aware . . . I've been caught up in my own affairs for some time. Please forgive me, Mr. Kropotkin, I've lost track of the time." She's struggling for composure; she knows she's had too much to drink. "It will be a cold ride home." She gestures towards the door.

"The Bakanevs have been so kind as to allow me the use of a carriage and coachman. So I won't have the cold to contend with on the way back. But of course, if you would prefer I leave immediately . . ." He puts his hand on her arm.

In spite of the faint buzzing in her head, Antonina is filled with shame. She has just complained about her indulgent, extravagant life, and feels she gave him an unflattering, perhaps even ugly, glimpse of who she really is. She feels the warmth of his hand, and looks at the ormolu clock on the mantle.

"It's still early. May I offer you cheese, or dessert?"

"No, thank you." Valentin is still standing very close to her. "I've had more than enough." He puts one hand on her waist.

"Shall we go to the drawing room?" She moves away, picking up her wineglass and finishing the burgundy. "I've asked Lilya to make sure the stoves and fire are kept going. It will be warm."

"Yes," Valentin says. "I'd like that."

In the drawing room, Antonina opens the front of a cabinet. She pours two glasses of vodka and holds one out to Valentin.

He shakes his head. "No, thank you, countess."

"You won't drink with me? You mean there is a man in Russia who says no to a glass of vodka?" She takes her own glass and slowly, unsteadily, walks towards him.

Valentin again holds her arm, this time to support her. "I'm sorry, but if I am going to play—if you wish me to, later—I perform better with a clear head."

"Not even one glass?" Antonina asks.

He shakes his head, smiling.

"I would like to hear of your childhood," she says, wanting the heaviness that has followed them from the music salon to the drawing room to lift.

Valentin looks towards the window, clearing his throat.

"If you don't wish to, I—"

"Certainly I will tell you, if that's your desire. But would you think me terribly bold if I troubled you for a cup of tea?"

She calls for Pavel, who waits outside, and asks him to bring tea. "Please. While we wait, let's sit by the fire." When she is settled in the deep velvet chair across from him, sipping her vodka, he sits as well.

"I was trained under the tutorship of a well-respected maestro, a man named Desyatnikov," he begins, with no preamble. "I have few recollections of my childhood before that time." The way he opens the story is as if he's reading the lines. Antonina suspects he's told his tale many times, to many women; men surely didn't share their pasts in this easy way. "I only know I was very young when I was taken from my family. My age remains a mystery." He smiles. "I was young enough—and perhaps frightened or confused enough—to forget the time before." He looks into the fire. "I only realized later, seeing the new boys come in, that we were given different names as we arrived. I had another, but that's gone from my memory as well."

After a moment of silence, Antonina asks, "Was it very awful for you? To be taken from your family? I think of . . . I worry for my son."

"Countess, that time—"

"Please. Please call me Antonina," she interrupts. It feels ridiculous, to be addressed by a title when Valentin is revealing the intimate tale of his former life.

"As you wish, Antonina." He smiles, and suddenly the air is lighter.

Her glass is empty. She thinks of the one she poured for Valentin, sitting on the cabinet shelf.

"While I don't remember my family or village, or how I came to be chosen, I later witnessed the procedure when I was older and travelled with Desyatnikov. Surely you know the process."

Antonina nods and clears her throat, then rises and goes to the cabinet and replaces her empty glass with the full one. She doesn't know why, but she would have felt closer to Valentin if he had accepted her offer of vodka, and touched his glass to hers. When she turns around, he's crouching in front of the fire, fanning the flames with the bellows.

After Antonina is again sitting, Valentin remains standing with one foot on the brass rail in front of the fireplace. "Every time I watched the maestro choose another boy, I tried to remember it happening to me: a man in fine clothes, the clean shirt and striped waistcoat and shiny boots, carefully looking at my face or hands. But I couldn't. I haven't even a faint memory of anything before practising for hours under Desyatnikov's tutelage."

She thinks of Mikhail. Surely he would remember this life, his life, at Angelkov. Would he ever really forget his name? Or her face?

"One of the other musicians, a boy I practised with for a number of years, told me that I didn't speak for a long time. I may have turned inward; I saw it with others, especially the youngest ones.

"My only comfort—and this I do remember—was the certainty that one day someone big and strong would save me. I was thinking of my father, I suppose, a little boy's dream that I would be rescued and taken home. Because I couldn't remember my home, I naturally made it the most wonderful place one can envision." He smiles ruefully. "Of course, nobody came. I became accustomed to the life, and grew up.

"Now you know the rather uninspiring story of my life." He gives a flourish of his hand and smiles at her. "I became Valentin Vladimirovitch Kropotkin. The little boy I was no longer exists, Antonina." Her name feels delicious in his mouth. He rolls it around as though it were a sweet cherry.

Pavel arrives with the tea tray. When he's gone, Antonina asks Valentin how long he remained with Desyatnikov.

"When I was fourteen years old, he sold me into an orchestra owned by Prince Yablonsky in the Smolensk province. We played at his musical evenings, and he rented us to friends and estates throughout the province and beyond." He drinks his tea. "As we came to be at your name day fete."

"It's terribly sad, Valentin."

"Not when you look at the lives of the villagers. Without the serf orchestra, I might have been nothing more than another labourer bent over in the fields, living a life of deprivation, never knowing the joy of music."

"Yes, I suppose so. And now you may play for whom you wish—where and when."

Valentin tries to keep the pleasant look on his face as he sets down the delicate teacup. Of course, he won't tell her what his life is really like: the struggle to find work, to hope he will be able to afford new strings and resin as needed. What of Madame Golitsyna—has she replaced him by now? Will he have anywhere to live when he returns to St. Petersburg after his job with the Bakanevs is over? "Would you feel comfortable telling me about your son?"

Antonina inhales and holds it. Can she talk about Misha? Valentin is sitting so still, and yet in a posture of waiting.

"If you can, Antonina." He says her name softly.

"He . . . he turned eleven in June. He's a musician. Like you," she says, trying to smile. "He's a truly gifted pianist—he's played since he was three years old. Like an angel." She thinks of the cherub that fell from the church roof.

"I'm sure he inherited this brilliance from his mother."

She smiles. "Actually, Valentin, you remind me of him." As she says this, she's surprised. Had she seen it on his first visit?

"Because I'm a musician?"

"Well, yes, but also because of your fineness of features, and the expressiveness of your face. When did you understand that you felt music within you?"

Valentin gives Antonina a rueful look. "That's gone as well. I only remember playing with the other boys under Desyatnikov. But I do know that I always had an odd quality, related to music: I see colour when I hear music. I know I must have always, because occasionally a shade is like a whisper from something in my past."

"I don't understand."

Valentin's face is animated. "Earlier in my life, I thought everyone saw it the way I did. When I hear certain sounds, I see colours. For example, when the cello plays, I see red. Depending on the ability of the cellist, the colour is clear and vibrant or in varying shades down to a rather dark and muddy burgundy. The colour pulses in the air or, if I close my eyes, inside my head." He continues to tell her about the colours he sees for each instrument.

"How strange and wonderful."

"Yes. Of course, I don't often speak of it—it would be seen as too odd by some, those who don't understand the power of music, and what it does to the mind. To the soul."

"I know that Mikhail, even as a very little boy, felt music more deeply than I have ever done," Antonina says, and Valentin sits back.

"How did he come to be taken?" he asks now, and Antonina blinks rapidly. Suddenly the objects in the room are too bright; they hurt her eyes. "I'm sorry. I see that I shouldn't have asked you."

"Valentin," she says. "What if Misha forgets, like you did? You said the child you were no longer exists."

"I'm sure I was younger than your Mikhail."

"Yes. Mikhail is eleven now. He won't forget me." Tears fill her eyes as she stands. "Will he?" She has trouble keeping her balance, and holds on to the arm of the chair.

Valentin steps close to her, taking her hands and raising them to his lips and kissing them. "Of course he won't.

He'll remember every lovely detail of your face. He knows his name, and the name of his estate. He will find his way back to you."

Antonina is moved by the compassion in his face, in his voice, and so dizzy. She holds on to him.

"He will be found," Valentin murmurs, putting his arms around her. "A child like yours—of the noble class, recognizable by his breeding and upbringing and talent—can't simply disappear. He's waiting somewhere, Antonina, perhaps playing his music." He kisses her. His lips are warm and soft.

But Valentin's lips make her think of Grisha and her immorality. She is drunk again, behaving abominably. She puts her hands on his chest and pulls her face away from his.

His arms are still around her, loosely. "I'm sorry," he says. "Please accept my apologies. You're so beautiful, and so sad. I want . . . please, I so want to alleviate your pain. I have no excuse for my behaviour but that I was carried away. By you."

She puts her fingers to her lips, then her throat. "I . . . I am not blameless. It's a confusing time for me. All I can think of is my son," she says, knowing this isn't entirely true. When she thinks of Grisha, there are moments when she isn't thinking of Mikhail. Grisha takes up so much space when he enters a room, and fills her head in the same way.

Valentin still has his arms around her. Antonina knows she should move away.

"I don't know of anyone who has the power to find my boy," she says. Again she thinks of Grisha. He has had the only contact with the kidnappers, although the last time was months ago. "Whoever returns my son, Valentin, would have my love and gratitude for life."

There is a muffled thump.

Antonina pulls away from Valentin to see Lilya standing in the doorway. Three logs are at her feet; she still holds two.

Lilya has been in the doorway long enough to see Valentin Vladimirovitch with his arms around Antonina. Did she see the kiss? She has heard what Antonina just told him.

"Excuse me, madam," she says, kneeling to pick up the logs.

Whoever returns my son would have my love and gratitude, Lilya repeats in her head. *For life.*

This is what Lilya has always wanted from Antonina.

34

*T*he next day, Lilya again sends for Grisha. This time there is no vodka, no plate of delicacies. As soon as he steps in the back entrance, she beckons with her head towards the pantry. In the alcove, she says, "We must do something."

"Tell me what happened last night," Grisha says. Without waiting for her answer, he adds, "He stayed?"

"The Bakanevs' coachman spent the evening in the kitchen, waiting to drive Kropotkin back," she tells him. "Kropotkin couldn't use the excuse of the cold to stay." She looks for something on Grisha's face, but it shows nothing. "Anyway, he told me that Kropotkin's position could go on indefinitely." She leans against a shelf and crosses her arms.

Grisha notices Lilya's hair. She's pinned it up at the back, and has cut wisps that hang around her face. She's trying to wear her hair as Antonina does. "Go on," he says.

"The princess's sister has decided she'll spend the winter with them. This means that Kropotkin will stay on as music tutor to the children."

"Until spring?"

Lilya shrugs. "Who knows? Maybe even into the summer. You know these people—they do as they choose." She reaches up to touch her hair. "You can see that Kropotkin has already become a regular visitor to Angelkov. And now it looks like he won't be leaving the province for a long time. Long enough, if you know what I'm suggesting."

Grisha is watching her face as if reading the words as they come from her lips.

"If only . . ." she says.

"If only what?"

"There was some way to get such an immoral influence out of Antonina's life. But what can we do? We'll have to sit back and watch it happen. Watch him seduce the countess." And then Lilya doesn't say anything more.

Grisha pulls an apple from an open sack on the shelf. He rubs it absently with his thumb as he walks from the pantry.

Lilya follows him. "Grisha!" When he doesn't respond, she shouts, "Antonina deserves love. Not what that man is trying to use her for."

Her words stop him. Finally he looks back at her, then tosses the apple onto the table. It rolls off and hits the floor as he leaves.

Lilya fingers her hair. Once she brings Mikhail Konstantinovich back to Antonina, the countess will give her all her love. That's what she said to Kropotkin: *Whoever returns my son will have my love and gratitude for life.*

Antonina is playing the piano when Lilya enters the salon with a tea tray.

Antonina stops, looking over her shoulder at Lilya as she sets down the tray. "You've still had no word from Soso, Lilya? You don't know where he is?"

Why is the countess asking about Soso now, so soon after Lilya has seen him? Is it simply a coincidence?

"No," she says.

Antonina stares at her. "Do you miss him?"

"My life is better without him." She arranges the cup and saucer, the plate of biscuits. "He drank too much, and was often ugly in his talk, and with his fists."

Antonina makes a sound in her throat. "At some time, maybe some years ago, did you care for him?"

Lilya shrugs. "He was a hard worker. And he never hit Lyosha, even though he wasn't pleased to have him with us."

"That was all, Lilya?"

Lilya stares at her. "I just said so. I have never loved a man, Tosya."

"But that's terribly sad, Lilya."

"Is it?" Lilya challenges. "Was it not the same for you and the count? Are you not the same as me?"

Antonina's eyes widen. "The same as you?"

"Neither of us will ever love a man fully," Lilya says. She wants Antonina to agree, wants her to see how it is for her. How it could be for Antonina, if she would only recognize it.

On the first day of November, Antonina readies herself for Valentin's arrival.

She thinks of Yakovlev's advice that she should pay a minimum amount of taxes as of the first of the month. And yet she has no rubles to offer. How long will it be before officials arrive at the door, threatening to take the estate from her? She will speak to Grisha about selling some of the antiques. Surely he will know how to begin the process of emptying the manor of the items that would bring the highest prices.

To help take her mind from the worry, she practises Chopin's Nocturne No. 20. She will play this piece for Valentin. She has decided she will not drink any wine or vodka during his visit. She will not.

By two o'clock, his usual time, he hasn't arrived, although the fire is dancing in the music salon and the samovar is waiting with the teapot and the best cups and saucers. Antonina goes up the stairway to the landing window, scanning the road and the clear sky. All is peaceful, quiet, as if readying itself for the long winter. Something has shifted for Antonina. In spite of the disrepair and ruin of the estate itself, she's seeing the beauty of her land for the first time in a long, long while. The thought of the taxes to be paid comes back to her. Will this be her last winter at Angelkov? In the next instant she thinks of Mikhail. He's subject to colds and sore throats during the winter. Who will give him hot milk with honey and butter? Who will have him soak his feet in warm mustard water?

She can't think about him being uncared for. It makes her want the vodka.

She glances at the timepiece pinned on her bodice. Valentin is close to an hour late. As she looks out the window again, a lone horseman appears far down the road, and she nods. There he is. But as the rider comes closer, she sees it isn't Valentin. This man is heavier and shorter. She goes down the stairs, and when Pavel opens the door to the knock, a stranger hands him a folded paper, bows his head and leaves.

"Madam," Pavel says, handing it to her. Lilya has also come at the knocking, and is standing beside Antonina.

"I hope he hasn't fallen ill," Antonina says, taking the note to the music salon. Lilya follows her, and Antonina unfolds the thick vellum square with the royal imprint of the Bakanevs at the top. She reads it then sits down, the note falling into her lap.

"What is it, Tosya?" Lilya asks, kneeling at Antonina's feet, the vertical line between her eyebrows deep.

Antonina swallows and refolds the paper, standing. "I will go to my room, Lilya. I don't wish to be disturbed."

Lilya jumps up, putting her hand on Antonina's forearm. "Is it bad news? He's ill, then—Kropotkin?"

Antonina looks into Lilya's face. "His name is Mr. Kropotkin, Lilya. And no, he is not ill. He has been called away."

Lilya is unblinking before Antonina's steady gaze. "What of the children's lessons?"

Antonina tilts her head. "You care about the children at the Bakanev estate, Lilya?"

Lilya won't look away. "I know you enjoyed the visits of Kr—Mr. Kropotkin, Tosya. I'm sorry if you're disappointed by his departure."

"What makes you think he's departed? I only said he'd been called away from the Bakanevs', not that he was gone from Pskov."

"I only meant—"

"Thank you for your concern." Antonina's back is straight as she leaves Lilya in the music salon with the dying fire and the cooling tea.

⁓

In her room, away from Lilya's questions, Antonina reads the letter again.

> My dear Countess Mitlovskiya,
> It has been brought to our attention that Valentin Vladimirovitch Kropotkin has been paying you social calls.
> Because Mr. Kropotkin was in our employ, we feel it our responsibility to be accountable for his actions. Mr. Kropotkin, as a former serf musician, has acted inappropriately.
> The prince and I offer our apologies for his wholly unsuitable behaviour. We understand that he has taken advantage of your kind nature and high standards. We have concluded that you are still in a state of distress, and we recognize that the difficulties you have experienced are capable of creating havoc with one's sensibilities.
> Mr. Kropotkin has been reprimanded and dismissed as of this morning. We will make certain that he does not go unpunished for his actions. He has not been given a good character reference, and this will ensure difficulty in finding future employment with the noble families throughout the province of Pskov, and hopefully further beyond.
> We have concluded that it would be fitting for all concerned if you allow some time to pass before you again grace Pskov's social milieu, so that the repercussions of

this unfortunate situation will have sufficient opportunity to be diminished.

With God's blessings,
Princess Eugenia Stepanovna Bakaneva

Antonina walks up and down the veranda for an hour before dusk. When she goes inside again, she passes Lilya on the way to her bedroom but ignores her. She orders Lilya to go away when she knocks, gently and persistently, on the locked door.

As darkness falls, Antonina adds more logs to the fire, crumples the letter and throws it into the flames. Then she retreats to her bed with the bottle of vodka from her wardrobe, Tinka beside her.

It is after eight o'clock that evening when Valentin arrives at Angelkov.

Pavel has fallen asleep in a chair in front of the stove in the kitchen, and there has been no sound from Antonina's room for hours.

When Lilya hears the dogs barking frantically, she goes to the door and opens it, peering into the darkness. As Valentin comes up the step and is illuminated by the lamp Lilya holds, she tells him, before he can speak, that Countess Mitlovskiya is asleep, and has left express wishes not to be bothered. By anyone, Lilya adds. She knows Antonina will have drunk herself into a deep state of unconsciousness by now.

"Where can I find the steward?" the man asks.

Lilya frowns. "Why do you ask about Grisha?"

"It isn't your business," Valentin tells her. "Where will I find him?"

"I expect he's in his house," Lilya says.

"And where is that?" Valentin struggles to hold his temper. He's seen how this woman hovers about Antonina, using any excuse to be present when he visits, giving him dark looks when she thinks her mistress isn't paying attention.

Lilya points with her chin. "Behind the servants' quarters. Follow the road past it. His house is the only one."

Without another word, he turns from her.

Lilya watches him go, her mouth firm. Grisha will make sure Kropotkin doesn't linger at Angelkov.

Grisha answers Valentin's knock.

"How did you know where to find me?" he asks.

"That miserable woman at the manor told me. May I step inside for a moment?"

Grisha moves aside to allow Valentin inside, then shuts the door behind him. "What do you want?"

It's obvious to Valentin that Grisha won't invite him to warm himself by the fire. It doesn't matter. What he has to ask Grisha will only take a moment. "I rode here to try to speak to Countess Mitlovskiya."

"I heard you'd left the Bakanevs'."

"Yes. I'm staying at an inn in the nearest village. The servant at the house told me the countess was already asleep. I suspect she is lying."

Grisha crosses his arms. "She creates her own truths."

"That peasant has made her feelings towards me obvious." Valentin's look pierces Grisha. "It's clear I haven't been welcomed at Angelkov by anyone except for the landowner herself, which is all that matters, really." His voice grows loud, angry, and he steps further into the room, in spite of the frown on Grisha's face. "Countess Mitlovskiya appeared cheered by my music and my conversation. And I have greatly enjoyed her company. And yet someone . . ." He stops. ". . . has been telling sordid tales."

Grisha says nothing. Valentin glances at the full book-shelf. Strange for a man who has probably spent half his life beating the serfs at Angelkov, he thinks. But from what Valentin has witnessed, there are now few left to flog.

"So you've heard I've been dismissed from the Bakanev estate." When Grisha still doesn't speak, he says, "Surely the whole province is enjoying this bit of scandal. I felt it necessary to speak to the countess. I want to make sure she's all right. The last thing I wanted was to cause her any more pain. She's had enough in her life to contend with without gossips trying to ruin her reputation. As for mine"—he gives a barking cough—"I'll be lucky to find a day or two's work in all of Pskov once the Bakanevs have finished their campaign against me."

"I don't understand what this has to do with me," Grisha says, fully expecting that Valentin has come to accuse him of spreading the lies. He and the steward at the Bakanev estate are friends. It only took a few words in his ear.

"I've written a letter to the countess. I thought I might post it, but then realized, as I said, how much I'd like to see for myself that she's all right. When that servant didn't allow me in, I didn't want to leave the letter with her. I knew it would be better to bring it to someone with authority, some-one who will ensure that the countess receives it."

It appears that Kropotkin isn't accusing him of anything after all. "You don't trust Lilya with the letter," Grisha states.

"That hard-faced woman? No. And although I know you don't think much of me, Naryshkin, you have the look of a solid man."

As Grisha goes to the fireplace to throw another log onto the fire, Valentin studies the bookshelf more closely. It's lined with neatly arranged volumes interspersed with a variety of small, charming objects. A *svirel*—a primitive Russian flute—sits on the top shelf. He picks it up, turning it over and looking at the name carved there. He puts the flute to his lips and blows a quick scale.

Grisha looks up at him, the poker in his hand. A chill runs through him. He drops the poker and snatches the flute from Valentin. Nobody has ever been inside his house except the count and Tania; the countess has only stood at the door once or twice. It angers him that this man is here at all, let alone touching his belongings.

Valentin's hands hang empty in the air. He shakes his head at the rudeness of the man, then, without knowing why, asks, "Who is Tima?"

Grisha's stomach contracts as if the buckwheat kasha he had eaten earlier has turned rancid. "Give me the letter for the countess." He sets the flute back on the shelf. "If you intend to get back to the inn before they lock the door, I'd suggest you leave now."

Valentin takes a square of paper sealed with dark blue wax from inside his coat. The cold has cracked the wax. He hands it to Grisha.

"It's very important to me that she receive it tomorrow morning. Early."

Grisha is angered by the man's gall. "I have my own plans for tomorrow. I'll see that she gets it when I have time to deliver—"

"In the name of all that's holy, Naryshkin," Valentin interrupts, his voice rising, "have you never felt anything for a woman?"

Grisha sucks in his breath, turns and puts the letter on the mantle. Not looking at Valentin, he walks to his door and opens it.

Valentin pulls down his hat and steps out into the cold. "Please, Naryshkin," he says. "All I ask is that you deliver the letter to Antonina tomorrow. It's not much, is it?" His voice is even, with no whisper of subservience, and this angers Grisha further. And that he calls her Antonina. "Can you not help me, Grisha?" he says, and Grisha's head pounds. Something about Kropotkin is troubling him, making him feel strangely unsteady. He wants him to leave.

That he would dare act as if they were old friends, calling him Grisha, talking of feelings for a woman, for *her*, Grisha thinks as he closes the door on Kropotkin.

The musician hardly knows her.

⁂

The next morning, Antonina unlocks her bedroom door when Lilya brings her hot chocolate and two sweet buns. "You must eat, Tosya," she says, setting the tray on the table beside her.

She glances at it. "I'm not hungry." Antonina's face is puffy and pale.

"If you're upset over Kropotkin, and whatever else the letter said . . . Tosya, it's not worth it to make yourself ill."

Lilya takes the empty vodka bottle from the bedclothes and sets it near the door. "He has nothing, Tosya. He's penniless, and useless, apart from making beautiful music. He's like a pretty songbird, designed to bring pleasure. Yes, he's well-spoken, but every word is surely rehearsed for you. To impress you." She holds her breath, ready to be reprimanded.

Antonina's silence makes Lilya bold. "Don't you understand, Tosya? For someone so clever, you don't see what's in front of you, do you?"

Antonina looks at her, waiting, knowing Lilya will tell her what's in front of her.

And Lilya will. But she has a different angle in mind than the one she used with Grisha.

"He knows you're far beyond his reach. Yes, he's a free man now, but that means nothing—all men are free in Russia. Does that mean you would take up with the village butcher or local blacksmith? With a merchant with a few bolts of cloth for sale, or a former steward with a patch of land to his name?" She is taking a chance on the last sentence, but Antonina's expression doesn't change. "You must continue to think of your class, Tosya. Nothing's changed in that respect. You've only been teasing him."

"Teasing him?"

"You've made him care for you, haven't you? It's clear he's taken with you." Lilya shakes her head. "What are you doing, Antonina Leonidovna?" she says, her voice almost a whisper. "What are you doing?" she repeats. "You put Kropotkin in an impossible situation. He cannot be part of your life. You are committing class treason, and in this way you are being unkind to him."

Antonina looks away from Lilya's steady gaze.

"There is no possibility of anything between you," Lilya says, her voice still low, but firm. "Surely you know this, Antonina. First impressions might be that he's a good man, but he's not. He's not the right kind of man, even if he was of your class. You will never find a man who will be able to deal with your strength, a man who understands what you've been through. What we have all lived through at Angelkov." She kneels in front of Antonina, taking her hands in her own. "Look how you've coped without your husband. He was useless from the day of the kidnapping, and you carried on so bravely. And now you must let the musician go. You know he's already suffered for it." Lilya's voice is low, soothing, full of sympathy.

"I never had feelings for Valentin other than friendship, Lilya. And I do not suspect he had the feelings you speak of for me. We simply enjoyed each other's company. That's all."

"Truly, Antonina?"

"Do you not believe me?" Antonina pulls her hands away, standing.

"No one knows you as I do, Tosya. No one," Lilya repeats, softly, still on her knees.

Antonina says nothing. She sits on her window seat and looks out over the dying garden.

35

The sky is full of stars, and a full moon lights the road. Tinka is asleep in front of the fire glowing in the music salon; Antonina has chosen to eat her dinner there. The rest of the house is in darkness apart from the kitchen, where the servants complete the last of the day's work. There's no reason to heat stoves and light fires when the rooms are empty.

Antonina looks at the new bottle of vodka Pavel set on the table near the door at her bidding, but, without touching it, she puts on a heavy cloak. She leaves Tinka sleeping and carries her cup of tea out to the veranda and looks up at the stars. She finds some of the constellations, and remembers pointing them out to Mikhail.

On the still air is the sudden echo of distant barking from the nearest village. Her two harriers, lying on the floor of the veranda near the door, rise silently. Hooves pound up her drive. As the horse and rider draw near, she can see by the moonlight that it's Valentin. She puts her teacup on the railing and goes down the front steps. The dogs crowd against her skirt; she rests a hand on each of their heads.

"You got my letter, then," Valentin says, dismounting and coming to her. "Thank you for waiting for me. I wanted to come earlier, but it was impossible."

Antonina shakes her head. "I didn't receive a letter. I came out . . . the stars are so . . ."

"Your steward didn't deliver my letter to you, to tell you I would come this evening?"

"No."

"I wanted to see for myself that you were all right after what happened with the Bakanevs," he says. Valentin believes he was very close to gaining some footing with the countess. He was prepared for it to take some time; he has rarely known a woman so reserved. "I don't know what they said to you, though I know they sent a letter. Were they insensitive?"

"They made their position very clear. But what of you, Valentin? Is it true that you won't get work anywhere in Pskov?"

"It appears that way. I had no luck today, even in the city itself."

"What will you do?"

"I'll go back to St. Petersburg. Nobody there will care about what happened—or didn't happen"—he smiles—"between an unknown musician and a beautiful landowner out in the provinces."

"Do you have friends there, somewhere to live?"

Valentin thinks of Madame Golitsyna. Will she invite him in when he knocks on her door? "I have my violin.

That's all I need. I'll find something, if not in St. Petersburg then in Moscow."

Antonina remembers Lilya's words in her bedchamber that morning. "I feel responsible, Valentin. I shouldn't have . . . encouraged you."

Valentin smiles again. "It was I who sought your company. I wanted to see who you had become." He pulls his collar closer against the chill.

"And did you?"

Valentin continues to smile.

"It's cold," she says. "Will you come in?"

Ah. It's not over yet, then. Valentin says, very quietly, "Have I not created enough turmoil for you?"

"It's still my home. Nobody can tell me what to do in my own home. And it's clear that you can't be damaged any further by gossip. Come." In a bold move, knowing she won't see him again, she takes his hand. In spite of the night air, his hand is warm, and his fingers wrap about hers.

In the entrance, she lights a candle. Olga is asleep in a deep cushioned chair in the shadows, her rosary looped through her fingers. Antonina points to her and puts her finger to her lips, and then leads Valentin to the music salon.

Tinka rises and comes to Antonina. "Could you build up the fire?" Antonina asks, and lights lamps as Valentin crouches in front of the fireplace and stirs the embers. He adds kindling and, when it catches, puts on two small logs. The air warms, and the glow is red and orange over their faces as she comes back to stand in front of the fire. She picks up Mikhail's journal from the mantle; she had been reading it again, for comfort.

He tries to put his arms around her; she moves away from him.

"Antonina," Valentin says, almost a whisper.

Holding the journal against her with one hand, she puts the other to her face, warm from the fire. She thinks of Grisha. She has known Grisha for more than a third of her life. She respects and understands him, his honesty and integrity, his strength of character. She knows so little about Valentin, even though he has recently told her more about his life than Grisha has of his. "All that consumes me is the thought of my son, Valentin."

"I can help you. If you open yourself to me, Antonina, and let me love you, you will see your darkness lift. I promise you."

Antonina turns away from him. She caresses the soft leather of Mikhail's journal, then lifts it to her mouth and kisses it. "There was word from him once, that he was alive. But that was months ago. I believe that he still lives, Valentin. I would know if he were no longer on this earth. Until I see him . . ." She faces him again.

They stand in silence, the distance Antonina had put between them still there.

Valentin has tried. She will not weaken. But there will be another woman, one who won't be as immovable as Countess Mitlovskiya. "I believe it's time for me to leave you, Antonina," he says.

They go to the veranda together. Antonina holds the dogs to keep them silent.

"Again, I'm sorry for what's happened to you because of me," Antonina says. "Will you leave for St. Petersburg soon?"

"Yes. There's no reason for me to stay. Is there?"

"Thank you, Valentin Vladimirovitch," is her reply.

"What do you thank me for?"

"For your friendship." At last she steps closer and allows him to hold her, but only for a moment.

It is too late, and will lead to nothing, he knows. He drops his arms, walks down the steps and mounts his horse. Just before he blends into the shadows of the trees on the drive, he turns and waves to her.

Lilya watches from the dark landing window.

The next morning, Lilya arrives with Antonina's breakfast. Antonina is already reading before the fire in her dressing gown. Her hair is tangled.

Antonina's lacy, delicate chemise is tossed carelessly on the bedcovers. Lilya imagines Kropotkin removing it in the music salon the previous evening. "There's a problem in the kitchen, Tosya. Raisa has found mouse droppings in the flour. She's very upset. The flour must last us through the winter."

Antonina puts down her book. "What's usually done when this happens?"

"Traps can be set. Or we can put a barn cat in the pantry at night."

"Well, can't it be seen to, then?"

"Raisa wishes to speak to you about it. She doesn't want to bring in a cat unless you approve," Lilya sees Antonina hasn't fastened the top buttons of her dressing gown, and that she wears no nightgown underneath. She has never known Antonina to be so dishevelled.

Antonina sighs, rising. "All right."

Lilya reaches to button Antonina's dressing gown. Her fingers graze Antonina's breast, and Antonina pushes her hand away and does up the buttons herself.

Once she's gone, Lilya picks up Antonina's chemise. She brings it to her face and breathes its scent. Thinking of Kropotkin's hands on it, she crumples it into a ball, holding it tightly with both hands.

She brings the fabric to her face again and smells it a second time. Then she bites at it with her sharp eye teeth. When she's created a small tear in the silk, she slowly rips it in half. She throws both pieces into the fire. The soft lace smokes for a moment and then catches, the flames leaping as they feed on it.

Lilya pushes the burning fabric about with the poker until there's no evidence of what she's done, then replaces the poker and sets out Antonina's breakfast. The cup rattles in its saucer.

Half an hour later, Lilya arrives at Grisha's house unannounced, and pounds on his door.

"He was with her, Grisha. *With her.* In the music salon. She snuck him into the house. I heard them, heard what they did."

Grisha is too shocked to speak, but fights for control in front of Lilya. He thinks of Valentin's face as he said: *Have you never felt anything for a woman?* Then he regains enough control to quietly ask, "And why do you feel it necessary to tell me this, Lilya?"

"It did no good to have him dismissed from the Bakanevs'. Do you really think he'll leave her alone, now that he's had a taste of her? He's ruining her reputation, and she's too blind to care. Next he'll be putting his boots under her bed. I *heard* them, Grisha," she repeats. "What will you do to stop him?" she demands, and by the colour in her face, the barely disguised fury, Grisha understands, with a start, what he hasn't before.

The woman isn't worried about Antonina losing Angelkov to Kropotkin. She's jealous, jealous in the same way he is. She wants Antonina as he does. How long has it been like this? How has he not seen it?

He feels weak at the thought of the musician making love to Antonina. "It isn't in our control to stop the countess from bringing whomever she wishes into her home," he says calmly, not wanting her to see how deeply he's affected. "It is still her home, Lilya. Don't forget that."

Lilya stares at him. "Fine. If I have to, I will stop him myself."

He turns away from Lilya's glare. "And just what do you propose to do?"

When she doesn't answer, he looks over his shoulder at her. She has an odd smile on her face, something that gives him a jolt of understanding even deeper than the one from a moment ago. *Something's not right with her. Surely she's ill in some way.*

"You'll see, Grigori Sergeyevich. If he returns, you'll see how I stop him."

⇥

Later that morning, as an icy, slanted rain falls, Antonina looks out her bedroom window at the garden below.

Almost all of the plants are dead, the leaves blackened and drooping, the soggy mounds of the flower beds like graves. The only survivors are a few beaten-down chrysanthemums with their tattered rust and dull gold blossoms, heavy with moisture. There are spots of brightness from the rosehips on their thorny stems: hard, brilliant garnets against the skeletal remains of the rose bushes.

And as Antonina surveys the sad remains of past beauty, the rain turns into the first snow. It falls onto the garden, slowly covering everything with a strange silvery glow. Antonina feels a sense of relief. She would rather it all be covered with pristine white than see it in such a state of ugliness.

She will never see Valentin again. She wraps her arms around herself, hearing him say that Mikhail would be playing his music somewhere. In her heart she knows this is unlikely, but allows herself the comfort of that vision: Misha at the piano. It's a better image than the one of him in a peasant's hut. She can't bear to think of her son cold and hungry. Hurt.

She doesn't want to stay in the house with these thoughts, so she puts on her cloak and walks out into the garden. But the snow switches back to rain, dissolving the delicate lacing of white. She becomes damp and chilled. Valentin said he'd given a letter for her to Grisha. Why didn't Grisha deliver it to her?

When Grisha opens the door to her knock, expecting Lilya again, he steps back, surprised.

"Grisha? Valentin Vladimirovitch told me he gave you a letter for me. I've come for it," she says.

Grisha's face is dark in the odd light of this third day of November. He studies Antonina, looking for anything about her that is different now that she's been with the musician. A slow-beating anger simmers as he thinks of them together, but Antonina can't know that he knows, that Lilya has been to see him. He needs Lilya to get to Soso. And to Mikhail.

"Countess," he says, and the word hovers oddly, like a presence, between them. He won't call her Antonina. "I'm sorry. I was involved in matters off the estate yesterday and the letter slipped my mind."

It's an outright lie. He didn't want to give it to her. He didn't want to face her. He's so tired of lying about Mikhail, about what he feels for her.

"May I come in?" she asks.

"Yes, please. Come in."

In the small sitting room, the curtains are open, letting in the soft daylight, and a fire of fir cones gives off a woodsy odour. The settee, covered in soft brown wool, is pulled close to the fire. A few lamps are lit, adding to the warm feeling of the room. There are many books, and a sense of comfort, of home.

"The letter . . ." Grisha says, looking around. "I put it somewhere."

Antonina picks up a book lying open, face down, on the settee. "Guiraud: *Les Deux Princes.* You read French, then?"

"My father taught me."

"How is it your father spoke French?"

Grisha is not about to disclose his past at this moment. He suddenly thinks that if he comes close enough, he will smell Kropotkin on her—and all at once he's furious with her. She's like a bitch in heat, spreading her scent, driving everyone within sniffing distance insane. Restraining himself, he says, "I've had that book since I was a young man. I carried it with me here, to Angelkov."

"Timofey Aleksandrovitch Kasakov," she reads from the flyleaf. It's Grisha's handwriting. Timofey. Tima: the name he'd asked her to call him the night in the dacha. *Call me Tima*, he'd whispered.

She looks up from the book. "Tima," she says, and he knows, by her eyes, what she's thinking.

He's trembling, although Grisha is not a man to tremble.

He wants to go to her, wants to hold her so badly that he finds it hard to breathe.

"That's the name you were once called?"

He's so raw. He knows what she's done with Kropotkin, what Lilya told him they had done in the last twelve hours. In that moment Grisha feels there will be no future and can be no consequences. He wants to say something meaningful, something that will make her understand it's him she should be with—him, not Kropotkin.

He says, instead, "Yes, that was the name I was given."

"You changed it to Grigori Sergeyevich Naryshkin."

"Yes," he says firmly.

She lets a moment pass, and then puts the book back on the settee. In spite of Grisha's curtness, it appears she doesn't want to leave. She picks up the *svirel*, putting her fingers on its six holes as Valentin had done, looking at the name Tima carved on one side. "Do you play?"

"No. It was a gift." Her questions turn the knife sharply in his gut. She must know what she's doing, talking to him as if nothing has changed. But everything has changed. Is she punishing him?

She puts the flute back. "Do you know something odd? Kropotkin told me that when he hears music, he sees colour. The sound a cello makes is red. The piano green, the piccolo yellow . . . He named what he saw when he heard each instrument. He made me think of Misha when he told me about it. Misha learned to play the piano as easily as he learned to say the letters of the alphabet or count his numbers." Remembering Misha learning to play makes her smile. "I sometimes thought—" Her smile falls away as she looks at Grisha. "What is it?"

He's gripping the mantle, his knuckles white, his complexion blanching.

"You don't look well."

"I'm fine."

"Have you ever heard of such a thing? Of music creating colour in someone's vision?"

Grisha makes a sound as if he's clearing his throat, or perhaps his breath is caught there. "What colour does he see when he plays his violin?" he asks, surprising her.

Her mouth is lovely, and as the muted light falls across her in streams, Grisha grows strangely weak in her presence. It's deeply confusing, the two elements coming together. As he's filled with desire for her, she's fitting in the final piece of something he hasn't allowed himself to believe.

He knows the colour before she says it.

"He sees gold when he plays. Certain tones make the gold shimmer, he said, like the sun through autumn leaves." She looks quizzically at Grisha. "Are you really quite well, Grisha? You appear . . . Perhaps you're falling ill?"

"No," he says, and straightens his shoulders. "I have work. The accounts . . ."

Antonina doesn't see any sign of the account books. "The letter, then, Grisha. Do you have the letter for me?"

"Yes," Grisha says in a vague way, as though he's suddenly very weary, or deeply distracted. He looks around, shaking his head ever so slightly, then pulls the letter from beside a small painting on his mantle and hands it to her. "Here it is. Good day," he tells her, making it clear it's time for her to leave.

Once she's gone, he sits, heavily, on the settee. He stares at the *svirel*. And then he rises, slowly, and goes to his desk and opens it. He takes paper, a pen and a bottle of ink. He stares at the paper for a moment, and then writes: *Dear Valentin Vladimirovitch Kropotkin.*

He stops, as if unsure of what he's about to say. It takes him a long time to compose three simple lines.

※

Antonina reads what Valentin had written to her two days earlier. His words tell her how much he had enjoyed her company. He would come to see her one more time, the following evening, but after that he would write to her from wherever he settled. That perhaps, whether in St. Petersburg or Moscow, she could one day come and hear him play again. "When you have your son back," she reads, "I would like to meet him. Please bring him with you."

Mikhail. *Is this why I wanted to be with you, Valentin— because you remind me so much of him?*

※

It's late in the afternoon when Antonina goes to the kitchen. She tells Raisa that she will ask Lyosha to bring in a barn cat for the mice. Raisa has asked if they should throw out the flour, and Antonina asked if there was any alternative. "We could sift it, madam, to get rid of the droppings. But it will take some time."

"I'll help," Antonina tells her. It feels wrong to sit, waiting to be served, when she sees how much Raisa and the others have to do.

Raisa tells her, as they work together, that Lyosha has ridden out to hunt rabbits. If he has luck, they will have rabbit stew the next day, Raisa says, smiling.

Neither Antonina nor Raisa know that Lyosha has already

returned with two large hares and dropped them outside the servants' quarters. Lilya is there now, skinning and gutting them.

Lyosha's rifle is leaning against the front of the house. He's in the stables rubbing down his horse.

Antonina is in the pantry, taking another sack of flour from a shelf, when she hears the dogs barking. She assumes it's Lyosha returning. She takes the flour into the kitchen and begins sifting again.

Lilya looks up from the skinned carcass as the rider gallops past the servants' quarters, down the road towards Grisha's house.

It's Valentin.

She throws down the rabbit, her hands bloody, and grabs the rifle from where it leans against the door frame.

⚍

The two men are inside Grisha's house. Valentin clutches the letter from Grisha. *Please come to my home when you get this. We must talk. I remember you.*

Grisha is holding the *svirel*. "What does this flute mean to you, Kropotkin?" he asks, handing it to him.

Valentin stuffs the letter into his pocket and runs his fingers over the carved name. "I played it when I left the letter for the countess with you," he says.

"But does it mean anything? From another time?"

"Another time? I don't know what you're asking. What are you saying, Naryshkin?"

Grisha swallows, gently taking the *svirel* from Valentin's hand. "I carried this with me when I left home. When I left Chita."

"I don't know Chita."

"It's in Siberia, far east of Irkutsk."

Valentin's face shows nothing.

"My little brother gave this to me," Grisha says. "He carved my name into it, and gave it to me for my name day. He was barely eight, and already played the violin as if he had learned in the heavens." Grisha's face is pale. "He saw gold when he played his violin. He was taken away, to become a musician."

Valentin's chest is rising and falling. "I don't remember my childhood."

"Nothing?"

"Bells." He swallows. "Church bells. And other sounds. Gongs, I think."

"Tibetan gongs."

Valentin wipes his forehead with his hand. "A glass of water, Naryshkin."

"You remember the gongs from the temple we attended with our mother."

"Our mother?"

"Yes, Kolya."

Valentin sits down, staring up at Grisha.

Grisha nods. "Kolya. You were Kolya. I was Tima. I am Tima. Your brother, Tima."

Valentin's mouth is open as he stares at Grisha. His breathing is erratic, and his face flushes. "You're . . . wait. Wait," he says, standing, putting out both his hands as if wanting to stop time.

The door is thrown open with such force that it hits the wall. It's Lilya with Lyosha's rifle. She aims it at Valentin.

Valentin looks from her to Grisha, and back to Lilya,

confusion on his face. Grisha sees what is happening, but before he can react, an explosion rips through the room.

Valentin, his chest blown open, flies backwards. He hits the settee and then the floor.

〜

Antonina hears the muffled report of a rifle. She glances at the window. It's dusk. Surely Lyosha isn't still hunting, she thinks. It's far too dark to be assured of a kill.

〜

When Lyosha arrives at Grisha's house, panting from running down the road at the sound of the shot, Grisha is on his knees, holding the musician in his arms. He is pressing a blood-soaked blanket over the man's chest. Lilya is slumped against the open door as if thrown there. Her eyes are wide with shock. The rifle, sticky with rabbit blood, is beside her on the floor. She is crossing herself compulsively, whispering prayers as she stares at the injured man.

Lyosha puts his hands to his head. There's so much blood. It looks like . . . it seems as if Lilya shot the musician. And Grisha . . . why is he holding the other man so closely, as if they're lovers? He's murmuring, pressing the dying man's head against his chest, his own face contorted in something frightening to behold.

Lilya is shaking violently, and as Lyosha looks at her, she whispers to him, "I heard an owl hooting last night. I knew something terrible would happen today." She says this as if she's telling him a secret. And then she continues crossing herself and muttering frantic prayers: *Forgive me, God in Heaven forgive me, forgive me Heavenly Father, forgive me.*

Lyosha drops to his knees. His hands are still on his head. Holy Mother of God. He has never seen a man dying like this. The musician is choking, a bubbling sound bursting from his throat. The blanket is saturated with crimson. Grisha is covered in it.

"You came," he hears the musician gasp. "You came, Tima."

Grisha tries to speak. He can't. He tries again. "Yes, Kolya, I came for you." His voice is hoarse, the words slow, fractured.

"As I dreamed you would. I knew you would come for me." The bubbling grows louder. Valentin coughs up a mouthful of blood and his lips move in what could be a smile.

After a long silence, Grisha looks up at Lilya and Lyosha. "He's dead," he says, slowly making the sign of the cross over the other man three times. His eyes are wet.

Lyosha has never seen Grisha sign the cross before. He looks at his sister, then back at Grisha. "Did you . . . do you know him so well, then, Grisha?" Lyosha asks, his voice sounding as though his throat has been burned. His hands shake violently.

"No," Grisha tells him. "I don't know him at all. But I could have."

36

*G*risha looks down at the body of the brother he had abandoned on the road outside Chita.

He remembers his one day in Irkutsk, and how he wouldn't stay any longer in case he actually did spot Kolya. How he got drunk and took his first woman. How all he wanted was to start his life with no responsibilities, no ties to a little boy who would only hold him back.

How easy it had been for him to betray that boy. He had betrayed him once, and now he is responsible for his death.

"Lilya," Lyosha breathes, finally getting to his feet. "Lilya, what have you done?" He lifts the rifle.

Lilya is staring at the body.

"Lilya?" Lyosha says again. She's still crossing herself and whispering prayers. She clasps her hands, raising them in front of her. Lyosha wants to shout at her, strike her, but it's all too frightening, too confusing. It is so quiet in

Grisha's house now, with Grisha holding the dead musician, looking at him in such a stricken way. "What happened? Why did you do this?" She doesn't answer. Lyosha looks at Grisha again. "Why has Lilya done this terrible thing?"

"I must go to church. I must ask for forgiveness." Lilya speaks aloud for the first time. "I . . . I didn't mean . . . I don't know what I was doing. I didn't even think it was loaded. How would I know? Why would you leave it loaded, Lyosha? I didn't mean to kill him. I wanted only to drive him away. To make him understand he could never come back to her. I must beg forgiveness. Will God forgive me, Lyosha?" She is crying now.

Grisha gently lays Valentin down. "Lyosha, take Lilya to the servants' quarters. Then come back and help me."

Lyosha is so pale. "Help you? But what about Lilya? Will she go to prison? I shouldn't have left the cartridge in the rifle. I never do that. I . . . I was tired. I got back and . . ."

"I'm not going to prison." Lilya's voice is unexpectedly loud, firm. She turns her head from Valentin's body, glaring at Grisha. "Bad things happen, but it's not always because one is bad."

Grisha stares at her.

"I only meant to frighten him away so that he'd never come back. But . . . but now . . ." Lilya's voice loses its strength, and she weeps. Almost immediately she gathers herself again. "Don't tell me you aren't glad," she says to Grisha. "I saved you the trouble, didn't I?"

Grisha wishes Lilya would be quiet. He's trying to stay calm, to think logically, but he can't. He wants to be alone with his dead brother.

"We'll bury him in the woods," Lilya continues. "Because how will we explain a man with a bullet in his chest? No one will miss him. He's been dismissed by the Bakanevs, his career ruined. It would make sense that he moved on to another province, where no one would know of his disgrace." Her words are stumbling, spittle flying from her lips. "And you can't tell what I've done, Grisha. If you do, I'll tell Antonina *you* killed him. Do you think she would suspect me? Do you think she doesn't know how you felt about him? That you hated him as much as I did?" She finally looks back at the body. "I'll tell her you did it," she says again.

"Lilya," Lyosha says. "Lilya, stop."

She ignores him. "Besides, if I'm arrested for his murder, you won't find Soso."

At that, Grisha steps up to her and puts his hands around her throat in one quick movement. He just wants her to stop her incessant chattering.

Lyosha grips the rifle. "Grisha, what are you doing?"

Grisha's hands are loose, loose enough for Lilya to speak. "Kill me then," she says. "Kill me and you won't find the boy. Kill me and you kill Mikhail Konstantinovich."

Grisha holds his hands up, away from her throat, and steps back.

"My God. My God," Lyosha repeats. "Tell me what you're talking about, sister. What in the name of God is going on?"

Grisha puts his hand to his temple. "Take her out of here."

Something in Grisha's voice frightens Lyosha more than if he'd shouted.

"Don't let her go to the countess," Grisha says, and Lyosha takes Lilya's arm. "And come back later to help me."

That night, Lyosha and Grisha dig a grave in the cemetery behind the Church of the Redeemer. Grisha has chosen a spot hidden by a thick stand of fir, where the newly turned earth won't likely be noticed. The ground is hard, although not yet frozen.

"Why did she do it, Grisha?" Lyosha asks, heaving clumps of hard soil out of the way. The area is lit by two lamps sitting on the ground. He glances at the wrapped shroud in the back of the cart. "And why are we burying him? Shouldn't we tell someone? At least Father Cyril."

Grisha stops digging. The harsh light from the lamps makes the bones of his face stand out. His mouth is grim. "Do you want your sister imprisoned, Lyosha? Sent to one of the women's camps in Siberia, to die after years of hard labour?"

"No. But it's wrong. It's wrong in the eyes of God. We have to tell the authorities in Pskov. It was an accident. You see that. Lilya didn't mean to do it." He glances at the body again. "I'll say I did it. I was hunting, and shot him by mistake. I'll say I did it, Grisha. It's my fault for leaving the rifle loaded. I'll take the blame."

Grisha looks at the young man, seeing what he is willing to do out of love for his sister. He has never known this kind of devotion. He didn't have it for his brother; he betrayed him for his own gain. As he betrayed Mikhail—and ultimately Antonina—for his own gain. Lyosha is a far better man than he will ever be.

"Wouldn't you do the same?" Lyosha asks, and Grisha turns away. He goes to the cart and lifts Valentin's body, carefully. With only a slight effort, he places him, gently, onto the cold ground beside the grave. He unwraps the shroud and kneels over Valentin, kissing his forehead and then making the sign of the cross on it.

As he gazes down at the man's face, he has a flash of understanding. His father wanted to give his younger son a chance at life that he never would have had if he remained in Chita. If he could have seen Kolya—Valentin—as a handsome and self-possessed young man, a powerful musician who brought joy to so many, he would have been proud. "I forgive you, Papa," Grisha says, crossing himself. "You were right," he adds in a whisper.

If he could only forgive himself; if only he had done something to make his father proud.

Grisha rearranges the shroud and, with Lyosha's help, lowers the body into the hole. He picks up a handful of dark soil and slowly crumbles it over Valentin's body, praying for him. Lyosha joins him, and then the two men begin shovelling.

There is snow through the night, and by morning the new grave is no more than another piece of lumpy ground in the neglected cemetery.

Just before dawn, while Grisha and Lyosha, alone and sleepless, wait for the night to pass, and Angelkov is still quiet, Lilya goes to Antonina's bedroom. She builds a fire and then awakens Antonina. She sits on her bed, holding Antonina's hand, and calmly talks to her.

"Yesterday, Tosya," she tells her, "Kropotkin died. He was killed by bandits on the road close to here. He must have been coming to see you. He was shot and robbed and left dead by the side of the road. The village is talking about it. He was taken back to Pskov and his body will be buried somewhere there. I found out in the evening, yesterday, but didn't want to tell you just then. I thought it best if you slept first."

Antonina pulls her hand from Lilya's. "What are you saying, Lilya? Surely you're wrong. Surely—"

"No. He's dead. It happened yesterday, at dusk. He was trying to come to you again, as he did the other night. The musician is dead because he loved you, Tosya."

Antonina's face is the colour of putty. She remembers the distant shot she heard, thinking it was Lyosha still hunting. She is trembling. "A drink, Lilya. I need a drink."

Lilya goes to the wardrobe and pulls out the bottle of vodka. She pours Antonina half a tumbler. "Here you go, *moya dorogaya*, my darling. Yes, you need something to help you. I understand what a shocking, unbelievable thing this is. But you know how violent some of the peasants are now. You, of all people, know what they're capable of. I wouldn't be surprised if Grisha had something to do with it."

Antonina stares at her, the vodka in her mouth. She has trouble swallowing. "What are you talking about?"

"You've never seen Grisha's temper, but I have," Lilya says.

"Why would Grisha harm Valentin?"

Lilya sits on the bed again, smoothing Antonina's hair. "Out of jealousy, simple jealousy, Tosya." Her voice is low, soothing. "We all understand what it can do to a person."

"Jealousy," Antonina murmurs. She thinks of how she had spoken to Grisha about Valentin in his house the day before. How odd—almost ill—he'd looked. She puts the glass on the bedside table. She'd rambled on and on. Does Grisha really feel so much for her? Did she do this, then? Make Grisha angry enough to . . .

She covers her face with her hands. Lilya is right. It's her fault this happened to Valentin. *I don't know why he was coming back to me . . . we'd said goodbye. But it doesn't matter. He was coming to me.*

"Oh, merciful God," she says. *I'm responsible for Valentin's death.* "Go away, Lilya," she says, but Lilya stays beside her, then puts her arms around her.

"No. You need me with you, Tosya. You need me." She covers Antonina's cheek with kisses. "I will stay with you and comfort you."

Antonina surrenders momentarily to Lilya's embraces. But there's something ghoulish on Lilya's face, something that Antonina finds appalling. It's as if the other woman is excited by this. Abruptly, Antonina pulls away. "I told you I want to be alone. Go away." Her voice is firm.

Lilya stands. "I'll bring you up some breakfast. We can eat together."

Antonina rises, her hands clenched. "Lilya, do you not understand me?" she shouts. "Leave me alone."

"I understand. You don't want your breakfast—it's the shock," Lilya says. "You'll be ready to eat later."

~

When Lilya leaves, Antonina falls to her knees in her prayer corner. She knows. It's her. She's the poison at Angelkov. Everything has happened because of her.

I am immoral and evil. I loved my son more than life itself, and he was taken from me because my husband didn't wish our child to be around me as I was. I am responsible for the death of my husband, because the night he fell ill, I was in bed with Grisha. Valentin died because I befriended him. And Grisha . . .

If what Lilya suggests really happened, then he will die at the hands of the authorities for his act of murder, and I will also be to blame for his death.

Antonina presses her forehead onto her clasped hands. "My God, You have seen my wickedness. I bring destruction to all those who come near me. This is the reason You keep my son from me. This is my punishment."

Her mouth is dry. She stumbles across the room, grabbing the bottle of vodka and drinking from it. Then she hurls it into the fire. It smashes, the flames roaring up in bright, consuming colour.

She is breathing heavily. She needs to keep praying for penance, and she needs to stop the evilness that is in her. The longer she stays at Angelkov, the more destruction she will bring.

She needs to be alone, and away from temptation.

⁓

Twenty minutes later, Lilya comes back, bringing a tray.

"I know you said you didn't want anything, but you'll feel better if you—" Lilya looks at the clothes scattered on Antonina's bed. A valise sits on the floor. "What are you doing, Tosya?"

"I'm going away," Antonina says, pulling a chemise from a drawer.

"Away? What do you mean?"

"Have Lyosha saddle Dunia, and an Arabian for himself."

"I asked you where you're going." Lilya looks at the clothing on the bed. Antonina has chosen oddly: it's as if she's taken whatever her hand first touched in the wardrobe. A shawl, a nightdress. A summer bonnet. What is she doing?

"Do you not want some dresses? And some slippers? You haven't taken—"

"It doesn't matter," Antonina interrupts. She sits at her dressing table, looking into the mirror, but to Lilya it doesn't appear that she sees her own reflection.

Lilya sets down the tray and sits on the purple velvet chair beside Antonina's. "Tosya," Lilya says, grasping Antonina's hand. "Ninochka." She kisses the back of the hand, and then turns it over and kisses the palm. Her lips are warm, damp.

Antonina shivers.

"I know you are grieving for Mr. Kropotkin," Lilya says. "I wish I could take away your grief. But there's no reason for you to leave. You'll feel better when you eat, and—"

Antonina stands. "Bring my valise downstairs."

When Antonina and Lyosha arrive at the dacha, there is a light layer of snow on the wooden steps.

Lyosha carries in her valise and the basket of food the countess asked Raisa to pack, then starts a fire with the bit of wood still left by the fireplace. He goes out to split more from the pile of logs behind the dacha, and carries in two armloads, leaving another tall pile on the step. He makes sure there is a full box of kindling near the fireplace.

Watching him, Antonina thinks that Lyosha doesn't look like his sister at all. His face is open and honest, whereas Lilya's has grown hard, everything becoming narrower: her eyes, her lips, her pinched nostrils.

"Are you certain you'll be all right out here by yourself? Do you know how to keep the fire—"

"Thank you, Lyosha. You may go back now. And take

Dunia—I don't want to worry about her in the cold stable. But please, remember that I don't want anyone to know where I am. Do you understand? *Anyone*."

From the look on his sister's face as she stood on the veranda and watched them leave, Lyosha knows Lilya is very angry at the countess's refusal to tell her where she was going.

Lyosha is exhausted and sick with worry. He can't stop thinking of what Lilya did the day before, of having to bury the poor man. But this morning Lilya appeared in control, as if nothing had happened. How could she murder that man— the quiet musician—in cold blood, and be so calm today? And what of the talk of Soso and Mikhail Konstantinovich?

"I'm sorry to ask you to do this, Lyosha," Antonina says. "But it's very important that you keep this secret. I know I can trust you."

"Yes, madam," Lyosha says. "When shall I return for you?"

"I have food for three or four days."

Lyosha touches his cap and mounts his horse. Antonina watches him ride away, leading Dunia through the narrow forest path.

Antonina looks around the dacha, remembering the last time she was here, with Grisha. She walks down the hallway to the bedroom. The bedclothes are still jumbled; no one has been here since. She lies down, pressing her face into the cold sheet. It smells faintly of leather and her own scent. She pulls the coverlet over her, and as she does, she finds the embroidered vest Grisha had worn when they were here together. She runs her fingers over the embroidery, telling herself that Grisha had nothing to do with Valentin's death. He did not. It was Lilya, spreading rumour. Not Grisha. She thinks of the many kindnesses she's witnessed from him over the years: to her son, to Lyosha, to so many of the servants. She knows that he doesn't punish with the knout, as Gleb had. She has heard this from the servants. They were mindful not to let Konstantin know, but she knows. Even Misha knew. He once talked of how he was glad Grisha wasn't cruel to the stableboys, as the steward he'd seen when visiting another estate had been.

She remembers the way Grisha took her here. Never losing awareness of her injured nose, he had pressed his mouth on hers softly and yet firmly. Valentin held her as though she were a treasured pet, and his one brief kiss . . . it was as though she was simply tasting something sweet and pleasing, something that would last only briefly on the tongue, like a summer ice. Grisha's mouth had substance.

She has convinced herself she will never again know Grisha's mouth, his touch. But at this moment she wants nothing more than to hear his footsteps on the wooden porch steps. She wants him to throw open the door without knocking, to stride through the dacha and hold her tightly, so she can forget, even for an hour, her grief over Mikhail, the sadness surrounding Valentin, her concern about the future of the estate. About her own future. So she can forget about wanting a drink so badly that without it she feels she can't take another step, another breath. With Grisha she would be able to forget, and live only in the moments when he took possession of her.

She must abandon her foolish thoughts. She goes back to the warm sitting room. From her valise she takes the letter Misha had written on the back of her notes to Glinka, as well as the two extra pages she found in his coat. She has read them all so often that she is almost afraid to unfold them again; they're creased and fragile. She thinks of all the tests that have been put in front of her: Konstantin, Grisha, Valentin. The vodka. She has failed them all.

The only thing she hasn't failed at is being a good mother.

She drops to her knees and, pressing the pages against her chest, prays out loud. "I am confessing to you, Heavenly Father. I have many sins, and I understand that You feel I do not deserve another chance. But I vow to You that I will try. I will try again. Perhaps You believe I don't deserve to have my son back. I was an unworthy wife. I am an unworthy woman. I accept your punishment of me for those things. But I am not an unworthy mother."

She sits back on her heels. She is thirsty, her hands shaking more all the time, her stomach cramping as if her time is arriving. She goes to the kitchen and empties the basket of food. There is a length of sausage, a loaf of bread, a jar of pickled cabbage and one of marinated apples, boiled potatoes still in their skins, hard-boiled eggs and bottles of buttermilk. She opens a bottle and puts it to her mouth. She drinks, grimacing at its thick taste. It makes her nauseous.

It is only noon.

Valentin has been dead for less than twenty-four hours.

~

Grisha had gone to the grave again that morning. He knelt and prayed for his brother. He feels such unrest, as if he should be doing something more.

He doesn't know which he feels more strongly: sorrow, or guilt, or anger.

He rides to the Bakanev estate to receive the agreed-upon price for the land he has sold back to the prince. The prince was annoyed at the transaction, giving Grisha only half of what he paid, but Grisha has no choice. His security is now gone, traded for Mikhail's freedom.

He returns in late afternoon, and goes to the manor's back door. It's locked, for the first time. When he knocks, Lilya answers, positioning herself in the entrance.

He asks her about the countess.

"She's fine," Lilya tells him.

"I'd like to see her. To see for myself that she's fine. I wonder what you've told her. I don't trust you." Grisha pushes past Lilya into the kitchen. Soon he won't have to worry about her. She'll leave Angelkov once Mikhail is returned and she gets her share of the money. "Did you tell her about . . ." It's difficult for him to say his brother's name. "Did you tell her anything? About what happened yesterday?"

Lilya looks around to make sure they're alone. "You can't see her. Do you have the extra money yet?"

"Yes."

"Good. It's growing colder and I don't know if Misha will be kept warm."

"Do you think I'm not as worried about him as you?"

"Were you worried when you helped to have him taken?"

Grisha's jaw is tight. "It's already growing late. Tomorrow you'll take me to Soso, and we'll get Mikhail Konstantinovich back. Go and tell Antonina I wish to speak with her." He won't tell her about what will happen tomorrow, just in case something doesn't go as planned. But he wants—needs—to see that she's all right.

Lilya refuses. "She's still asleep."

"What do you mean, still? It's late afternoon."

"You know how she gets," Lilya says, and mimics lifting a glass to her lips. "I'm not waking her."

"Tomorrow morning, then, Lilya. I'll be back tomorrow and we'll go to Soso."

Lilya shrugs, turning from him.

By five o'clock Antonina is sick to her stomach, and by early evening she's moaning, clutching her cramping abdomen, alternating between chills and fever, her body slick with sweat. She has already torn everything apart in the kitchen, looking for the bottle of vodka she had shared with Grisha when she was last here. When she finds it—empty—she screams and hurls it at the stove; it shatters. In despair, she drops to her hands and knees. A piece of the glass from the broken bottle pierces her finger. She picks it out, sucking away the blood, then lies on her side on the cold kitchen floor, wanting to weep but unable to.

Grisha returns to the manor the next morning. Raisa and Pavel are working in the kitchen. He asks Pavel to fetch Lilya.

"How is she today?" he asks, when Lilya comes into the kitchen.

Lilya ignores his question. "You've left the door open. Close it. It's cold, and look—the snow." She crosses her arms over her chest, hugging herself and stepping closer to the stove.

Grisha shuts the door firmly. The snow had started in the night, just a dusting at first, but now the wind has picked up. Heavy, wet flakes are coming down so quickly that Grisha's footsteps are almost covered by the time he reaches the back veranda. It's only the beginning of November, and yet it appears winter is trying to get its icy grip earlier than usual.

As he turns from the door, he sees, with an unpleasant start, that Lilya is wearing one of Antonina's gowns.

Raisa is stirring a pot of barley porridge on the stove and Pavel is back at the table, polishing silver: a chafing dish, candlesticks, fish knives.

Grisha recognizes this tea gown: a soft, creamy fabric cut in a fashion that emphasizes the waist. Antonina had been wearing it the last time he saw her, when she came to his house and spoke of Valentin. It had brought out the translucence of her skin. It makes Lilya sallow. The fabric is pulled too tightly, buckling across her hips: Lilya's body is not shaped like Antonina's. She also wears Olga's ring of keys—the housekeeper's keys—on a thick leather belt, incongruous on the delicate dress. "The countess gives you permission to wear her clothes?"

Lilya looks annoyed. "It's none of your business what I wear." There is rouge in careful circles on her cheeks, and a tortoiseshell comb hangs crookedly in her hair.

"I want to see her, as I wanted to see her yesterday."

"You can't," Lilya says.

Grisha still studies Lilya. She's a little shorter than Antonina, and wears flat boots; Antonina always wears heeled slippers. The hem of the dress drags on the floor; bits of dust and grit are caught on it. The rouge is too livid on her cheeks. "Is she ill?" he asks then. "Is that it? Raisa, is the countess ill, and doesn't want to see anyone? I'll fetch the doctor."

Raisa opens her mouth, frowning, but Lilya says, "She's not sick."

Grisha doesn't want to imagine that Antonina is drinking so heavily this early in the morning. "Then I will see her whether you like it or not," he says, and starts across the kitchen.

"No!" Lilya cries, and moves towards the doorway that leads into the house.

Grisha pushes away Lilya's outstretched arm. He walks through the hall, his wet boots hitting the wooden floors with hard, purposeful thuds.

All the doors on the main floor are shut. He opens each one quickly, methodically, looking for Antonina in the dining room, the morning room, the library, the study, the drawing room, the music salon. Each room is dark, the curtains drawn against drafts from the frosty glass, and no stoves or fires burn anywhere. The air is dry and cold. There isn't enough firewood in the once-huge stacks outside to heat more than a few rooms at a time. They are surrounded by forest, but there are no longer men to cut and cord the timber.

Old Olga is asleep in a corner of the main vestibule on a straight wooden chair with a heavy blanket wrapped around her shoulders, her chin on her chest. She lifts her head as Grisha's footsteps wake her, blinking in a confused manner, and watches him start up the stairs. Nusha, the last of the young servants to remain at Angelkov, is on her knees, sweeping the carpet with a small, hard brush. She jumps aside as Grisha takes the stairs two at a time.

Lilya follows him.

He stops outside Antonina's door. "Madam," he calls, knocking. "Countess. It's Grisha. May I enter?"

He turns the crystal knob and pushes open the door. "Madam?" he says in a wary voice. But when he steps over the threshold, the room is like the others, the curtains drawn and the fireplace dead. He turns and faces Lilya.

"Where is she? Tell me where she is," he says, coming close to Lilya, towering over her.

Lilya doesn't step back, or flinch. She looks up at him. "The countess is gone, Grisha," she says calmly. "Gone away," she repeats.

"What do you mean? Where?"

As Grisha's face has grown agitated, Lilya's has become serene, unreadable. "She had Lyosha take her to the city, where she was going to hire a carriage and driver." She's furious with Lyosha for his silence. That he would show allegiance to Antonina and not to her has caused a further rift between them. They haven't spoken since the horrible event in Grisha's house. She's thinking quickly but speaking slowly. "She's gone all the way to St. Petersburg," she finishes, and is rewarded by Grisha's pupils dilating, the sudden colour in his face.

"St. Petersburg?" he repeats.

Lilya has the upper hand. She was able to get Valentin out of Antonina's life, and now she will do the same with Grisha.

"Yes, St. Petersburg. She said there was no reason for her to remain at Angelkov at the moment. There's nothing here for her, she told me."

Lilya is enjoying this little game, watching Grisha's face. Her hours are long and dull without Antonina.

*T*he snow keeps up, falling fast and heavy. The wind grows steadily colder.

Lyosha is thinking of Antonina alone in the dacha, burning up the wood faster than either of them would have thought. By eleven that morning he goes to the stable, having to push through snow midway up his shins. He saddles the Arabian and starts down the road. It's more logical, in this weather, to hitch the Orlovs to the troika: they're bred for pulling the sled through snow at a fast pace. The three of them abreast are fine on the main road, but he knows they couldn't get through the narrow path in the forest that leads to the dacha. He plans to bring Antonina back with him on the horse, if she'll come. If not, he'll chop more wood for her. Maybe he'll even stay with her, to ensure her safety.

The snow is blinding by the time he reaches the turnoff for the dacha. It's another half-hour ride through the forest.

The horse struggles, attempting to lift its legs as high as it can, then shies nervously, whinnying. It refuses to go forward, no matter how Lyosha urges it on. He's so cold he can't feel his hands on the reins. His *ushanka* is pulled over his eyebrows, and a thick scarf is over his nose. But his eyelashes are coated with ice, his eyes burning from the stinging snow.

Finally, he turns the horse. It slowly picks its way back through the trail it had broken. Lyosha can't see the road. All is white and blinding. Were it not for the horse's determination and sense of direction they might have wandered into a field and died of exposure. Lyosha has been gone six hours on a journey that should have taken less than two. Darkness is falling as the horse struggles up the long road to the manor.

But the Arabian is too exhausted to break through the rising drifts to the stable. Lyosha squints, trying to see where they are. All he can make out is the looming square of the house, but the smaller outbuildings have disappeared. He slides off the horse and, taking its bridle, bent in half against the wind, trudges to the manor.

He collapses on the front steps, and it takes him a few moments to gain enough strength to crawl up them. On his knees, he pounds on the locked front door. In a moment it's opened by Lilya and Grisha, with Pavel, Olga, Raisa, Fyodor and Nusha—the only servants left at Angelkov—crowding behind them.

As Lyosha half falls through the doorway, Grisha brings the horse into the wide, high entry hall. The poor creature has icicles hanging from its nostrils and whiskery jaw, its mane so beaded with ice that it's hard as stone. It shivers violently.

While the women take Lyosha to the kitchen, Fyodor

brings blankets, and he and Grisha rub the horse vigorously. Grisha leaves Fyodor to finish the job and goes to the kitchen.

Lyosha lies on the floor near the stove, completely spent. A thick blanket covers him. Lilya is kneeling beside him. His boots and socks are off, and she is briskly rubbing his feet.

When Lyosha hadn't come into the house for his noon meal, Lilya had gone to the servants' quarters. She looked for him there, then in the stable. She was still angry with him, but seeing the Arabian's empty stall frightened her. Where would Lyosha go in this snowstorm? She fought her way down to Grisha's house and told him that Lyosha was missing. They both had the same thought: after what had happened to the musician, he didn't want to be at Angelkov anymore. He had decided to say nothing to either of them— who would blame him?—and leave. Lilya wondered if he had gone to the home of Anya Fomovna. But wherever he went, he wouldn't get far in the storm, they also knew.

Grisha had returned to the manor with Lilya and sat at the kitchen table, staring at his knuckles. The servants prayed in front of the icon over the stove for Lyosha's safe return.

Now, finally, Lyosha stirs. He struggles to sit up. Lilya hands him a steaming cup. Grisha stands over him. "Tell me what you thought you were doing. You know better than to take a horse out in this weather," he says sharply, hiding his concern over Lyosha by talking about the horse.

"I was trying to get to her. The countess," Lyosha says. The end of his nose is frostbitten. "I knew she would need more wood, and—"

Lilya interrupts him. "Where is she?"

Grisha looks from Lyosha to Lilya. "But you said she was in St. Petersburg."

"She's in a dacha. About six versts from here," Lyosha says. "It's in the woods, off the—"

"I know where it is," Grisha says. "Why did she go there?"

"I don't know, Grisha. I took her there as she requested."

Grisha turns to Lilya. "Why did you lie to me?"

"She didn't know," Lyosha says. "I wasn't to tell anyone. Lilya didn't know," he repeats.

Lilya shrugs. "What's the difference? For all I knew, she *had* gone to St. Petersburg."

Grisha shakes his head in annoyance. "So she's been there . . . When did you take her, Lyosha?"

"Early yesterday morning, after . . ." Lyosha stops, the image of the dead musician still too clear. He can't shake it away, nor the picture of his sister with her bloody hands. "I tried to go to her today because I'm afraid she doesn't have enough wood."

"How long did she tell you she'd stay?"

"She said to come back for her in three or four days. But how could we know about the storm? And I don't know if she had fuel for the lamps. I wasn't comfortable leaving her, Grisha, but she insisted." He covers his eyes with one hand.

"I'll go to her," Grisha says.

"But it's dark, and impossible for a horse right now," Lyosha murmurs.

Grisha is all too aware he will have to wait until morning.

In the warm, brightly lit kitchen, with a fragrant soup bubbling on the stove, they are all thinking of Countess Mitlovskiya, alone in the middle of the forest, in the dark, and cold. "There are wolves in the forest," Nusha says.

The storm blows itself out by midnight, and Grisha sets out as soon as there is a glimmer of dawn. The snow sparkles in the rising sun. It's a struggle for the horse, and the journey is difficult.

When he arrives, there is no smoke from the chimney, and a myriad of wolf prints around the foundation of the dacha. He clears away the deep snow in front of the door to get it open. When he does, he finds Antonina on the floor in front of the fireplace, empty but for a high pile of ashes. She's under blankets and a mouldering bearskin he knows was nailed to the wall of the small back veranda. As Lyosha predicted, there is no more wood, and it feels colder inside the dacha than out. He can't see Antonina's face, but her breath curls into the air above her.

He quietly shuts the door and goes back outside to chop an armload of logs and split kindling. As he comes in with it, Antonina is sitting up, her hand to her throat. There is dried blood on one of her fingers.

"Grisha, is it really you?" she cries, a sob in her voice. "I heard the axe. I'm cold, Grisha, and I was afraid. The wolves . . . Grisha, they were howling and scratching."

She is so pale and drawn that Grisha feels a thump of dread. There are dark smudges under her eyes, and her lips are raw-looking.

"Are the wolves gone?" she asks, and he nods, stepping over her and setting down the wood. Kneeling, he clears the heavy ash from the fireplace and looks back at her.

"Are you all right, Antonina?" Of course she's not. It's more than being cold and afraid. It's something else, something that has taken hold of her.

Her teeth are chattering. "Lyosha told you I was here?"

Grisha nods again, turning away to start the fire. As the kindling catches, he sits back on his heels, watching the flames as they tentatively lap and sizzle around the damp wood. "He tried to come to you yesterday, but couldn't get through."

"And so you came," Antonina states. There is snow, like tiny melting gems, in his dark hair. It sits on his wide shoulders.

"You're ill, Antonina," he says, looking back at her. "What is it?" Her lips are torn, as if she's been fiercely biting them.

How to tell him without humiliating herself? There is no way but the simple truth. "I came here to do penance, Grisha, and to be away from . . . from . . . temptation."

"Temptation?"

"The drink, Grisha. The wine. The vodka." She tries to lick her lips, but her tongue is so dry. "I can't . . . not anymore. I can't use it to make my life bearable, because it doesn't. It doesn't make it more bearable. It only makes it worse. What it did to me . . . how it made me weak. I told myself it made me strong."

Suddenly she's shivering fiercely, bending forward and clutching her abdomen. She lies on her side again, her knees up to her chest, closing her eyes with an almost imperceptible groan.

As the fire grows stronger, Grisha watches her. She seems to have fallen into something like sleep, although she's twitchy and stiff.

She opens her eyes again, crying out when she sees him. "I forgot . . . I thought you were a dream. I dreamed you would come and rescue me."

Grisha has to turn away so that Antonina can't see how her words affect him. Did his own brother not say this same thing, only days ago, as he lay dying? But Antonina is not dying. Is she? He *can* still help her, as he couldn't help his brother.

"Yes. I'm here. I'm here," he says, looking at her again, picking up one of her hands. It's icy, although the palm is damp. Her fingers feel boneless. "Are you growing warmer?"

She nods, but her teeth are still chattering.

As he pushes aside the blankets, he sees that the front of her dress is stained where she's been sick. He also sees his vest; she's been sleeping holding his vest. This gives him a surge of emotion. He gathers her to him and holds her tightly. She rests her head against his chest as though she were a trusting child.

Then he stands, carrying her to the settee. She is even lighter than he remembers. He lays her down, wrapping a blanket around her. She pushes it aside, fretful, and sits up.

"Lie down, Antonina," he says. "Try to sleep."

"I can't. Every time I close my eyes, I see terrible things. They're like nightmares, but I don't think I'm asleep."

"They'll stop."

"Sometimes my eyes are open and the nightmares come, too. I'm frightened, Grisha," she says, and again he puts his arms around her. "When will I feel better?"

"Soon," he says. "I know it will be soon." He doesn't know with certainty, but surely the alcohol is gone from her body—this is the third day. Her body is only remembering it, and wanting it. He knows how long his own body wants what it had once, with her. How long the memory holds.

He brushes back her hair. It's tangled, combs sticking out at all angles.

She reaches up and begins to pull them out. He sits beside her, watching. When the last long strands of her hair fall down her back to her waist, he takes a deep breath. He runs his fingers through it. It is so fine, and yet it has such weight.

He knows what she's doing: she's letting him see her in a state of complete weakness. No, perhaps it's not weakness, but strength. It's her way of telling him she trusts him. She is giving the last of herself to him, which takes strength.

"I'll make you some tea."

As he stands to go to the kitchen, she grabs his hand. "Don't leave me. Don't go, Grisha."

"Only to the kitchen, Antonina."

She's trembling again, biting her chapped lips, opening a tiny crack in the bottom one. A bead of blood appears.

Grisha wants to lick it away, and curses himself for such a thought when she is so clearly ill and vulnerable. In the kitchen he sees the untouched food Antonina has brought. He lights the stove and fills the kettle, then comes back to stand in the doorway, looking across the room at her.

"I tried to stay brave by reciting poetry last night," Antonina says. "Do you know Pushkin's 'Winter Evening'?"

He nods.

"Isn't it odd? As I spoke it aloud, I realized it was about my life. *The storm wind covers the sky*," she recites,

"*Whirling the fleecy snowdrifts.*
Now it howls like a wolf,
Now it is crying, like a lost child.
'*Let us drink, dearest friend,*
'*To my poor wasted youth.*
'*Let us drink from grief—where's the glass?*
'*Our hearts at least will be lightened.*'"

Antonina makes a faltering attempt at a smile. "Even Pushkin is urging me to drink. A poem about winter and wolves and lost children and drinking. Ha," she says bitterly. "It's a difficult thing, is it not? Here I have no choice. The vodka is not here. But when I return to Angelkov . . . can I do it, Grisha?" The kettle is making slow popping sounds. "It must be for always. It must."

He looks at her for another minute, then goes to prepare the tea and a plate of bread and slices of sausage.

The tea is steaming in the glass, sweet with chunks of sugar he's broken off the cone. He gestures at the bread. She looks at it, then picks it up and takes a tiny bite. She chews, but struggles to swallow, gagging, and then covers her mouth as she empties the half-chewed bread into her hand.

"I'm sorry. I can't eat yet, Grisha. My stomach . . . I've been so sick."

"Bread is too hard, and the sausage . . . Of course not. Drink the tea."

She manages a few mouthfuls.

"I'll make you some soup," he says. "Soup is the best thing for you now."

"You know how to make soup?"

He puts a hand on her shoulder. "Sleep now, and later, when you wake, there will be hot soup."

After she has fallen into what appears to be a restless sleep, Grisha uses the sausage and potatoes and cabbage Antonina brought with her to make a thick soup. He looks around the kitchen, knowing the dacha is no longer his. It again belongs to Prince Bakanev; it is on the land Grisha had owned, so briefly. He doesn't let himself dwell on what he's lost. He goes out to chop more wood, making sure the fire is burning fiercely, keeping the sitting room warm. Sparks fly up the chimney and the wood crackles. He sits on a chair beside the settee, watching how Antonina's body twitches. Her face and throat are damp. She frowns and moans and at one point cries out. He takes her hand. "Sleep, Tosya," he murmurs, wiping her forehead and neck.

It's late afternoon when she finally sits up. "My head," she says. "It doesn't stop throbbing." Her pupils are slightly dilated.

"It will help if you eat. Can you try some soup?"

She nods, and he holds the bowl while she puts the spoon into it, but her hand is too unsteady. He feeds her four spoonfuls, then she shakes her head.

"It's a good start. You'll have more later." He carries the bowl to the kitchen.

"Grisha?" she calls. "Could you bring me a glass of water?"

When he hands her the glass, she looks at it. "This is what I will drink from now on, Grigori Sergeyevich. I have made a pact with God."

"Good."

"Do you believe me? Do you believe *in* me?"

"I believe in you, Antonina Leonidovna," he says, feeling such a rush of tenderness for her—her expression and voice so earnest—that he can't stop himself. He cups the side of her face in his palm.

She leans into his palm, putting her own hand on top of his. They stay like this for a long moment. "I need a bath," she says finally.

He warms water in two cauldrons, bringing in the big tin tub that hangs on a hook in the back veranda. He puts it in front of the stove, which is radiating its heat into the kitchen.

"I'll come and get you in a moment, Antonina," he calls as he's pouring the warm water into the tub. But she comes on her own, slowly, holding on to the door frame for support. She looks at the steaming water, and then, as if very old, or very weak, unbuttons her dress and slides her arms out of it, letting it drop in a heap behind her. She peels off her stockings and pantalets, and then pulls her chemise over her head. She is looking at him the whole time. Her top lip quivers.

She is far too thin, a slender, pale flower suddenly un-sheathed, her abdomen concave, her hip and collar bones jutting.

He holds out his hand. She takes it and steps into the tub, then sits down, her knees up. He moves behind her, bending over to gather up her hair with one hand, scooping water in a dipper with the other and pouring it over her shoulders. She rounds her back and drops her head. The back of her neck is so white, so susceptible. He can see all her vertebrae. He wants to press his lips to each one. Instead, he takes a flannel and wets it, passing it over her back as though her skin were the thinnest paper.

He gently washes her neck, her shoulders, her upper arms.

Antonina leans her forehead on her knees, wrapping her arms around her legs. Her body is still, finally, her breathing soft and even, and Grisha wonders if she's fallen asleep again. He puts down the flannel and slowly lets go of her hair and picks up the clean blanket he's left warming over a chair near the stove. "Come," he says, spreading it wide, and she lifts her head and looks at him. Her pupils are still slightly enlarged. With his hand for support again, she steps out of the tub. He wraps the warm blanket around her and holds her against him.

He recalls Lilya's words to him in the kitchen: *She deserves love.*

"I want to love you, Antonina," he says, so quietly she has to move her head, lifting it so that her ear is near his mouth.

She doesn't answer. Did she hear him? He has never said this to a woman. He doesn't know what he means: make love to her, or love her? Suddenly it's the same thing. She's so small in his arms, so fragile. How did he take her, in September, without hurting her?

"Can we go back to the sitting room?" she asks, and he picks her up as he did earlier. Again she leans against him, into him, in such a trusting way that he feels stronger than he's ever felt. He can carry her forever.

He puts her down on the settee, and builds up the fire again.

"Grisha?" she says, and he turns. "Please. Come and sit with me."

He does, and she takes his hand—this time she takes *his* hand—and says, "You mustn't love me, Grisha."

She heard him, then.

"And I mustn't love you."

"You wanted me once before, Antonina. You wanted me, and then you didn't. Is it because I'm a steward?" He feels the old confusion, the first beat of anger. "It didn't stop you with Valentin Vladimirovitch. You gave yourself to him, in spite of his class." He works very hard to keep his voice even.

A line appears between her eyebrows. "Gave myself to him? No, I didn't. He kissed me, once. It meant nothing."

She squeezes her eyes closed, then opens them. "Poor, poor man," she says, and Grisha knows Lilya has told her that Valentin is dead. He's not surprised. "But why do you think there was anything more between us?"

"Because Lilya—" He stops. "Ah," he says, understanding coming. In his mind he sees the grave behind the stand of fir. Once this is all over—once everything has come out—he will put up a headstone. He will give his brother the burial rites he deserves. "Yes. Poor Valentin," he says, and something in his voice makes Antonina sit very still.

"But . . . *you* didn't hurt him? You didn't, did you? Lilya said . . ."

Grisha stares at the fire. "Of course I didn't hurt him. Why would I? Lilya is not to be believed, Antonina. She has her own reasons for creating lies, for turning us against each other."

"It was just a robbery, then? A terrible crime, as she told me? But the fact is that Valentin was coming to see me," she says, without waiting for his answer. "If he hadn't been coming to see me, he wouldn't have been killed."

"He wasn't coming to see you, Antonina." The flames are pulsing gold. It's almost as though Grisha hears something, a faint melody in the quiet dacha.

Antonina frowns. "Of course he was. And for that I can never forgive myself."

Grisha looks back at her. "You can't hold yourself accountable for Valentin's death, Antonina. You shouldn't feel blame, or guilt."

"Don't you see? I *am* guilty. Everything terrible that has happened at Angelkov is my fault. Everything. Any man who comes near to me is punished. Konstantin. Valentin.

Even my own son. It's because . . . whenever I drink, I am not myself. And then bad things happen."

Grisha closes his eyes.

"I came to the dacha to be alone, to make atonement for my evilness."

"Do you think you were evil when you were here with me, before? Are you saying it was a bad thing, us together?"

"It was adultery." She is silent then. "But it felt right, Grisha. It felt too good. It made me want you more."

"And now?"

"If I am with you again, bad things will happen to you. If I let you touch me, Grisha, you will be poisoned."

He wants so badly to tell her that nothing is her fault. The kidnapping was waiting to happen: if not the day it did, it would have been another day. Soso and his men had nothing but time. Valentin came back to Angelkov because Grisha wrote the letter telling him to come. It had nothing to do with Antonina. But how can he tell her this without telling her that he was involved in the kidnapping? Without telling her that Valentin was his brother?

"I think you should forgive yourself for all the trouble you believe you have brought, Antonina. You are a good woman. A good person." It's all he can say.

She doesn't answer for a moment. "Have you ever done things you can't stop thinking about, things you wish you could change?"

"Yes." His voice is low. "I have."

"Things you could never go back and make right."

He nods.

"And did you forgive yourself?"

He thinks of Valentin's face, of his words. *You came as I*

dreamed you would. I knew you would come for me. "No.
I haven't been able to forgive myself."

"Not yet?" she asks. "Or ever?"

He envisions Mikhail's face when he rode into the clearing with the ransom money. It haunts him—Misha's pale little
face, so like Antonina's. He remembers the vision of his own
brother's face like this, a child in the back of the tarantass.

. He's done the same thing to two little boys who trusted
and loved him: he betrayed them.

It's too late for one of them, but he must make it right with
the other.

He gets up and goes to his jacket and reaches into the
pocket. He brings her Mikhail's last letter—the one Soso
gave to Lilya. Before he left Angelkov to come to the dacha,
he forced Lilya to give it to him. He's ashamed that he used
physical force, twisting her wrist until she cried out, saying,
All right, let me go. I'll give it to you. But he knew he would
need Antonina to have hope. To believe him when he tells
her he will get her son back for her.

"What is it?" she asks, looking at the folded paper in
Grisha's hand. But she knows. Her face shows that she
knows. She recognizes her notes to Glinka. This one is
newer, not so wrinkled and worn.

She reaches for it. The trembling has begun again, but
this time not from the last traces of alcohol leaving her body.
This time it is from both fear and hope.

"Read it, Tosya," Grisha says. "It came only recently."
He hopes she doesn't ask how.

Antonina slowly unfolds the page. *"Mama, I miss you so.
They told me Papa is dead,"* she reads aloud, and draws in a
deep breath. *"I'm sad. I pray every day."* Now she is shredding

the bits of skin on her bottom lip. Grisha fights not to pull her fingers away. *"I still have the rest of my notes to Glinka. Please keep this one for me until I return to you, dear Mamushka. I will look after you now. Misha."*

She looks up at Grisha, her eyes full of tears. "Is it really happening? Is God forgiving me? Has He seen how much I want to change, and is already rewarding me?" She thinks of the cherub falling from the church ceiling. "Can it be true that He loves me enough to do this for me?"

Grisha doesn't want to hear about God. For him, God plays no role in the evils of man. In the evils of a man like himself. "I will get Misha back for you, Tosya. In the next few days I will know where he is. I will bring your son to you."

Antonina is weeping. "Grisha, oh, Grisha, let this be a real, true thing. Tell me I'm not asleep."

He puts his arms around her. "You're not asleep, Tosya. You can feel my arms, can't you?" He holds her more tightly, stroking her hair.

They sit like this for a few moments, as her crying slows and then stops. She takes a deep, shuddering breath, but before she lifts her head, he speaks against it, into her hair.

"I must tell you something, Antonina. I will bring back your son, but you need to know something of great importance. I have to tell it to you now, before you feel you are grateful to me in any way." He wasn't going to speak of this today, but he can't commit the sin of omission, or pretend to himself that his own guilt and remorse have countered the wrong he has done. He knows that once he says the words—*I too am responsible for your son's kidnapping*—she will turn from him, and never want anything to do with him again. He knows with such certainty that she will hate him that he's filled with a deep, deep dread he has never before felt, even when he held his dying brother in his arms. He knows that once she has her son, she has every right to tell the authorities. And he will be imprisoned. Tortured, or sent to Siberia. He may never see her again. He knows all of this. But it doesn't matter; nothing that might happen to him matters. The important thing is that Antonina has her son back. He never again wants to think of her as she is right now. He wants to think of her laughing at the piano, with her son.

"Antonina, please. Listen to me. When Mikhail was kidnapped, I—".

She puts both her hands on his arm, looking up at him. "Please, Grisha. Don't spoil this moment. Don't talk of that terrible day. Right now I feel something wonderful. Don't spoil it," she repeats. "Please, Grisha."

"But I need to tell you that I—"

"You can tell me another time, later, when I hold my son. You can tell me whatever you must tell me then. Do you understand?"

What is she saying? Is this some kind of acknowledgment, something that indicates she suspects he was involved?

She reaches up and puts her arms around his neck. The blanket falls away. He sees the pulse beating in her neck. He sees her chest rising as she breathes. He knows what her breast feels like in his mouth. He knows the smoothness of her skin, the scent of her.

Grisha pulls her arms from his neck and stands. "Are you well enough to ride back to Angelkov before night falls? You should be in your own bed, in your own warm room, tonight."

He looks down at her. Her face is open: she sees only a good man. He will not be free to love her, and to take her love, until she knows and accepts the truth about him.

38

*A*ntonina sits on the horse in front of Grisha as they slowly ride back to Angelkov through the snow, blue in the waning light. She leans against him, feeling his comforting width and the warmth of his arms around her as he holds the reins. The air is crisp; with each deep breath the ache in her head dissipates a little more.

As the manor comes into view at the end of the long drive, Antonina says, "I don't think I should keep Lilya any longer. I've been thinking for a while now that it would be better—for both her and me—if she was no longer on the estate. She's changed so much, and she almost . . ." She stops. She was about to say *frightens me*, but that's not it. Lilya doesn't frighten her, but there's something about her now that is overbearing. Almost possessive. "Life changed her. Life has changed us all," she finishes. "Nusha can learn her position."

"Yes," Grisha says. "I think this would be the best thing. Lilya should have her own life, somewhere away from you."

"I would help her," Antonina says, watching the lowering afternoon sun glint off the windows of the big house. "I still have a few good pieces of jewellery left. She could sell them, and perhaps buy into a small business in Pskov or one of the bigger towns. She's an excellent seamstress, and makes lace of the highest quality. I don't want to leave her with nothing. She deserves to have a good life. Just not near me."

"Don't speak to her about this today. Not until . . ." He stops.

"Until what, Grisha?"

Until she takes me to Soso, Grisha thinks. He doesn't want any problems between Lilya and Antonina until Misha is safe with his mother. Once the child is back at Angelkov, Lilya can go. And then he will confess everything to Antonina.

"Please don't say anything to her just yet," he requests.

She looks over her shoulder and up at him. "Why?"

"Please. Just trust me."

She stares at him a moment longer. "All right," she says, and faces ahead again. "There is no hurry, I suppose. But she won't go easily."

After a moment, Grisha says, "Remember, Antonina, that no matter what she says—or does—you are the countess. Angelkov is yours. You are the one who holds power over your land, your life. Not Lilya."

⌒

Lilya hears a whinny and runs to the front door. She opens it to see Grisha swing down from his horse and then help

Antonina. She sees how Antonina clings to him. Antonina can't see Grisha's expression, but Lilya can. Lilya suspects they have shared more than this ride on the horse. No, she thinks, God, no. Don't let it have happened again.

Lilya is still wearing Antonina's tea gown. She folds her arms over her chest, rocking slightly, watching Grisha put his arm around Antonina's back as they slowly walk towards the front veranda.

—

Antonina has taken off her cloak and hat and is propped against the pillows on her bed with a light blanket over her legs. Grisha sits on the edge of the bed, holding her hand, when Lilya comes to the open doorway. She'd waited, out of sight, until they were upstairs.

"You can leave now, Grisha. I will care for her," she says from the doorway. They didn't even have the decency to close the door, leaving it open as if they have nothing to be ashamed of. Her stomach roils at the way Antonina's fingers curl over Grisha's. She now can see that Antonina's dress is stained, and her hair . . . her hair is completely loose, falling over her shoulders to her waist. Antonina has never let anyone see her with her hair down. Even when she had given birth to Misha, and Konstantin waited to come into the bedroom to see his son, Antonina had insisted that Lilya pin up her hair before he was allowed in.

Antonina hadn't shown her hair to her husband. Only Lilya has seen it in its true beauty. The sickness in her stomach rises, thick and sour, into her throat. "Go, Grisha," she says, louder. "I know what the countess needs."

"No," Antonina says. "I want Grisha here. He's getting

Misha back, Lilya, perhaps as soon as tomorrow. Leave us alone. I'm fine."

Lilya doesn't move from the doorway, and Antonina studies her.

"Why are you wearing my dress, Lilya?" she asks, frowning. When Lilya doesn't respond, she shakes her head and tells her, "Go and put on your own clothes and take that to the laundry. I'm surprised at you. Please leave. Now."

"All right, Tosya," Lilya finally says. Before she leaves, she stares at Grisha. We need each other right now, she thinks. But just wait. You have no idea what is about to happen to you.

⌁

Lilya stands in the shadows of the upstairs hall until she hears Grisha's footsteps going down the stairs. It's after eight o'clock. The front door closes. He's so bold he doesn't even go through the servants' entrance in the kitchen, she notices.

She goes into Antonina's room. There is one lamp glowing softly, and the fire is well built up. Antonina is in a deep sleep. Lilya takes off her boots, then Antonina's dress and the belt with the keys, and puts them at the foot of the bed. She lies beside Antonina in her cotton petticoat. As the mattress dips with her weight, Antonina stirs and reaches out, her hand touching Lilya's bare arm.

Lilya holds her breath. She sees Antonina's mouth move in a smile. "You're still here, Grisha?" she murmurs. Her eyelids flutter but stay closed. The smile fades, and she sleeps again. Lilya lies still, taking in Antonina's peacefulness.

⌁

Eventually, Antonina moves, opening her eyes, and gasps at the sight of Lilya's face, almost touching hers. She struggles to sit up, moving away from her.

"Shhh, shhh," Lilya says, trying to stroke Antonina's cheek. "Shhh, my darling, it's just me. I've come to be with you, to help you sleep through the night. I'll stay with you."

Antonina blinks, pushing back her hair. In the lamplight, her eyes are too wide, and her mouth trembles.

"Why do you look so distressed? Don't be upset, my lovely. It's all right. Once you feel better, I'm going to show you that I can love you more than he'll ever know how." Lilya picks up a strand of Antonina's hair and brings it to her face. She closes her eyes and inhales.

Antonina slides off the bed, holding on to the headboard. "Get out, Lilya," she says, her voice low. "Don't speak of love to me in this manner. You shame yourself. Do you hear me?" She points at the door. "Get off my bed and leave my room at once."

Lilya stares at Antonina as she climbs off the other side of the bed. Her face looks as if she's been struck.

"And don't come back unless I ask for you." Antonina looks at her dress and Lilya's belt on the end of the bed. She picks up the belt and unhooks the ring of keys. "You are my servant," she says, folding her fingers over them. "Never forget that." She throws the belt onto the floor.

Lilya is weeping now, tears running down her cheeks. "Tosya," she says softly. "Please. Are we not friends? More than friends, after all we've been through together. Don't treat me like this. After what happened to Lyosha, and to me, so long ago, how can you—"

Antonina won't let Lilya play that old game. "I demand

that you leave," she interrupts. "We'll talk about this tomorrow, in daylight."

Lilya wipes her cheeks with her palms. "Yes, tomorrow. We'll talk tomorrow. It's been a long and difficult day, Tosya. You're not thinking clearly." She picks up her belt and boots and, in her petticoat, goes to the door, then looks over her shoulder. "You're making a mistake," she says. "Soon you will see your mistake and beg for my forgiveness. And I will forgive you. I will forgive you," she repeats, and then is gone, in her stocking feet, into the dark hall.

Antonina walks to the door. She shuts it, turning the lock, then collapses against it, breathing hard. She doesn't care what Grisha said, she must dismiss Lilya immediately. The woman is dangerous, she thinks, recalling Lilya's face as she stared into hers on the bed. Dangerous.

~

Early the next morning, while Antonina is still asleep behind her locked door, Grisha comes to the house.

"It's time, Lilya," he tells her. Her face is blotchy, her eyelids swollen and red. "Today you'll take me to Soso, and then we'll get Mikhail Konstantinovich. Today he will be reunited with his mother."

Lilya blinks, studying Grisha. Then she says, slowly, "No. We'll do it tomorrow."

"Why tomorrow?"

"I must have time to tell Soso we're coming. There are things he will have to do—he and the others . . ." She pauses. "It must be tomorrow. And Lyosha will come with us."

"No. Don't involve Lyosha in this. He knows nothing, and need know nothing."

Lilya's lips grow even thinner. "I don't go without Lyosha."

Grisha grabs her arm. "First thing tomorrow morning, then. No later."

"Yes. First thing," she says.

When he's gone, she listens at the foot of the stairs to make sure Antonina is still in her room. Then she goes into Konstantin's study, quietly closing the door behind her. She sits at the broad desk, opening a drawer and taking out a pen and sheet of paper with the Mitlovsky crest at the top. She lifts the lid of the inkwell.

It takes her a long time to compose the simple letter; twice she crumples up the page and takes a fresh one. When she is done, she waits for the ink to dry, then folds the paper and ties it tightly with the fine twine from a spool in the drawer.

She replaces everything with care. In the kitchen she burns the two ruined sheets of paper in the stove. She puts on her cloak and trudges across the yard to the stable.

⁂

"Lyosha, there are some errands you must do."

He puts down the curry comb and looks at Lilya.

"First," she tells him, "ride to Borzik. As you enter the village, you will see an izba with a donkey tied outside. This is where you will find Soso."

"Soso is living in Borzik?"

"Yes. Tell him that we will come for him—Grisha, you and me—tomorrow, mid-morning. Tell him the plan is finalized."

"Plan? What do you mean?"

"Don't question me, Lyosha. Just do as I say. If Soso

doesn't agree about tomorrow, or you can't find him, then come back to me. But if he is there, and says he will wait for us tomorrow morning, then ride on, into Pskov." Lilya pulls the tied letter from inside her cloak and holds it out to him. "You will take this letter to the authorities on Fedosovoy Prospekt. You must not tell anyone."

Lyosha looks at the letter she holds out to him. All these secrets. He doesn't like it. "Sister, I don't—"

"It is to help us get Mikhail Konstantinovich back to his mother," she says sternly. "Do you not want this?"

Lyosha remembers the chilling statements Lilya made after killing the musician: *Kill me and you won't find the boy. Kill me and you kill Mikhail Konstantinovich.* "Of course I do, Lilya. But why must everything be done with such stealth? How is Soso involved?"

"This is all I can tell you. Should you not do as I ask of you, the countess will never see her son again. Do you understand?"

Lyosha nods, and takes the letter.

"No one can know," Lilya repeats. "The letter must go directly into the hands of the authorities." Her face is blank. "I can trust you, can I not?"

"Yes. You know that, Lilya."

―――

Lilya knocks on Antonina's door and the countess tells her she doesn't wish to see her.

"But last night you told me we would talk today," Lilya says, her lips against the door.

"Send Nusha with warm water for me to bathe," Antonina says, "and tea. Do as I say," she orders, and Lilya leaves.

Later, after she has bathed and dressed and done her hair as best she can, Antonina goes downstairs. Wrapped in a warm cloak, she walks up and down the veranda. The yard is empty and still, the snow beaten down by horses' hooves. The sky is a pale blue, streaked with cirrus clouds. She goes down the steps. Halfway across the yard she sees Fyodor. "Is Grisha in the stable?" she calls.

The man shakes his head. "I saw him earlier, but I don't know where he is now."

Surely Grisha has gone to get Mikhail, as he said he would. Antonina returns to her room. The waiting is so difficult. Once, she goes to the wardrobe. She knows there is nothing there—she threw the last bottle into the fire—but it makes her feel better to see nothing but her dresses and hats and slippers. She drinks many glasses of water, and manages to eat a few bites of the now-cold breakfast Nusha brought. She pins up a few loose strands of hair. She tries to rub a little colour into her cheeks. When Misha comes to her, she wants to look as well as she can.

The day passes. Grisha does not bring her son to her.

She refuses to give in to despair. She comforts herself with thoughts of Grisha coming to her with Misha the next day.

It's all she has to hold on to.

Lilya is waiting for Grisha early the next morning, and as soon as he comes to the back door, she silently changes from her house work boots into her warm felt *valenkis*. She puts a heavy cloak over her shawl and ties her kerchief more tightly under her chin. "Show me the rubles," she says.

"I have them. Just take me to Soso."

They go to the stables. Fyodor and Lyosha are there.

Lyosha had done as his sister instructed. He looks from her to Grisha. There is such a terrible feeling surrounding his sister now, and it's clear that things are very bad between her and Grisha. He can feel the tension hovering in the air, so tight it's almost vibrating, like a thin wire in the wind.

"Fyodor," Grisha calls. "Hitch the three Orlovs to the troika."

On the way to Borzik, Lilya demands the money from Grisha. He's brought his own money from the sale of his land, as well as the packet of rubles that belong to the countess—the amount he didn't hand over to Lev in Tushinsk. He'd divided the rubles, and now takes out a small amount and hands it to Lilya. She sits alone on the back seat of the troika; Lyosha is driving. She opens the packet and looks through it. "This is all?"

Grisha doesn't answer. He's hoping that she and Soso and the others will take what they can get. This is their last chance: they will take it, because they want to leave Pskov. They don't want to keep on hiding the boy. Better to take something than nothing.

"I know this can't be all. I know you had land."

Lyosha's head turns towards Grisha, his lips slightly parted. "Grisha?" he says, but Grisha is looking at Lilya.

"Land without serfs to work it is useless," he says. "Take the money before I change my mind and tell the countess."

"If Soso doesn't see enough money, he won't take us to Mikhail. I know you must have more. Give it to me," Lilya says again.

"Why should I trust you? Do you think I haven't thought this out? Don't I know you might simply take the money and leave with Soso? No, Lilya. I hold anything more until I have the boy."

Lyosha looks at Grisha again, then over his shoulder at Lilya. "Sister, what—"

Lilya is staring fiercely at Grisha. "Just drive," she tells her brother, and he and Grisha turn to face the road ahead.

Lyosha steers the troika with the four reins, one for each outside trace horse and two for the centre horse in the shaft, under the *duga*. The *duga*—a semicircular wooden bar that connects the main shafts over the centre horse—is decorated with blue rosettes and hung with the traditional one hundred bells. The bells and fresh winter air remind Lyosha of happier times. His face is flushed slightly from the cold, but more from his concern about the conversation between his sister and Grisha.

Forty minutes later, they arrive in Borzik. Grisha and Lyosha wait outside while Lilya goes into the low hovel. A pig snuffles around its foundation. The donkey brays at it crankily, lips drawn back over its long yellow teeth. Soso comes out with Lilya after a few minutes. There is dried food in his beard, and his hair is sticking out at all angles, as though he's been asleep. He looks up at Grisha. "You have the money?"

"I have it. Hurry up before I lose my patience."

Soso looks at Lilya. "You saw it?"

"Yes," she tells him. "Here is some of it." She opens the packet and Soso looks at the rubles. "What of Lev and Edik?"

"I'll divide the money with them later," he says after a brief hesitation. And with that, Lilya knows that Soso doesn't intend to share the money with anyone. They don't know about this transaction. They may even have left the province. "Why is he here?" Soso asks, raising his chin at Lyosha.

"I wanted him with me." Lilya is holding Soso's bearskin coat.

Soso grabs it from her and shoves his arms into it. He kicks at the pig. It squeals and lumbers away. "We go towards Pskov," he says, glancing at Lilya again, and something about the look Soso and Lilya exchange triggers a warning in Grisha.

"That's where Mikhail Konstantinovich is held?" he asks.

"Why else would we go there?" Soso climbs into the front of the troika and pushes Lyosha out of the way, taking the reins. Lyosha moves into the back and sits beside Lilya.

As they pull away from the izba, Grisha takes out the loaded pistol he put inside his tunic before they left Angelkov. He has had it since he came to Angelkov from Moscow, but has never used it. He sits sideways on the front seat, facing Soso, and can also see Lilya, behind Soso. He holds the pistol low, aimed at Soso. Soso glances at it. "Just so that you understand, Soso," Grisha says. "We are going to the boy."

Soso shouts at the horses and they break into a trot.

＊

After forty-five minutes, when the city is only a few versts away, Soso sharply turns the troika onto a narrow road leading into the forest. The horses have to make their way slowly, the trace horses swatted or scratched by encroaching branches. Nobody has spoken since they left Borzik.

They painstakingly travel through the scrubby forest. Grisha can smell Soso; the coat is filthy and matted. He doesn't want to think it's another trap: is Soso actually taking them to the other two men, to be robbed and beaten, or worse? He grips the pistol more tightly. He's prepared to use it the instant he feels a threat. He can only hope—pray, as he did earlier—that they will see Mikhail Konstantinovich.

He can see Lilya looking into the trees and occasionally behind the troika. The anxiety is thick in the air. He wants the boy to be alive so badly, wants to return him to Antonina. What if Mikhail is not where Soso is taking them? Grisha's worst fear is that he will die without knowing what happened to the boy or if he is ever reunited with his mother.

Grisha can't bear to think of Antonina's face should he not be returned. Instead, he envisions her expression when she sees her son. He knows that he will do anything for this to happen: he will give his life if it comes to that. And as they travel through the forest, he feels an unexpected and surprising exhilaration. It's not just that he's unafraid, but he's actually anticipating what will happen next. Knowing that this will be the end of the whole mess brings its own relief. And he will accept death graciously if it means Mikhail can be returned to Antonina.

There is a wooden cross nailed on a tree to the right, with a rough sign announcing the Ubenovo Monastyr, and a track that looks like no more than a path for mushroom or berry picking. Soso pulls on the reins to stop the horses.

"They can't go any farther," he says, and climbs down.

Lyosha harnesses the horses to the trees. Then he and Grisha and Lilya follow Soso along the tiny rutted track, frozen and snowy. Within a few minutes they arrive at a clearing. The trees here have been cut back in a wide swath. There is a low round chapel with a small domed roof. The outbuildings have padlocks on the doors. It's quiet, apart from the tinny calls of the hooded crows hunched against the cold in the bare birch and aspen.

Grisha still holds the pistol on Soso, glancing around the eerie place. Lilya too is looking around as if expecting to see someone.

"Father Saavich," Soso calls into the still air, then again, louder. "Slava Saavich!"

A middle-aged priest in a threadbare cassock and crude boots, a wooden cross on a leather strip around his neck, opens the door of the chapel. His long grey hair and beard are greasy and stringy, his skin yellowed as if he suffers from a liver disorder.

"We're here for him," Soso says, and the priest looks from him to Grisha. His eyes rest on the pistol. "Did you hear me?" Soso asks. "We're here for the boy. Bring him out."

The priest is frowning at Soso as if he doesn't recognize him.

"Saavich," Soso says, his voice gruff, "are you deaf? Get the boy."

Finally, the priest steps back inside the chapel. They all wait, heralded by the crows. It is a lonely and desolate place, the buildings ancient and rundown, the whitewash flaking.

"What kind of monastery is this?" Lyosha asks, his voice low.

Nobody answers.

"Soso, what kind of place is this?" Lyosha repeats.

"It's for peasant boys, to train them into the monkhood so they can return to their villages as priests."

"And they must be locked in?" Lyosha gestures to the huts.

As he finishes the sentence, the priest reappears, his hand clutching a boy's shoulder.

39

At the sight of the boy, a deep pain grips Grisha's throat, and he moves the pistol behind his back so as not to frighten him. He doesn't know if, until this moment, he really believed he would ever see Mikhail Konstantinovich alive.

It is Mikhail, but not the vivacious child he remembers. This boy is taller, his wrists knobby as they protrude from the sleeves of the black robe, his hands red and chapped in the cold. His jaw is sharp, his chin pointed. His hair is a golden stubble.

His expression . . . it's unfamiliar, stiff. But as Mikhail sees them—sees Grisha, and Lyosha, and Lilya—everything on the rigid face changes. It softens and loses the tightness, and he is once more Misha. He jerks forward as if to run to them as voices ring in the air, him calling them, them calling him, but the priest keeps his hold on the boy's shoulder. His fingernails are long and dirty.

Silence again falls. Soso moves to stand in front of the priest and Misha.

Mikhail moves his head, trying to see around the bulky bear coat, staring at Grisha. Misha's eyes glint, but he doesn't cry. He straightens his shoulders and lifts his chin, and in spite of the ragged black robe with a rope around the waist, the shorn hair, he is once more the child of nobility. Grisha sees he wears only bark shoes; there are chilblains on the boy's thin bare ankles. He feels a rush of pride, as if the boy were his. For the first time in his life, he wishes he had a son, a child of his own. "Mikhail Konstantinovich," he says.

"Yes, Grisha. It's me," Mikhail says, his voice sure, but the words are heartbreaking, as if they all might have forgotten who he is. He breathes in short, shaky puffs, white in the frosty air.

Grisha understands that the boy is fighting to stay in control. Soso is between Mikhail and Grisha. The boy has learned to fear, and he understands this is a pivotal moment, that he mustn't ruin what is so important. He is only eleven, but he is a child of good breeding. He understands this, Grisha thinks, in spite of what he must have been through.

"Now," Soso says, looking back at Grisha. "You see for yourself that the boy is alive. Give me the money."

"We have come for you, Mikhail Konstantinovich," Grisha says, ignoring Soso, holding out his free hand, the other, with the pistol, still behind his back. "Come."

"Not without the money," Soso says.

Grisha takes out the packets of rubles, but at the same time he brings the pistol in front of him. He can't point it at Soso; Mikhail is too near. He throws the packages on the ground.

Soso is looking behind Grisha. There is surprise, perhaps incredulity, on his face, and this makes Grisha turn to see what he's looking at.

Lilya is holding a pistol at chest height with both hands. She points it at her husband. Soso reaches inside his bearskin coat, frowning. He takes one step. "Give me that, you fool woman."

"Stay there, Soso," Lilya says.

Soso stops, but shows his teeth at Lilya. "Lilyanka," he says, drawing out the pet name. "Come. It's me, Soso. We're in this together, sweetheart. Are we not?"

"No. We're not."

"How did you get my pistol?" Soso yells, and Lilya jumps.

"Do you suppose it was that difficult? You always slept like a boar. It was an easy matter to take it out of your coat before I woke you."

"Lilya," Soso says again, lowering his voice with something like a chuckle. As if she were a small and clever child.

Lilya cocks the hammer of the Cossack pistol the way she saw Soso do it in his izba. At the sound, so loud in the cold, still air, Soso's chuckle fades. Lilya knows, by the look on his face, that the pistol is loaded, as he had boasted.

"Do you not believe I'll shoot?" she says. "I've killed before. I'll do it again, if I have to." She steps back. "Lyosha, pick up the money."

Lyosha does as she orders, and then Soso takes another step towards Lilya. Lyosha calls out, "Soso! Stop! It's true. She's already . . ." He glances at his sister, then back at Soso. "You must believe she'll do it. I'm telling you, Soso, she'll shoot."

Something about Lilya's expression and the confident way she holds the pistol, her thumb steady on the hammer, or perhaps what Lyosha has just said, makes Soso stop.

Grisha still holds his own pistol. Before anyone can antici-
pate what will happen next, Soso turns and grabs Misha, pulling him from the priest and dragging the boy in front of him.

Misha struggles, kicking backwards, trying to wrench
himself free of Soso's grip. "No!" he shouts. "Let me go!"

At his loud cries, a burly man in a long greatcoat and grey
fur hat appears behind the priest, from inside the chapel. His
hat has a white star, and the words *Pskov Captain* are embroidered under it. He is followed by a second and then a third
man, both as tall and wide as the first, wearing the greatcoats
and fur hats of the police. They all hold their own revolvers.

Grisha doesn't understand.

"Good," Lilya says. "You're here."

"You're Lilya Petrova?" the captain asks, and when she
nods, he adds, "Put down the weapon. And you." He looks
at Grisha. Grisha hesitates for a moment, then carefully sets
his pistol on the ground in front of him.

Lilya still holds hers. Her hands remain steady, her face
composed.

"Let the boy go," the captain says, and Soso spits onto the
priest's boots with an expression of disgust as he drops
Mikhail's arms. Mikhail runs to Grisha, who is nearest to him.
Grisha pulls Mikhail close, his arms tightly around him.

A sob comes from Misha's throat. He knows it's not over
yet. He stares at Lilya, and the pistol, but she hasn't looked at
him. Her eyes are fixed on Soso.

"Put the pistol down," the captain says again.

As Lilya keeps the revolver aimed at Soso, Lyosha slowly
holds out one hand to her, palm up. "Sister, what are you
doing? Look. It's Misha. We have him now. Don't hurt
anyone. You're upset, Lilya. That's all. Give me the pistol,

and let's take Misha home. Let's all go back to Angelkov, to the countess."

At that, a strange look comes over Lilya's face, one of sudden clarity, followed by horror. She looks at her hands holding the revolver as if they are someone else's, and lowers the pistol so that it points towards the ground at her feet. For the first time, she looks at Misha. He's turned his face against Grisha's chest, and his hands are over his ears. "Misha," she says. "I'm sorry, *moya malysh*, my baby, I'm sorry. It's all right. Don't be afraid. You don't have to be afraid anymore."

As Misha lowers his hands, he half smiles at Lilya, a tremulous, trusting smile, and Lilya attempts to smile back at him. Then she says to Lyosha, in a small voice, "I loved her, Lyosha. I always loved her. But she doesn't want me. I know that now. I saw it, so clearly on her face. Even if I bring back her son, she won't love me."

Lyosha doesn't understand what she's talking about, but he needs his sister to be calm, to not hurt anyone. She's still holding the revolver. " I . . . You know I care about you, Lilya." He has never used the word *love*, and can't now.

She blinks and looks at him as though he's a stranger. "You love Anya now. I didn't want you to love anyone else. But you do, don't you, Lyosha? You will love her just as she loves *him*. She loves *him*, not me."

"Lilya, please," Lyosha urges, confused.

Suddenly Lilya smiles, the natural smile Lyosha remembers, and relief goes through him. He smiles back at her, nodding encouragingly. "That's right, Lilya. That's better. Give it to me." He takes a step towards her, his hand still out, palm up.

She puts the revolver into his hand. He stoops, setting it on the ground, as Grisha did.

"You said there were four of them," the captain says.

Lilya shrugs. "There are only two now, Soso and Grisha. Not him," she says, putting her hand on Lyosha's arm.

Soso waves his arms in the air. "What's she talking about?" His voice is loud, indignant. "She's crazy. You can see she's crazy. We've come to free the countess's son. We heard he was here, at the monastery. We came to bring him back—"

"You are Iosef Igorovitch, known as Soso," the man states, and Soso closes his mouth and lowers his arms. "We have spoken to Father Saavich. He corroborated with the woman's story: that you would be coming for the boy today. That you have threatened him unless he hid the boy these past months."

Soso looks at Father Saavich. "Bastard. Traitor," he says, and spits at the priest's boots again.

"And how were you involved?" the man asks Lilya.

"She wasn't," Grisha says. The boy has stopped trembling, and is looking up at him. "She wasn't involved. It's as she told you. It was Soso and me. Grigori Sergeyevich Naryshkin. Go to Lilya, Misha," he says then, and the boy does as he says, but looks over his shoulder at Grisha.

Lilya takes off her cape and wraps it around Misha, holding him against her and kissing his cheeks, his bristly head, his cold ears.

"Give him your *ushanka*, Lyosha," Grisha says, and Lyosha takes off his hat and sets it on Mikhail's head.

At the police station on Fedosovoy Prospekt in Pskov, Soso and Grisha are led inside, their hands tied behind their backs. Lilya and Lyosha and Mikhail follow; a report on the discovery of the Mitlovsky child must be filed.

Lilya retains her composure during the laborious writing out of many details. She answers all the questions slowly while sitting with her hands held loosely in her lap.

Lyosha waits with Mikhail in an outer room, the boy still wrapped in Lilya's cape. He holds the *ushanka*. Someone has found an old pair of felt boots for him.

At one point, Grisha is led past him, and Misha draws a deep, shuddering breath. Lyosha puts his arm around the boy's shoulders. Grisha stops in front of them and says, "Lyosha. Please. Make sure all the money is given to the countess. With it she can pay her taxes and keep Angelkov for a while longer." As Lyosha nods, Grisha looks at Misha.

The boy stares up at him. "Grisha?" he whispers, a question in the name.

"Mikhail Konstantinovich," Grisha says. "I'm sorry. This is not what I wanted to happen to you. Ever." As the captain and another policeman try to pull him forward, Grisha asks, "Will I be allowed to write a letter?"

"Not now," the captain says. "Later you will be allowed one communication."

"I will write to your mother, Mikhail, to explain. Can you tell her I will write to her?"

Misha reaches down the loose front of his robe and pulls out a small leather booklet. He opens it and tears two pages from it, walking towards Grisha.

The captain takes the pages of music, turning them over and frowning.

"It's her notes to Glinka," the boy says, "so Grisha can write to my mother."

The captain nods, and they lead Grisha away.

The captain says he will accompany Lilya and Lyosha and Mikhail back to Angelkov. "I'll follow by horse," he tells them in the waiting room. "I must ensure that the boy is returned safely to Countess Mitlovskiya, and present her with the official report."

Lyosha stands straight, his hand on Misha's shoulder, and dips his head at the man.

As the captain follows them outside, he tells them to wait while he brings his horse from the stable.

Before Mikhail climbs into the troika, Lilya again hugs and kisses him. She holds him for so long that Lyosha touches her arm. She lets Misha go and turns to her brother. He puts out his hand to help her up. She takes it, but then brings it to her lips and kisses it, laying her cheek against it.

"Come, Lilya. Climb in."

"Make sure you give the money to the countess as Grisha instructed."

Lyosha puts his hand inside his jacket. "Here. You take it. You should be the one to give it to her."

"No. You must do it. I'm not coming with you."

"You're not coming back to Angelkov?"

"No. There is only one thing left for me now."

"What are you talking about? The countess will need you even more now that Misha—"

"No," she interrupts. "It's as I said. The countess doesn't need me anymore. There is no place for me at Angelkov."

Lyosha studies her face. It is pale, but calm. Resolute. "You know that God loves you, Lilya," he says.

"No. Not since I did the unforgivable at Grisha's house."

"But He is forgiving. He will forgive you."

"I will devote my life to asking for His forgiveness. Goodbye, Lyosha."

"Where are you going?"

"To where I can do only good. To Seltocheeva."

Lyosha frowns. "The convent?"

"They have welcomed me. They await me," she says.

Lyosha knows she's too old to be a novice. Besides, they take only members of the nobility into the sisterhood. But what can he say? He understands Lilya well enough to know there is no use in trying to change her mind. It appears she's already arranged this. He thinks of her, again, in Grisha's house, with the bloody rifle. He remembers how only a few hours earlier she aimed the pistol at Soso.

"If you change your mind, come back to Angelkov."

She shakes her head, but her eyes and mouth are soft. "This is part of my repentance, Lyosha. I must be punished. Never again seeing those I truly love will be my greatest grief." She looks at Misha again. "Goodbye, Mishenka, my darling."

"Goodbye, Lilya," Misha says. "Your cape," he adds, "you must have your cape back." He starts to take it off.

Lilya puts her hands out to stop him. "Keep warm. Stay warm until you are in your mama's arms."

Mikhail and Lyosha watch Lilya walk away. The cold November wind ruffles her skirt and light shawl. Her kerchief is slipping off the back of her head, as it often does, and Lyosha sees the part in her hair.

Her scalp looks vulnerable.

"Goodbye, sister," he says, although she is already too far away to hear him, and then he climbs into the troika beside Misha.

At Angelkov, Antonina had awoken to a quiet house. When she went downstairs to the kitchen, Raisa and Pavel and Nusha were there. She asked Raisa about Lilya, but Raisa told her she hadn't seen her. And Grisha? Again, Raisa shook her head.

Antonina waits for something to happen. For Grisha to come to her with Mikhail. Or even for Lilya to appear. But nobody comes. By mid-afternoon she has a terrible feeling that something has happened, something that will be unbearable.

She goes to the stable, but only Fyodor is there. He tells her that Grisha and Lilya and Lyosha all left together in the troika that morning. She walks down the winding road to Grisha's house. It is cold and empty. She builds a small fire and sits there, looking at his books and the items on his bookshelf. After some time she wanders around, staring at the small, tidy kitchen and at his bedroom. She sits on the bed. She imagines him here, filling the space. She lies down and covers herself with his thick quilt.

An hour passes.

When the fire in the sitting room has gone out, Antonina starts back to the manor. She is adrift. At this moment she feels more alone than she can remember. They are all gone: Misha, Konstantin, Valentin, Lilya. Grisha. Even Lyosha.

She looks around her as she trudges up the snowy road, studying the beauty of the snow embracing the pines, hearing the calls of the white-backed woodpeckers and nut-hatches from their branches.

As the manor comes into view, she sees the troika and an unknown horse. She walks faster. She makes out two tall figures. Please, she pleads, let one be Grisha. Let one be Grisha. But it isn't. Lyosha and a uniformed man stand on the veranda. She hurries. As she comes up the steps, she looks into Lyosha's face, but can't understand what she sees there. She glances at the other man. By his clothing, he looks to be a member of the police force. Suddenly she doesn't care, because now she hears it.

Music. It comes from inside the house. Antonina pushes past Lyosha, who reaches towards her, his mouth moving as he speaks to her. But she can't hear his voice. She only hears music. She pushes open the door and runs down the hall, her snowy boots sliding on the wooden floor.

She runs towards the music salon, towards the Glinka music, and her son.

ONE YEAR LATER

New Year's Day, 1863

SELTOCHEEVA CONVENT, CITY OF PSKOV

Seltocheeva Convent is quiet for the holidays. The Little Sisters of Righteous Elizaveeta celebrated the birth of Christ on the eve of Christmas, but the New Year passes unnoticed.

Lilya is one of the unpaid women who earns her keep in the convent by offering services the sisters are unable to perform. The sisters clean the convent and work the gardens. They preserve and prepare food and serve it, and they do the laundry. But there is a need for delicate lace for the holy surplices, and none of the sisters have Lilya's skill. And so she sits, every day, in a small nun's cell with a cot and icon. She works on the tiny, intricate patterns she creates under a high window where the light streams in. As well as the room, she is also supplied with two meals a day. Although not a nun, she wears only black, a representation of repentance and simplicity. She attends the services in the chapel morning and evening, praying reverently through the Little and Great Entrances, the Epistle and Gospel readings, the Divine Liturgy, the Anaphora, the distribution of Holy Communion, and the Dismissal. In her cell-like room, she falls to her knees every hour and prays with the ringing of the chapel bells.

She finishes her work as the final daylight fades. This is not for a surplice; it is a gift. She stands, stretching, and then runs her fingers over the finely embroidered cloth belt she has created. She smooths her hair and pinches her cheeks to bring colour to them. The last hourly bells have finished ringing, and in the hush there is a lovely sense of peace.

Lilya venerates the icon and walks down the long, narrow hallway. She raps, lightly, on the low door of Sister Ludmilla. The door opens. The young sister looks at her and smiles.

"Lilya Petrova," she says.

Lilya smiles back. She has taken a vow of silence, even though the Little Sisters are under no such order. She holds out the belt to Sister Ludmilla. As the sister reaches for it, Lilya lets her fingers touch the nun's.

Sister Ludmilla draws back her hand, her smile fading. "You made this for me?" She studies the belt, a symbol of the vow of chastity to be worn on feast days.

Lilya's gaze never leaves the young woman. Sister Ludmilla's face is thin and pale, and a pure light shines from her grey eyes. A tiny wisp of blond hair emerges from under her black *klobuk*, just at the temple. Lilya reaches up and touches it.

She knows that under the wimple the sister's neck will be long and white.

She would like to know it someday. She dreams of that moment.

Iliychiv Prospekt, St. Petersburg

The Novogodnaya Yolka—the New Year's tree—is beautiful, with its bright star on the top bough. Sweets and gold-painted nuts are scattered among the branches; the cherub from Angelkov, with its wing repaired by Grisha, is tied onto a branch with a red satin ribbon.

In the St. Petersburg apartment, there isn't room for a tall, wide tree such as they had in Angelkov, but this one is a lovely symmetrical pine with soft, sweeping branches. Lyosha cut it himself, taking Misha with him to find it in the forest on the edge of the city. They dragged it home behind Lyosha's horse on Christmas Eve, and set it up in a bucket of stones in a corner of the sitting room. It lists slightly, but nobody mentions that.

There is a New Year's present under the tree for Misha—a new leather music composition book—although of course he is far too old to believe that Ded Moroz and Snegurochka, the Snow Girl, have brought it. Had he believed in Father Frost and his granddaughter the year he was taken? That time is hazy to Antonina. It's been over a year since she and Misha started their new lives.

In the autumn, Mikhail was accepted into the St. Petersburg Conservatory, founded that year by the young musician Anton Rubinstein. It's Russia's first school focused on teaching the arts, under the sponsorship of the Imperial Russian Music Society. Mikhail Konstantinovich Mitlovsky is one of the youngest students, and he's alive with excitement every day as he heads to class.

The year 1862 brought another new school to St. Petersburg: the Free School of Music, founded by Mily

Alexseyevich Balakirev. Antonina Leonidovna Mitlovskiya is one of three female teachers hired to instruct talented young women unable to pay for private tuition. It is as Valentin Vladimirovitch told her: new options and opportunities are being born.

Every morning, she walks with her son to the Conservatory. Then she goes on to her own job at the Free School, where she teaches for the morning. In the afternoon, she gives private music lessons in her apartment. She makes a small sum from both her work at the Free Music School and the private tutoring, enough to pay the rent and buy what they need.

The sound on the British upright piano she bought is good, although it isn't like the beautiful square rosewood Érard, far too large for the small sitting room. With the money Lyosha gave to her, she's managed to ensure that she can keep the estate at least for a few years. At Angelkov the windows of the manor are boarded and what furniture remains has been covered in sheets. Antonina worries about mice gnawing the books and making nests in the body of the Érard. Someday she may want to live there again. Someday there may be a reason, but for now her life is in St. Petersburg.

Misha walks home from the Conservatory with his new friends when he's done his classes, and in fair weather he and Antonina take Tinka and Dani to the nearby park. Dani is Misha's dog. He is small, brown and white-spotted with long, soft ears, and he sleeps at the foot of Misha's bed at night. Tinka is too old to walk far now, so Antonina carries her.

After the park, they have dinner and talk about the music they have heard and made that day. Misha does his homework, or practises. The apartment on Iliychiv Prospekt, two blocks from the Fontanka River, is small but warm and inviting.

"Mother," Mikhail says—at twelve, he no longer calls her Mama—"when can we go out to the square for the fireworks?"

Antonina pictures Misha watching the display Konstantin put on every New Year at Angelkov; she still can recall the wonder on Misha's face.

"Soon, my son. Lyosha? What time are the fireworks scheduled?"

Lyosha glances at the clock on the piano. "We should leave in fifteen minutes."

"We will leave after the toast. If you will, fetch Anya from the kitchen. Ask her to bring the good glasses."

Lyosha married ten months ago. Anya Fomovna is small and winsome, with chestnut hair that gleams like wood. They came with Antonina and Misha to St. Petersburg, and they live nearby. Lyosha secured a well-paying job in the military stables. Anya comes to Antonina's apartment every morning to help out with the housework and laundry while Antonina works. On the weekends she teaches Antonina how to cook.

Little Nusha returned to her parents in one of the local *mirs* with the gift of a bag of rubles. Antonina secured Pavel a job at the Bakanevs'; she gave him permission to take anything he wished that had belonged to Konstantin.

Fyodor and Raisa look after Angelkov. They live in the house with blue shutters. Olga went with them; she was too old to start a new life. She died only last month, and Antonina went back to Angelkov to attend the funeral and see the old woman buried behind the Church of the Redeemer. While there, she supervised the erection of stone markers for both Konstantin's and Valentin's graves, and she alone stood by the violinist's grave for his prayers.

She knows everything that happened in those last, terrible months at Angelkov. She glances at the desk where Grisha's letter sits in the top drawer: the letter, written in his firm hand, on the back of her notes to Glinka. The two pages were delivered to Angelkov a week after Misha came back to her. The letter tells her everything. She knows it by heart, she has read it that often.

She is working on forgiveness, and finds it is easier to forgive when looking ahead instead of back.

Now the four of them—Antonina, Mikhail, Lyosha and Anya—raise their glasses and toast the New Year. The wine is cheap but glows, ruby, in the crystal glasses Antonina brought with her to St. Petersburg.

"*Za vashe zdorov'e!*" Lyosha says. Antonina echoes, "To your health," and the four of them clink their glasses. Misha grimaces at the taste, but looks proud to be given wine on this special occasion. God knows, Antonina thinks, he has been through enough to be thought of as a young man now.

On this special night, she thinks of her parents and brothers, of Konstantin and Valentin—poor Valentin—of all those who tried to care for her in their own ways. She thinks of Lilya.

Lyosha tried three times to visit his sister in Seltocheeva, but was turned away. Lilya Petrovna, he was told, has devoted her life to God, and has permanently left the outside world. Lyosha has accepted that he will never see her again.

After the toast, Antonina sets down her glass, the wine untouched. She has kept the promise she made to God and to herself in the dacha.

As they dress warmly to go to the square for the fireworks, Antonina notices with a start that Lyosha is putting on a quilted coat that Grisha wore in the stables. She runs her hand over the sleeve and smiles at Lyosha.

On the way out, she kisses the icon and crosses herself. *To faith*, she thinks, and then follows Lyosha and Anya and Misha out into the cold January air, closing the door firmly to keep in the warmth.

ZERENTUY KATORGA, SIBERIA

The men in Hut 83 are finished their labour for the day, and have been given a ration of potato vodka to celebrate the New Year. Thirty-two men are crammed into the wooden shack. There is a narrow corridor between the sixteen stacked cots, with the door at one end and an open bucket for a toilet at the other. Tonight the hut is even more raucous and malodorous than usual.

"And what are your plans for 1863?" the new man—his name is Bogdan—asks. Then he smiles, a grimace, really, at his own attempt at a joke. "Plans," he repeats with a rude snort.

Grisha rolls the tin cup with the two inches of potato vodka between his palms. "The only thing possible," he says, looking into the other man's red-rimmed eyes.

Bogdan was among the most recent shipment of prisoners brought to Zerentuy. He is a Sybiraks—a Pole. He was assigned the bunk over Grisha's. The man who had formerly slept above Grisha died three days before Bogdan arrived, coughing up blood and wasting to a thin layer of flesh over bone. A few others, noticing the unnatural quiet from the top bunk, had stealthily made away with the dead man's blanket and clothes and boots before morning, when the guards were alerted and hauled the body away.

Grisha had been the first to know that the man, an elderly cellist who had once played for the Tsar, was dead. He'd liked and respected him, and so instead of taking what the dead cellist no longer had use for, he'd made the sign of the cross on the man's forehead, covering the cold, waxen face with the blanket before the others crept up to take it away. He didn't hold it against them; he'd done the same.

Bogdan, his head half shaved in the way of all new prisoners, still has some weight on him. As yet there are no rough, frostbitten patches on his cheeks. Grisha eyes his boots, surprised the guards haven't taken them yet. But they will. He again wants to feel supple leather wrapped round his feet, instead of the newspaper-lined felt boots of the prisoners. He wonders, absently, what this man, Bogdan, did to end up here, in the Siberian work camp. He also knows it's unlikely he'll find out.

The men do not discuss their crimes, or what they've been deemed guilty of. Too much talking in a *katorga* is not a good thing. Some of the men Grisha works with each day are murderers and thieves. Some simply had too much to say about the new regime taking over Russia: those with the belief that the Tsar's will should not arbitrarily be understood as Russia's law.

"To get out of this place," Grisha finally tells Bogdan. "That's what I plan."

A short, wizened man with a deep limp, on his way to the bucket, passes the lower cot where Grisha and Bogdan sit.

"You are a dreamer, Grigori Sergeyevich. You know you won't survive."

"I will." Grisha's voice is quiet and sure.

The older man shakes his head, his lungs wheezing like

bellows as he laughs. Bogdan drains his cup. He grips it with his huge, scarred hands.

"Because it is the New Year, Naryshkin, I will humour you. Suppose you escape from the camp. The old bastard," Bogdan says, looking at the wheezing man's back, "has given up. He knows there's no chance for him. But let's say you escape. Then what? How will you cross Siberia? Where will you go?"

Grisha puts his cup at his feet and digs under the frayed coat tied with rope and inside his layers of patched tunics. He pulls out a hard chunk of dark bread, and with some effort tears it in half. He hands a piece to his new friend. The man grabs it, nodding his thanks, and carefully puts it to the right side of his mouth, where six teeth—three on the top and three on the bottom—remain. Grisha knows, by the cautious manner in which Bogdan gnaws the bread and the awkward way he forms his words, that he has only recently lost most of his teeth.

"Go on, Naryshkin," Bogdan urges him. "It's the New Year, and the night for seeing the future. So tell me what you predict for yourself, my friend."

"I will walk out," Grisha says, picking up his cup again. "I have walked across Siberia before, and I was hardly more than a boy. I did it once, and I will do it again."

"All right," Bogdan says, still gingerly chewing. "Where will you go? Do you have a family who waits for you? A home?"

Grisha thinks of the house with blue shutters. "I don't know. But I know whom I will walk towards. Whom I will look for, and hope she still waits."

The other man's face softens. "It is always good to think of someone waiting," he says quietly. "What is important in a place like this is the hope." His cup is empty, but he raises it.

"To hope," Grisha murmurs. He crosses himself, raises his cup towards Bogdan and then upwards. "To hope," he repeats, picturing Antonina's face, and he drinks.

ACKNOWLEDGEMENTS

I grew up hearing pieced-together stories of life in Russia in the early part of the twentieth century; I listened to my father and grandmother speak Russian at the dinner table, and my grandmother whispered her language to me in bed at night. I parroted back her words, not understanding them, but loving our furtive, hidden connection. Because of the suspicions and distrust surrounding the Soviet Union during the Cold War, having a Russian heritage was something I was taught to suppress. But the intrigue surrounding my grandparents' lives in villages near Odessa and St. Petersburg before they fled in the hopes of a brighter future filled me with a longing to understand what was—inexplicably to me as a child—dark and secretive. It was this part of my past that drew me to write about Russia decades later. I started with an incident from my grandmother's life, which I've fictionalized for the novel: she watched her five-year-old brother being stolen by Cossacks on a muddy road outside her village home. He was never seen again.

Studying Russia in the mid-nineteenth century, with its contrasts of extreme wealth and extreme poverty, its all-encompassing religious overtones, its emerging literary and musical giants and its long history of serfdom, was both wildly exciting and tremendously challenging. To help me in my search to capture the aura of that time I relied on fiction and poetry, from the classic offerings of Gogol and Pushkin, Dostoevsky, Tolstoy and Chekov to the slightly more contemporary works of Ahkmatova, Pasternak, Nabokov and Soltzhenitsyn. Memoirs such as *Up from Serfdom: My Childhood and Youth in Russia, 1804-1824* by Aleksandr Nikitenko and *Days of a Russian Noblewoman: The Memories of Anna Labzina, 1758-1821* offered intriguing details of a past life. Of great assistance were *Village Life in Late Tsarist Russia* by Olga Semyonova Tian-Shanskiaia; *The Pearl* by Douglas Smith; *Echoes of a Native Land: Two Centuries of a Russian Village* by Serge Schmemann; *Serfdom, Society, and the Arts in Imperial Russia* by Richard Stites; and *Life on the Russian Country Estate* by Priscilla Roosevelt.

Big thanks, as always, to my agent, Sarah Heller, for suggestions and encouragement. Thanks to Anne Collins, publisher and editor extraordinaire, for her insight and gentle direction. Thanks to John Sweet for astute copy-editing and asking the right questions; to Terri Nimmo, for the jacket and interior design; to Caleb Snider, Deirdre Molina, Marion Garner and Ashley Dunn of the Random House Canada team.

To Zalie, Brenna and Kitt, thank you, as always, for so graciously putting up with your mother's wild mind and sudden flights of fancy. Special thanks to Brenna, who shared long train journeys across Mongolia and Siberia and into Western Russia as I sought to make this story right. Thank you to Vialetta in Ulan Ude, Valeriy in Listvyanka on the shores of Lake Baikal, Tamara in Irkutsk, and Irena in Yekaterinburg who opened their homes to us, giving us a taste of true Siberian life. Thank you to Randall, Tim and Shannon and your families for the endless encouragement and love. In this year of change for all of us, with arrivals and departures, your caring presence has been more meaningful than ever before. Thank you to my friends—you know who you are—for your endless patience and your interest and support in the way I have chosen to live my life. Each of you brings such a rich weave to the tapestry.

Finally, loving thanks to Marty, who has taught me so much about story—both real and imagined—and the joy of sharing creative lives and hearts.

LINDA HOLEMAN is the author of the international bestselling historical novels *The Linnet Bird*, *The Moonlit Cage*, *In a Far Country* and *The Saffron Gate*, as well as eight other works of fiction and short fiction. Her books have been translated into twelve languages. A world traveller, she grew up in Winnipeg, and now lives in Toronto and Santa Monica, California.